Mafia Beauty

The Mancinelli Brotherhood

Sabine Barclay

OLIVERHEBERBOOKS

A special thank you to Dr. Zachary "Bones" Alexander for letting me examine the world of radiology.

Subscribe to Sabine's Newsletter

Subscribe to Sabine's bimonthly newsletter to receive exclusive insider perks.

Have you read *The Syndicate Wars*? This FREE origin story novella is available to all new subscribers to Sabine's monthly newsletter. Subscribe on her website.

The Mancinelli Brotherhood

Mafia Heir

Mafia Sinner

Mafia Beauty

Mafia Angel (8.22.23)

Mafia Redeemer (10.17.23)

Mafia Star (12.12.23)

Do you also enjoy steamy Historical Romance? Discover Sabine's books written as Celeste Barclay.

Chapter One

Matteo

8 months ago

"Maria? Wake up."

I nudge my best friend's sister, but her head lolls on her pillow. I've lived on adrenaline for the past two days and slept maybe three hours. We've spent every waking minute searching for Maria and getting her away from those pervs. We found her pretty easily after the first night. We don't know where her abductors had her before that, but her tracker started pinging by midafternoon. That was after my best friend, Marco, and his brothers, cousin, and his cousin's best friend arrived from New York. We went straight to three nightclubs as soon as we left the airfield and spent the morning at bars interrogating staff.

"Maria, I need you to wake up. Can you hear me?"

I shake her a little harder, and her eyes flutter, but she doesn't wake. I look at Marco and his brothers, along with their cousin Carmine and his friend Gabriele. None of us knows what to do. Cuban sex traffickers snatched Maria and her best friend, Veronica, from a nightclub bathroom while I was her guard. When I went to look for them, these guys took the two other women, who are—were—attending the same medical conference as Maria.

Understandably, the guys want to know what the hell happened now that we aren't frantically searching for her.

"We got off the plane, and the car service was there waiting for us. The driver helped me load everything into the SUV while Maria and Veronica sat inside. They were chatting, and I watched the driver the entire time. He was never out of my sight. I even watched him through the car windows as he walked to the driver's side, and I walked to the front passenger side. We went straight to the hotel and checked into the suite. It was three bedrooms, so the girls each had their own, and I had one. We got cleaned up, then went downstairs, so Maria could check in at the conference registration table. She got everything she needed, and we were headed back to the elevators when she spotted two friends from med school. They invited us to join them for dinner, which we did. Maria wanted to go to a club she and Veronica didn't hit the last time we were down there. She convinced her friends to join her. There was a crowd, but not horrible."

I pause as I collect myself.

"Veronica needed to go to the restroom, and Maria said she may as well go, too. We left her friends at the table. I stood outside the door. Some women went in and out, but fifteen minutes went by. I called out to Maria, but she didn't answer. I immediately pounded on the door. No one answered. I went in, knowing it should have only been Maria and Veronica in there. I checked before they went in, so I knew when they were alone. No one was there. I saw the closet and the earring. It led me outside, but there was no one around. I went back in through the front door, and the two doctors were gone too. I looked around as I called the hotel to see if they'd returned. None of them had. I tried getting a ping from Maria's tracker, but nothing happened. That's when I called Uncle Salvatore."

I watch Maria, in my mind begging her to wake, as I continue to explain the worst night of my life.

"I looked throughout the club, even pushing my way into the manager's office and the backrooms. I canvased the block, but there was no sign of them. I kept trying to ping Maria's tracker, but it was complete radio silence. When I was certain I'd done everything I could in the area around the club, I started walking back to the hotel. It was four miles, but I wanted to be sure I didn't miss them on some side street. Nothing. The four of them just vanished. I got back to the hotel and waited until I got Luca's call that you guys were ten minutes out. I called the driver and went to meet you."

I shake my head and run my hand over my face.

"I heard nothing, and I was right by the door. Neither Maria nor Veronica had a chance to scream, and there was never the sound of a scuffle."

Once the others arrived, we went straight back to the club. We searched the clubs next door. Then we tried the bars in the morning. *Tres J's* called a few hours later. Marco and I staked out the place they told us to look while Luca, Gabriele, and Carmine went to the bank once the *Tres J's* called to tell us they knew where a woman matching Maria's description was. A Cuban man offered the Colombian brothers the first chance to buy her. The moment he described her as a rich, hot, Italian princess from New York, they called us. Lorenzo stayed in the car, trying to hack the tracker. Maria's tracker came back on just as we got to the villa the *Tres J's* told us about.

Maria and her friends were out cold. We got her out, but we had to leave the other three. Carmine could only negotiate a ransom for her. We didn't wait around to test our luck. Once we got Maria in the SUV, the others pulled away. Marco and I stayed back to keep watching the house from the empty villa next door. After the two Cuban motherfuckers left, men came to get Veronica and the two doctors. We intercepted them and grabbed the women. We knew we couldn't go back to the hotel with four unconscious women, so Lorenzo and Gabriele did some looking on Airbnb and VRBO and found some empty rentals. We helped ourselves. We broke in and laid the women down in the bedroom with the two double beds.

Maria's been out of it for the past seven hours. Veronica and the two doctors are in the same shape. Whatever these fucking traffickers drugged them with is powerful. Likely horse tranquilizers for all I know. It's meant to keep them knocked out through an international flight. That much I'm sure of.

All three women need medical attention, but we don't know anyone down here. Maria and the two women we don't know are doctors, but they're in no condition to heal themselves or anyone else. Veronica's an admin assistant to some old stockbroker she's sucking cock for under his desk. That was a story I could have lived without last Christmas. But as much as I dislike her and don't know the other women enough to care, none of them should be like this.

I've been in a state of panic since I realized Maria was gone. I want nothing more than for her to wake as I keep nudging her. Why isn't she—or any of them—conscious after so long? I haven't cried since I was eight, but I'm close now. Most of it is the adrenaline crash from my guilt and shame. A good chunk of it is from fear. I can't sit still. I move out of Carmine's way and return to staring out the window.

Marco's older brother, Luca, holds out his phone, and a Colombian accent floats out. It's a nephew of the Colombian Cartel's *jefe*, who's usually our adversary, asking how she is. They go back and forth, and Luca asks if there's a doctor who can make a house call. Luca rattles off the address of the house we broke into.

One of the *Tres J's* poses the same two questions we've wondered from the get-go.

"Do any of you know how Fernando picked Maria? Or did he go for her friends, and she got swept along?"

I'm back to pacing as I answer. I haven't calmed down since the moment the others got off the jet. Since the moment I realized Maria was gone. I blame myself entirely. I can tell the rest of the guys blame themselves for letting Maria travel with only me. I snap at the guy.

"Are you new? You've seen how beautiful Maria is."

There's silence at the other end of the phone, and I'm guessing the *jefe's* nephews, *Tres J's*—Javier, Joaquin, and Jorge—are reminding themselves that none of us are in our regular state of mind right now. Maria is beautiful on the inside and out. She's kind, funny, generous, and she tries to see the best in everyone—which is no small feat when you're the New York don's niece.

I watch Maria as the man who's been our enemy for years speaks again.

"We'll dig more into what's going on while we're on our flight back from Bogota. The *puto cubano* obviously didn't do this alone. Do you know where any of those other women were from?" Fucking Cuban.

Lorenzo, Marco's younger brother, was the only one who heard any of the traffickers speak while we were negotiating Maria's freedom along with her friends. The negotiations didn't go well. The piece of shit leader realized who Maria was and decided to ransom her, rather than sell her to someone else. He wanted to sell the other three women. We barely got them all out. Lorenzo speaks up.

"Eastern Europe, but I'm not sure where. None of them really talked."

Our nemesis comes back on the line.

"Then that begs the question: Do we get Maks involved?"

My friends and I look at one another, and I shake my head. I think we should keep this contained. We don't need the Russian bratva involved. Carmine did all the negotiating while we met with the fucking traffickers, so he answers.

"No. I'm going to go back tomorrow to see if I can strike a deal. Fernando and that little guy—Pedro—think they're going to score with me since they know I own five strip clubs."

I get distracted for a moment thinking about how I get the feeling he wants to sell those clubs to me since he has a girlfriend. Fuck no. I want nothing to do with those. There's someone I'm into, and she would never forgive me.

I don't like how suspicious a second Colombian pain in our asses sounds when he speaks next. Doubt fills his tone as he picks up the conversation with Carmine.

"Are you going to buy their freedom?"

My best friend's cousin snarls his response.

"Of course." Carmine takes a breath. "Then we'll figure out where they're from or where they want to go. But money exchanging hands is a last-ditch thing. I don't want to actually buy a human being. I don't want anyone—even those motherfucking pieces of shit—to think I want a sex slave. I'm betting I can get Fernando to take the other captives to the warehouse where he said he was going to take Maria and her friends. He said he's leaving tomorrow night and heading back to Cuba."

I pause as I rein in my temper because talking about this is about to make me explode. I want to speak up, but I let Carmine continue.

"I paid Maria's ransom, and we got her out of the villa before he took her to another location. Once Fernando left to do God only knows what, we slipped back in and got Veronica and the two doctors before anyone moved them. He'll think Veronica and the other two women went to the Texan guy he sold them to. Once these other captives are at the warehouse, we'll get them out."

I don't appreciate it when anyone questions what any of us are going to do with the other women. Of course, we'd buy their freedom. Then we're setting them free. We don't keep sex trafficked women. The call ends, and we all look at each other. There's nothing we can do right now, and for men who survive by being in control, this is driving us nuts.

I don't think Maria's or any of the women's condition is so urgent that they can't wait thirty minutes for the doctor *Tres J's* arranged for, but I'm worried. We only know how long ago their captors drugged them because I beat it out of one of them. I dragged the guy away while Carmine spoke to Fernando. He told me what he'd heard. The kidnappers put sacks over their heads but didn't gag them. When they tossed them in the van, they hobbled them but didn't restrain their hands. They wanted to let the women know they could scream or beg, but it would do no good. They wanted the women to know they could fight, but they couldn't get away. They mindfucked them from the beginning. There are several hours between their abduction and their rescue that we can't account for because no one at the villa knew. The women were already unconscious when the guards we saw arrived.

"Matty?"

"Maria!"

She must be out of it. She hasn't called me that since she was eight. I was ten and made it very clear I was Matteo. I practically yank Carmine out of the way to sit next to her. I'm a big guy, just like the rest of us, but I'm as gentle as I can be when I take Maria's hand. I help her sit up, but she shakes her head and lies back down. She covers her eyes with her hands.

"Where are we?"

"We're still in Miami. I'm so sorry, Maria. I'm so sorry I let them take you. What do you need?"

"You didn't let them do anything, Matty. Can I have some water? That's what I need most."

Gabriele thrusts bottled water at me, and I unscrew the cap. I help Maria sit up while she sips. I glance over at the other women, but they're still out. I pull the bottle away from her mouth after three sips.

"Slowly, or you'll be sick."

"What time is it?"

I glance at my watch.

"Six in the evening."

"How many days have I been unconscious?"

"Just today. We couldn't get a read on your tracker for hours. *Tres J's* gave us a tip, and once your captors took you to the villa, it came back on."

"Yeah. That makes sense. I was in a warehouse basement for several hours. Then I was at some house on the water."

"We know. We went there to negotiate your release based on the tip. The man wouldn't budge at first. But while he and Carmine went back and forth, your tracker came back online. That's when Carmine steered the conversation to a ransom rather than buying you back after he sold you to someone else. We got you out by paying, and we got the others when he left."

She looks at the three other women and flinches. That alarms me. I need answers. Now.

"Maria, what did they do to you? We have a doctor coming, but do any of you need more urgent care?"

"No. They did nothing to us but threaten us. Matteo, they're sex traffickers."

"We know. We saw other women there."

We all listen intently to Maria when she speaks.

"I don't think all of those women want to go back to their homes, but they don't want to stay at that villa. That man—Fernando—already has a buyer lined up for the women. Some guy in Texas, I think.

Maria continues, her eyes misty as she remembers what she endured.

"There was one woman, Larisa, who was so brave. I know she was terrified, but she looked out for the other Russian women. She knows no one here. I tried to offer her some clothes one man tossed at me. But the guy got pissed and threatened to strip us all naked. When he left the room, I gave them to her, anyway. It was obvious she'd been in the same outfit for days."

"Was she the blonde one you were next to?"

We saw a group of women walk into the villa from a speedboat, but most of them were in some stage of being drugged. Maria, Veronica, the two doctors, this woman Larisa, and four others laid passed out on mattresses in a guest bedroom. When I saw Maria, I wanted to kill the fucker on the spot. But the priority was getting her out alive immediately, then going back for her friends.

"Yeah. They took her from her apartment in Moscow and got her to Cuba, then Miami. That's all I had time to learn before they knocked us out."

Larisa had been more awake than the rest of them. She looked right at Carmine, and his face said everything once we left. He'd never felt guiltier than he did when he turned his back and carried Maria out of that room. She and the other women weren't there when Luca, Marco, Gabriele, and I went in for Maria's friends. Lorenzo and Carmine stayed with Maria in the SUV we arranged—by that, I mean stole and put fake plates on that we brought with us.

Carmine shakes his head.

"If she winds up there, it'll be practically impossible for anyone to find her. She's more likely to wind up crossing the border back and forth as a mule. She'll probably die from cocaine poisoning rather than anything else."

Drug transporters are often poor people no one would guess are mules. Sometimes, they're young people who look like innocent tourists or older day workers who cross into the U.S. to work and go home to Mexico each night. They swallow little baggies of coke. But they don't have long to get to their destination and vomit them up before the bags disintegrate and release an overdose of coke into their systems. An Eastern European woman crossing the U.S.-Mexican border more than once will look suspicious. Her life expectancy will be short.

Luca inhales deeply enough to hear him before he looks around.

"If there are Russian women involved, we may need to call Maks. He might have connections."

Lorenzo's usually the quietest of all of us. The observer. He speaks up now.

"He might. Or it could put him right back into the Podolskayas' crosshairs. Aren't three of them headed to Moscow soon? Something about going to a funeral with their dads for one of the older guys' KGB friends. Is this the right time to get them involved?"

None of us have a good answer. Maria struggles to move to the edge of the bed. I help her stand, and I figure she wants to go to the bathroom. Instead, she moves around the bed and comes to stand in front of Veronica. She feels for her friend's pulse before examining the unconscious woman's arms and legs. I know she's looking for track marks or any puncture sites.

When she finds nothing, she moves to the other bed and examines the other two women.

"They forced us to swallow some pill. It doesn't look like they gave us anything else. But I could just be missing it. My guess is it was some type of benzodiazepine and not an opioid. Either way, we've all been out for—what—six or seven hours? If I woke up, they should too. We're all different sizes, but these types of sedatives don't depend on body weight. It shouldn't last that much longer in some of us than others. Let's see if we can get them up."

She tries to rouse Veronica while Lorenzo and Gabriele try the other two. Veronica clings to Maria as she comes round, but the two doctors scream when they wake to find a hulking man leaning over each of them. The doctor closer to Veronica and Maria swings her legs over the edge and looks at Maria.

"What happened? I mean, besides being drugged."

Maria looks at her brothers, then back to the woman.

"Someone kidnapped us from the nightclub. Four men dragged Veronica and me from the restroom through a broom closet to a van outside the back of the club. They must have gotten you two while Matteo was waiting for us."

The woman squeezes the bridge of her nose as she speaks again.

"I remember feeling really off and wanting fresh air."

The second doctor confirms it when she adds to the story.

"I felt the same, so we went outside for a couple minutes. We stepped aside, so we didn't get in the way of the line. Next thing we knew, someone was dragging us around the building and throwing us in a van with both of you."

Luca's been as patient as he can be. He pulls Maria into his embrace and envelopes her in a hug. She burrows against his chest and clings to him. I see the doctors looking at Luca's left hand with its wedding ring. I step in as I see the women shift from curious to confused to wary. *What do they think? Maria was out looking to cheat on her husband?*

"I'm Matteo, Maria's brother's best friend. She's hugging Luca, her oldest brother." I point to each person. "Marco—my best friend—and Lorenzo are her other brothers. Carmine's their cousin, and Gabriele is a close family friend of ours. We know Veronica. What are your names?"

The woman who explained what happened shifts her gaze from Luca and Maria to me.

"I'm Tammy. This is Lynette."

Maria pulls back and turns around.

"Neither of you wanted to go out last night, and I convinced you. I'm so sorry."

Lynette stands and wobbles, but once she's sure of her footing, she offers Maria a hug.

"It wasn't any of our faults. I'm just grateful your family came to our rescue."

A knock sounds at the front door, and Gabriele lets the doctor in. The Miami doctor examines all four patients and gives them clean bills of health. Each of the women showers, even though we didn't bring any fresh clothes for them. There are enough bedrooms in the house we broke into for each of them to have their own room and two more bedrooms for the men to take turns sleeping and guarding. The men set up a schedule to keep watch. Carmine takes the first shift with Luca, but I can hear them. I wish I were the one Luca thanked rather than being the one to blame. I really wish no one needed thanking.

"Carmine, thanks for today. You read Fernando and totally knew what to say. We wouldn't have Maria if you hadn't stepped in."

"We would have, and it would have saved us twenty-thousand dollars. But I wasn't willing to wait another second to get her out of there. None of us gives a shit about the money."

"I still appreciate how you handled it."

Guilt and remorse stab at my heart and gut as Luca shoots him a tired but genuine smile. Carmine offers him a rueful one before he responds.

"I know his type. I've pretended to be his type in negotiations before. He did nothing I wasn't already prepared for."

Carmine's come a long way from the shitbag he once was. Luca blows out a long sigh before continuing. What he says next is my fault because I failed to protect Maria.

"We brought enough cash to pay a reasonable amount to help the other women. But there may be more of them than we realize. What then?"

After Carmine's past, his reasonable answers still surprise me.

"The *Tres J's* help us. Or we involve the Kutsenkos. We do our best to manage this ourselves and keep word from spreading that anyone took Maria. We can eat our slices of humble pie if we have to. But we call Uncle Sal before we do either of those things. No more going behind his back."

"Good. I'm going to call Olivia."

Luca pulls out his phone to call his wife.

We give the women a few more hours to sleep off the effects of the drugs. Lynette and Tammy go straight to the hotel and leave the conference. Neither asked us questions. They just accepted how we got them free. Odd. But definitely better than having to lie to them. We head back to Fernando's villa and everyone but Lorenzo and Carmine goes into a coffee shop. They go inside the villa to negotiate for the other women. But it doesn't work because they aren't there. We drive straight to the airport. Not soon enough, I'm walking into Maria, Luca, Marco, and Lorenzo's parents' house.

It's inevitable that we have to debrief Uncle Salvatore the next morning. The shame rushes back to me. Telling the senior members of our *Cosa Nostra* branch what happened is like salt and lemon juice in my open wound filled with guilt. When Marco sees me struggle to go on, he chimes in with more of what Maria told us once we were all aboard the plane.

"Since none of their kidnappers spoke the entire way to the villa, Maria wasn't certain who had them. She told herself not to automatically assume Russians since that's a shit stereotype. But she couldn't figure out if they were random Americans or a rival. Once they reached the villa, the men spoke Spanish. I doubt they realized Maria's fluent, though she said they knew her name. She believes they looked at all of their IDs. She figured they would have thought she's Latina given her name and coloring. Perhaps seeing her last name meant they knew she wasn't. Or they targeted her from the get-go."

Uncle Salvatore nods along with what Marco said.

"Does Maria remember enough from before they drugged her to give you any hints?"

Luca answers for us.

"No. They said nothing to the women. They did it all in complete silence. Maria knows there were at least four men because she and Veronica reached the van at almost the same time as Lynette and Tammy. It was highly coordinated, so their captors didn't have to say anything. This was obviously not their first time. From how efficient they were and from the number of women at that villa, they're pros."

I run my hands through my hair for the umpteenth time. My guilt is like an extra person in the room. It consumes so much space and is such a heavy presence. Lorenzo's been quiet, like usual. But he's a keen observer of people and has situational awareness like a hawk.

"Their nasal accents and some of the slang they used made it clear they're Cubans. They never told us that, but I could tell. Never mind that we were in Miami, and Cuba is pissing distance from there for sex trafficking. Fernando mentioned selling to a Texan. I don't think their buyers intend them all to become forced sex workers. Many of them were going to be mules. The women we saw didn't fit the mold for forced prostitutes. They clearly came from different socioeconomic groups, which makes sense if they want some to pass as drug smugglers."

There were about three dozen women in the villa. Some in the upstairs bedrooms, drugged and unconscious. Some on the patio, just arriving. Others were in various parts of the downstairs. There were women of all races, body shapes, height, and, as Lorenzo mentioned, socioeconomic backgrounds. I'm certain Fernando would claim he was giving some a better life by getting them out of poverty or dangerous countries. Bull-fucking-shit.

Our *consigliere*—Luca, Marco, Lorenzo, and Maria's dad—looks at Uncle Salvatore, his face grim.

"When we take out Fernando and his colleagues, what do we do about the women? We could just leave them to figure shit out on their own, but we all know that wouldn't sit right with any of us. But if we get involved, we risk at least one of them going to the authorities and naming us. A group of men who sound like Italian New Yorkers makes it pretty obvious. We won't have the luxury of remaining silent."

It's the *consigliere's* job to state the obvious and not so obvious, to question all situations, sometimes including Uncle Salvatore's decisions. If they weren't brothers, it would have come to blows on a few occasions. But he never, ever does it where anyone but the men in this room can hear. He can be both the devil and the angel on Uncle Salvatore's shoulders, but he always does it with what's best for our family and the ones we protect in mind. If anyone can process a load of information and make a judicious decision on the drop of a dime, it's him.

Uncle Salvatore taps his fingers on his desk in a rhythm I've heard my entire life. It's not as simple as just pinky to index finger and back again. It's ring finger, index finger, pinky, middle finger. Three taps each. He said it came from hours of piano practice being drilled into him. It's like playing an arpeggio. There's something reassuring about it because I know it means Uncle Salvatore is methodically planning a solution. I can't wait to be as vindictive as possible as we act on our vendetta. Both vindictive and vendetta come from Latin. We Italians gave the world those words, and we will show those Cuban sacks of shit that we know exactly what they mean.

Chapter Two

Maria

Today

Matteo's been my second shadow since we returned from Miami. It's a blessing and a curse. I love it, and I hate it. He breathes down my neck when he's assigned to my security detail, which irks. But I miss him when he's assigned to Luca's wife, Olivia, or Carmine's wife, Serafina. I hate that too because missing him irks just as much. But I love when we're able to chat and just hang out. No one believes me when I say he's hilarious. Not even Marco, and they're practically twins. Seriously. Matteo's two hours younger than Marco. Our parents are best friends. We call them Uncle Domenico—because that's easier than Second-However-Many-Times-Removed or Third Cousin Domenico—and Auntie Carlotta.

Matteo's dad is my dad's closest friend and has been since they were in second grade. He's my dad's adopted second cousin. That was a whole scandal eleven years ago. Fucking Irish prick released Uncle Domenico's sealed adoption records just to spite us. It hit Uncle Domenico really hard that he and Matteo aren't really our blood relatives.

Marco and Matteo used to nap together in the same crib and have been besties since they were three. Matteo has spent the night at my family's house as often as Marco's spent the night at his. By the time they were six, each set of parents set aside a spare bedroom for their honorary son. I'm used to Matteo walking around my parents' house in pajamas, and it used to feel like he was my fourth brother. Not so much anymore.

Things definitely haven't been the same between Matteo and me since I was kidnapped in Miami. I thought we were making progress at Carmine and Serafina's wedding in South Africa. She noticed, and I think Marco has questions. But Matteo's gone back to being frosty with me, so I guess not. We're just not as comfortable around each other as we once were. I'm back to being his best friend's little sister who needs looking after. I appreciate it, but it annoys me at the same time. I liked it better when we were friends with no qualifiers or caveats.

Now I often feel like a burden to him. A constant reminder in his mind that he failed as a *capo* and as my brother's best friend. Neither Marco nor I blame Matteo in the least. Not a single person in my family does. But I get how it is. Something happened on his watch, and he couldn't stop it, and he didn't solve it on his own. He's not prideful by nature, and that's not what it's about. He's worried people will question his fitness to be a leader in our branch of the *Cosa Nostra*, and he's terrified of reflecting poorly on our family and Uncle Salvatore in particular.

I've tried to ease his guilt, but he offers me that placating smile, as though I'm the one who needs calming down. That especially grates on my nerves. It's like he wants to wallow in the shame at times because he thinks that's his penance. No one—not God or the devil or anyone in between—is punishing him except for he himself. But I know my extra security detail doesn't help at all.

Giuseppe has always been the most inconspicuous of my guards, so I can almost forget he's around. I can see out my bedroom window that he just stepped outside my apartment building, as though he's waiting for a cab. But I know he's keenly aware of everything going on. Why couldn't all my guys be like that? The others are great, but they rarely try to blend in. That has its pros and cons. Right now, having two of my guards, Matteo, and his two guards standing in front of my building is drawing stares as I peer down at them. Mostly because there isn't an average one in the bunch, and they're all huge. But they also are brooding as fuck, which makes the pack of them appear menacing. That's not by accident.

I take a last look at myself in the mirror as I snap the back on my earring stud. I brush my hands down my floral dress and hope I didn't err picking something pastel. I grab my high heels and go to my front door. I live alone now that I'm done with med school. I can't expect anyone to live with my rotation schedule as a radiology resident. Besides, I like my little apartment in Manhattan. It suits me. I slip my shoes on, then my coat.

I'm headed to a hospital fundraiser for the oncology department. I'll know all the other doctors there, but I won't know any of them well unless they're from my department. I love being a radiologist, but we're not the most social group. We spend our time looking at imaging, so we're not making rounds or in surgery like so many other doctors. I climb into the town car waiting for us. My other guard's driving, and Giuseppe is in the front passenger seat. Matteo and his guys follow us in an SUV.

When we arrive at the hotel where the event's being held,

there's already a crowd. Since it's New York City, and there are some major donors here tonight, there's a step-and-repeat. I'm certain my guys are crawling out of their skin at the idea of me mingling in the crowd outside and standing in front of what's basically a massive target to have my photo taken.

My driver will have to park, which means only Giuseppe will walk over with me. It's normal for only one guard to escort me if the other is also my driver. But I can tell they're both uneasy about the crowd I can now see, thanks to the privacy glass being down now. Alfonso maneuvers onto the next street and pulls up. Giuseppe gets out, and I wait for him to open my door. I know to never get into or out of a vehicle without one of my guards at the door. I don't even open them myself. It's a precaution. They check the exterior and scan our surroundings before I go anywhere.

It takes Giuseppe a little longer to open the door than I expected, and it makes me anxious. When he does, he thrusts out his hand and practically pulls me from the vehicle. He usually just holds my hand as a courtesy. He wraps his arm around me and hurries me to the entrance. I scan the crowd for Matteo and the others, but I can't see them. Now I'm nervous. I assumed they were right behind us.

"Beppe, what's going on? Where's the SUV?"

"They got caught at a light a couple blocks back, but they should be here in a moment. But Alfonso and I don't want you out here without more of us. There are too many people for me to watch by myself, and he can't just leave the car at the curb. Come on."

I catch sight of Matteo getting out of the SUV just as I pass through the circular hotel door. I squeeze my eyes shut for a second, then ease one open. I lean forward to look out of the glass. Matteo has his arms crossed, and his suit strains across his back. I know his legs are like tree trunks within his trousers. His suit coat hides it, but I also know his ass looks amazing. That's an aside for my own sake. But he appears unmovable. He's blocking the sidewalk to the hotel doors, and I realize that's no accident. He wants me to get inside before anyone else passes.

I want to wait for him, suddenly feeling calmer for knowing he's here, but Giuseppe's practically herding me across the lobby. I scan the crowd and feel more assured that my dress for tonight wasn't a mistake. There are plenty of women in little black or red dresses, so I definitely stand out. But the pastel floral cocktail dress isn't out of place. I wear scrubs most days and have my hair in a messy bun. It's not that I can't be stylish. I just have little practice these days, so I get nervous. I'm always aware I represent the Mancinelli family, especially since I'm the only girl in my generation.

I spot Carmine and Serafina, and I relax even more. I point them out to my guard, and we make our way over to my cousin. It only takes me a moment to spot Carmine's best friend, Gabriele, who's assigned to Serafina for the night. Carmine and Gabriele have been best friends since they were ten, and Gabriele moved here from Palermo. I made friends with him when he knew no one and spoke little English; that way, he had more than just Carmine.

"Car, Sera."

Serafina and I exchange hugs and kisses on each cheek before I do the same with Carmine. We've always been really close since I'm six weeks older than him. He's a different man than he was a year ago, but we've always been close. He's made more shit choices than I can count, but I've never once believed he was a shitty person. Now he's with Serafina, and he's happier than he's ever been. They're still newlyweds, having only gotten married five months ago. They've kept to themselves a lot since then, and who can blame them? They haven't attended many social events since last Easter, so it doesn't surprise me when Sera stays close to my side when Carmine joins my brothers and Matteo. Gabriele stands behind us, now watching over both of us.

We both shift when the doors open again, and I turn into a statue. We watch as a group of men enter the ballroom. They're ruggedly handsome, in a devil-may-care sort of way with an arrogance that would be unappealing on most men but somehow works for them. Serafina whispers to me as she sways closer, her eyes never leaving the new arrivals. She can sense the shift in the air and the change in my attitude.

"Who are they?"

"The Irish."

"The O'Rourkes? I don't see their leader or his right-hand man. They both terrified me at our uncle's wedding."

It always feels funny to say "our" when we talk about Uncle Salvatore and Aunt Sylvia. My brothers and I, along with Carmine, are related to the couple through Uncle Salvatore. Serafina's related to them through Aunt Sylvia. We use the English aunt and uncle, but since Serafina grew up in Italy, *zio* and *zia* will always be their titles to her.

"The leader you met is dead, and so is his best friend. They messed with the oldest Kutsenko's wife. The guy who inherited the leadership messed with the youngest Kutsenko's wife."

I offer Serafina nothing more, since I'm certain there's nothing she wants to know that won't give us both nightmares. She watches as they move toward a table, and her brow furrows. Her next question reminds me I really need to tell Carmine to do a better job of teaching Serafina about our rivals. But I know they dealt with enough shit when they were dating, so I get that the Irish probably haven't been on his mind much.

"Who's who?"

"The one in front is Dillan. Don't go near him. He will hurt women and children. He has no boundaries or hard limits."

"Doesn't that break the code?"

I flinch, then force myself to nod.

"Apparently, no women and children are a thing of the past for the mob. The twins are Sean and Shane. Sean has a freckle on his throat. That's the only way I know how to tell them apart. Finn is their older brother. They may as well be triplets from how much they look alike. Just like their mother. What I heard when we were all kids was that caused quite a stir on both delivery days. Finn is the one in the back. He's the only one I sorta trust. Their cousins on their mother's side, Seamus and Cormac, are between the twins and Finn."

"Sorta? Why him?"

"We were at a party a few years ago, and neither of us knew the other was going to be there. We would have avoided it if we'd known. Donovan sold a ton of Fentanyl to the guys hosting it, and the girl Finn was with took some when he went to get them another drink. It was my first year of med school, and I was home for a vacation. I did what I could. But no one had Narcan with them. I carry it everywhere with me now. The girl died. I sent Finn away and dealt with the police for him. I never mentioned him. No one else did either. The hosts didn't want to lose their drug dealer, and the guests didn't want a visit from Seamus and Cormac."

"Doesn't saving his ass get you some protection from his family?"

"Yes. At least, I think so. But I never want to test that theory."

The O'Rourkes take their seats, and I scan the crowd for any of the other syndicates. It's easy to recognize the Ivankov bratva since the six Kutsenko and two Andreyev men are always the largest in the crowd. All but Sergei and Anton are married now, and the wives are as equally beautiful as the men are hot.

While the O'Rourkes have the devil-may-care attitude that makes them appear arrogant, the bratva men exude an aura of silent but deadly. I spy the Diazes already at a table and nod when their *jefe*, Enrique, and I lock gazes. I nudge Serafina away before she spots them. She's not fond of them. Enrique might be the only syndicate leader to laugh often, but he's ruthless, just like Uncle Salvatore, Dillan, and Maksim.

I feel bad for Serafina and for Luca's wife, Olivia, since there are so many names and faces to memorize. I drew them family trees a few months ago, but this is the first time Serafina is putting several faces with names.

Now that every leading family of New York's underground is in the same room, we'll all play nice for appearance's sake. It confuses the fuck out of people, since I think most people expect some Godfather-style shoot-out whenever we're together. But that'd be bad for business. People might guess—even know—who and what we are, but not a one of us will admit it.

"Stay close."

I gasp when Matteo comes to stand behind my right shoulder. I nod as I look back at him. He's so close I can feel the heat radiating from him, smell the hint of his cologne, and practically taste the mint on his breath.

"I know. I will. Can you try to have a good time tonight?"

"This is work."

My smile falters, and I know my gaze hardens.

"I'll endeavor not to be too tedious then."

"Maria, that isn't what I meant, and you know it."

"Oh? You're only here because you're assigned to me, and you refuse to have a good time because you're at work. Easy to piece together that means you won't have fun because you're stuck with me."

"Don't start with me. You know that wasn't what I meant.

I'm not interested in whether or not I have a good time. I'm interested in you making it home tonight. Nothing is more important than that."

His tone sends a shiver coursing along my spine. It's so definitive, and when he tells me nothing's more important than my safety, I can't help but relax. I know I'm safe with him.

"Matteo, I just feel horrible that you're still so stressed about me going anywhere. You haven't let yourself relax in eight months. I know you take your duty seriously, but I miss hearing you laugh."

Our gazes meet, and we stare until people moving around us snap us out of our trance. When a server comes by with a tray of hors d'oeuvres, it surprises me when he picks out the things I like most and hands me a plate. He avoided the olives— I know, I know. How can I be Italian and not love olives?—and doubled up on the salami and prosciutto. He discreetly bumps the tomatoes off the bruschetta and onto his own plate. Again, I know. I love tomatoes in things. I really just don't like them raw. Firm on the outside and mushy and watery on the inside. No thanks.

But he's known me all twenty-nine years I've been alive. I know he knows what I do and don't like. We grew up together. It just makes me feel special that he made sure I got what I like and not what I don't. Our fingers brush as he hands me the plate.

"Thanks. We remind me of Jack Sprat and his wife."

"He could eat no fat, and his wife could eat no lean. Between the two, they licked the plate clean. Sounds like us plenty of times when we were kids and during the holidays."

He flashes me a smile that reminds me of the Matteo from before "the incident." That's how I think of it. Air quotes and all. I try not to think about it at all.

"This is delicious. You should have yours before I take it."

I savor the first bite of bruschetta made with *taleggio* instead of mozzarella. It's one of Italy's smellier cheeses, but it has a mild and slightly tangy fruit flavor. I could make an entire meal out of just this. I watch Matteo and offer him an appreciative smile in return. I still can't believe he made a plate of just what I like. We've attended tons of events like this, and he's never done that before. It makes me feel all warm and gooey inside.

When it's time to sit for dinner, he pulls my chair out for me and sits to my right. Gabriele's between me and Serafina, who's to my left, and Carmine is to her left. Luca and Olivia are farther down the table with Lorenzo, while Marco is on the other side of Matteo. Even though it's a plated meal that'll be served by course, there're bottles of wine along the table. I reach for the one in front of us, but Matteo gets to it faster and picks it up. Every man in my family is chivalrous to the nth degree. Their fathers would never let them forget if they weren't. I find I love listening to him speak Italian as he keeps his voice low and continues.

"*Gradisce del vino?*" Would you like some wine?

"*Sì, per favore. Ma non troppo.*" Yes, please. But not too much.

"*So che questo rosso ti fa venire il mal di testa.*" I know this red gives you headaches.

I chuckle as we continue in Italian.

"It also gives me a hangover, which you know since you were the first person to ever get me drunk."

"That wasn't on purpose, and shh. Thirteen years later, and Marco still doesn't know it was me. It's one of two secrets I've kept from him and why I'm still alive."

It was my freshman year of high school, and I was a competitive rider. I went to practice with my first hangover and fell from my horse. I injured myself so badly that I was in the hospital for weeks. Carmine used to come every day to tutor me and keep me company when the others had jobs Uncle Salvatore gave them. He was so kind to me when I cried during physical therapy. For a while, I felt closer to my cousin than my three brothers. I broke my arm and fractured ribs to go along with a nasty concussion. But it was those injuries that made me interested in radiology and set me on the path to my career.

"Your secrets are always safe with me."

He glances over at me, and I practically melt. I know what that other secret is, and it's also one I'll always keep. My brothers would likely kill us both. Matteo would definitely already be in his grave if they knew. I sip my wine, barely tasting it as I shift my attention to the hospital's CEO as she makes a speech I've heard several times before. It's always the same smoke being blown up donor's asses before she practically sticks her hand beneath everyone's noses to gather checks with at least six zeros on each of them.

I know he's trying to show he can relax around me when he focuses on me rather than striking up a conversation with Marco.

"Did you have a busy day today?"

"Yeah. There were two gnarly MVAs that came in, so a lot of rushing imaging before the patients went into surgery. I hate knowing that it comes from car accidents, but they are often the most fascinating x-rays I read."

I shrug and blush. I wish I could swallow my words since it sounds fucked-up even to my ears.

"I bet you see some crazy shit from those. But I bet they also test you to find the tiniest irregularities, and doctors count on that."

"True."

The meal begins, and he turns to Marco. Serafina and I lean forward to chat, and Gabriele and Carmine talk over our heads. We're used to it. Our seating arrangement is always on purpose to ensure every woman has an armed male family member on either side. Annoying, but it's proven wise plenty of times. I look past Gabriele and Serafina to find Carmine watching me. I'm uncertain what to make of his speculative expression, and I'm uncertain I want to. I offer him a smile before shifting my attention to my food.

Conversation flows around me, and I regret turning my attention away from Serafina. She's occupied talking to Carmine, so she doesn't need me to keep her company. But we both grin and sit back as dessert arrives. I look at them and recognize several of Matteo's favorites. The chef tonight clearly knows Italian cuisine, and since my family is the largest donor at the event, it's a damn good thing that they do.

I reach for the plate a server placed in front of us and pick out the Italian wedding cookies with the glaze and sprinkles. I put three on the plate. Then I grab two *pignoli* made from almond-paste and topped with pine nuts. I skip the sesame biscuits. I don't care for those either. I grab us each a *brutti ma buoni*—ugly but good. They're meringue-based cookies with hazelnuts inside. They're both crisp and chewy. They tend to have an uneven texture on the outside, so hence the name. I didn't expect the catering department to serve something so— unrefined, but I don't care.

I hand over the heaping plate, and Matteo grins like he did when we were kids. This is the most at ease he's been in ages. I suck in a breath when Matteo's knee presses against mine as he reaches forward to pour more wine for me. I shift to give him more room, but his leg still presses against mine. What am I supposed to do with that? For a moment, I thought it was an accident, but he hasn't moved it.

I'm trying not to make too much of it since it's not the first time we've sat this close. But it is the first time we're spending an entire course secretly touching beneath the table. I bite into my dessert, then force myself not to reach for more. I focus on that until his hand dips beneath the tablecloth. He rests it on my thigh for only a moment before he pulls it away as he leans toward me.

"I really should have told you how beautiful you look when we got here."

"Thank you." I glance around. "You always look amazing in your suits, but I really like the tie. It makes your eyes appear even greener."

"I am having a good time tonight, and the sky hasn't fallen and the walls haven't crashed down around us. I'm enjoying your company."

"You talked to Marco most of the meal, and I was chatting with Serafina."

"But I'm sitting next to you. I didn't pick out your favorite antipasti by accident, and you didn't pick out my favorite desserts by chance. We both know that."

"That's true."

What else do I say? We've known each other our entire lives, so it would surprise no one that we know what each other prefers. But I picked out the items to make him happy, and I think he did the same for me. The conversation hits an uncomfortable lull when neither of us knows what to say next. I'm wracking my brain for anything, but I come up with nothing in time. Serafina leans forward again, drawing my attention back to her.

"People danced at the Easter dinner. Will people dance at an event like this? I know if I ask Carmine, he'll indulge me. But I don't want us to be the only couple out there."

I smile at my newest cousin. She and Carmine have nearly as complicated a past as Matteo and me. But last Easter, I maneuvered them to sit next to each other. They hit it off after being nemeses since they were twelve. They danced together, and I'm pretty certain they fell in love that night.

"Yeah. The quartet should start playing soon, and some people will head out there."

I watch Carmine wrap his arm around Serafina's shoulders and whisper something to her. She presses a quick kiss to his cheek before nodding. Somehow, I don't think they're talking about dancing. At least not the upright kind they can do in public. It's only a couple minutes later, and the string quartet's just started playing. People are stepping onto the parquet temporary dance floor, and Carmine stands to help Serafina out of her chair. I watch them make their way out to where other couples are dancing. I try not to sigh as I watch them, so clearly devoted to each other. It's not quite envy that I feel. More like longing.

"Would you like to dance?"

I turn toward Matteo and nod. Our parents made us all take ballroom dancing classes as tweens, so Matteo and I fall into a natural rhythm. We've been partnering for over a decade. But this time, he holds me a little closer. Or am I just imagining things?

"What are your plans for tomorrow night? I'm on your detail again."

Well, fuck. I didn't know that. Something must have changed because Alfonso and Giuseppe were supposed to have the night shift. Neither Matteo's parents nor mine, nor Uncle Salvatore and Aunt Sylvia, attended tonight. But everyone our age is here, so if it hadn't been Matteo guarding me, it would have been Marco. I know Carmine prefers Gabriele to guard Serafina. Lorenzo is Olivia's extra body-guard tonight, so only Marco is truly free. I figured Matteo would have his own plans for tomorrow since he's technically working tonight.

"Not much. I was just going to hang out and watch something."

Matteo does *not* need to know I was going to hang out at my BDSM club and watch other people have sex. He definitely does not need to know what I planned to get up to while I was there. Alfonso and Giuseppe are the only ones who know about my secret membership. I trust them, and they've always been discreet when they accompany me. I know for a fact that I'm not the only person in my family who likes their sex kinky. I've overheard the guys talking before. Luca and Carmine both had memberships to pretty exclusive clubs. I don't know if they canceled those, but... I suspect my new sister and new cousin share proclivities similar to their husbands'.

"Sounds low key."

"Uh-huh."

It's going to be. But that was hardly what I planned. Well, fuck all over again. I'm going to have to text the guy I was going to meet. We're definitely not dating since we don't see each other socially outside of the club, and we don't have an established relationship of any kind other than we like to meet there a few times a month if our schedules work out. It's not always easy since our rotations don't always line up. My gaze darts across the ballroom to the very man I'm going to text later. He's standing with three other doctors, none of whom have any clue he and I have an arrangement.

When I shift my gaze back to Matteo, I realize he's been watching me. The look in his eyes has hardened, and he's definitely suspicious. He guides us along with the music until we've turned, so he can now see where I was looking.

"Are you having company over?"

"I wasn't planning on it."

"Were you hoping to?"

"No."

That was easy to answer honestly. I hoped and planned to be tied up and fucked tomorrow night. Neither of those is happening.

"Someone you know over there, Maria?"

"I know most of the doctors here. I'm a radiologist. There isn't a department I don't work with."

His fingers press into my lower back, and I'm certain his arm just got tighter around me. It's not wishful thinking. His warm breath tickles my ear.

"Who is he?"

"Who's who?"

"Which man are you dating that you don't want anyone to know about?"

"Matteo, I'm not dating anyone. Seriously."

I'm just fucking him at least once a week when we can.

Matteo looks completely unconvinced and almost angry, which makes no sense to me. I realize he doesn't want anyone to hear him grilling me, so that's why he pulled me closer.

"It's someone over there. Fine. You don't want to tell me, but you know your brothers will find out eventually. If you have a boyfriend, you should tell them now."

"I don't have a boyfriend. I'm not even dating anyone seriously. You know that. I just recognized some colleagues, and they caught my attention for a moment."

He peers down at me skeptically, but he nods. The song ends, and I move to step away. His arms drop, and I regret moving so hastily. Instead, he leads me off the dance floor, and we quickly let our family know we're headed out. I say I'm tired and have to be at the hospital by six. I notice Carmine's helping Serafina into her coat, and Olivia already has hers on. The two couples arrived together in the same limo. I look around for my guards, and spot Alfonso and Giuseppe by the main doors.

"Goodnight, Marco. Goodnight, Enzo." I hug both of my brothers, then turn to Matteo. "Night. You guys have fun."

His brow furrows.

"I have the night shift all the way through. Francesco will meet us at your place."

"I figured you were off the clock and going with Marco to Enzo's club."

My next older brother owns one of the hottest nightclubs in New York, and if Marco and Matteo didn't drink for free, they could probably pay Lorenzo's mortgage. Neither ever gets drunk. None of my relatives or I get intoxicated in public. That's hazardous for our health. Alcohol impairs reaction time and decision making. That only makes the target on the guys even bigger.

Matteo, Marco, Lorenzo, Luca, and Carmine are all over six feet tall and probably between two-ten and two-twenty-five. Gabriele's the same height, but he's gotta be two-fifty, two-sixty. They're all lean muscle without an ounce of fat to spare with metabolisms like they're still seventeen. They can hold the liquor they drink.

"Not tonight."

I hear suspicion in his voice, and I wonder if he thinks I planned to slip out tonight after this event. I shrug and let him help me with my coat. I can't wait to get home and take off these heels. Blessedly, this hotel isn't too far from my Upper East Side apartment. We say nothing as we walk through the lobby, his hand resting at the small of my back. Alfonso already has the car out front. He opens the back door, and I slide in.

Matteo rides in the back of the town car with me while Alfonso drives and Giuseppe sits up front. I spy Francesco already parked on the street when we arrive. Alfonso stops close to the elevator in the underground parking lot. The people in my building know who the town cars belong to, so no one ever says anything when my guys park a little less than legally when they're picking me up or dropping me off.

"Goodnight."

Matteo offers me a loose hug as he speaks. I don't know when he slipped another mint, but his spicy breath wafts across me. I return his hug, then I'm watching him walk up the ramp to the street as my guards and I wait for the elevator. I recognize the restlessness that I suddenly feel. It's something only Matteo creates. Shit. His plans are changing tomorrow night, not mine.

Chapter Three

Matteo

Maria wasn't telling me the truth tonight, but it's none of my business who she's dating. But she definitely spotted someone at the party. I saw the recognition flash in her eyes, and it wasn't like she spotted a colleague or an old friend. It was something—I don't know—more intimate. I hated it. Like passionately and almost violently. I know the emotion. It was jealousy. It's not one that I've felt often in my life, but only one thing—one person—causes it.

Marco and I are pretty much fraternal twins. We've shared everything since the day we were born. Our moms delivered in the same room. We used to share cribs when they visited each other, and it was our nap time. If he wasn't over at my house every night, then I was at his, even on school nights. I have an older brother, Emilio, and Marco has his two brothers. I've always shared with them. Carmine's mom is Uncle Salvatore's younger sister. Marco's dad, Uncle Massimo, is the middle sibling. So, I've shared pretty much as often with Carmine as I have Emilio, Marco, Lorenzo, and Luca. Once Gabriele moved here, he became Carmine's fraternal twin. Add him to the mix, and I've had very few things that are only mine.

And I've been totally okay with that. I haven't liked Carmine or Gabriele much for—what—like—seventeen years. But whatever shit was between Luca and him is over. Some heavy shit's come out about how Carmine's grandfathers used to treat him as a kid that makes his piss-pour attitude for the past twenty years make way more sense. Now that I actually understand him, I like him. Gabriele was never that bad. He was just always with Carmine. Guilty by association.

So, there's only one person on our confusing and sprawling family tree who elicits any sense of jealousy from me. And it's not that I'm jealous *of* her. I'm jealous of anyone *with* her who isn't me. But I'd give my left nut before I admitted that to anyone. Obviously, she's not into me if she was checking out some guy while dancing in my arms. And Marco would flip his fucking lid. She's supposed to be my baby sister too, but she's so not. Not since she was fifteen and stopped looking like a girl and suddenly looked like a woman. She sure as fuck stopped feeling like my baby sister when we discovered Papa—and therefore Emilio and I—aren't Mancinellis by blood. She's not truly my whatever kind of cousin.

But I'm certain plenty of people would think my attraction to her is fucked-up incest. So, I keep my mouth shut and make sure no one knows. I thought maybe she'd figured it out by how attentive I was after the fucktastrophe in Miami, and I was almost certain she shared my feelings when we were looking at each other during Carmine and Serafina's first wedding at the courthouse. Serafina definitely sensed something, and it confused Carmine enough that his expression showed. Marco saw Carmine's face, which made him look at us. I was scared he guessed, but he's given no hint that he has.

Maria's safely tucked away in her apartment, and I'm staked out in an SUV halfway down her block with Francesco. We've said nothing to any of the women, but there have been some extra rumblings with the Irish lately, so we're keeping the women in our family closer than usual. They fucked up a deal we had with the Boston Albanians, and we struck back three months ago.

Someone unexpectedly searched several of their ships, and the cargo got turned over to the DEA and ATF. Kilos of drugs and crates full of guns. The feds were dancing a fucking jig at the Irish's wake with that score. None of the mob's top leadership, the O'Rourkes, went down for anything. Fuckers are slicker than a greased pig. But they lost at least a dozen men during the raid, and several more are at Rikers still. Fuck around and find out.

We know they're raring to strike back at us, but they also have their eye on the bratva. Right now, they're more pissed at the Russians than they are at us. But we know better than to lower our guard when things are this heated.

So, that means I'm spending the night in the car with Francesco. Luckily, I really like him. I don't mind the other members of Maria's detail, but Francesco's wife is an insanely good cook, and she always makes sure he brings tons of food. He's also just a really good guy. He knows when to be chatty and when to entertain himself.

The next six hours pass quicker than I expected, and Martin arrives just before dawn to relieve me. Alfonso and Giuseppe will be back at noon for their shift. No one's getting much time off, and I know it sucks for all the guys. But they're all Made Men, except for Martin. His family's not Italian, so he can never rise higher than an associate. But my dad and Uncle Massimo, Uncle Salvatore's brother, trained him. He's been

Maria's guard the longest and even went away to college and med school with her.

"Ms. Mancinelli warned me yesterday that today's gonna be a long one."

Martin's stretching as we stand together outside Maria's building. That must mean they're cycling at least ten or fifteen miles before Maria puts in a ten-hour shift at the hospital. I'm about to leave in the SUV Martin arrived in when Maria walks outside. Her hair's up in a messy bun, and she's got only one earbud in. She knows better than to go out anywhere with both in. It's not safe. It's January, and the morning is fucking frigid. She's bundled up against the wind that'll be in their face for most of their ride. She leans her bike against the wall as she stretches, too.

"You ready?"

She grins at Martin, who's in as good a shape as all of us. He's the only guy who enjoys cycling. He just doesn't enjoy how close Maria gets to the cars sometimes. He's terrified he's going to be scooping her off the pavement and rushing her to my mom, who's a general surgeon at the same hospital where Maria works. He's more scared of Maria's mom, Auntie Nicoletta, than he is of Uncle Massimo, Maria's dad. Rightly so. All the moms are way more terrifying than their mafioso husbands.

"Yeah. You ready, Ms. Mancinelli?"

"Born ready."

I watch them mount their bikes and clip their shoes in, then they're off. I watch until they're out of sight, then I head home to catch a few hours sleep. Except I'm lying in bed with my eyes wide open. Something's gotta give and soon. I need to know if it's all in my head or if what I've thought are subtle hints are real. If they are, then I'm not going to ignore them. And that means batten down the hatches. Hurricane Marco's going to make landfall.

I should have tried harder to sleep. I'm trying not to fall asleep as I deal with payroll. I rarely come into my strip clubs' offices, but I do once every two weeks to supervise payroll. I want to know just how much each of the women makes and how much the clubs bring in. I don't give a shit if the women report like two percent of what they earn. I'm not the IRS. But I do demand to know we're turning a profit. Carmine used to do this, and he was as strict a taskmaster as I am. But the moment he and Serafina decided to get married, I knew he was going to hand them over to me. I'm never a patron, but they're great places for us to launder our money, and that's why I check the books regularly.

"Hi, Mr. Mancinelli."

"Hi, Reba."

"Can I get you anything?"

She's a gorgeous blonde, but I'm not interested. I can't say the disinterest is mutual. But I know she doesn't give a shit about me as a person. She's angling for better days and hours, so she's after me as the owner. She probably also wouldn't mind bragging rights to fucking the owner. Carmine warned me about her.

"Nope. Just headed to the office. Make sure everyone knows I'm not to be disturbed." I turn away, then twist back to look at her. "By anyone."

She pouts, and I want to roll my eyes. She's in a g string and pasties, and my cock doesn't stir a bit. I get to my office and picture Maria in the floral dress she had on last night, and I'm a fucking tent pole. It takes at least a half-an-hour of looking at Profit and Loss Statements before my dick goes back to sleep. I glance at the sofa in the corner, and I'm seriously tempted to take a nap. The office door's locked, so no one's going to bother me.

Fuck it. A cat nap will get me through since I'll be spending another night outside Maria's place. If I sleep for an hour-and-a-half, then I still have enough time to approve payroll, grab dinner, then head to her apartment. I slip off my suit coat jacket and pull my gun from the holster at my lower back. I recline on the sofa, my arms crossed, and the gun resting in my right hand on my chest. I'm just drifting off when someone pounds on the door.

"Busy. Go away."

"Let me in, Matteo."

I'm off the sofa in a heartbeat and across the room. I practically yank the door off the hinges before I pull Maria into my office.

"What's wrong? What happened?"

She looks completely freaked out.

"I headed out to run an errand during my break, but Alfonso wasn't at the end of my hallway. I looked around, but I couldn't find him. I waited five minutes, thinking maybe he'd gone to the restroom. When he didn't come back, I called Beppe. He didn't answer. I tried my brothers and Carmine, but none of them answered."

I try not to let it sting that she didn't call me. But I'm more concerned about why Alfonso and Giuseppe weren't at their posts.

"How'd you get here? Did you drive to work?"

"Yeah."

I see she's trembling, so I pull her into my arms. The moment her head hits my chest, she sags against me. I stroke her hair to where it ends mid-back. She has her arms pulled up between us, but she shifts and wraps them around me. I barely hear her when she speaks again.

"I couldn't get here fast enough. I just kept praying you were still here."

I'm the one she came to. She called the other guys, but she came here. She didn't go home. She didn't go to her parents or anyone else.

"How'd you know I'd be here?"

"Because today's the second Tuesday of the month, which means payroll. You check on the other clubs, but this is the one where you work. It's the quietest. Though that bitch downstairs fucking squawked like a pissed off goose when I insisted upon coming up here."

"Reba?"

"Yeah. How'd you know?"

"Because you described her perfectly."

"She's fucking pissed as shit. She insisted you wouldn't see me, and I laughed in her face. I was too upset to argue with her. I told her to find out who the fuck I am before she speaks to me like that again."

Maria never talks to people like that. Ever. She never throws her family name around, and she never uses her privilege as a Mafia daughter to get anything. She works for everything she has and has earned it all. She'd rather no one know her connections than brag about them. She hates intimidating people. She's super freaked out.

I ease her over to the sofa where I'd just planned to take a nap. We sit, and I keep my arms wrapped around her. She tries to burrow closer, but the position's awkward. I don't think what I'm doing until I've done it. I pick her up and place her on my lap. She immediately curls into me, and I glance down to see her eyes are closed.

"Can you track them? Can you find out where they are? They would never abandon me. I'm terrified something's happened to them."

I pull my phone out of my pocket, trying not to jostle Maria while I do it. I unlock it and pull up the tracking app we use for our guys and our vehicles. I tap on Giuseppe's name first. His phone's pinging in Queens; it's in South Jamaica—one of the city's most dangerous neighborhoods. I look up Alfonso next, and he pings in the same place. It doesn't surprise me when the town car shows up there, too. The problem is there's not shit in that area except for a park. There's no reason for them to be there, especially not when they're on duty.

I send out a group text that has all the guys on it, plus Uncle Salvatore, Uncle Massimo, Uncle Cesare—Carmine's dad—and my dad.

Me

911 Maria got separated from Alfonso and Beppe. She's with me and fine. They're in the center of Baisley Pond Park.

The place is like a hundred acres with a fucking thirty-acre pond. Their phones are pinging near the water, and the town car's GPS has it in the closest parking lot. Maria's not asking for more info, so I'm not offering it. I suspect she assumes they're already dead.

LUCA

I'll come and get her.

Luca's response is almost immediate, and a moment later, another text comes through.

LORENZO

Carmine and I'll go to the park. Marco meet us there.

I know Lorenzo and Carmine are headed to the garage right now. It's where we take people when we need to have a private chat. Sometimes these people need some convincing. I'm certain they all wish they'd cooperated before they arrived because they leave as ash or ooze.

UNCLE MASSIMO

I'm calling you.

The time it takes the text to come through must be the time it takes to hit the phone icon.

"Uncle Massi, Maria's all right. She's here with me at Whiskers."

Ridiculous name, but two owners before Carmine came up with it. Whiskers as in on cats as in pussies. So stupid.

"Papa?"

Maria sits up, and I hand her the phone.

"Papa, I'm okay. I came out of the MRI room and looked around for Alfonso, but he wasn't there. He didn't come back, so after I waited five minutes, I called Beppe. He didn't answer, and neither did Alfonso when I called him. I had hospital security walk me to my car, and the town car wasn't parked next to me anymore. I came straight to Matteo. I tried calling the others on the way, but no one answered."

She didn't come here because she couldn't go anywhere else. She only wanted to come to me. I'm seriously messed up to be happy about that when she's in danger. Someone got to her guards, and there's a good chance they're dead. But she's done nothing to move off my lap, and I won't suggest she does.

I can hear her dad, even though the call isn't on speakerphone. I know he's trying to stay calm, but I'm certain his fear for her is back just as strong as it was while we didn't know where she was in Miami.

"Come to the house. Mama will meet you there, and I'll be there as soon as I can."

She looks up at me and mouths, "will you come?"

I nod.

"Okay. Matteo'll bring me."

"Can Matteo hear me?"

"Yeah, I can, Uncle Massi."

"Who do you have with you today?"

"Raphael and Luigi."

"Good. How soon can you leave?"

I help Maria to her feet and stand. I holster my gun, then snag my suit coat and slip it on as I answer. I take the phone and text Luca not to come while we stay on the call.

"We're leaving right now. Donny can finish payroll."

"Good. I may make it to the house before you."

We hang up, and I huddle Maria against my side as we head downstairs. My guys spot me immediately, and they can tell it's urgent. As we approach a group of dancers, Maria's arm wraps around my waist under my suit coat. My arm tightens, enjoying what felt like a territorial move. I'm not interested in any of the women here, and I would never date an employee. I figured Maria knew that, but I don't mind her staking a very public claim. She may regret it later. I may too if word gets back to her brothers. But for now, I'll relish the moment.

She points to her BMW SUV.

"Did you drive here? Should we take mine? I parked right over there."

I hold out my hand.

"Give me your keys."

She already has them out, a habit I know she's had since she learned to drive. She leaves nowhere without her keys in her hand if she's driving herself. I toss them to Luigi. He knows I want the car checked before Maria goes anywhere near it again. I pull my keys from my pocket.

"We're going in my car."

I drive a Yukon Denali, so basically a tank. It's big enough for the guys to pile in, and it sits up high, so I have good visibility. I open the passenger door for Maria, then hurry around to the driver's side. Raphael's right behind me when we pull out of the parking lot. We ride in silence to her parents' house here in Queens. They live four streets over from my parents. I open one of the garage doors, and Maria knows to stay in the car until the door shuts all the way. I turn the engine off and reach for the door handle, but she puts her hand over mine.

"You'll stay, right?"

"If that's what you want."

She nods, and tears finally well in her eyes. But none fall. She wills them away. I'm certain she cried after her abduction, but no one saw her. She's never liked to cry in public. She once told me it was the same as hating anyone being near her when she throws up. She doesn't like to feel out of control in front of other people. It makes her feel too vulnerable. I cup her cheek, and she leans into it.

"Cry if you want to. I won't tell as long as you don't tell anyone if I cry."

"You cry?"

"Yeah. I'm fucking freaked out, Maria. I can't go through another Miami. I can't live with being that scared again, and I'm halfway there."

"No one blames you for what happened."

"I know, but that's not it. I don't fear being blamed. I fear never seeing you again."

She nods as a single tear slips down her cheek. My thumb brushes it away. I know we have to get inside because her parents know we arrived. Her parents' cars are parked next to mine. Since we're in the closed garage, she doesn't wait for me to come around to her side. She slides out of the car and meets me at the door leading into the house. I open it and wait for her to walk through. My hand goes to the small of her back, and her next step brings her closer to me. But only for that one step. She catches herself and puts an appropriate distance between us.

It cannot be my imagination anymore. But now's not the time.

"Papa!"

She rushes into Uncle Massimo's arms, and he engulfs her. Auntie Nicoletta is there a moment later, and he holds the two women he loves most in his embrace. I suddenly feel out of place when I never have before. It's because I know I have no claim to her. When her parents finally let her go, we head into the family room. I move to the loveseat, and Maria follows me. She usually sits on the sofa while Uncle Massimo and Auntie Nicoletta have their recliners. It puts her closer to her parents, but I sense she still wants me close.

Uncle Massimo's and my phone ping at the same time. We get the same message.

CARMINE

Found them alive but had the shit kicked out of them. Both were unconscious and the car's totaled. Someone ran it into a light pole on purpose. It got nailed from the back too.

ME

What happened? How'd they wind up there?

MARCO

Three guys dressed as doctors jumped Alfonso in the restroom. They took him out through the laundry loading dock. Two more guys went after Beppe. Shot him in the arm and busted the windows before they tied him up and gagged him. Both wound up in the backseat with a bag over their heads. The guys in the garage wore balaclavas and the ones looking like doctors had on ball caps and sunglasses. None were recognizable and none spoke the whole time.

UNCLE MASSIMO

So we have no idea who did this.

LORENZO

Nope

LUCA

I'm pulling up to the house now.

LORENZO

We need Auntie Carlotta. We're ten mins out.

I open the text thread to my mom.

Me

We need you at Uncle Massi's. A couple guys got jumped. One got shot.

I wait for a response, and it feels like forever.

MAMA

How bad is it? I still have rounds for another two hours.

ME

I don't know yet. Lorenzo said we need you.

MAMA

Luca may have to take the bullet out. Is he there?

ME

He will be.

Luca trained as a paramedic during college. Auntie Carlotta taught him to remove bullets and to suture more complicated wounds than his classes taught him. He's who we go to when it's not bad enough to need my mom. We only go to the hospital if the Reaper is waiting at the door. Gunshot wounds and stabbings equal the cops. No one needs that added shit when they're injured.

MAMA

Keep me posted.

ME

Will do. Thx.

MAMA

Love you.

ME

Love you too.

Maria fidgets, and I watch her looking out the window.
"Do you want to go outside for a few minutes?"
"It's safe, right? Yeah."
I hate hearing the uncertainty in her voice. That she would even question being safe in her family's home makes me want to torture whoever did this, so they can experience the same fear Maria does. I walk with her. When we get outside, she looks around and leads me to a corner near the BBQ grill.

Guards patrol the grounds, but we both know we're tucked away. She keeps her voice low.

"Will you hug me again?"

"Of course."

I press her head against my chest and wrap myself around her. I murmur to her between light kisses on her head.

"You're safe now. No one can get you here. No one will let anyone come close to you. I'm here, and I'm not going anywhere."

"Good."

I don't know which part of that statement she's reacting to. We stand together for ten minutes, but all too soon it's over because we hear Luca bellowing for his sister. She pulls back and offers me a timid smile.

"Thank you. I've always known I'm safe with you."

God, how I wish that were true. But I've already proven it isn't. What the fuck will I do if I fail again?

Chapter Four

Maria

The men disappeared into my dad's study about an hour ago. Aunt Sylvia, Auntie Carlotta, and Auntie Paola—Carmine's mom and my dad's younger sister—have all called to check on me. My mom's making dinner, and I'm soaking in the tub. I got to see Alfonso and Giuseppe, and they look like shit. I'm the one who took the bullet out of Giuseppe's arm. Luca would have done it, but I insisted I was up to it. I love and respect my brother, but for fuck's sake, I'm the one who's the doctor. I'm shaken up but not catatonic.

I probably could have gotten here faster than Whiskers, but my gut didn't tell me to come to my parents. It told me to get to Matteo as fast as I could. I was ready to tear that bitch Reba apart when she tried to stand in front of me. I don't think of myself as haughty or snobby. But I sure as shit can act the part when I need to. I might have done more than just insinuate I'd hurt her because I'm a Mancinelli. I might have told her that no one would ever find her body if she didn't move her fucked up tits and fat ass out of my way. I might have also shoulder checked her too.

I remembered Carmine bitching about her one time and how he wished he could fire her, but she makes the club a fuck ton of money. Her pissed-off attitude wasn't about protecting what she had so much as not wanting anyone to have what she didn't. I know she and Matteo aren't screwing around, but even if they were, I still would go to him. He's not any better trained or stronger than the other guys. In fact, Gabriele's the biggest and strongest of them all. But Matteo's looked out for me my entire life. I was closer friends with Carmine than Matteo, but it was Matteo who always made sure they included me in the group whenever I wanted to be.

But I can admit—at least to myself—it would royally suck if Matteo were with the bitch. He wouldn't have hugged me the way he did, and he definitely wouldn't have pulled me onto his lap if he was involved with someone. Propriety wherever or whenever someone might find out has always been important to him. Except for the aftermath of my kidnapping, when Matteo looked like shit warmed up, he always appears ready for a board meeting. Sophisticated is how I think of it. I know plenty of guys who think he's arrogant. Maybe he is, but he pulls it off. To me it's not cockiness or bravado. He has the strength of will and body to carry out the air of authority he exudes. It's fucking sexy as all get out.

I'm soaking with my eyes closed, picturing him from last night as we danced. Then I'm remembering how it felt to sit on his marble hard thighs and have his iron-forged body wrapped around me. It was like my own manly cocoon to burrow into. It was the safe place to hide until the world was ready for me again. My left hand squeezes my breast while the heel of my right hand runs over my pussy. I press it against my clit and shift restlessly. I imagine his hand in my hair, fisting it and keeping me in place just how he wants me. My nipples harden, and my index finger starts rubbing. I keep the image in my mind and behind my closed eyelids. He's holding me, and now he's kissing me. I'm creeping closer to coming. I'm so close that my body is straining toward it. My legs tense, and I rub faster.

"*Stellina?*" Little star.

Fucking-a. My mom would knock on the door and ruin the moment. I fist my hands under the water and silently scream. Two more fucking minutes. That's all I needed.

"Yeah."

"You all right? You've been up here for nearly an hour. You never take baths this long."

"I'm fine. I'm just tired, but the hot water feels good."

I've had to let water out four times to make room for more hot water. I know I'm hiding, but I couldn't have tried to rub one off anywhere else. I mean, I could in my room, but clearly my mom came into that to get to my bathroom.

"Are you feeling okay?"

"Tired, but I'm better than I was a couple hours ago. I'll be down in ten minutes. Just let me wash my hair and get dressed."

"Okay. Dinner's ready."

I consider using a few of those ten minutes to get myself off, but the mood's gone. I hurry, and I'm walking down the last three stairs when all the men come out of my dad's study. I hear other voices, and I realize everyone's here. Olivia, Serafina, Auntie Paola, Auntie Carlotta, and Uncle Cesare. Just how big a deal is this, really? I ask Carmine when he steps next to me.

"We don't know yet. We don't have any clues about who did this."

"The Diazes took care of Fernando, and you took care of Pedro."

Took care of. That's all I know and all I want to know

about the men who abducted me. I don't need the details because it's likely to give me nightmares. I also don't want to test my conscience and the whole "doctor will do no harm" Hippocratic Oath. I'd feel compelled to help anyone who might be injured and feel guilty if I didn't. But I can separate patients, even ones I never meet, from people who intend harm to my family. Those fuckers get what they deserve. I believe everyone is entitled to affordable and adequate healthcare. But if you play stupid games, you win stupid prizes. In a lot of men's cases, that's death—however that comes.

"That's why we're not sure who this is. The bratva handled Yuri, and Besnik knows better than to even sniff, let alone breathe, in our direction."

Russians and Albanians who were indirectly connected to my kidnapping.

"O'Rourkes?"

"That's the obvious guess, but it doesn't feel right. They would have gone for you, not your guards."

"That leaves the Diazes or the Kutsenkos."

"And the Mexican Cartels are trying to grow here. We've had no trouble with the Triad in ages, but we can't rule them out entirely. The Yakuza aren't too fond of us either since they didn't invest in time in Luca's casino out in Reno."

Invest. I suspect that's a front for paying my family to run drugs for them. I'm not ignorant of their less than legal businesses. I just don't get involved. I won't risk my medical license in front of an ethics board. As is, it took a fucking deep dive into my background check to approve my medical license. I'm certain they investigated the rest of my family, but I'm also certain they didn't find shit about them. It helped that Auntie Carlotta is already a well-respected surgeon. It's no secret we're related, so I think that helped vet me.

"What about the Albanian Osmani here? Didn't you have trouble with them when you first started dating Sera?"

"Yeah. It could be, but they're highly unlikely. They already found out what happens when they come for us. It didn't work out well. They took a restaurant, and we took everything else."

"Do you think it was just a warning? They didn't kill Alfonso or Beppe, and they never came near me."

"That's what we figure, but we don't know who or why."

"The list is rather long."

Carmine shoots me a sardonic expression before he walks over to Serafina. Luca's sitting with Olivia, who I suspect has a secret she'll be sharing in a few weeks. I know Auntie Carlotta guessed at the same time I did, but we're not giving away any hints. Though it wouldn't surprise me if Mama and my aunts haven't already guessed too. We're from a massive Italian family, and Mama had four kids. But it's not my place to say anything.

Lorenzo and Marco are looking at Marco's phone, and my guess is they're watching some game. Matteo angles himself beside me.

"How're you doing? Do you feel better after your bath?"

Now there's a loaded question.

"Pretty much."

He shoots me a questioning look, and I feel myself blush. His brow furrows, then his green eyes bore into mine as though he can read my mind, see into my soul. But all he does is nod. I wish more than ever that I was going to my club tonight, but there's only one person I want to scene with. Since neither going nor fucking *him* is happening, I'm going to have to settle for one of Serafina's pies that she brought from her bakery.

Once dinner's over, people filter out and head home.

Matteo keeps darting glances at me while he plays some video game with Marco that they haven't touched since college.

"I'm wiped. I'm headed to bed."

I truly am. I can barely stifle my yawns, and my eyes are dry and itchy. When I stand, my parents do too. My dad'll help my mom finish tidying up the kitchen, though all the guys took care of the dishes and put away leftovers. I head toward the stairs while Marco and Matteo keep playing. I hear my brother when I get halfway up.

"You gonna just crash here?"

"Are you?"

"Yeah. You may as well, too."

Marco's so intent on winning that he doesn't notice Matteo looking at me again.

"Uh, yeah. I'll stay."

My parents' room is downstairs, and my brothers have the right half of the second floor. I have the left along with the three spare guest rooms. Matteo's room is next to Marco's and across from Luca's. Marco's is across from Lorenzo. My parents figured that, as the only girl, I should have some privacy. Our house truly is enormous, with eight upstairs bedrooms and a master suite downstairs. I was four when we moved in here, so Marco and Matteo were already glued at the hip. It meant there were basically five kids in the family, so we needed the space.

I can hear the guys joking as I close my door. I'm quick to brush my teeth and take out my contacts. It's been ages since I climbed into this bed, but it's still comfortable and familiar. I strain to hear anything, but it's blissfully quiet. Except I'm not out as fast as I expected. I'm lying here ready to count sheep. The minutes tick by, and I'm still not asleep. It's not that I'm restless or that my mind is a beehive. I'm just not as sleepy as I thought.

I hear Marco and Matteo come upstairs and their doors close quietly. Now my mind really is jumping. I know why I went straight to Matteo, but I don't understand why the need was so visceral. And I don't get why the moment he touched me, I felt so comforted and protected. It was like nothing could get to me as long as he sheltered me. I haven't sat on anyone's lap since I was a junior in high school, and some friends and I went to see Santa. But the moment he lifted me onto his, it was like I'd slipped into my favorite jammies and could just relax despite my fear.

We've hugged plenty of times over the years, but he hasn't held me like that before. Even when he hovered over me in the safe house in Miami or when I sat with him on the flight back. We were keenly aware of everyone around us. Now I can't stop wanting to be right back where I was a few hours ago. Nestled against him, inhaling his fresh scent of cologne, shampoo, and body wash.

I pick up my phone from the bedside table and wake the screen. 1:42 a.m. The guys have been in their rooms for twenty minutes. I debate texting him. What would I even say?

ME

You awake?

The response is almost instant.

MATTEO

What's wrong? Are you okay?

ME

I'm fine. Just wondering if you were awake.

MATTEO

Barely

ME

Sorry. I'll let you go.

MATTEO

Tell me what you need.

Well, shit. That's a loaded statement. I take too long to answer.

Matteo

WHAT DO YOU NEED?

Fuck me. Like literally. That's what you can do. I blow out a breath, and I'm still taking too long to answer.

MATTEO

Don't make me ask a third time. If you don't answer I'm coming to you.

He didn't exactly ask the first time, but I can hear his voice in my head. And I'm wet. And the word coming. Fuck my life. I'm questioning my sanity for texting him and for what I want to answer. I finally tap in the word just as I hear his hand on the doorknob.

ME

You

He doesn't knock. He just walks in. I suppose he gave me as much heads up as I was going to get. Good thing I still have clothes here; otherwise, I'd be sleeping naked. I take in his chiseled body in just pajama pants as he stands in the doorway. It's rippling muscle upon rippling muscle. There's so much contained strength, and I totally get the phrase "animal magnetism". I feel it drawing me to him. I sit up, and I see his eyes drift down to my tits. I'm certain my nipples show through the light tank top. It may be January, but I'm always too hot when I sleep.

"Close the door before Marco hears you."

He steps into the room, and I'm glad he's on the right side of the door. But he doesn't come any farther into the room.

"Did you have a bad dream?"

"No. I haven't fallen asleep."

He walks to the foot of the bed but says nothing else. What do I do? I pretty much invited him in here, so I'm certain he's waiting for me to make the next move. I push back the covers farther until he can see the boxers I'm wearing. I see his abs contract as he sucks in a breath.

"Aren't those mine?"

"They were. You left them in the laundry room ages ago, and I liked them."

His gaze hardens, and my pussy aches.

"Come here."

I can't disobey him. Like even if my mind wanted to rebel, my body isn't. I can't remember the last time I was this compliant. Just the opposite. I think he's often ready to throttle me because he usually can't bend me to his will. But this is different. Despite the command in his voice and the heat in his gaze, there's something gentle about his presence. I push back the covers all the way and shift to the end of the bed, so I'm kneeling before him.

I smell the toothpaste on his breath, but there's a faint hint of beer. He and Marco must have had a few while gaming. He slides his arm around my waist band pulls me closer. My hands rest on his chest as our bodies press together. My sigh feels like it comes from my soul as I rest my head against him. He hugs me until I pull back. Then he fists my hair, keeping my head in place. Just like my fantasy in the bath.

"You haven't answered my question, and I asked three

times."

"You demanded once. Then you asked once."

His hand slides precariously close to my ass, squeezing the top of my hip. His grip is firm but not painful. But it tightens when I don't move. Our eyes lock on each other, and I'm certain he can feel my nipples against his bare skin. I can feel he's hard. My hands slide up his chest to rest on his shoulders. I look down between us to where his cock is pressing against the front of his pajama pants, and my eyes widen.

"You flatter me... *piccolina*."

Little girl. I freeze. I've tried not to hear it for the sake of my brother's and my cousin's privacy with their wives, but I know they call their wives that. Matteo has never called me that. At least, not since he was ten, and I was eight, and he told me not to call him Matty anymore.

"Matteo."

My voice is a hoarse whisper. I try to see past him to the door, as though I can see down the hallway to Marco, who will shit a brick if he hears Matteo call me that or notices his best friend's hand on his little sister's hip.

I swallow, growing nervous that someone might hear us even though my parents are downstairs, and Marco is at the other end of the hall. And surely my cheeks are fire engine red because they're feeling like a five-alarm blaze. It's a herculean effort, but I don't shiver and let him know how aroused I am. He still hasn't moved his hand from my hip, so I rest mine on top of his. He must think I intend to move it because he starts to pull away. I wrap my fingers around his palm and nudge it back. I even press it a little lower and closer to my ass.

"I know you've had at least one beer, but you never get drunk. Not even a little tipsy."

"Maria, I'm as sober as the day I was born."

"Matteo, what's happening?"

Chapter Five

Matteo

That's a damn good question that I can't answer truthfully because I'll be dead with a bullet between my eyes if a single man in our family overhears me. I can't tell Maria that my lascivious thoughts grow kinkier every time I'm near her and she makes my dick grow, too.

"I'm here for whatever you need."

I purposely speak slowly, bringing her closer to me. Her whiskey brown eyes peer into mine, and I could drown in them. Her right hand tightens around my left one on her ass, even as her other hand remains resting on my shoulder.

"I know I texted you, but now we're like this. Why tonight? You've been distant for months. Last night, you made it sound like guarding me was a chore."

"And I explained it isn't. I told you, nothing is more important to me than keeping you safe. And that's not just because it's a duty. It's not just because I still feel guilty. Nothing's changed, Maria."

But it has. So fucking much has changed since she was eighteen and I was twenty. We've both changed, but not enough to forget what's been quietly simmering on a back burner.

"Matteo, you were the one who told me to forget all about that. You were the one who told me—"

"I know what I said. And it was the right thing, even if it sucked back then. But we're real adults now. Do you want to keep ignoring each other, pretending?"

"Do you want to die? If Marco finds out, he'll never trust you again. If Luca, Lorenzo, or Carmine find out, they'll castrate you."

"Or they could remember they want us to both be happy."

"Yeah, but not together."

"But what do you want, *piccolina?*"

I swear her eyes just darkened, and she inhales enough that her tits press harder against my chest.

"The same thing I wanted that night."

"You told me it was because I was safe. That you could trust me and know that I would never take advantage of you. Is that why you want another night with me?"

"There is nothing safe about wanting anything with you. Not now and not back then. You were those things to me, but I thought the same thing back then as I do now."

"What's that?"

"You're the hottest man I've ever seen."

"You flatter me again, little one."

"Take it that way if you want. I just see it as the truth. I didn't want to go to college completely inept with guys, so I asked you. But you had to know how much I wanted you back then."

"And I said I'd take your virginity because I was a better choice than some random asshole in a dorm room or frat house.

I couldn't stand the idea of another guy touching you. I wanted to make sure that while other guys might come and go from your memory, you'd never forget me."

"And I haven't. I know I wasn't your first, Matteo."

But you're the only one I've ever loved.

"True. But you were the only virgin I've ever been with."

She grimaces.

"Wonderful. The only woman who didn't know what the hell she was doing. Great memory."

My arm pins her against me. Not even a hair's breadth is between us. She can feel I'm hard for her. My fucking balls ache.

"It's the best memory I have."

"Don't tease me, Matteo. That's cruel."

"I'm not. I'm not lying either."

"Why tonight? Why are you confessing all of this tonight?"

I stare past her shoulder, not able to meet her gaze. I saw the way she looked at the doctor last night, and I know there's something between them. I also know she's been out with a different guy for the past two months. I've had to accompany her twice.

"Because you've been out with Patrick four times, and I hate it."

"Are you jealous?"

"Insanely. My need to know you're safe is stronger than the pain of seeing you with someone else. But I don't enjoy it."

"And you think I enjoy hearing you talk about going out with Lorenzo and Marco? Enzo owns one of the hottest clubs in New York, and you own like fifty strip clubs."

"Five, and only because Carmine sold them to me when he got together with Serafina. I was a silent investor before that. And you know I don't go to strip clubs, even if I own them. I've never been into that."

She stiffens.

"Don't lie. I know for a fact you go to them. You all go to them. And I went to you at one today."

"For business, not for pleasure. Maria, you know as well as anyone in our world that those establishments are where respectable men do business with men from families like ours. They're the ones measuring dicks, not us. And I'm not there for the entertainment. I don't need to pay a woman to get naked in front of me."

And now I want to swallow my tongue. She narrows her eyes and glares at me.

"Oh, I know. I know more than enough about the women you hook up with that you meet at Enzo's club or while you're traveling for work. I know what you used to do in Miami."

"I didn't mean that the way it sounded. I meant, I don't enjoy strippers. They do nothing for me. And as for what I do or don't do or have or haven't done in other clubs or while out of town, I've been single since high school. You have not."

"Yeah, I have. You can hardly count an eight-date limit—which is usually closer to four—as having boyfriends. The conversations with guys always go the same way, eventually. 'Oh, you're a Mancinelli. Like swimming with the fishes Mancinellis?' Or 'What made your family move here from Italy? Business. What does your family do? This and that. Do you have to have bodyguards? Yes.' I'd hardly call my dating experiences relationships."

"I don't want to think about my past when I'm with you. Neither of us has had long-term relationships since we were teenagers. Our lives aren't conducive to it. But we both know this life. We both know our family. We—"

"Family. We all know you and Uncle Dom aren't related to us by blood. But you're as good as a fourth son to my parents, and Uncle Dom and Auntie Carlotta think of me like the daughter they'd trade you and Emilio for."

She shoots me an impish grin, and it's the same one she's had since she was a baby. She shakes her head as she looks over my shoulder again, and I know she's picturing Marco in his room less than a hundred yards away.

"Matteo, everyone will freak if they think there's something between us."

"Think? There is something, Maria. There has been for years. That's why you came to me today. That's why you texted me in the middle of the night. That's why we're both half naked and holding each other in your childhood bedroom for fuck's sake. I'm fucking fed up with hiding it. You said at the fundraiser I'm even more brooding than ever. What the fuck do you think I've been thinking about? What do you think's been going through my head all fucking afternoon and night? That I could have lost you. That I've been a fucking idiot for letting so many years go by. That I hate not holding you like I am now. That I don't want to keep lying to everyone about how I fucking feel."

I sweep my gaze around as if Marco or Auntie Nicoletta or Uncle Massimo can tell I'm here since I'm getting heated. She shares my nervousness.

"Should we be having this conversation here? What if Marco overhears us?" Her expression grows sad. "But honestly, I don't want you to let go."

"Where and when? Your place or my place? Tomorrow—or rather later today?"

She considers that because there are logistics since she has guards parked outside her building overnight. If I walk her up to her apartment tomorrow evening after work, they'll notice that I don't come down. If I leave but turn around, they'll see me come back. It'll be just as complicated if she comes to my place because her guards will accompany her.

"We're all having dinner over at Aunt Sylvia and Uncle Sal's tonight. Can I say I want to leave right after we're done because I have an early shift tomorrow, and you offer to take me home? Then we can go wherever. The night shift will get there just after we would. For all they'd know, you walked me to the door and left before they arrived. They won't come up. We could tell whoever drives us we're good, and they can go since you're with me."

"They know I would never leave you without knowing someone was in place. They'll know no one drove me home."

"Can't you say you wanted to give the guys an early night off, so once you knew I was safe, you Ubered or something?"

It's not like we don't take cabs or use rideshares, but it's rare. Why would be when we have a fleet of town cars, limos, and SUVs?

"I could say I walked home. It's only six blocks."

"Six New York blocks at that time of night? You wouldn't do that alone."

"*Piccolina*, don't get mad."

"That's a surefire way to piss me off."

"Alfonso guessed something was up after that night right before we both left for school. I've denied it more times than I can count, but I'm certain he knows. I saw him watching us in Cape Town at the wedding. He'll never breathe a word."

"You trust him that much?"

"Yes. And he knows I'll kill him if he breaks that trust."

"I trust him, too. But won't he feel obligated to tell Uncle Sal or Luca at the least?"

"We aren't breaking any rules or doing anything wrong, so there's nothing to tell."

"All right. Can we say goodnight to everyone tonight, and

Alfonso can drive us to my place, assuming he's up to it? Would he lie and say he took you home when he didn't?"

"Do you want me to spend the night?"

The look she shoots me is my answer, and I'm practically ready to drag her to the town car and say fuck it to anyone finding out we sneaked out tonight. I lift her, then sit down where she was just kneeling.

"Tell me what you want, *piccolina*."

"You."

She whispers, but she's decisive.

Eleven years of repressed desire flows through us as our lips meet. She runs her fingers through my hair as I nip at her bottom lip. She sucks my tongue into her mouth, and I'm trying not to come. Fuck. I want her lips and mouth doing that to my cock, and she fucking knows it. That's why she's doing it. I pull away.

"Behave, little girl. I am not fucking you in your parents' house."

"Really?"

"*Piccolina*."

Most men wouldn't cross me when they hear that tone, but her impish grin is back.

"What if I don't want to behave? What if I'm not that patient?"

"Maria, I'm not that young man anymore. My tastes run differently. Don't tempt me to show you what I want to do if you misbehave."

I see the interest in her gaze, and there's a challenge there too. But I'm unprepared for what she says next.

"Are you a Dom? I'm a sub."

I sit there, blinking. That's all I can do for a moment because the thoughts in my head scatter and nothing comes together.

"Yes, and what the fuck do you know about that?"

She shifts to straddle me, so she doesn't have to twist to look at me.

"I know plenty. I got curious about BDSM in college, and I realized I enjoy it enough to belong to a club. Most of the guys I've dated are too vanilla for what I like. Or they figure out about our family before it can go that far."

"Have you been in a Dom/sub relationship before?"

"No. Just what I do at my club. You?"

I hesitate.

"Yes."

I know she can see it in my eyes. She sucks in a breath.

"You have a sub right now, don't you?"

"I did until Miami. That changed everything. But she wasn't the first sub I had."

"Why'd it change things?"

"Maria, I haven't been with anyone since before Miami. I can't."

She glances down at my crotch, and she cocks her left eyebrow. She shifts, and her pussy rubs against my dick. Her smile is pure seduction.

"That's not what I mean, and you know it. My body can just fine. My mind can't. I don't want anyone else."

"What're you saying? Do you want a Dom/sub relationship with me?"

"Absolutely not. No."

She leans back.

"You're pretty fucking adamant about that. Are we really going to talk about all this here? I thought the whole point was to wait until tonight."

"We can talk just fine right now. It's everything else that'll have to wait. And no, I don't want to be your Dom. I want us to be equals in everything. But I want a relationship. This has been brewing for years, and we both know it. Something's had to give for ages. But after almost losing you, I don't want to waste any more time."

"Is this about your guilt? Do you feel you need to have me by your side to make sure you can always account for me?"

"No. You make it sound like I want to date you or fuck you out of duty. The shit that went down made me realize I hate that I couldn't hold you until you woke up. I couldn't hold you while you explained everything or while we flew home. I hate that you aren't curled up beside me in bed every night, so I can hold you while we sleep. Someone nearly ripped away from us all the possibility of what we can be. I'm fucking fed up with thinking about what everyone else thinks or wants. It's not just about what I want and me putting that ahead of everyone else. What I want most is to give you what you want."

"And what I want is you. It has been since we were teenagers. I had such a crush on you for so long. Then I thought I was over you once we slept together, and I went away to college. I thought you were out of my system. I was too busy and tired to think about much of anything but studying and rounds while I was in med school, but I think about you a lot, Matteo. Like a lot, a lot."

"I hate knowing when you have dates, and they're not with me. I'm trying not to lose my shit thinking about you fucking other guys at a BDSM club."

"I hate when you go out with my brothers, and I know you're going to hook up with someone. I definitely hate knowing you've been other women's Dom."

"*Piccolina*, I do not hook up half as much as you seem to think."

Her eyes trail over me before our gazes meet again.

"I'm certain it's not from lack of offers."

I turn my head and look out the window. This conversation escalated fast. But what the fuck do I have to lose at this point?

"I haven't been with a blonde or redhead since before our one night together eleven years ago. Part of why I enjoy BDSM is because I can blindfold and gag my partner. When I don't have to hear them or have them look me in the eye, then it's easier to picture who I really want."

She stares at me for a moment before she kisses right beside my mouth. I turn my head and snag her lips in a fiery kiss that threatens to send us up in a blaze of glory. When we pull apart, our foreheads rest against each other.

"We are so fucked up, Matteo. That's why I like to be blindfolded. It can be whoever I want—*you*—when I don't have to actually see them. I'm a sub, but the one thing I insist upon is whispered commands. It's harder to tell it's not your voice. It's easier to imagine it is."

"*Piccolina*—"

"Why do you keep calling me that? I know Carmine and Luca say it."

"And that's where I got the idea. You know I'm protective of you and have been our whole lives. But I think you get that I definitely don't look at you like you're my little sister. I want to take care of you in a way I've never been allowed to before. I fucking hate that anyone scared you today, but I won't lie and say I'm not fucking pleased you came to me. You want me to take care of you. You want to lean on me, and that's what I want too. Now that I know you're into kink, I don't suddenly think you're a little. I'm definitely not a Daddy Dom, but you're smaller than me. You're also more vulnerable than I am. It's a term of affection because of that, not how I see you."

"And if I want some term of affection for the man I look to, the one who takes care of me and protects me. The one I can count on to make me feel safe. What do I call you?"

We stare at one another, and the energy's even more charged between us than it was a moment ago. Our dynamic's done a one-eighty tonight, and it's shifting again.

"Say it, *piccolina*."

I pray she's thinking the same thing I am.

"I've never called any man that."

I think I'm right.

"No woman's ever called me it either."

"Are you sure we're thinking the same word?"

"Say it then."

"Yes, Daddy."

"Goddamn, that's hot."

Before either of us knows what's happening, her arms are over her head as I strip her tank top off. I turn us, so she's lying on the bed, and I'm yanking her—*my*—boxers off. I'm standing again and admiring the single-most alluring woman I've ever seen.

"You look like the Big Bad Wolf, Daddy. And I'm one of the three little pigs you're about to devour."

"Say it again."

It's not a request. It's a command, and I watch her shiver.

"Daddy."

I pinch her left nipple hard as I lean forward to suck her right. She makes a stifled noise, and I glance up to see she's covering her mouth with both hands. I return to licking and sucking one nipple while I roll and twist the other between my fingers. I squeeze both tits until her back arches as I kiss my way up her neck until my lips are against her ear.

"I'm still not going to fuck you in your parents' house. I still have some common sense and respect. But I'm also going to leave your little cunt aching to know what I feel like inside you."

Her eyes flash a challenge, and I know she's never going to

be my sub, even if she submits to me.

"And when you jerk off tomorrow—which you'll need to because you won't be able to stand being hard without being in agony—you're going to wish your hand was my pussy."

"Is that so?"

I slide my left index and middle finger into her, and her hips lift off the mattress. I press on her belly, flattening her back against the bed.

"Yes, Daddy."

"Maybe we'll have to see which one of us can last longer without needing to get ourselves off."

I lick her pussy before drawing her clit into my mouth. I swirl my tongue around it before flicking it over and over. I watch her every breath, every tremble. She covers her mouth with her right hand while her left clutches the comforter. When I graze my teeth against her clit, she weaves her fingers into my hair and presses my head to her. I pull back. I capture both of her wrists in one hand and raise her arms over her head. I slide my coated fingers into her mouth. I know she doesn't like the taste of herself as much as I do, but she sucks my fingers. Once more, the challenge is back in her eyes even as she lets me control her body. She knows I'm wishing it was my cock, not my fingers, in her warm, soft mouth.

I climb onto the bed, lowering my weight onto her but holding myself up on my forearms. I grind my dick against her pussy, not relenting as I know I push her closer to coming. Her knees bracket my hips as I dry hump her. I whisper to her.

"You will never be my sub, but you will submit to me. You know those aren't the same thing. If you can't live with me leading when we fuck, then tell me now. We aren't as compatible as we think."

I pull my fingers from her mouth.

"I want you to lead, and I want you in control. In my mind,

even when I challenge you a bit, you're still in control. You decide what happens when I do. All I have to think about is right now, being with you. Knowing I'm safe and desired. Knowing that you'll take care of me and give me what I need."

"Always, *piccolina*."

We watch each other, and the air shifts. My fingers entwine with hers, and I press a soft kiss to her lips before nuzzling along her neck. Once more, I whisper to her. Partly because I don't want anyone to possibly hear us, but also because I want the intimacy in a way I've never longed for before now.

"We will go as far as you want later. If it's not sex, that's fine. If it never comes to that, that's fine. But if we do, if I'm ever inside you, I will never let you go. You will be mine."

Her smile is so relaxed, and she looks happier than I've seen her in ages.

"Can we go somewhere right now, so that can happen soon?"

"Do you want me to claim you, little one?"

"You did that eleven years ago. It's just time for you to hold on to what's always been yours."

"Maria, I'm serious when I say you'll be mine. I won't share you, just like I'll never expect you to share me. Once we do this, there's no going back. If you ever want out, I won't force you. But I won't be the one who walks away."

"You assume I'm the one who will."

"I don't assume this is going to end. I pray it doesn't. But I will not trap you into staying with me if that's not what you want. If you change your mind, or it isn't working for you, then I won't hold you captive. But once you're mine, I want all of you. Need all of you. Mind, body."

"Heart and soul?"

"Yes."

"And what do I get in return?"

"All of me, *mio piccolo cigno*." My little swan.

Her nostrils flare as she sucks in a breath.

"Swans mate for life, Daddy."

"I know."

Doubt creeps into her eyes.

"Matteo, is this all for real? This isn't some scene or prelude to one, is it?"

I roll off her and sit up. When she follows me, I bring her onto my lap. God, how I wish I was buried inside her while we have this conversation. Maybe then she'd feel how sincere I am about what I want for us.

"We will never scene without us both being on board with it. We'll both know when we're doing it. This is real, Maria. I'm telling you want I want. What do you want?"

"All of this. That's why I need to make sure I'm not making more of it than it is. I don't want to share you either. I want to know that you're as into making this work as I am."

She shifts, rubbing her pussy against my cock. I can't help but groan. My hands grip her ass as she watches me. She bites her bottom lip until I pry it loose.

"What, *piccolina*?"

"I just have this sudden urge to have you inside me without us fucking. Just to sit here like this, but to know what it's like to feel us like that."

She shrugs one shoulder.

"I know what you mean. I feel it too. We'd finally be one again. But we both know that it might start as us just sitting together, but there's no way the first time I'm inside you again won't lead to us trying to get each other off."

"I test regularly."

I didn't expect that to be her next comment, but okay.

"So do I. I have to for the club I belong to and just to be safe."

"Same. I've never had sex without a condom, and I have an IUD."

"Neither have I."

"Knowing all that, do you want to wear one when we do have sex?"

"Only if that makes you feel more comfortable."

"I don't want you to."

I rest my hand on her belly.

"I know enough to know an IUD is probably the most effective birth control short of abstinence. Are you prepared for the possibility?"

"I don't think we're Auntie Paola or Uncle Cesare."

Carmine's parents were dating when they were nineteen, and Auntie Paola got pregnant. They weren't that serious, but their families forced them together. There's never been a more mismatched couple to live under the same roof. The day after Carmine went to college, they separated. They're actually good friends now, but only because they live separate lives. However, we're Catholic, so they'll never divorce. They just— ignore stuff.

"No, we're not. But are you prepared for what could happen if you get pregnant?"

"No one's going to force us to marry. But I wouldn't agree to this—I wouldn't suggest this—if I weren't prepared to make things permanent. None of us would have children out of wedlock, and there's never been a divorce in the Mancinelli family. I know what that would mean for us. Are you prepared for what could happen?"

"Work isn't the only reason I've stayed single, Maria."

"Oh?"

Her eyebrows shoot up her forehead.

"You know I haven't had a girlfriend since college, and the few I had were never that serious. There's only one person I've ever wanted to commit to. Only one person I would have a family with. Only one person I've ever considered marrying."

Her smile is timid as she waits, but I say nothing more.

"Who, Daddy?"

"*Mio piccolo cigno.*"

"*Stresso.*" Same.

Everyone in our family learned to speak Italian before English, even those of us born in America, which—at this point—is everyone but Aunt Sylvia. We switch back and forth with ease, using Italian even more than Sicilian.

Maria's phone buzzes, and I see the screen light up. It's already close to 2:45 a.m.

"You have to be up in a few hours for your shift. Are you sleepy yet?"

She stares at me as though I've lost my mind. I stand with her wrapped around me and walk to the head of the bed. I ease her down and slide onto the bed beside her. I prop myself onto my forearm while my other hand slides between her legs.

"I'll stay with you until you fall asleep."

I press two fingers into her as my thumb rubs her clit. Our kisses are languid, but I withdraw my hand and wrap it around her wrist when she tries to pull my cock out.

"I'm not trying to take control, Daddy. I just really want to do this for you. I don't want to just take."

"It's not taking when it's freely given."

"You know what I mean. I really want to touch you and please you."

"You already please me."

"Stop twisting what I'm saying. If you're going to refuse, then just tell me no. But I don't want this to be only about me."

"And if my pleasure comes from yours without you doing anything?"

Her lips tighten into a pucker before flattening into a line.

But she doesn't argue with me.

"Maria, the moment my dick is out of my pants, it's going to be inside you. I'm holding onto the last minuscule, frayed threads of my honor and resolve not to have sex with you in your parents' house. We aren't married, and we're sneaking around right now. I won't humiliate you in front of your family if they find out, and I won't throw back in their faces the way I've always been part of this family."

"I understand, but then I'd rather wait. I don't want to come if you can't. I want that to be something we do together."

I gaze into her eyes, and she's truly beautiful inside and out. Her expression is sincere, and it makes me melt. I'd do absolutely anything for this woman. I'll give her everything she needs and hopefully most of the things she wants. And I'll destroy anyone who ever threatens her again.

"Get dressed, *piccolina*."

She slips her tank top and boxers back on before she climbs under the covers. She nestles against me, her head on my chest. She slings her arm around my waist and closes her eyes. I'm going to have to fight not falling asleep with her. I've never been so comfortable. Her sleepy whisper drifts to me.

"I wish every night were like this."

"They will be."

"Promise, Daddy?"

We both know I can't. There will be nights when work keeps me away. And who knows how our family's going to react when they finally find out? The logistics of being together and being discreet are already giving me a headache.

"Maria, I will do everything I can to make that happen. I can promise that."

"That's good enough for me."

I pray it is, but nothing about our life says it'll be that easy. I can already feel it.

Chapter Six

Maria

Last night has played on a loop in my mind all day. I'm in the cafeteria for lunch, sitting with a friend of mine who's a pediatrician and another who's an endocrinologist/oncologist. We started our residencies together, so we've known each other for a while. I'm trying to pay attention to the two guys, but my mind wanders to Patrick, the guy I've been seeing, and Jordan, the doctor I scene with.

Did Matteo and I commit to being boyfriend and girlfriend? That's sure as fuck what it sounded like to me. He said I would be his, and he wouldn't share. He didn't expect me to share either. He wants me mind, body, heart, and soul. He already has three out of four. Giving him my body is the last thing I'm holding onto. And it's not like he hasn't had it before, and he was well on his way to having it again early this morning.

"Maria?"

I pull myself back into reality.

"Sorry, Jimmy. Lost in thought."

"The little boy?"

Huh? Oh, shit.

"Yeah."

"It never gets easier telling a family their kid has leukemia. Has it gotten any easier seeing it on CT scans?"

"No. Part of me wishes it would because it's hard to see so often. But another part of me prays I never become desensitized to it. I'd rather read broken arm and leg x-rays."

I'm going to have to text Patrick and end it. And I definitely have to tell Jordan that our plan to reschedule is off. I saw him enter the cafeteria, so I hope I can pass his table on the way out to talk. Alfonso and Giuseppe are back today, and they look exhausted. I can't believe it. When I saw them this morning, I insisted they go home. But they refused. They're even more low profile than usual since they have black eyes and busted lips from getting attacked. I feel horrible that they aren't getting any time off, but all the men my family trusts with the women are working overtime. Alfonso's eating near the door, and Giuseppe's stationed outside my office.

I'm in la-la-land again when Thomas nudges my arm.

"You ready to go?"

I look down at my half-eaten meal and shake my head.

"You guys go. I'm going to finish up. I need to stop thinking about it."

My "it" isn't the same as they assume, but let them live in ignorance. This'll give me a chance to talk to Jordan, anyway.

Jimmy and Thomas nod, and we say goodbye. I hurry to finish and am carrying my tray to the trash when Jordan and the people he's with stand. I brush his sleeve and glance up at him. He knows where to meet me. We've tried a roleplaying scene or two here, but it's never felt right. I see his surprise. It's only going to grow. I nod to my guard, and he gives me space as

I slip into a storeroom. Lovely. Colostomy bags and catheters. This is probably going to go to shit, so I suppose it's appropriate.

"Hey."

Jordan steps in and closes the door behind him. He's deepened his voice from how it is conversationally. He reaches for me, but I take a step back and shake my head.

"No."

"No?"

He cocks an eyebrow, and I know how he expects me to answer.

"Jordan, no. We're not doing anything in here but talking. Briefly."

I tack that on at the end.

"You could have just texted me the time and day. I know you've been busy."

I hear the annoyance in his tone. Well, fuck you, buddy.

"I'm not available anymore. I won't be going to the club."

"You getting serious with that guy?"

"Sorta."

I don't want to say it's a different one.

"Just let me know when you're free again in a few weeks."

He shrugs because that's how it's been for the past two years.

"No. I mean, we aren't going to keep seeing each other at the club. I'm not arranging anything with anyone."

"You're that serious with Patrick?"

Fuck.

"No. It's someone else. I'm letting him know next."

"Do you have a full-time Dom now?"

"Jordan, I just won't be going to the club to meet up with anyone."

I might go with Matteo. I can hope. I don't want to give that up, but I don't know if he would go to a club where he might run into someone I've had sex with. Not just sex, but BDSM sex. I know I'm not thrilled to go to his club and meet someone he's been intimate with. That makes my stomach hurt.

"You really mean it, don't you?"

"Yeah."

"I hope this Dom is good enough for you. When he isn't, you have my number."

Asshole.

"It's done, Jordan. No more. Period."

His arrogance fades, and now he looks annoyed again.

"I enjoy our time together, Maria. If you change your mind, let me know. You know we have fun. We already know what each other likes and wants."

"I've enjoyed it too, but things change."

He inhales, then sighs. There's nothing else to say. He eases the door open and peers into the hallway. He leaves, and I wait a minute before I open the door and do the same thing. Except I want to slam it shut. There's an enraged man staring at me, and now he's stalking down the hallway toward me.

Matteo pushes the door open, forcing me to take a step back. He shuts the door a little too hard and spins me around. He pins me to it, his hand at my throat. He nuzzles my neck and sniffs. He wants to know if I smell like a man's cologne. His free hand captures my jaw before he kisses me. It's primal and possessive, and I'm here for it. I respond immediately, my hands going to his belt and tugging him forward. His hand tightens around my throat, reminding me I don't tell him what to do. He tells me.

But I need to tell him what happened. I know what he's thinking, and I can't blame him. I'd be going apeshit if the situation were reversed. I turn my head and break the kiss. He tries to pull me back, but I resist.

"He's the guy I meet at the club. I just told Jordan we're done. I told him there's no chance that we'll meet up again. Even if you and I don't work, I don't want him anymore. I don't know that I'll ever want anyone else."

"That's because you're mine, *piccolina*. You always have been."

"I know, Daddy."

I test the word again, and it feels so right. Matteo thinks so too, because his hand leaves my jaw and tugs at the drawstring to my scrubs. His hand slips beneath my panties and into me. His green eyes darken when he finds me wet—soaking, actually.

"Daddy, it's because of you. You did that. Matteo, please. I need you."

"I'm not fucking you in some storeroom for the first time after eleven years. *Eleven.* That's how long we've fucking tortured ourselves."

"All the more reason to stop doing it. I don't care where we are. We could be here or a suite at the Four Seasons. I don't care about that. I care about finally being with you again. You're pissed, and I know it. But I want it like this."

"Angry sex?"

I press my lips together, and my brow furrows. I can barely speak above a whisper.

"I want you to claim me."

His gaze turns entirely predatory.

"You want me to take."

"Only because I give it freely."

"I don't have to fuck you for you to know you're mine."

"I know, and I don't disagree. But I want it like this."

"You want me possessive and controlling?"

His eyebrows shoot up.

"Not all the time. Just right now. Just for this first time together again."

"Turn around and pull down your pants, *piccolina*."

"Yes, Daddy."

I hope I'm right about what's coming next because I really don't want him to fuck me from behind. I want to see him.

"Uh!"

His hand lands across my bare ass. I pulled down my panties when I dropped my scrubs pants.

"Widen your legs and turn your feet in. Push your hips back."

"Yes, Daddy."

He lands another smack across my ass.

"Count them."

His hand connects again.

"Three."

"No. That was one. I didn't tell you to count the others."

"Yes, Daddy. One."

Smack.

"Two."

Smack.

"Three."

Smack.

We continue until we get to ten. My ass burns, and tears well in my eyes. He wraps his arm around my waist and pulls me back against him. His pants are unfastened, but his boxer briefs are still up. I feel his cock through the cotton. Fucking hell. He's bigger than I remember.

"You could have texted him. You don't go into storerooms with anyone, Maria. You know that. But you especially don't go into one unless it's to fuck me."

"Yes, Daddy. I wanted to tell him in person, so he knew there was no convincing me to see him again. I wanted him to see how serious I was. But we don't talk in public. We keep our distance, so no one could guess we've been together. It wasn't a conversation I wanted anyone to overhear. Alfonso's out there."

"And after what happened yesterday? How'd you know he'd still be there?"

"True."

He's still pinning me between the door and his wall of muscle that most people would call his chest and abs.

"Turn around and kick off your pants."

I look down at his cock, and I know what his command was. But the floor is going to be fucking freezing. I bend my knees and start to lower myself, but his hands immediately catch my upper arms and yank me up.

"No. Absolutely not. I am not your Dom, *piccolina*. You do not have to repent on your knees or thank me for my forgiveness by giving me a blow job. I give it unconditionally. You took the spanking, and that made amends. I only spanked you because of the danger you put yourself in. I hate knowing you were in here with another man, but I hate the risk even more. I've given in to you about a lot of things over the years, and I will probably keep giving in because I want you to have everything you want. But only within reason. I've never wavered on your protection. If we're together, you know I'm only going to be more demanding about that because I can. As your friend, there were limits to what I could order. Now there aren't."

"I ended things with Jordan, and I am going to text Patrick. I planned to do it on the way back to my office. But what are we, Matteo? Are we a couple like we talked about last night?"

"Yes. I don't have a fucking clue how this is going to work out with everyone. But you and I know that there is no one else. I told you last night. I will not share you, and I don't expect you to share me."

"I don't want anyone else, Daddy. And I couldn't do this if I knew you could be or are with anyone but me. It would hurt too much."

"Same. Take me out, little girl."

Finally. I push his pants farther down his hips and pull down his boxer briefs. He springs out, and I practically salivate as I kick off my clogs, pants, and thong.

"When we have more time and are in a better place, I'm definitely giving you a blow job."

I have never said those words in my life. I don't mind blow jobs, but they've never been the first thing I've offered. But there's something about Matteo. I want it all with him. I want to give him everything because I know he'll give me everything I need and want. I just know.

"You said no condom last night. I have one if you've changed your mind."

"I haven't."

"Good. I want you to remember you're mine with every step as my cum drips down your legs and leaves you sticky all day."

I whisper beside his ear as he leans forward to kiss me again.

"Fuck, Daddy. That's hot."

His hand goes back around my throat and squeezes, but it's not enough to be breath play.

"This one time, you can come whenever you need to. You don't have to ask. After this, your orgasms belong to me. I give them, and I withhold them. Can you live with that?"

"Yes, please."

I'm shivering with need, and there are goosebumps on my arms. He lets go of my throat and lifts me until I wrap my legs around him. He's so hard that it's easy for him to line us up. He thrusts as he presses me down. Fuck. I might go cross-eyed.

"Goddamn, *piccolina*. You're so fucking tight. Fuck...God, this feels good."

"Daddy, rough."

He's thrusting hard as he guides me up and down. I'm practically bouncing as he drives his cock into me. His left arm wraps around my waist, and I tighten my legs. His right hand goes into my hair, clutching a handful.

"There's no going back, Maria. Not now, not ever. I won't force you to stay with me, but nothing will be the same as it was."

"Good. I don't want to go anywhere. I've wanted you since I was sixteen. It's been a long fucking wait."

"Yes, it has. I've wanted you too."

Our kiss is a battle at first, and I love it. He lets me try to take control, but ultimately, I relent. I don't want to lead. I don't want to think about what to do next. I just want to enjoy. I want to feel my boyfriend inside my mouth and my cunt. I pull away when I'm breathless and lean to whisper to him.

"I'm about to come, Daddy. Harder...So hard... Fuck. Like that... Yes...I'm coming. I'm coming."

This is the best orgasm of my life. I feel it all the way into my toes. He keeps rubbing my clit against his pubic bone, prolonging the ecstasy. I cling to him as his hands grab my ass.

"Every inch of you is mine."

"Yes, Daddy. Take all of it."

His fingers bite into me, and there are bound to be marks. His marks on me. I love it. I've never allowed that before, but I crave it now.

"Please. I want to make you come. Tell me what you want."

I'm desperately begging. I want him to feel what I did. I want to know I did that.

"Not until you get off at least once more."

We're kissing again, and it's sloppy and passionate. My

fingers go into his hair, and I clench a handful as I come again. I Kegel and hold on to his dick as tight as I can, not wanting this to end. I feel him pulse inside me, which keeps me going.

"You made me come, little girl."

"Don't pull out!"

Fuck. I practically wailed that.

"I'm not. Not until I can't stay in there. I don't want this over yet either. I need to hold you."

We cling to each other until I suddenly feel chilled. My endorphins, oxytocin, and dopamine are wearing off, and I'm left feeling depleted instead of replete.

"Your arms must be getting tired. You can put me down."

"I can carry Gabriele. Believe me, if I can carry his two-sixty ass, I can hold *piccolina mia*." My little girl.

I sigh as my head rests against his shoulder, and I kiss his neck.

"I have to get back to work. I've got to be late by now. People are going to be looking for me."

"I know."

He lowers me to my feet, but he hugs me, and I don't want to let go. Finally, I do. I could practically cry. I feel completely drained even if I am happy. I reach down to where I left my pants and clogs I kicked off. I look up when he grunts.

"No panties. I will shred them if you wear them. Nothing between your pussy and whatever part of me wants inside."

I pull them off my left leg, and he takes them from me. He sniffs and shoots me a wolfish grin before tucking them into his pocket.

"No more boxer briefs."

His laugh is dark, and I can imagine him as a real Dom. But then he grins, and it's the Matteo I've always known.

"If that's what you want. But I'm warning you. If I don't

wear them, everyone will know the moment you give me a hard on."

"I'll just have to stay out of arm's reach."

I laugh as I tie the drawstring. At least, I try to. He pulls me back against him.

"All I have to do is think about you, and I get hard. Seeing you? Hearing you? It won't be a secret for more than thirty seconds. Even once everyone knows, I doubt a single member of our families will want to know what you do to me 24/7."

"You exaggerate."

"I do not. The only reason you don't know is because I wear boxer briefs. It's on purpose. It helps hide what you do to me, little girl."

"Do you have any idea how much I love hearing you call me that?"

"I do because that's how much I love hearing you call me Daddy."

"Do you think anyone else in our family would understand that? Like if any of them ever accidentally overheard me say it, would they think we're fucked up?"

"You cannot tell anyone, but I've heard Olivia call Luca that. And Serafina's caught herself a couple times. I know neither of those guys is a Daddy Dom. That's not what they've ever been into, and it's not what they'd want now. They appreciate their wives' independence and how much they can lean on them to give sound advice at all times. But I think they have what we talked about last night. I think they each take care of their wife, and I think each wife knows she can depend on her husband. I think Olivia feels completely safe with Luca, and Serafina feels the same about Carmine. I think it's purely a term of endearment rather than a title."

"Is that how you see it with us?"

"Absolutely. I may call you *piccolina* and little girl, but I don't think of you as being any younger than you are. I don't think I need to take care of you because you can't or don't want to do it on your own. I want to take care of you to share the load."

"I think you also need to feel in control. There's so much in our lives that we don't control. It depends on all the other players in this fucked-up game. The control you have without the fight to stay alive—I can let you have that without a power struggle. I can give you the reassurance that everything's going to be okay because you're in charge. That's how I think I can take care of you."

"That's exactly what I need. I don't think anyone else would ever understand that. I mean, no other woman I'd consider. I suppose Olivia and Serafina get it."

I cup his cheek as he fastens his pants.

"I never want you to feel like this is a one-way street. You've told me all the things you want to do for me, and I just told you what I can offer. If you're ever not getting what you need, tell me, Matteo. It's not because I won't give it. It'll be because I don't know. I'll give you everything I can."

"I know. I will never abuse that trust. The same applies to you. Tell me what you need and what you want. I will give you all that you need, and I will do my fucking best to give you all that you want."

I want to tell him I love him. I have for as long as I can remember being interested in boys. If he's still this into me after eleven years, then I think he feels the same. But it's not the right time. It sure as shit isn't the right place. But, hopefully, soon. I don't want to keep that secret from him. Not when we're going to keep a huge secret from our family.

He brushes a soft kiss against my cheek then my lips.

"We'll figure something out about tonight. I relieved Alfonso. Marco took over for Beppe."

"My brother's here?"

Panic bursts through me.

"Shh. He's outside your office, but you can tell him you got delayed talking to someone. It's not a lie."

I snort.

"Talking. We did a little of that."

"I think we did a lot of it. And we needed to say what we did."

"How long's your shift?"

"I said I would stay till morning. Marco's off at seven."

Matteo opens the door and checks the hallway before stepping out, his hand at his gun holstered against his lower back. When he sees nothing, he sticks his hand back to me. I take it, and he guides me out of the storage room. We walk to the elevators with an appropriate distance between us, nodding to the other people on it. When we get off on my floor, I spy Marco six doors down. I nearly jump out of my skin when Matteo whispers to me, still looking straight ahead.

"Do you feel claimed?"

"Enough...For now."

Chapter Seven

Matteo

It's been three days since my interlude with Maria in the hospital storage room. Not my finest moment for places, but the best fucking sex I've ever had. But the universe is conspiring against us. And it's driving me fucking batshit bonkers. Lorenzo showed up that evening to relieve me since there was a fight at one of the strip clubs. The manager got hurt breaking it up, so I had to step in. The two guys soon realized how big a mistake that was. Needless to say, they won't show their faces in any of my establishments ever again.

The next day, they assigned me to Serafina, so I was at her bakery near Maria's place. It was Maria's day off, so she dropped by. We got some small talk and a few glances, but I wasn't Serafina's only guard, and Gabriele was with Maria.

The day before yesterday, I was in Jersey all day with Luca at one of his casinos. While I own the strip clubs, my real job is as an architect. I design everything Mancinelli Developers builds. Luca's doing some renovations and expanding the buildings at the resort, so that it's more than just a casino and hotel. I had to oversee the meeting with our foreman and Carmine. He's a structural engineer and pretty much handles everything from me handing over the blueprints and the groundbreaking until the end of the project.

Yesterday was agony. I was stationed at her apartment, but Maria moonlights. She reads radiology images and sends in her findings to a board-certified doctor who checks them and sends the final report. It's helping her pay down her student loans faster. Yeah, our family is rich as sin. Our parents all paid for our undergraduate degrees, but graduate degrees are on us. Could they afford it? Absolutely. Did any of us want to live off Mama and Papa once we were adults? Fuck no.

I was there the whole day, but she was swamped. Fucking universe. It's seriously fucking with us when all we want is to be fucking each other. But we're bound and determined tonight. The others think she has a date, but he's going to conveniently cancel right before the movie starts. I'll be her date. We're on our way now, and I'm driving. Francesco is in the town car too. Maria's in the back with the privacy glass up. I teased her and warned her I would know if she got herself off while waiting for me to take her into the movies. She blushed, and I think I busted her even though I hadn't been serious.

I park as close to the theater as I can. It's freezing again tonight, so no one expects Francesco to stay outside. He can see the entrance and get to it within twenty yards. I hand him the keys, and he looks up at me. I suppose he assumed I was staying in the car since I drove.

"I'll take her in, Franco."

I don't wait around. Instead, I open Maria's door and help her out. She's in jeans that look amazing on her athletic legs and juicy ass. The things I'm going to do to and with it. Spanking her almost made me come. Watching it jiggle. Fuck me. I know she has a fitted top on under her coat since I helped her put her coat on. She's wearing calf-high boots or whatever they're called. Even with a heel, she's still six or seven inches shorter than me.

I want to wrap my arm around her, but I can't. At least we have the excuse of ice for her to wrap her arm around mine. We pick our way over to the doors. I already bought our tickets and picked our seats. We head inside, and I immediately steer us toward the concessions.

"Large popcorn with extra butter all the way around and inside. Reese's peanut butter cups and Thin Mints, please."

She looks up at me when I finish ordering, her guilty expression adorable.

"I promise I'll share."

"That's what you said the last time and the time before that, and all the times since you were five, and I was seven. I'll be lucky to get three handfuls of that popcorn. And I definitely know better than to ask for a Reese's. I'll lose a damn finger. I'll stick to the Thin Mints."

I know I exaggerate, but she loves movie theater popcorn. She rarely has it since she doesn't come very often, so it's a treat for her. I'm happy to indulge her with whatever she wants on our first date. I order drinks for us too, and we gather our food. As we grab straws and napkins, she leans toward me.

"I like that you already know my favorites."

God, how I want to kiss her. Even if it's a peck on the forehead while she gazes up at me. But we can't risk it.

"I like that I can get you what you like."

We walk to the theater, once again keeping an appropriate distance since we never know who we might see or who might recognize us. The one good thing about hating having anyone sit behind us is we're all the way at the top. Alone. No one joins us, so we're soon reclining with the popcorn between us.

I pull out my phone because it's the responsible thing to do.

ME

The asshat didn't show. I'm in the movie with M. We'll come straight out when it's over. I have my phone on my lap. Text or call if you need me.

The response is almost immediate.

FRANCO

Good. I didn't like the douche anyway.

"Franco doesn't like Patrick?"

"None of us like any of the guys."

"Why?"

"Because none of them are good enough for you."

"Until now."

She rests her hand high on my thigh. I keep my voice low as I cup her pussy.

"Next time, you wear a skirt and no panties. I want what's mine when I want it."

I squeeze, then pat it before pulling my hand away, but she catches my wrist and presses my hand back to her pussy.

"I'll freeze if it's still winter. But I like your hand there."

"Claiming you again?"

"Something like that. Or it's just arousing as fuck."

The first previews begin, and she leans her head against my shoulder, but only for a moment. My gaze darts to the ramp from the door, but I'm also watching the movie. I intend to enjoy my time with Maria. If Francesco comes looking for us, he'll know to look for us up here at the top. Even if Maria really was on a date, she knows to sit up here. I would just be off to one side. Francesco would spot us before I spot him.

I stifle my groan when she sits up, and I know she doesn't

like it either from her resigned sigh. As the lights completely dim, we continue to share the popcorn before she has her peanut butter cups, and I have my chocolate mints. I'm not surprised that she chose a horror film. She loves them. I jump more than she does, and that's embarrassing considering my line of work. I don't jump in real life, but somehow, movies still get me. She stifles her giggles each time, patting my leg or my arm reassuringly. My hand eventually moves from her pussy to her thigh. But we're back in our own space as the lights come up. People are standing and looking around. We'll wait until the crowd is gone, but there's a chance someone will recognize one or both of us.

Speaking of...

"Isn't that the doctor you..."

Maria lifts her head from fastening her coat and freezes. The guy is staring at us and looks ready to beat the shit out of me and grab Maria. My hackles go up when he lets his friends go ahead of him, but he doesn't leave his row.

"I don't want to talk to him, Daddy."

My guard really goes up now that she called me that in public, even if I'm the only one who can hear her.

"Stay behind me, *piccolina*. If you don't want to talk to him, then you won't. Does he know who we are?"

Cosa Nostra.

"He's guessed, but I've never confirmed nor denied. That's confirmation on its own."

"Okay."

I lead the way to the aisle, and Maria stays behind me until we're nearly to this fucker. I reach back with my right hand and ease her to that side and away from Jordan. He looks like a Jordan. An All-American prick from some Long Island old money family.

"Maria."

She says nothing, but I sense she nods to him.

"Is this who you replaced that other dick with?"

I get his double entendre, and I'm not impressed.

"I'm her brother's best friend, and her guard tonight. Don't speak to her like that."

Never have I hated that title—brother's best friend—more than right now. Boyfriend. That's what I should be called. Her future would be even better. My hand moves to her lower back as I usher her forward, putting me between her and the real dick.

"You'd rather go to a movie than what you could be doing?"

Maria doesn't miss a step, but I feel her go rigid. I know she doesn't like her past being thrown in my face, and I don't care for it either. I'm sure the guy thinks I don't know what he means. He wants me to ask Maria or him. He wants to humiliate her.

When he takes a step too close, I smile. Maria's completely blocked by me when I turn to face him. I don't have to put my hands on my hips or cross my arms for him to realize just how much bigger I am than him. I inhale, and my chest expands as I push my shoulders back. I played Division One football for Cornell. I'm a smart jock and always have been. I've been working out twice a day most days since I was in middle school. Sometimes the workout is at the garage rather than a gym. Swinging a pipe or bat at someone is just as good a way to stay in shape as anything else I can think of.

"We're leaving. You're going to wait until we're gone. She told you things are over. She won't meet you there, and you won't approach her at work. You won't text her or give her shit because she's moved on. You will leave her the fuck alone. There are six of us in her family who will find you. That's not even including her bodyguards who work for the family or her father and uncles. Back off."

I see the shock. He didn't think I would know anything about her extracurricular activities since I've never been one of her guards at the club. I still don't know who is, but I suspect it's Giuseppe and Alfonso. They're the most discreet, and given Alfonso already figured out our past, it wouldn't surprise me if he's also keeping other secrets for her.

"I know who you are. And now you know who I am. Back off. I won't say it again."

I wrap my arm around Maria's waist and guide her out of the theater and into the lobby. We cross it quickly and make our way outside. She wraps her arm around mine like earlier as we pick our way back to the car. Francesco gets out as we approach and opens the door for Maria. We have no choice but to let go of each other. The privacy glass is up as always, so I can no longer see her once I'm up front.

"Was she disappointed?"

I glance over at Francesco as he speaks. He's driving now, and I'm looking out the window.

"I think she was relieved. She said she was ending it with the guy. This made it easier."

I hate fucking lying to any of my guys, but he's not high enough on the food chain to know what's going on yet.

"I recognized a doctor coming out right after you. I've seen him at the hospital before."

"Yeah. We ran into him."

"He looked pissed, Matteo. Like really pissed."

"He didn't enjoy seeing us together. He's into her, and she's not into him."

I shrug and try for nonchalance.

"Do you think he got the point?"

"Unless he wants to be a patient at his own hospital, he better."

It's his turn to shrug, and I can tell it's a "we'll see" kinda move. We stay quiet until we reach Maria's place. We pull into the garage after seeing a couple of our guys who aren't regulars for this kind of duty. But I've known them since we were all kids together. I trust them to stay down there and monitor the building. I don't love that they're the only ones here.

"I'm going up with Maria. Hank and Stevie are set, but I want to be sure."

"Sounds good. Have a good night."

I open Maria's door, and we watch Francesco drive away as the elevator doors close behind us. We both glance up at the camera in the elevator. Fucking inconvenient, but there expressly for Maria's safety. Pete's in the security room downstairs, watching all the feeds. There's always another guy who works for the building's management company, but we keep a guy here around the clock. Nothing happens near any of our properties that we don't know about. Those who have houses have security who patrol the grounds. Those who live in condos have security outside the building and in rooms watching camera feeds.

"Daddy, what's wrong? Don't let him spoil the night."

"I wasn't thinking about him."

"Then what's the matter?"

The cameras don't record audio, but she still keeps her voice low.

"I was just thinking about all the security precautions we have in place here. It was ridiculous that we went to Miami with just me guarding you. We did it twice. We got lucky the first time."

Maria and her best friend, Veronica, went down to Miami last winter and had a great time until Maria got called back because half her department was out with the flu. I own a place in the Keys, so we went there for a while. Small. Remote for the most part. And peaceful. Maria and Veronica swam and laid out. When Maria needed to work, she could do it all on her laptop. She didn't have shifts at the hospital, but she still moonlighted a few days. I'll buy a fucking house in Miami if she ever wants to go again. And we'll bring a full fucking entourage. No more hotels, and no more only having one guy.

The elevator doors open, and we stay quiet as we walk down the hall to Maria's penthouse. The luxury is only part of the reason those of us who live in Manhattan have the top floor units. Getting through the roof is much harder than going through a ceiling. We also have more time to spot someone on their way up if they have more floors to travel in the elevator or take the stairs. It's also closer to the roof if we need to use a helo to get in or out. There's only one other unit on this floor, and the owners live in Boca Raton most of the year. They're retirees and only come back up here periodically.

"You do still blame yourself for this. It wasn't your fault. If anyone had a problem with only you going with Veronica and me, then some of the other guys would have come too. We all thought it would be fine. I shouldn't have insisted upon going to such a crowded club."

"And I shouldn't have indulged you."

"You make me sound like a spoiled child."

"No. But I gave in, and you could have died for it."

Maria hangs up her coat and purse while I lock the door, then hang up mine.

"Stop being a martyr."

I stare at her, blinking. I can't think of anything to say that won't escalate this.

"I'm sorry. That came out way harsher than I meant. I just don't want you to keep blaming yourself and falling on this sword. Even if we had six guys with us, so all of my brothers, Carmine, Gabriele, and you, only one of you would have come to the restroom with Roni and me. They still would have gotten us, and they still would have left before anyone could have done anything."

"No. With more guys, there would have been someone out front and someone out back."

"Who probably would be dead now. Matteo, I need you to let this go. I need you to know I don't blame you for any of it at all. Just the opposite. I'm the one who put everyone in danger. I put you in a position where you couldn't possibly have won. I scared the shit out of everyone, and we could have all died. All of that was because of me. I'm the one who's guilty. I can't handle you taking any of this onto your shoulders. I'm the one to shoulder this."

"But—"

"Stop, Daddy. Enough. There are no buts except that one you can spank. Seeing you hurt like this is worse than anything they could have done to me, any future they could have forced upon me. Stop punishing yourself. Punish me instead. You haven't said a damn thing to me about the role I played in this shit except to placate me. Is that the punishment? Making me feel like shit? Because it's more effective than anything my parents ever did when I was a kid."

"No. Of course, it's not a punishment. I hold nothing against you."

"Then why can't you see I hold nothing against you? Matteo, we're finally together. *Finally.* We are going to face a straight-up shit storm soon. I need you completely with me to face this. I know you. If you don't let this go, they'll fucking guilt you into breaking up with me. Or your fucking conscience will tell you to. I'm not fighting that battle along with whatever our family throws at us."

I slide my arms around her waist and pull her against me. I look into the same eyes I've been peering into for twenty-nine years. The day she was born is my first memory. I was barely two-and-a-half. I remember Mama sitting with me, Emilio, Luca, Lorenzo, and Marco and telling us stories in the hospital waiting room. I kept asking for Papa because he'd told me he would take me to McDonald's that day. That part I know because plenty of people have told me over the years. I remember sitting on Mama's lap, then I remember going to see Maria. Marco, Lorenzo, and Luca climbed onto the bed with Auntie Nicoletta while Uncle Massimo stood beside her. Mama held me up so I could see. Emilio stood on his tiptoes, hanging onto the bed railing.

When Mama leaned over because I begged to get closer, I reached out to touch her hair because it looked so shiny and soft. She batted my hand away, then grabbed my finger. I'm pretty sure that's when I fell in love with her.

"It's us against the world, *piccolina*. From now on and always."

"That's right, Daddy. Can you let it go?"

"For us, there's nothing I won't do."

She opens her mouth as though she's going to say something, but she smiles instead. She rests her head against my chest.

Was she going to say the one thing I need to hear but am too chickenshit to say first?

Chapter Eight

Maria

Another frustrating week of only catching moments with Matteo has passed. It's driving me crazy, and I know he isn't much better. I overheard Marco comment on his crankiness—pissiness, as my brother called it—and I know how he feels. We've shot each other a few covert glances, but this won't work for us if we don't tell our family, like right now.

We're at Uncle Salvatore and Aunt Sylvia's house for Sunday dinner. My aunt's the matriarch of this family. Not just because she married the don. She's a leader because it's innate to her. People know that, and it means the women follow her. There's not a man in the Mancinelli *Cosa Nostra* who wouldn't follow her orders if it ever came to that. We trust her as much as we do Uncle Salvatore and Luca. I've respected her since the first time we met. I hope I can have her poise and grace one day.

I glance around the living room as I stand next to Serafina

and Olivia. The latter nudges her chin to where Uncle Salvatore and Aunt Sylvia's girls, Pia and Natalia, giggle.

"It looks like Carlotta and Domenico are keeping them occupied."

"They think Uncle Domenico walks on water. He tells them funny jokes and slips them candy. He was my favorite, too."

I remember sitting on his lap and listening to his stories when my brothers and Matteo were off doing "man stuff" as they called it when we were little. Basically, it was them playing sports they didn't want me to beat them at. While they're all stacked and were athletes since childhood, I'm still the most naturally athletic. Apparently, I was prone to rubbing that in when I was younger.

We make our way into the dining room, and I listen to the conversation going on around us until Uncle Salvatore blesses the food. There's a moment of silence after the Amen, then voices flow as people continue to chat. Matteo sits across from me, and we exchange surreptitious glances. I bite my bottom lip when he puts down his wine glass and looks around. We talked about it, and we're making the announcement now. We agreed there was no point in tiptoeing through the roses.

"Maria and I are together."

Those five words hang in the air.

Marco leans forward to see around Lorenzo, Carmine, and Serafina.

"What did you just say about my sister?"

I want to speak up, defend us, but they need to hash this out.

"Maria and I are dating. There's been something between us for years that we've ignored. We're not anymore."

I sip my water and nearly spew it across the table when my dad speaks.

"About damn time. You've been sneaking around for two weeks, but it's been obvious since Maria was eighteen. Something happened back then. I don't want to know what, but it shouldn't surprise anyone with eyes."

Silverware clatters on plates as my brothers plus Carmine and Gabriele shift their gazes between Matteo and me. My head whips around when Auntie Carlotta enters the fray.

"Mimmo and I are glad it's finally out in the open. Matteo, we want you to be happy. We've waited patiently and haven't interfered, but it wasn't easy."

No one but Auntie Carlotta calls Uncle Domenico Mimmo. Everyone else will use Dom, but that's hers alone. It's like how only Luca calls Olivia Livy, and only Carmine calls Serafina Fina. My name's not really long enough for Matteo to have something that's just his.

Aunt Sylvia grins at everyone, and I can only imagine what's coming next.

"You boys have been living under rocks big enough to be Stonehenge. Maybe you really are that oblivious, or maybe you really didn't want to see it. But the rest of us are happy for them. Sal, you owe me my vacation in the Maldives. I told you it would be out before the end of dinner."

I gawk at my aunt before I find my tongue.

"You bet on us?"

My mom wraps her arm around my shoulder, and I turn to her.

"We all did. I lost last week, and Papa lost yesterday. Uncle Dom and Uncle Sal guessed at least another month. Auntie Nicoletta guessed tomorrow."

I'm not sure how I feel about that. They not only talked about us behind our backs, but they made a joke out of this. That hurts.

"So, you all think this is funny? You've been laughing at our expense for years, and now you finally wager on us. Why not just tell us after the fundraiser? I'm assuming that's when these bets started. Why let us think we should be scared to say something?"

Marco's fuming.

"You should be scared. You're my best friend. She's my sister. What the hell? She's supposed to be your little sister, too."

Matteo's voice is far more controlled than mine.

"But she's not. We're not even cousins by blood. We've stayed away from each other for eleven years, for everyone else's sake. Isn't that long enough for us to have considered everyone else ahead of ourselves? Marco—all of you—might be pissed. Fine. Don't support my happiness. But don't get in the way of Maria's. You should want her to be happy. If you're going to claim to defend her because you love her, then you should support her when she is."

Three people sit between Marco and Matteo, which is a good thing because I think my brother's hands would be around Matteo's throat otherwise. But I want to slide under the table when my cousin speaks.

"Before you went to college, right? Now I get it."

I glare at him. Luca leans all the way forward to see past Olivia, Marco, Lorenzo, Carmine, and Serafina.

"What's he talking about?"

I can't take it. I will not have my sex life discussed in front of my parents, uncles, or aunts. Only Uncle Cesare and Auntie Paola have remained silent. Considering they got married at nineteen because Auntie Paola got pregnant, they won't weigh in on anyone's romantic and sexual relationships.

"Stop."

I push my chair back as I put my napkin on the table. I step around it, and my mom reaches for me, but I shrug off her hand.

"You five can have your temper tantrums. And you six can have your bets at our expense. I'm done."

Pia and Natalia watch with eyes as wide as saucers. I shoot them a smile that I hope reassures them after my icy tone. I turn toward the doorway, and I know Matteo stands too. More chairs move, but Uncle Salvatore's voice gives the command.

"He goes. You stay."

As though Matteo would have listened if Uncle Salvatore said otherwise. I know that when I see his expression as he wraps his arm around me. I want to leave the room, but I'm not ready to leave the house. We can't just run away or storm out. I twist to look over my shoulder.

"Talk amongst yourselves and figure this out. We'll be in the living room. If you can't say anything nice, then don't say anything at all."

Matteo and I walk into the living room, and I steer us toward a window. It's only seven, but it's pitch black out. A handful of stars are visible, with lights from the other houses dimming them. Matteo slides his arms around my waist, and I lean back against him.

"I thought that went well. Considering everyone in that room is armed, and I'm still breathing, I count it as a success, *piccolina.*"

All the men are armed. You'd think they'd take the night off since we're at Uncle Salvatore and Aunt Sylvia's, and there's security all over the property. They're even more vigilant any time we're all together. They only relax when there's a few of us together, or they're at their own homes. Aunt Sylvia has a pistol tucked away in each room that she can handle, and the girls can't reach. Mama, my other aunts, and I all have some type of weapon with us in our purses. We often carried weapons, but once a Mexican Cartel started pursuing Olivia, and she entered our family, all the women never leave home without a knife or pistol now.

I blow out a breath.

"When you put it that way..."

"It'll be all right. I'm actually relieved your parents and mine already know. I think Uncle Sal and Aunt Sylvia would have been easy to bring around, and Uncle Cesare and Auntie Paola will always support any couple if they're happy together. They'll only speak up if the wrong people are forced together. I didn't think your parents or mine would be okay with this."

I turn in his arms and rest my hands on his chest before deciding to wrap them around his waist. I rest against him, absorbing the heat he puts out. It's like having an electric blanket wrapped around me. It calms me immediately.

"I know you were worried my parents would feel you betrayed them after being a fourth son and spending so much time at their home. I'm glad that's not how they see it. I think they see you as finally officially being their fourth son."

"Is that where this is headed, Maria?"

"I hope so."

I lean back.

"I love you, *piccolina*. I have this entire time. That's the real reason I agreed back then. I was a glutton for punishment, but I needed to be with you. Even if it was only ever once. I couldn't live without knowing."

"I love you, Daddy. It was the same for me. I knew I could trust you, but I used the whole going to college as an excuse. I didn't want to move away, unsure how often I'd see you, without knowing, without that memory."

We press a soft kiss to each other's lips, then we rest our foreheads together.

"Between college and you going to med school and me in

grad school, it wouldn't have been the right time for us. We've also had time to figure out what we do and don't want with a partner. We've figured out what we need, and now we can build our future together."

"That's true. And I think if I'd been any younger when this came out, it really wouldn't have gone over so well with our parents and the others. My brothers and Carmine will come around. I think Gabriele gets it. At least, that's what I thought from the way he looked when I stood up. I don't know."

There aren't any raised voices, and no one's sent Pia and Natalia out. I'll take that as a good sign.

"Little one, how about we go out after this?"

"What do you want to do?"

"The questions are who—that's you—and where. That's a surprise."

I lean back again, and I see the hunger in his gaze as he purposely stares at my tits. When our gazes meet, my eyebrows shoot straight up.

"Oh."

"Yes, oh."

"Where, Daddy?"

I whisper since I definitely don't want any part of this conversation overheard. He hesitates.

"You belong to a club, too. I figured you would if you've been a Dom. Where did you go?"

"Lab.Oratory."

Shit. That's some hardcore kink and BDSM there. It makes Threshold look like a kid's party.

"Daddy, I could cancel my membership. We could go there instead."

He pauses for a moment.

"I don't want to take you somewhere where you'll run into women from my past. I don't love the idea of Threshold, knowing you've been there with other guys. There are other clubs we could join."

"That's what I want."

I do. I don't want to give up this lifestyle, especially since now I know we both enjoy it. But I don't want either of our pasts lurking while we're trying to be intimate. He tucks a strand of hair behind my ear as he speaks.

"Do you want to wait however long it'll take to join a new one? That could be a few weeks."

"Not really, but I will."

"It's Sunday, so I doubt Threshold will be crowded. You're comfortable there, so we can go there. If you don't enjoy it, we leave immediately. But I'd like to share this with you."

"I want that too. I know we can and will do a lot at your place or mine, but I told you I'm a sub. You know how I wanted things in the storeroom and what I said at the movies. I guess I want to go into this with that dynamic already set."

"I'll never be your Dom, Maria."

"No. I get that. That's not what I meant. I know you can be dominant without being a Dom. I know I can submit without being your submissive. Those roles don't carry on beyond sex. I know you'll always treat me as an equal. I know you'll never punish me for disagreeing with you or not doing exactly what you say, as long as it's not about my safety. I don't want to act out to get your attention, and I know I never need to, to get your affection. But we've been friends my entire life. That's already established and why we love each other. I want the new part of our relationship to start off—I don't know. Special. With a bang."

"Oh, I'll bang you, *piccolina*. Don't you worry about that."

I laugh and nod.

"Does any of that make sense, though? Or did I just ramble?"

"I get it. I also think it'll be a meaningful way to move from just being friends into a couple with a future together."

"Are we truly all in?"

"I am, little one."

"I am too. If we weren't so compatible, we wouldn't be such close friends. I know there are times you disagree with me, and I've brushed it off. But every time that's happened it's because it put me in a position where I would have been close to you and couldn't do anything about it. It hurt to know that. I thought you'd reject me."

"*Amore mio*, I thought the same. I wouldn't have." My love.

"Neither would I."

Our conversation ends when we hear voices approaching. Matteo doesn't let go of me, but we turn to see who's coming. Luca lets go of Olivia's hand, and she enters the living room. Serafina's with her. My oldest brother looks at us, and I can't read his expression. That doesn't happen often.

"Let's talk in Uncle Sal's office."

Matteo hesitates to let go, but his arms drop from around me. As my parents and his enter the living room, along with our aunts and uncles, I figure I'll be staying here. Conversations that happen in Uncle Sal's office are usually things kept far from the women's ears. Archaic in some ways, but I certainly appreciate it. I don't need to know the things they do.

"Maria, come too."

Matteo slips his hand into mine and entwines our fingers. We bring up the rear behind Carmine, Gabriele, and my brothers. The six amigos, except I'm not so certain any of them still consider Matteo a friend.

Lorenzo stands beside the door and closes it behind Matteo and me. The office is a converted den since it needs to be large enough for at least these six plus Uncle Salvatore and Papa to fit in here. There's usually closer to ten large men when they're strategizing or whatever.

Marco walks right in front of us, the toes of his shoes nearly close enough to touch Matteo's.

"You going to marry my sister?"

I open my mouth, but Matteo's answer is immediate.

"Yes. But I would have liked to tell her that before you."

I look up at Matteo. That's what I want, but it's definitely not how I wanted to hear he wants it to. All in and a future didn't necessarily equal marriage. I look at Marco.

"*Stronzo.*" Asshole.

"He's not screwing my sister and just walking away."

"I'm pretty sure *Nonno* said something similar to Uncle Cesare when he found out Auntie Paola was pregnant."

I glance at Carmine. I didn't put that tactfully. But while none of us exactly liked our grandfather—my father's father and Carmine's mother's father—we loved him as family. He was atrocious to Carmine though, and I've heard the stories about him forcing Uncle Cesare and Auntie Paola to marry. It was ugly.

"And what if I walked away? Would you defend Matteo's honor?"

"Yes." Marco snaps at me. "If you break my best friend's heart, I'll be just as pissed at you as I would be if my best friend breaks my little sister's heart. That's why this is a bad idea."

Matteo sighs, but I'm encouraged by what he says.

"I've been hinting at this since we were eighteen and leaving for college. I told you there was someone I wished I didn't have to leave behind, that I wished I could tell them that. Maria is who I was talking about."

Lorenzo stalks forward from the door as he spits his words.

"She was fucking sixteen. You were an adult. Did you fucking touch my sister back then?"

Lorenzo lunges forward. I'm dumb enough to step between Marco and Lorenzo, and Matteo. My boyfriend literally picks me up and moves me. He leans over and whispers in my ear so quietly I almost don't hear him. I'm sure no one else does.

"Never do that again. If you do, you won't sit for a month. You can defend me and us with your words, but you never put yourself between two men who know how to kill. Do you understand me, *piccolina*?"

"Yes, but—"

"The only but will be yours. Promise me, Maria. Right now."

"I promise not to do it unless I absolutely have to. I'm not going to not defend you and your life."

I glare up at him, challenging him to correct me again. Carmine hoots, and I shoot him a dirty look.

"Nothing's changed between them. God bless the man for taking her on. We're the idiots who didn't see it."

"*Fanculo*." Fuck off.

I hurl at Carmine while I keep looking up at Matteo, who wraps his arm around me and pulls me close. We stop short of kissing.

"Only if your medical opinion believes I'll die. Otherwise, you stay out of the way, Maria. Not negotiable." He looks up at my brothers. "Ever get that close to me again like that while Maria's next to me, and I won't stop."

Fucking hell. This is escalating if Matteo's saying he'll fuck up either or both of my brothers the same as he would anyone he perceives as a threat to me. Luca steps next to Marco, and Carmine and Gabriele walk to Lorenzo's other side. Fucking one brain in five bodies when they all speak.

"Good."

I narrow my eyes before looking up at Matteo, who looks

about as pleased as I do. I step forward and beside Matteo, careful not to be a hair's breadth in front of him.

"You did all of this for posturing. Our parents placed bets on us and humiliated us. You had to measure your dicks to put us in our place. Fuck all of you. Matteo, I want to leave."

Gabriele is usually silent but deadly. He's a natural leader, but he doesn't need to use his voice to impose his will. It surprises me when he's the voice of reason.

"Maria, we all love you both. If this doesn't work out, none of us will take sides, which will only leave us all adrift. We don't want to see either of you hurt. It's not that we assume things will end between you, but we're nervous about what will happen if it does. There's no one any of us respects or trusts more than Matteo to be with you. In many ways, it's perfect. We know you're safe, and he won't stop making you happy. We're happy Matteo is with you because he deserves the best, and you're hands down it. Shut up, Luca. Shut up, Carmine. We know what you think about your wives." He doesn't even bat an eyelash at that aside. "But we also have to wrap our heads around how this changes things, and it does. We're all feeling a little stupid for not having noticed, and we sure as shit all feel guilty that you've hidden how you feel for eleven years. That's a fucking long time. We're sorry about that."

Gabriele moved to America when he, Carmine, and I were ten. He barely spoke any English, and he was taller than everyone else in our grade. Kids used to pick on him because he was a gentle giant. That didn't change until much later. All the guys changed as they stepped into their roles in the *Cosa Nostra*. But at heart, he's still as kind and gentle as he's ever been.

I made friends with him because he understood Carmine, who was already alienated from everyone else. I was Carmine's only ally among the kids in our family back then. When they became besties, I didn't feel like I had to look out for Carmine as much, and I didn't worry about my cousin being lonely anymore. That was all because of our fucked-up shared grandfather and his paternal grandfather. I trusted him with Carmine, and I've always trusted him to protect me. He's just an all-around amazing friend.

"Thanks, Gabe."

Luca pulls me in for a hug and whispers to me.

"We just want you to be happy. If that's with Matteo, we'll figure it out. We just want what's best for you both, and we're scared that either of you will get hurt. I hope you can understand that."

I step back and nod. I look at Marco, who's watching Matteo. There's something going on between the two of them. They've been like this since forever. Carmine and Gabriele are similar, but maybe it's the whole being born on the same day and sharing a crib since birth thing. They communicate with utter telepathy half the time. When they both nod, I breathe a little easier. Matteo wraps his arm around my shoulder, and I wrap mine around his waist. He speaks up next.

"We are family, even if we found out we aren't related by blood after all. Do you think this is incestuous?"

Once again, one voice out of five bodies.

"No."

Lorenzo shrugs. He's the most mellow of the men, taking after Mama. Funnily enough, my dad's considered the most mellow among him, Uncle Salvatore, and Auntie Paola. Lorenzo has the patience of a saint, but when he's done, he's done. Fucking hold on for dear life because when Typhoon Lorenzo rips through, he destroys everything not nailed down. He's the one I was most worried about.

"We're adults. You can both pick who you want to be with. We've never thought of Uncle Dom, Matteo, or Emilio as anything other than family. But it's not fucking incest. Let people say it is. Perfect excuse to be done with them."

Luca flinches at the mention of Matteo's older and only brother, Emilio. There's a nasty history there that no one really knows except for Luca, Emilio, and Carmine, who was somehow involved. Suffice it to say, the scar that runs down my brother's cheek, neck, and under his collar is a reminder of why Emilio is no longer part of our family's inner circle. Fucking hell. This means I'm going to have to make nice to him. I've always been on Luca's side, but if I'm with Matteo, then Emilio is another brother to me. From the way Matteo squeezes my shoulder, I know he's thinking the same thing. We'll sort it out later. There's other shit to worry about.

"You know people are going to say shit about Matteo and me being together. You can't lose your shit every time they do."

Lorenzo's brow furrows, and he frowns in mock disagreement.

"Why not? There isn't a person in this world who doesn't know that picking on you is a sure-fire way to face us all. No one's come out the winner yet doing that."

"We aren't in high school anymore. That melee you guys got into with the others won't just be teenagers trying to prove themselves. At least one of you is likely to wind up dead. Don't do that again."

When we were all in high school, one of the *Tres J's* called me a flat-chested bitch because I thought he was being a jerk to my friend who had a crush on him. The Irish made the mistake of laughing, and the bratva came to my defense. The Kutsenkos and Andreyevs have no tolerance at all for bringing women into syndicate business, and they saw it as that.

It happened at a party at one of the O'Rourkes' houses. I got out with my friend, and everyone not associated with a syndicate fled. Uncle Salvatore has never been so angry in his life. We all wound up back here, and I could hear him screaming in English, Italian, and Intanglese—a blend of Italian and English. All the guys from all four families got into a shit ton of trouble from their respective leaders because it wasn't just a fist fight. Guns and knives were involved.

Matteo kisses the top of my head, and I enjoy being shorter than him, so he can do things like that. While I smile up at him, Carmine reassures me.

"Don't worry. It won't come to that. The bratva won't say anything, even if they have an opinion. The O'Rourkes can't afford to say shit to anyone right now. There aren't any female cousins in the Diaz family. At least not ones who live in America, so *Tres J's* didn't realize how we'd react. But we've all known each other since we were kids. Just like you are with me, you've always been tolerant of the three brothers—even if I think they're criminally insane. They learned their lesson back then."

Tres J's—Javier, Jorge, and Joaquin—came to America not knowing much English when they were teenagers. They were in a similar situation to Gabriele then, so I was nice to them. That's why it didn't go over well when Javier insulted me. My family felt like it was more than just a rude comment but a slight to how welcoming I'd been. All of us know how to make nice in public, and that's supposed to extend to the women. Always. That was the rule even as teens. At least, whenever we ran into them at events our parents dragged us to. Each syndicate likes to flex in front of city officials, which means more black-tie cocktail parties and fundraisers than any teenager should have to endure. *Tres J's* fucked around and found out.

Marco reassures me a little more, too.

"Finn's still appreciative that you lied for him at that party. His voice carries weight now. I don't think he'd let his brothers or cousins say shit to you."

"Okay."

I guess I feel a bit better. I'm leaning against Matteo now, and I like the feel of how his chest rumbles as he speaks.

"We good now? For real?"

"Yeah."

"Yes."

"Sure."

I don't catch all the responses as the others speak over each other. Matteo and I each get a hug from the guys, and I get a kiss on each cheek. That wasn't as painful as we expected, but it still wasn't fun. Matteo must be thinking the same thing because he whispers to me as we leave the study at the back of the group.

"You handled that well, *piccolina*. Now you get a reward."

Chapter Nine

Matteo

I had a quick word with Giuseppe and Alfonso after I walked outside Uncle Salvatore's house. Maria admitted a few days ago that they were the guards who went with her to Threshold. Maria was still saying her last goodbyes. She's hurt about the bet, even if I know she can see some of the humor in it now. I don't love it either, but I know there's no point in getting pissed over it. I don't want to make it worse for her, and I know there was no harm intended, even if it was completely thoughtless. Aunt Sylvia feels horrible, and I know that made Maria feel worse. She was still promising Aunt Sylvia everything was fine between them when I headed out to talk to the guys.

They took it all in stride, so it didn't faze them when we stopped by Maria's place for her to change. She grabbed the masks the guys usually wear, and she had one she hadn't unwrapped yet that she gave to me. We kept the foreplay pretty tame as we rode in the back of the town car. My fingers wandered up her leg and slid into her. The angle wasn't great, so she straddled me as I got her off. I looked at the privacy glass when I noticed the car wasn't moving anymore. Once she was back on her half of the seat, I glanced at her, ensuring she was properly covered. We put our masks on, then I rapped my knuckles against the window, and Alfonso opened the door. I reached in and helped her out, and she was careful not to flash the world before I placed my hand at the small of her back.

We entered Threshold incognito. People might recognize Maria and her guards as patrons who've been here before. But they won't recognize any of us as Mancinellis. We're hardly the only people here disguising our identities.

We're in a room I can tell Maria enjoys. It's set up like a dining room. A gorgeous chandelier hangs down over a long wood table. There are three chairs, none of them pushed in. They're against each wall that doesn't have a door. The wood table's polished without feeling slick or sticky. I don't love that she's been here before with at least one other person, but she's comfortable and at ease. That's what's most important to me right now.

The smooth texture is cool beneath her back as I wrap a rope around her left wrist. There are two loops that are snug enough to keep her from getting up without feeling as though she has no movement. I prowl around the table after I toss the rope beneath it. I pick it up and bind her right wrist.

"What shall I do with my *piccolina?*"

She knows it's a rhetorical question. I press her tits together and lean forward, swirling my tongue around her right nipple. I squeeze both, making her arch her back. Then I begin the first course of my feast. I alternate sides as I suck until each nipple is a tight little dart, and she's trembling. I kiss along her neck to behind her ear.

"I've only just started. That was an appetizer. What's your safe word?"

She thinks about that for a moment, and I feel a surge of happiness that she needs to come up with something.

"Truss."

My lips quirk as I shake my head. She picked something for me. Only she would choose an architecture term.

"That sounds too much like trust. I don't want any chance I could confuse them."

"Transom."

She grins at me before I press a quick kiss to her lips before picking up the flogger she pointed out. We're not using anything that she didn't ask for, since this is our first time sharing BDSM together. We need to learn each other, and since we aren't in a Dom/sub relationship, I want to know exactly what she wants. I don't want to decide and do things *to* her, but *with* her. We both want to do this together.

I flick the flogger across her belly, judging her reaction to that amount of pressure. Her abs tense, but she shows no other reaction. I bring it down across her left nipple, and now she jumps. I'm quick to do the same to her right. She turns her head to look at me, and I'm not sure what I expected to see. She definitely doesn't want me to stop. There's some pleading in her gaze, but it's more like patient waiting. I keep watching her as I take a step to my left and press her right leg open wider. I switch implements, then bring the crop down on her cunt. She moans. Her hands flex.

"Little one, I want to be clear that this is entirely about pleasure. I know I warned you earlier when you stepped between me and your brothers, but that's over and done."

"I know, Daddy."

The crop lands against her clit again, and her hips lift off the table. I'm quick to press them down with my free hand. I keep flicking it as I lean to suck her tits. She moans and writhes, but I don't stop. She can safe word if she needs to, but I know she won't. At least not for this. I nip at her before grazing my teeth over her nipple and biting. Enough to hurt without real pain. Her labored breathing and repeated moans tell me she's down for this. When I straighten, her hand pulls against the rope as though she wants to catch my arm, but she can't.

I move to stand between her legs at the end of the dining room table. Because I still wanted to have the option to move her legs around, I hadn't bound her ankles, but now I do. Her legs dangle off the end of the table, and rope wraps around her ankles and table legs. I slide my hands under her ass and lift her hips to my mouth as I blow cool air on her pussy. Then I dive in, starved for her taste.

"Fuck, baby."

My tongue slips inside her as my lips presses against her clit.

"Do you like how I taste, Daddy?"

I grunt as I move my tongue inside her cunt. When her hips try to lift higher, bringing them even closer to my mouth, if that's possible, I pull back.

"Nooo!"

I chuckle. I kiss the insides of her thigh before latching onto her clit. I work it, flicking my tongue and sucking until she's whimpering.

"Do you need to come?"

"Yes."

"Don't."

She tries to kick her feet, but there's no slack for her to do that. I return to my main course, knowing that I keep bringing her to the edge, then pulling her back. That's why they call it edging.

"I decide when you come."

"I know, Daddy."

I keep going until her breathing changes. I know we're on

the cusp of this going from erotic foreplay to her frustrated and withdrawing from me. I drop the crop on the table where I'd placed it before we started. I'm quick to release her wrists and ankles before helping her up. I lift her from the table and put her down, holding onto her until her legs are steady.

"How're you doing?"

"I'm all right. Give me a second."

I pull her in for a hug and stroke her ass while she catches her breath. It's not just about giving her reassurance. It's affection. I want to share that with her when I've never done that before with any other woman.

"I don't want you to let go, but I also want to do whatever you have planned next."

"Safe word if you need a break again. You know I'll never get frustrated or be disappointed."

"I know. That's one thing I will never fear."

I turn her to face the table.

"Bend forward, *piccolina*. Hold on to the sides of the table."

"Yes, Daddy."

I brush the hair from her back, leaving it exposed. I move to get something that I know she can't see because she has her eyes closed as she rests her right cheek on the table. She shivers as a Wartenburg pinwheel glides down the left side of her spine. It's right next to the vertebrae without being on top of them. I trail it over her left hip, down to the table and back up. I do the same on the right side, moving from her hip back up to her shoulders. I'm certain she's so focused on the pinprick sensations and goosebumps they give her she's unprepared for the paddle to land across her ass.

"Ugh!"

Immediately, her ass turns pink. I squeeze her left cheek before kissing it. I do the same to the right. Then I land a slap with my hand on one side, then the other.

"Can you take more?"

She knows I mean more force not more spanks.

"Yes. Harder."

I oblige, but I'm careful not to forget my own strength. This is my girlfriend—the love of my life—not some shitbag who's wronged my family. I will always be conscious of not being too rough, even when she asks for more. She must sense what I'm thinking.

"Matteo, I can take more. I know you'll never forgive yourself if you harm me. But I like the way this hurts, and I can take more pain. I will never put you in a position to doubt being able to share this with me. You need to trust me to say stop as much as I trust you when I say keep going."

"All right. But if I take it even a smidge too far, and you don't tell me, I'll have a hard time getting over that."

"Yes, Daddy."

I paddle her until the light pink of her ass darkens, but before it can turn red. I never want to bruise her when I use any type of toy or implement. I know she enjoyed seeing my fingerprints after our time together in the storage room. But that's different. I put the paddle and pinwheel down and walk to the chair where Maria left her clothes earlier. I strip and prowl back toward her. She watches me as she continues to rest her cheek against the table. She opens her mouth, the invitation clear. One of these days, but I can't wait much longer.

"Daddy, are you going to make me come?"

I don't answer with words. Instead, I fuck her. I grip her hips as she continues to hold on to the table. I pull her back toward me as I thrust forward. Our sounds of pleasure and need fill the air as they create their own melody. When the fuck did I become a poet?

If they hadn't bolted the table to the floor, it would be clear across the room. I lean over her, my longer body draped across hers as I rest on my elbows by her ears.

"Daddy, don't stop...Please."

"Not until you come."

"I'm close."

I keep pounding into her as the table creaks beneath us. When it shakes a little too much, I pull out, and she wails, scrambling to stand up. I spin her around and hoist her into my arms. She wraps her legs around me just like she did at the hospital. She slides down my dick, and I struggle to keep from coming.

"You are going to take my cock and my cum. Tomorrow, you're going to think about me with every step."

I walk with her to a chair and sit. She moves her legs out of the way, bringing her feet back to loop over my thighs. She grasps the chair back, using it to gain more leverage.

"I'm definitely going to be sore, Daddy. Deliciously and gloriously sore. May I come?"

"Yes."

She rises and squeezes her knees against my hips as her pussy contracts around my cock. She throws her head back as she orgasms.

"I want to make you come, Daddy. Please. Tell me what to do."

"Just like this, *piccolina*. Don't stop."

I'm ready to explode as pleasure coils in the pit of my stomach before it radiates into my limbs. She doesn't slow down, and neither do I. Rather, I work harder to rub her clit with my pubic bone, circling her hips each time I go as deep as I can. Another orgasm builds inside her as I feel her inner muscles spasm. She's already squeezing her eyes shut. She whispers to me as my hand shifts to run my fingers through her hair.

"I'm close again."

"I can't hold out much longer."

"I want to make you come, Daddy. So much. I want you to enjoy this as much as I am."

"If I enjoyed this any more, I'd have a heart attack. Maria, I'm barely holding on to make sure you get off again."

"Don't hold back. Now, Daddy. I want to feel your cum inside me. I want to know I did that."

Our mouths crash in a messy kiss that sustains us as we both go rigid, her cunt holding me deep inside while my cock pulses my cum into her. She's fucking mine. All mine. She was the moment we admitted what we wanted. We made certain of that the first time we fucked. Now there's no denying it.

She collapses against me, panting. She kisses my neck over and over as I stroke her glorious ass again. I love that it's soft and round. I like that there's more than enough to hold on to.

"How're you doing, little one?"

"Never better."

She laughs, and I do too.

"I could hold you all night, but I can already feel you getting cold. Let's get dressed."

"But that means getting off your dick."

She pretends to whine as she shakes her head against the top of my shoulder. I hold her tighter against me until neither of us has a say, and only my dick does. I stand with her wrapped around me and carry her to the table. I ease her down, but we keep our arms wrapped around each other.

"Do you want to stay?"

We'd planned to spend the entire night here once she traded shifts with another doctor. She doesn't have to be in until midmorning.

"Not as much as I thought I did when we made plans earlier."

I nod as I cup her jaw, my thumb brushing her cheek as I speak.

"I'd like real privacy to hold you for the rest of the night. Whose place do you want to go to?"

She bites her bottom lip, and I know she feels the same way I do. Either way, someone has to leave in the morning. I mean, figuratively. Obviously, we'll both have to leave for work. I just don't know if it'll be harder to walk out her door or watch her walk out mine.

"Where do you want to sleep, little one? If it's your place, then we swing by mine, and I grab some stuff for a few days. If it's my place, then we stop by your condo and get your stuff. We are not going to be apart."

"Good in theory. But you have work, and so do I."

"Maybe during the day, but we are coming home to each other, Maria. We are going to figure us out and start living like a real couple."

"Can you just decide? I'm suddenly so exhausted that all I want is to curl up and fall asleep."

She yawns as if to prove her point, but I know she can't help it. After the stress of worrying about how to tell our family, the mess that was, and now good, hard sex, I'm not surprised that we're both worn out. We get dressed quickly and step into the hallway. I nod to Alfonso and Giuseppe. Alfonso leads the way with Giuseppe on Maria's right while I'm on her left. When we get to the car, Alfonso opens the door. I tell him we're stopping by Maria's place then going to mine before I follow her into the backseat. As soon as the door shuts, I lift her onto my lap, then my hands are in her hair. Our kiss might be the most blissful experience of my life.

We pull apart, and I press a kiss to the tip of her nose. She seems happy, but I need to check.

"Did you have a good time?"

"Yeah. Did you?"

"Best time ever, little one."

"I'm glad. I was nervous going there, but I'm glad we did. I'm glad we shared that."

"Me too. We'll work something out with another club, but it's obvious we enjoy doing scenes together. If you want to go again, then we'll pick a quiet time and go straight to whatever room we want."

"I'll think about it."

"Was being in there distracting?"

"No. Not at all. I didn't think about anything but us. That's why it was so wonderful. I was completely focused on what you were doing and how you made me feel. My mind never wandered. You were in control, and I could just relax. Did the spankings hurt? Fuck yes. But it was also blissful. I've never experienced it like that. It was because of you."

We're at Maria's place, and I know Alfonso or Giuseppe will wait by the door in a moment. The privacy glass is always up by default, and neither of them will open the door until I rap on the window. But they'll know if we dawdle. I help her off my lap, and she straightens her clothes. I adjust my suit coat, and as soon as I'm standing in the parking garage, I button it. It's the only way to hide my hard on. I reach back into the car and help her out.

Alfonso leads us to the elevator as though he doesn't notice how my arm is around Maria's waist. I mean, he just accompanied us to a sex club. He says nothing when we get to her door. They wait until I've swept the place, gun drawn, before she comes inside, and he closes the door behind her. Maria's quick to gather clothes for work and to hang out at my place for a few days.

We head back to the car and repeat the entire arrival process at my place. Thankfully, the town car windows are so tinted that the men stationed outside my place for the night can't see it's Maria with me. It was enough dealing with our family tonight and admitting to Giuseppe and Alfonso that not only are we together, but we were also headed to her BDSM club. We managed that much. We'll survive the rest of the world's opinions tomorrow. And I'm sure there are going to be a ton of them. Fuck them. She's mine, and that won't change. But I'll fuck some shit up if anyone upsets my *piccolina*. God help them. I was protective before. There's nothing stopping me now.

Chapter Ten

Maria

The past week has been awesome. Every morning, I wake up, and Matteo is spooning me. It's like a toasty cocoon being wrapped in his arms. I'm in no hurry to move. Every night, we fall into bed and are soon asleep, but we wake up at least twice to have sex. Sometimes he wakes me the first time, and I wake him the second time. Neither of us can make it through the night. I'm glad we don't. Whenever I'm barely awake and move my top leg, I feel that soreness I want. It's not painful. It's just a reminder that he's home and that we're finally together.

Matteo and I go our separate ways once we're in the below-ground parking garage. Sometimes we drive ourselves, and sometimes we take town cars. I drive more often than Matteo since he's often picking up Marco. We do what we do at work, then we meet each other back at Matteo's place. We've made dinner together every night except for one. We went to a family favorite, Donatelli's, and definitely turned a lot of heads since we walked in hand-in-hand. I can only imagine what people thought if they don't know that Matteo and I aren't related by blood. Everyone who frequents the restaurant knows who we are. It's Uncle Salvatore's favorite place.

The nights we've stayed in, we've binged shows or movies on streaming networks, or we've read. Sometimes I was reading radiology images and completing my reports, but we're both avid readers. It shocked the shit out of me to discover he was halfway through a popular Women's Fiction book. He tried to hide it on his tablet, but I caught sight of the title. He just shrugged and said it was a good story.

I'm headed to his place now to get changed before we head to Uncle Salvatore and Aunt Sylvia's for Sunday dinner. All of us call her aunt instead of auntie because we were adults when she joined the family. Auntie just came naturally when we were kids. This'll be the first time we're all together since last week when we announced our relationship. I'm nervous.

"Hey, I'll be home in a couple minutes. I'm just about to pull into the garage. Could you grab the green dress and leave it on the bed for me? I need to shower."

I always shower as soon as I get home. I also shower in the morning because I run or bike most days. Showers. Oh, the sex we've had in the master bathroom. It usually looks like fog's settled in there by the time we get out of the steamy shower. We've tested the limits of our balance, and the feel of the water cascading over us is beyond erotic. It's not like I've never had shower sex before, but it's never been fulfilling before Matteo. Only the guy would get off. I'd enjoy it, but I never came. Matteo—the things that man can do with his fingers, tongue, and cock. He could be an Ironman triathlete.

"Sure. Which shoes do you want?"

"The flats. I've been on my feet all day. It was extra busy. It's like every kid in New York decided to fall off their bike or skateboard today."

"I'll rub them better in the car."

"I thought you were driving tonight. Are we going in one of the cars?"

"I can drive if you want. But it's been fourteen hours since we've seen each other."

I chuckle.

"Fourteen hours since we've touched each other. Do you need to get off before our family sees you with a hard on?"

"That's what suit coats are for and why I still wear boxer briefs."

He's not exaggerating. I convinced him to go commando the night we went out for dinner. It was one of the rare times he didn't wear a suit. He was smoking hot in the slacks, fitted button down with the rolled back sleeves, and loafers. But it was hard for him to hide every time he got a hard on when we touched. I teased him about being worse than a fourte-year-old boy with the wind blowing up his shorts. When we got home, he showed me he was no teenager. The man has the endurance of—I don't even know what to compare him to. It's unreal.

"I suppose I can accept that. If you wore jeans, then it wouldn't be so obvious."

"If I wore jeans, I'd suffocate it."

I laugh outright this time.

"You make it sound like it's its own living, breathing entity."

"It is. It has a mind of its own. It won't be tamed anytime I think of you or hear you or see you or smell you or touch you or taste you."

"I get it. All five senses."

I roll my eyes as I wait for the garage's security bar to rise. I drive down to my spot. Matteo moved his Yukon Denali to a garage our family owns, and now only has his Mercedes at his place. I back into the spot, just like my family always taught me. In case I ever have to flee, I should always have a clear line of sight and not have reversing slow me down.

"Maria."

I spin and almost drop the phone as I pull my backpack out of the backseat of my BMW. Since the car's off, Bluetooth switched off too. I know that voice. I also hear Matteo say my name through the phone.

"Maria?"

"Yeah. Hang on a sec."

I press the phone to my chest and try to cover the mic. I watch from the corner of my eye as Francesco and Martin approach. They were my guards today and followed me home. Nothing about this scenario is going to be good.

"Jordan, what are you doing here?"

"Visiting a friend. I thought I recognized you."

Bullshit. What's he doing in the garage? It's strictly for residents. Guests are supposed to go through the front door and check in with security. My senses heighten, and I cant my head slightly to the left. Martin and Francesco hurry toward me, reading the sign.

"Have fun. Goodnight."

Once my guards are close enough that I'm comfortable to turn my back to Jordan, I head toward the elevator, but he persists.

"What're you doing here?"

I have never told him where I live. For all he should know, I could live here. He should think I do since I have a parking spot.

"Coming home from work." I put the phone back to my ear to speak to Matteo. "I'll see you inside."

Matteo says bye, and I shove my phone in my pocket. Jordan stands behind me at the elevator. Neither of my men like that, so they shift to block him from seeing me or getting any closer. When we get on, I hit the button for the lobby. I don't hit Matteo's floor. Martin and Francesco position themselves, so there's no way for Jordan to touch me. When the doors open, no one moves.

"Jordan, you need to check in with security."

"Oh, my friend said I can come straight up."

"That's not how it works here."

There's a person who sits at a front desk around the clock. There's also extra security in a little room beside the elevator. That's where two of our guys hang out while they watch the security cameras. No one comes into the building without them knowing, so I'm certain they already saw Jordan. In fact, Aurelio steps out of the room as I press the button to hold the elevator door open.

"Sir, come with me."

Jordan frowns.

"Why?"

"You need to check in before you go up."

Jordan looks like he doesn't plan to budge. He's making a huge mistake, and he's about to make a scene as people come home from work. People step out of the second elevator, and I can see others pass through the front door.

"Jordan, you need to go with them. They won't let you go up."

"What're they going—"

I wince as I see Aurelio speak into his earpiece. Paulie comes out of the security room, and I recognize a guy named Simon who works for the building manager and was sitting at the desk. Martin grabs Jordan's right arm and yanks him forward. He's unprepared to be manhandled, so Jordan stumbles forward a step. Aurelio and Paulie are clearly armed. They don't hide it and don't have to since they have permits to carry. Their hands rest on the holsters at their hips.

I hear the other elevator ping. Then Matteo's standing in front of us. I've known him every day of my life, so I can read him with ease. He doesn't intend to appear menacing. Just the opposite. He's trying to appear relaxed. He just can't help it. His aura of authority and restrained strength radiates from him. He doesn't have to put his hands on his hips or cross his arms. He just looks at Jordan, who Aurelio and Paulie are practically dragging from the elevator. Once Jordan passes through the doors, Matteo holds his hand out to me. I don't hesitate.

He pulls me into his arms, kisses my forehead, and whispers to me.

"What's going on? Aurelio said a man he didn't recognize was in the elevator with you."

"He was in the garage when I got out of my car. The guys shielded me, but he wouldn't get off when I told him he had to check in. He didn't move when Aurelio told him to."

"He's who I heard and why you hung up."

"Yeah."

"The guys'll take care of him. Let's go."

"We're going to be late."

We step back into the elevator, where Martin and Francesco remained. Martin flicks the lever, allowing the car to move once he hits the top floor's button. We're standing with our arm around each other, and I realize my heart was racing. Matteo's hand is rubbing the outside of my arm, and I lean my head against him.

"What're they going to do to him? He said he was here to visit a friend."

"If he is, they'll escort him to the unit. If he isn't, he'll be out on his ass."

"I don't know how he got into the garage. I didn't see his

car, so maybe he walked in behind one Maybe he followed someone else in if he parked down there."

"He was waiting for you, Maria."

"We don't know that for sure."

Matteo shoots me a look that says don't be stupid. I nestle closer to him, then I stretch to whisper in his ear. He leans closer, so neither of us has to strain.

"Daddy, I don't want to think that he was. I want to enjoy our evening. I'm already worried about it."

"*Piccolina*, no matter what, I'll deal with it. You don't need to worry about this or being with our family. The guys have been completely normal, even when they've heard us on the phone or know we're texting. They all know you're staying here. None of them has said or done anything about it. I guess the shock didn't last long once they really thought about it. The signs have been there, and I think Carmine might have suspected something a while back."

"I'm pretty sure Sera gave him an 'I told you so' after dinner. She guessed at their wedding."

Matteo grins down at me and drops a quick kiss on my lips.

"I know. I was scared she was going to say something right then and there."

I don't dare say that I was jealous and wished it was us. We've talked about marriage in a roundabout way as an inevitability. But I'm not sure I want to admit I was pining for that months ago. I think he was thinking the same thing, though. I saw the longing in his eyes when we gazed at each other at the end of the ceremony. I think my expression matched his. But that was as close to confessing feelings as we were going to get.

I try not to think about Jordan as we walk into Matteo's penthouse. His is twice the size of mine, and neither of us has ever lived with anyone. But Marco's here as often as Matteo is at his place. And before Luca got married, he came over a bunch, too. Lorenzo flies solo the most. It was never a surprise that all the guys got such big places, despite being bachelors. They're all huge and take up too much space. When they're all together—well, it's a good thing I'm a lot smaller than them. I can squeeze in. Now that I'm staying here, it's a perfect size to keep us from tripping over each other while still being close.

"Do you need me to scrub your back, *piccolina?*"

"As much as I'd like to say yes, we'll never leave if you do. We can't show up for just dessert."

"No, but we can definitely come home for it."

I giggle.

"Are you serving my favorite *cannolo?*"

"Absolutely. You can have my *struffoli* too."

Honey balls. God, the man does have a high opinion of himself, well-earned as it may be.

"I got nothing. Mmm. *Panna cotta?* Is that the closest thing to a dessert you can call my—"

Matteo cuts me off with a passionate kiss before he spins me and taps my ass, pushing me toward the master bedroom.

"Don't get me thinking about your creamy goodness."

I haven't laughed as much in years as I have since we finally came clean with our feelings and started dating. The weight of the world feels so much lighter these days. I think about that as I hurry to shower and get changed. I don't bother reapplying my makeup, and we head out with my hair still wet. I'll twirl it in a bun before we get to my aunt and uncle's.

"Relax, little one."

Matteo senses me looking around the parking garage as we head out to the town car. We'll go in a vehicle with a driver, so neither of us has to worry about having wine with dinner. The last thing any of us needs is for one of NYPD's finest to pull us over and claim we're driving while intoxicated. A cop tried to pull that bullshit with me the night we held my college graduation party. I'd had half a glass of champagne and one glass of wine.

He claimed I was swerving. I was—because I didn't want to kill that fucking squirrel that darted out in front of my car. The guy gave me a breathalyzer and a sobriety test. When I passed both, he tried to come up with something else. The thing is, he was completely mellow when he walked up to my car and greeted me. Then he saw my name on my license, and everything changed. Carmine passed me and doubled back. He made sure the cop understood harassing me wouldn't be good for his pension.

"I know. But it freaked me out. I just wasn't expecting him, and he made it sound like he knew I don't live here."

"But you could."

I'm about to duck into the town car's backseat when he drops that little gem. I look over my shoulder and meet his gaze before getting in. He follows me and helps click my seatbelt buckle. I wait for him to do his own and cock an eyebrow when he doesn't move to get his seatbelt right away.

"You want me to move in with you?"

"Or I could move in with you if you prefer your place."

"You want us to live together after only a week?"

"It hasn't been a fucking week. It's been twenty-nine years. And it's not like we haven't practically lived together before."

"You spending the night at my parents' house almost every other night since you and Marco were three isn't the same as living together as a couple."

"True. But we both know how the other one lives. We know when we need space and when we want company. We know what we like to eat and watch on TV. You know what to do if I come home and say I need space."

I nod. If he tells me he needs space, it's because shit went sideways. It means he needs time to calm down and switch out of mafioso mode to boyfriend mode. It probably means he needs to shower and dispose of his clothes, too. I've known what that meant since I was a toddler, and it was my dad coming home, needing space. Then once they were teenagers, it was my brothers, cousin, and friends along with my dad saying that. They'd all come back to my parents' house, or Matteo's parents', or Carmine's. It made it easier to have just one burn pile and one or two bathrooms that needed disinfecting.

"We do know more about how each other lives than most couples when they move in together."

"Maria, I won't tell you to get rid of your place if you move in here. Or I won't get rid of this place if I move in with you. There'll be an out if you need it."

"If I need it? What if you're the one who wants to leave?"

He looks at me as though I'm slow.

"Matteo, it's possible that we aren't as compatible as we think. I don't want you trapped and miserable, and I don't want you to give up a prime piece of Manhattan real estate only to regret it afterward."

"We don't have to decide our entire future right this minute, but I want you to know that's what I want."

Our gazes lock, and I watch him for several heartbeats. I know when he's lying better than anyone, even Marco. I see nothing but vulnerable honesty. I cup his jaw and press a kiss to his lips.

"You know no one in our family lives together before they're married. Only Luca and Olivia, and they had extenuating circumstances. Don't you worry we might push everyone past their limits if we move too fast?"

"I only care about what you want. I'll deal with whatever

shit your dad or brothers give me. Whatever will make you happy is what matters most to me."

If I were a normal girl—one who isn't a Mafia daughter—then he'd be saying he's picking me over the *Cosa Nostra*. But he can't get me without my family. We come as a package deal. Same way for him. So, picking me doesn't make me a higher priority than the *Cosa Nostra* or *famiglia*. He's lucky, and so am I.

"You know what my dad's going to ask and what everyone's going to expect if we live together."

"Maria, do you have reservations? Or are you just pointing out the obvious?"

"The latter. But if we aren't as compatible as we think, then I don't want to cause the very situation the guys were worried about."

"Will you consider it?"

"Daddy, I've been considering it since I was sixteen. I might have some concerns, but that doesn't mean I'm saying no."

"If we live together, and it goes well, then I am going to marry you."

It's a definitive statement, not just a passing thought. It fills me with excitement, and I'm practically ready to propose to him right this minute.

"If I move in, how long do you think we need to know whether marriage is the right next step?"

"An hour."

He gives me a lopsided grin, and it's the same one I've been looking at my entire life. But it's become rarer and rarer over the past ten years. I cup his cheek again and brush my thumb over the creases beside his mouth.

"I love you, Matteo."

"I love you. You're the only one I ever have. I've always

loved you, but I've been in love with you since we were teenagers."

We look at each other before we're both hopelessly smiling. Our kiss begins languid and affectionate, but it takes very little for it to heat up. All the years of longing and denial come out whenever we kiss, as though we want each one to make up for all the lost years. He burrows his fingers into my damp hair and cradles my head as he deepens the kiss. Both of my hands cup his face as his free hand rests low on my throat, just above my collarbone. I love the feel of him holding me in place. That even in the tender moments I know he's in control. I can just enjoy. I know I'm loved and safe, desired and needed. It's everything to me.

"Daddy, we both live in Manhattan and not that far from each other. Convenience to things isn't a concern. Really, I think, it boils down to which place do we like more? Mine's cozy, and it would be great for two. But your place is better for when all the guys come over."

"That shit's stopping. Luca's the underboss. If we need to get together, then it can be at his place. I'm not living in a bachelor pad anymore. You're entitled to privacy and not constantly having your house full of guys. I want you to be comfortable going wherever you want and never feeling like you have to stay out of the way."

"You'd rather do that to Olivia?"

"They have a house, and he has an office well out of the way. Olivia can move around their place however she wants and never see us. My office at my place isn't big enough for all six of us. None of the bedrooms, except for the master, at your place would be big enough either. If Luca doesn't like the idea of his place being our meeting spot, then Lorenzo, Marco, or Gabe can have us over. They have plenty of space. None of the wives have to be inconvenienced. But eventually, Olivia will have to get used to it. Uncle Sal's won't always be an option."

I nod. Luca has a nice house in Queens with four bedrooms, but I suspect they're going to move into something bigger soon. It'll be a good investment in their family's future. But I'm still keeping that to myself for now. If they haven't said anything yet, then it's not my place to.

"I don't want you to feel like they can never come over, no matter where we live. Marco hasn't been over once since I started staying with you."

"True. I think he thinks of you as my houseguest. He doesn't want to intrude while I have a visitor. He's going to have to get used to seeing you when he sees me."

"Do you think he doesn't want to see me that often?"

"Of course not. But he's gotta get used to a new context. You're the only one none of us ever minds coming over whenever you want. You're the only one whose company we enjoy unconditionally."

"Because I come around the least. I haven't worn out my welcome."

Matteo smiles and shrugs as we drive into the Queens Midtown Tunnel. It goes dark as we pass beneath the East River. Because of that, it becomes obvious when headlights shine way too brightly into the backseat. Someone is far too close. Traffic's relatively light, so there's no reason for this person to be up our ass. It's never a great idea to follow so closely. One accident can close the entire side of the tunnel. No one wants to be caught in a tunnel or on a bridge because of a fender bender.

It's Matteo's men with us tonight, and Severino's driving. He must notice the headlights being too close because he changes lanes. The headlights follow us. That's no coincidence. I know what to do. I unfasten my seatbelt and slip to the floor.

Matteo draws his gun. The privacy glass drops, and I hear Nino.

"Can't tell who it is. The headlights are keeping us from being able to see through our side-view mirrors."

He dropped the glass, so he can use the rearview mirror. He must feel like it's urgent because he didn't use the intercom to warn us he was lowering it. Only the passengers lower the glass without warning. It's a standard rule in our family, and the drivers know better when there's a couple in the back seat. I don't want to imagine how many of us were conceived in the backseats. Gross.

Matteo rests his hand on my shoulder.

"Cover your head, *piccolina*."

Someone must be approaching the side of the car. We wait, but nothing happens. We emerge from the tunnel, and the light makes me blink a couple times. I look up and see Matteo staring out of the back window, but he soon shifts to see me. He sticks out his hand, and I climb back onto the seat. He pulls me close, and I fasten the belt to the middle seat as I lean against him. He has his gun on his lap, and I heard the safety flip back on. He doesn't think the threat is imminent anymore, but he's prepared.

"Did you see who it was?'

I'm asking any of the men. Nino and Giancarlo shake their heads. Carlo is Matteo's other guard tonight and in the front passenger seat. I glance up at Matteo, and he shakes his head too. He explains what I couldn't see.

"He whipped past us just before we left the tunnel."

"Is he ahead of us?"

I lean forward to look between the two front seats. Carlo points toward a car in the lane to our left.

"The blue Beamer."

I strain to see.

"*Fottuto figlio di puttana.*" Motherfucking son of a bitch. "I know that car. It's Jordan's. The license plate holder. SUNY Downstate Medical School. The day I met him, he was bitching about doctors who think they're better than everyone else when they go to the best med schools. We're all doctors once we pass our boards. That was his argument. It was uncomfortable when I said I went to Wash U."

Washington University in St. Louis has a top ten radiology program and is consistently in the top twenty for research. Both Matteo and I moved away for college and for our advanced degrees. He went to Cornell University for their five-year architecture undergrad program and then moved to Boston to attend Harvard for their MBA program. He came back to NYC when he was twenty-six. I'm two years younger and returned to NYC at the same age after doing my undergrad at Duke for three years—I graduated a year early—and Wash U for med school for four years. I'm almost done with my second year of residency. We might have hooked up eleven years ago, but we lived apart for nine of them.

"We'll sort it out later."

Matteo's rigid next to me as he speaks. The moment I said Jordan's name, he turned into a statue. I know what he wants to do, but he won't. And that's entirely for my sake. Scaring me twice in one day is punishable by death in his mind. But he knows I wouldn't want to cause that. He'd reasonably argue that Jordan caused it, and I'd agree to a certain point. I swore to do no harm. I don't want to know Matteo tortured and executed a colleague and now former friend because of me. I'm not naïve about what the men in my family do. I may not know the details, but I know the gist.

"All right."

What else am I supposed to say? The privacy glass remains down the rest of the way into Queens and into the neighborhood where my aunt and uncle live. I noticed both Nino and Carlo keep their guns on their thigh, just like Matteo does. This isn't the first time I've had a car ride like this, and it's undeniably not the last. But it still blows.

What the fuck is Jordan doing?

Chapter Eleven

Matteo

I grit my teeth as I listen to Carmine three days after Jordan accosted Maria in the parking garage, then rode our asses through most of the Queens Midtown Tunnel. I don't like what I'm hearing.

"Matteo, none of us knew. I don't even know the fucker."

"Maria and I are going to have a little talk about anyone else from her past who might need a background check running."

It's not her fault. But I want to make sure there's no one she thought was insignificant who could become a major problem. Carmine's voice remains calm as he explains, but I see the worry in his furrowed brow.

"It wasn't as simple as just running a DOJ or FBI background on him. I had to fucking dig into his ancestry to discover Jordan and I are related."

Yeah. That wasn't such a fun surprise. It's through

Carmine's dad's side of the family. The Ciccones. Carmine's great-grandfather on his dad's side was the don until his great-grandfather on his mom's side had him killed and took the title. Needless to say, when Auntie Paola wound up pregnant with Cesare Ciccone's child, it apparently didn't go over well. I was barely a year old, so I don't remember firsthand. Andrea-Mario Ciccone claimed Auntie Paola got pregnant on purpose to make the Ciccones the Mancinellis' bitches and that she just wanted to escape her father.

Vicenzu Mancinelli claimed Uncle Cesare got Auntie Paolo pregnant to trap her for her inheritance. I think there were even rumblings that Uncle Cesare planned to kill Vicenzu and Uncle Salvatore. It's not like he doesn't have the skills or the training, but anyone who knows Uncle Cesare knows that's not in his nature. He doesn't kill needlessly, and he's never aspired to be the don. He likes his quiet life as an insurance agent. He prefers behind-the-scenes action and has made the Mancinellis millions.

"I know. You said you're third cousins. It's not like you were having Sunday dinners with them instead of with us."

Carmine and Fuck-Face share a great-great-grandfather through Carmine's dad and Jordan's mom. It just doesn't look good that anyone from a former don's family did anything to threaten the current don's family. That shared great-great-grandfather was the don back then. There are still people who believe the Ciccones should lead our *Cosa Nostra* branch. But they're ancient and dying off.

I turn toward Lorenzo as he speaks.

"It could be purely coincidental. He may not know his ancestry any better than we did before this morning. He could just be a shitbag who doesn't take a breakup well."

For Maria's sake, we said that they'd flirted and been

talking at work. Instead of admitting that they fucked at a BDSM club, we said they had lunch together a lot. A few pointed looks made the others realize that wasn't the truth, but that's the story we're going with. It makes everyone a lot more comfortable, even if I can't stop thinking about Jordan doing things to Maria that I wish only I shared with her. We'd talked about going back to her club, but Jordan made that an impossibility. I didn't even have to say it.

Maria refuses to consider going anywhere where she might run into him. She avoids him at work. Since radiologists work with all departments, she's able to track his schedule more easily than she would if she were another type of doctor. She's changed hers to keep them apart as much as possible, and when she can't, she takes her lunch at a completely different time than before.

I hate the inconvenience this is for her, but I know she feels guilty that she didn't tell anyone, so no one dug into his past. She didn't think it was that serious since the hospital hired him after doing an extensive background check, and she kept her interactions limited at work and only saw him at the club, where they also run background checks. What I had to remind her of was once done, the background checks don't get repeated without reason. Who knows what may have changed?

Marco's standing next to me in Luca's office. Maria's off today, and I don't want to have this conversation where she might overhear. He asks what everyone's thinking.

"So, what do you want to do?"

"Depends. Carmine, is there anything else you can dig into? Any way to find out if the rest of his family thinks they should still be running things?"

"As best I can tell, they don't. They watered down their connections after having a bunch of daughters in the family.

They married men outside the Mafia. It's only my dad's immediate family that's still connected because they were the only line of sons from my great-great-grandfather. No one has ever mentioned family on Long Island that the rest of you don't know about, too."

I twist my mouth from side to side then sigh.

"If that's the case, then we just keep an eye on him for now. We can't take him to the garage without good reason."

The garage is where we handle things. Anyone who needs a little extra convincing to talk or anyone who needs punishing goes there. It's like the fucking Hotel California. You can check-in, but you'll never leave. The only way out is as ash or ooze that winds up in the East River. Only the don's family, our *capos*, and the senior-most Made Men know where it is here in Queens.

Our *soldati*—soldiers—and associates—the non-Italian version of a Made Man—are on a strictly need-to-know basis for where it is. We trust only a couple from each group. It's not traceable through deeds or city records. We pay the people in the area well to forget we're there. They're all pretty old-school Italian families, anyway. They know it's a short walk if they don't stay the fuck quiet.

Luca types something into his computer before he looks at me.

"I'll adjust the schedule and have men follow him for the next few weeks. If he tries to get too close to Maria again, he'll realize he goes nowhere alone. He won't even shit in his own house alone."

"Thank you. That's what I was hoping for, and Maria knows it. She asked that we start with that."

She was the one who brought it up. She asked me to have him followed, but to do nothing unless it was her life or his. I see "her life" as anything to do with her not just her still breathing. I doubt she'd agree with that, but she knows enough not to argue.

Luca looks around and nods before he spins his laptop around for all of us to see. He changes the subject since there's really nothing else to say.

"Things aren't quiet with Enrique, and that's excluding Carmine's ongoing feud with Alejandro."

That started years ago over a woman Carmine didn't even know Alejandro was that into. He walked away, so Alejandro could pursue her, but the damage was already done. More recently, Alejandro stirred up some shit, and Carmine retaliated by taking away Alejandro's favorite possession—his private jet. There's been some petty shit since then, like Alejandro had one of Carmine's cars booted. Carmine had all the gas siphoned from Alejandro's motorcycle while the guy was in the worst part of the Bronx one night. But Luca's talking about real stuff right now.

"Enrique's guys set up a pot shop right on the border of Astoria Heights. Creeping a little too close for my taste."

Jackson Heights is the hub for the Colombians, and Astoria Heights is one of our neighborhoods. Bensonhurst in Brooklyn used to be the home of the big name mafiosos, but we enjoy running things in Queens these days. Less obvious.

Marco oversees that neighborhood, so he'll coordinate whatever happens there. But only with Luca's go-ahead.

"What do you want to do?"

Luca grins before he explains.

"Since Enrique's guys have infiltrated the Department of Environmental Protection, they can clean up some shit. A burst sewer line that backs up into the store might remind them we don't need them stinking up the neighborhood."

Marco nods as he pulls out his phone, and I see him scrolling through his contacts.

"I can get guys on that as soon as tonight. Do we want to strike now?"

"Not yet. They haven't set up everything. They're still moving in. Wait until it'll really damage the building and contaminate all their products. The OCM won't let them sell anything that's even remotely exposed to sewage."

The New York State Office of Cannabis Management makes a tidy little profit from turning a blind eye to the *Cosa Nostra*. They ignore all the syndicates, but we pay the best and have the strongest ties to the governor right now. From the ground up, we have people on our payroll who know what's best for them and their families.

I know Marco needs to make some plans, so his next question doesn't surprise me.

"How long?"

"Two, maybe three weeks tops. Just long enough for them to get a little smug."

I glance at my watch. Maria's probably just waking up. I suggested brunch, so I want to get this meeting over with.

"What else do you have for us?"

Luca hesitates. What now?

"I need you to go to Reno. The new casino's having some trouble getting planning approval. The city wants some changes to the proposed restaurant, and I may need you to redesign some of it. They said the kitchen in the main restaurant isn't big enough for the number of diners we expect."

"Isn't big enough? What the fuck? It's bigger than most Vegas kitchens. Who the fuck's bribing them to hold this up? Yakuza?"

Luca and I had a meeting with some Japanese investors a few months ago. They had the chance to buy into the project, but they dragged their feet. Turns out the woman who showed up as part of the delegation was not only the daughter of the *oyabun* but someone Luca fucked in grad school. They missed their opportunity and are still pissy about it. Not smart. The only reason we entertained letting them invest is because we already have a deal to run drugs for them up the Pacific Coast from Mexico to Washington State before getting the product on container ships to Japan. It was a good way to hide their down payment and first installments.

Luca shakes his head and rolls his eyes.

"Some local official who knows who we are. He thinks he can put a squeeze on us."

"If he knows who we are, how can he think that's a good idea? Is he married? Kids?"

"Neither."

"Fine. He wants to fuck around in our house? We can return the favor. We have a construction team with demo experience who like to be paid under the table for shit no one needs to know about. I'll figure out something once I'm there. When do I go?"

"Day after tomorrow."

I can practically sense everyone wincing. I roll my eyes.

"I can be away from my girlfriend for a few days."

Now it's their turn to roll their eyes. Lorenzo smirks at me.

"Aren't you going to be late to brunch with your girlfriend? My sister values punctuality."

"No shit. I've known her as long as you have, down to the minute. Luca, you need anything else from me?"

"Nah. Head out. Say hi for me."

"Will do. The rest of you?"

Carmine grins at me, and a few months ago, I would have wanted to smack it off him.

"Go before the rest of us get texts telling us to stop delaying you."

"Yeah, well, I don't see your wife sending any texts worrying about you."

"Worrying? Is that what you think Maria's doing? Hah. You better hurry up before she gets hangry."

I flick him off on my way out of the office. I drove myself today, but I have guys following, so I let them know I'm headed back to my place. After Sunday dinner, Maria and I swung by her condo. We did some impromptu packing and rearranging. We separated out her living room and office furniture into a group that she wants to bring to our penthouse, and what she'll leave behind as a furnished rental. She had some boxes broken down and stored under her bed from when she moved in. She said she saw no good reason to get rid of moving boxes she'd just have to pay for again. I reminded her the *Cosa Nostra* owns six moving companies, and Gabriele owns a hardware store. She doesn't have to pay for any of that. She just told me, "waste not, want not."

We boxed up clothes, kitchenware, and linens that she wanted. She's pretty minimalist, so it didn't take long. We laughed over several of the photos she had on her walls as we packed those and her ornaments that she's collected during her travels. We already have those placed around the penthouse we're sharing. I dropped hints at the beginning of the meeting, and the guys said it didn't surprise them. Marco even said they were waiting for Maria to tell them when to load the moving trucks themselves. We're having the boxes delivered this afternoon, so we can unpack during her day off. If I have to be out of town for a few days, I want her to feel at home.

"Maria?"

I don't hear her as I enter the condo, and Nino isn't outside my door. I look around and notice Maria's mountain bike is still against the wall, but her street bike is gone. I walk toward the kitchen and notice a piece of paper on the counter.

Gone for a ride. Be back at 11. Decide where we're eating. I'm going to be starving.

I glance at my watch, and it's eleven-fifteen. Maria is punctual to the point of annoying. I pull my phone out of my pocket to see if I missed any messages or texts. Nothing.

ME

Are you on your way back?

I know it may take her a moment to answer, or she may not even get it until she's in the elevator on the way up. Five more minutes pass, and I'm getting nervous. I'm about to call Nino or Martin, who'd be out riding with her, when the door opens.

"What happened?"

I rush forward to take Maria out of Nino's arms. Martin's right behind them, guiding the bikes inside. There's a noticeable dent in Maria's, and the front tire is practically shredded.

"I got clipped."

I glance down at Maria, then I'm staring at Nino and Martin. That isn't even close to the whole story. They'll tell me because they fear me. Martin speaks up as he props the bikes against the wall and closes the door.

"Ms. Mancinelli had the right of way as we made a U-turn to head back. There was a no turn on red sign, but the *stronzo* turned anyway and hit the front of her bike. It took her down. He didn't stop."

"*Piccolina*, are you all right? You should have gone to the hospital."

She stares at me as though I've lost my mind.

"For them to give me a few band-aids. And before you say I could have broken something, I'll stop you right now. I may not be able to see under my own skin, but I know nothing's fractured. I need some soap and water then some antibacterial oint-ment. I'll be fine."

I'm not convinced, but she's the doctor, not me.

"Martin, are you okay? Did the guy hit you too?"

"No. I was on the inside when we turned. He only struck Ms. Mancinelli. He didn't stop, but there's no way he didn't know what he did. Other cars did, and a couple people came to check on us."

"I suspect that kid's going to be googling some of those words he heard me say. He'll need to translate them."

I look down at Maria. The woman can swear in English, Italian, and Spanish. Her French isn't that shabby either.

"Did you see who it was?"

I ask the next obvious question as I put Maria down on the sofa. I'm listening as I head into the kitchen for one of my first aid kits. I have a much bigger one in the master bathroom. I've sewn myself up more than once. I'm glad neither Maria nor I are going to have to do that for her. But I can already tell she's going to have some nasty road rash.

I lean sideways to look into the living room when no one answers. Maria's looking at Martin, and I know that expression. It's her don't tell on me look. I glance at Martin, who looks like he wants to be ill. Nino is conveniently looking out the window.

"Maria?"

I carry the kit to her and open it before going back to the kitchen to get a towel, soap, and a bowl of water. When she has everything to clean up her knees and elbows, I sit beside her and try to stay out of the way. I want to hover like a mother duck, but Maria is not someone who wants her hair held back or people fussing over her. I know she's keeping how much pain she's in and how pissed she is in check. I know she feels like the situation is out of her control, so what she does with her body and the control she has over it is important to her right now.

How do I know this? I took a punch to the nuts when she got drunk at her twenty-first birthday party. The guys and I flew down to Duke to surprise her. I tried to help her when she ran to the bathroom. She was heaving, and I went to hold back her hair. Her fist went sideways and nailed me in my junk.

That doesn't change the fact that I want answers.

"Maria, did you see who did it?"

"I think I did. But I can't be sure. Maybe I just want someone to blame."

I narrow my eyes. That could be any number of people in the Diaz or O'Rourke families. I know the bratva families would never hurt Maria, so none of them are at the top of my list.

"It was Fuck-Face, wasn't it?"

Maria looks at me over her shoulder as she washes her left knee. I hand her the towel to pat it dry. It's one of the few bloody items that will ever get washed in this place instead of burned.

"I couldn't be certain. It wasn't his car, and I only caught a glance for like a second. It could have been some other blond guy. New Yorkers aren't known for being the world's best drivers when it comes to giving way or yielding."

"Martin, what did you see?"

"I didn't. He had no turn signal on, so we thought he was going to go straight when he got the green light. Like I said, I was on the inside and looking ahead when it happened. Ms. Mancinelli braked and swerved toward me. I focused on her, hoping to keep her from falling. I saw nothing but the back of his car."

"License plate number?"

"Delaware."

"What?"

That's odd. I'm looking back down at Maria, who's watching me as she holds gauze to the still bleeding gash across her knee. She sighs.

"Can you get the other kit? I need stitches after all. This is deeper than I thought."

"Do you want me to do it?"

She shakes her head.

"You've never given your—"

"Yes, I have. More than once."

My face sets into a hard expression that usually intimidates most men. Martin and Nino back away, Nino mumbling about going back to his post outside the door, and Martin saying he'd deal with the bikes. Maria just stares expectantly at me.

"The first aid kit? Are you going to get it?"

"What do you mean you've given yourself stitches before?"

She points to a scar below her kneecap, only inches above her current wound.

"I got drunk at a Halloween party in med school. I made it to my car and got the first aid kit from the trunk. I sat on the backseat and stitched myself up while two friends hurled and couldn't watch. Both women are surgeons now."

She pulls up her biking shorts on the opposite side and shows me a faint scar along the outside of her thigh. I've seen both but never knew how she got them.

"Remember when I did the zipline? The carabiner got me. Took out a chunk. I wasn't about to go to some hospital there, so I did it myself."

She was in a touristy area in South America, but it still wasn't somewhere I'd want to wait around in a hospital.

"Any others?"

She appears sheepish. I just nod. I don't want to know after all. I let her work as she sews up a gash on her left knee and glues together a cut on her right forearm. Her resilience and pain tolerance both astound and terrify me. She bandages them to keep them dry before I help her out of her clothes and into the shower. I wash her hair and soap her down. She's got some gnarly road rash on her left side, and it takes everything in me not to lose my ever-loving mind. She says she's starving and still wants to go out to eat. While she puts on some makeup, I text Carmine because Maria gave me the time and cross streets.

ME

I need you to check the street cameras. Maria got clipped on her bike at 10:45 on the corner of Hubert and West. Near the dog run.

He responds immediately.

CARMINE

Is she ok where is she and yeah I can do that

ME

She's here. She stitched herself up and still wants to go out for lunch.

CARMINE

Can't you make her rest or something

ME

Can you

Carmine shoots me the eye roll emoji.

CARMINE

Fine I'll send you a screenshot when I have it.
I'm home so I'll do it now.

ME

Thx

As Maria comes out of the bedroom in a skirt, I can see the fresh bandage covering her stitches, and my heart pounds. It could have been so much worse. Luckily, Nino had an SUV and went to pick them up. I'm pissed no one called or texted me, but I can accept that Nino and Martin were more concerned about getting her here than talking to me. I think Maria also told them not to.

"Ready, Freddy? I'm starving. Did you hear my stomach rumbling in the shower?"

Maria grins as I help her slide on her coat.

"No. The world's finest ass distracted me. Are you going to be warm enough?"

"Yeah. I don't want anything rubbing against the bandage today. I'll be fine. And it's not the world's finest anything."

I spin her around, careful not to hold her too tightly since I saw the bruises forming on her ribs and hip, but I grab her ass with both hands.

"*Piccolina*, if I say it's the finest ass, then it's the finest ass."

"I bet my brother and cousin think the same thing about their wives."

"They can think it all they want. Not the first or last time they're wrong."

I give her a searing kiss that threatens to have us staying home instead of going out, but I hear her stomach this time. We pull apart laughing and head out the door. We're just walking into the restaurant in Tribeca, just far enough from my apartment that I didn't want us to walk, when Carmine sends me a text.

I open it and tap the photo. I zoom in, but the driver's face is unclear. But I can see the accident and how Maria's falling in the shot. Another photo comes in with the license plate easy to read. The third one Carmine must have intentionally saved for last. It's Fuck-Face. It's a head-on shot from the next street camera. I jerk to a stop, and Maria takes a step forward, almost tugging me since we're holding hands.

"Matteo?"

"Yeah."

I show her the phone. She must already know because she just watches me.

"It was him, wasn't it?"

"Yeah."

We sit in a booth and thank the host for the menus. We're quiet as we read and decide what we want. We're holding hands across the table as we make our choices. Once we've ordered, Maria lets go of my hand.

"Will you sit next to me, Daddy?"

She keeps her voice low. She uses the term during sex all the time, and we both love it. She'll call me that when she's tired, too. But I know she's upset if she's saying it in public. I move around the table and slide in beside her, careful not to jostle her leg. I wrap my arm around her, and she sinks into my side.

"I'll take care of it, *piccolina*. I promise."

"He comes from money. He didn't do as well on his MCATs as he wanted, so that's why he went to Downstate for med school. His parents wouldn't buy his way into something better. But he's not someone who can just go missing, and no one can do anything about it. His family has resources and can make some noise."

"I know. I found out more about him today. He's distantly related to Carmine through the Ciccones. They're third cousins."

She sits up and stares at me as the waiter drops off our drinks—hot chocolate for us both with whipped cream.

"What?"

"Yeah. Through Carmine's dad and his mom. But from

what we can tell, they've had nothing to do with the *Cosa Nostra* in almost three generations. Once your paternal great-grandfather ousted Carmine's paternal great-grandfather as don, Jordan's side of the family had a bunch of daughters who married out. We don't know if Jordan knows the connection."

"He knows who my uncle is. Do you think he knows his family once led New York? Could that be an old family tale?"

"It wouldn't surprise me if he's the type who enjoys knowing he fucked a mobster's daughter."

She frowns. None of us care for that term. That's the Irish. We're the Mafia. *With a capital M.* Sure, people throw those terms around, but Mafia—with the capital M—is specific to Italy, and more specifically Sicily. The Irish are the mob. So fucking original. Unorganized fuckwads. They have no chain of command like the other syndicates. They just dog pile on shit like a mob of angry farmers.

I sigh. I'm just getting pissy. This has nothing to do with the O'Rourkes, the mob, or the Irish in general. My mind needs a scapegoat since Jordan isn't within reach. But he will be.

"I'm sorry someone from my past is causing us problems. I'm sure you don't want the constant reminder of someone I was with."

"It's not your fault, little one. He's doing this, not you. Don't apologize for someone else's fuck-ups."

"I know, but maybe I could have handled it better."

"How? You weren't dating. You had an arrangement not a relationship."

"Yeah, but he hinted at more recently. I didn't think much of it at the time. I didn't even really think about it until just now. He'd suggested we move things away from the club, but I told him I didn't want a Dom/sub relationship. He said he meant just my place or his. I skirted the issue and just said the club was more fun. He tried bringing it up a couple more times, but I changed the subject both times. I thought he got the message."

"What was he like those times that you shot him down? Was he passive aggressive about it? Harsher than he needed to be?"

She thinks back and slowly nods.

"Sorta. Maybe. I thought he was trying harder to prove himself not to punish me. But that could have been it. I really don't know. If I'd thought of this sooner, maybe... I don't know."

"Even if you had, neither of us knew he'd lash out and actually hurt you. But, Maria, this changes things. I might not be able to make him disappear, but I can make him understand he needs to stay away from you."

"Thank you, Daddy."

"You know I don't mean a conversation."

"I do. I don't think a conversation would be enough at this point. Maybe take my brothers to really prove the point."

"I'll at least take Gabe."

He's the biggest of us all and always has been. He's the same age as Maria and Carmine, so two years my junior. But even when he was ten and just moved here from Sicily, he was bigger than me. Luca and my brother, Emilio, are almost two years older than Marco and me. Gabriele was as tall and nearly as broad as an almost fourteen-year-old Luca and Emilio. We all caught up to him, but it took a while. He's just a Hulk. The only men he matches in size are the ones from the bratva.

"You and Gabe are definitely enough to scare him."

Gabriele's been our chief enforcer for years because he's the strong, silent type who gets the job done with no fuss, no muss. His loyalty to Carmine during Carmine's misbegotten years held him back. It delayed him going to law school, and it kept him from taking his place as a *capo*. An enforcer is usually one of the lowliest positions, but because he's so good and because of his close family ties, Uncle Salvatore elevated him to somewhere between a high ranking Made Man and a *capo*. Uncle Salvatore just promoted him to *capo* two months ago. Now that all of Carmine's secrets are out about why he acted how he did, not only do we understand both guys better, we appreciate Gabriele a hell of a lot more. He deserves his position.

"If the others are available, then I'll ask them to come too. I know I'm enough to stop him. Two of us are enough to convince him he'll die. All six of us will ensure he goes straight to hell. No God's waiting room for him."

Purgatory. As good Catholics, we all believe in the divine holding cell. We live in that limbo on Earth. Our lives aren't truly our own, and we're far more likely going to hell than heaven. We're just waiting for our turn. However, we send our enemies straight to hell.

"Thank you, Daddy."

She kisses my cheek as our food arrives. We don't talk about either of our jobs; instead, we plan for the upcoming week. There's an exhibit at the MOMA I'd like to take her to. I know she'll tolerate it for my sake. In return, she got us tickets to a boxing match in Madison Square Garden. She hesitated when she asked if I would come since she knows that's a little too much like parts of my day job. She's been wanting to go to a live match for years, but she never asks any of us guys, and she doesn't want to just go with her guards. They'd be working not hanging out with her.

And her best friend, Veronica, would dissolve into hysterics at the first sight of blood just for the attention. Her father and brother are Made Men, so she's no idiot when it comes to *Cosa Nostra* life, especially since they made some poor choices and are living with chronic pain to remind them that playing stupid games wins stupid prizes. She's an attention seeker of the worst kind. Thank God Maria hasn't subjected me to her yet.

As though my girlfriend can read my mind.

"I know you won't want to come, but I was hoping to go out with Roni tomorrow night."

"You sound like you're asking rather than telling me. You don't need my permission."

"I know. But we've spent every night together since we got together. You'd never tell me I can't see my friends, but I know we've been really happy in our little bubble. I just feel guilty neglecting her."

"Who said they'd go with you?"

"I haven't asked my brothers or Gabriele."

It would be Marco, Lorenzo, or Gabriele who accompanies her. For outings like this, she's definitely not going somewhere without a male family member. For bike rides or runs, or to go to work, her bodyguards are enough. But when she, or any of the other women in our family, goes somewhere, at least one male family member goes too. We just don't feel like anyone—no matter how loyal the man is—will ever be as protective as we are. We don't want to think that any of our men would hesitate to take a bullet, but they might. No one in our family would think twice about putting ourselves in harm's way to keep the women safe.

"I'll come if no one else can, but I get you want a girls' night out. Veronica won't want your boyfriend tagging along, even if I promise to just be your guard."

"Thanks. I know none of you like her. I know how she is, but she's awesome with me. She doesn't drink nearly as much as she used to, and she actually has a boyfriend."

"She does?"

"Yeah for about two months now. Maybe we could double date."

"Sure."

That's sounds like a fucking dream come true. I can't think of too many worse ways to spend an evening. Until I take care of Jordan, the worst way is to keep fearing something's going to happen to the love of my life.

Chapter Twelve

Maria

I already know my phone is dead, and I don't have a charger. It was something I didn't think to grab. Of course, I have the one phone that isn't compatible with anyone else's chargers. Carmine and I got our first cell phones together and got a killer deal, or at least we thought so back then. We didn't realize what a pain in the ass it would be that everyone else uses a different operating system than us, but we're used to it, and our phones sync with our other devices. But right now, my phone is dead and the chargers in the town car don't fit. Matteo is going to lose his fucking mind.

Veronica and I had a great time tonight. We went to Lorenzo's club and danced our asses off. We know all the bartenders and bouncers, so we tip well since we don't pay for drinks, and we always feel safe. I'm sticky and sweaty now, and my knee is throbbing, but I had so much fun. The DJ was on fire, one song after another that kept us shaking our asses until we could barely stand. For four hours, I didn't think about work and the bad news I'm usually relaying to doctors. I didn't think about Jordan and the shitshow he's become. I didn't think about what happened in Miami—I had a mild panic attack the first time I went clubbing after being kidnapped in Miami. I just had a good ass time tonight.

But I told Matteo I would call him on the way home, and I haven't. I know the guys probably have, so he knows I'm safe. It's not entirely the fact that I said I would and didn't. It's that I let my phone die. I have my tracker bracelet on, which I never take off. I've worn it pretty much every day since I was fifteen and got a new one because the one I wore when I was younger got too tight. My parents gave it to me, and it's beautiful. I get compliments all the time. There's a little latch on the back that if I hit it, it sets off a panic alert. Matteo knows I'm safe because of that. But for part of the time when I got separated from him in Miami, my tracker wasn't pinging. If that ever happened again, the hope is that I would still have an operating phone.

I bite my bottom lip and brace myself before I open the door to our condo. Matteo's on the couch watching TV. He mutes it and turns to look at me. Fuck. Fuck. Fuckity fuck. I should have asked one of the guys to use their phone. Hopefully, he can forgive that I haven't called.

"I heard your voice on the recording. I know I called the right number."

So, we're going for passive aggressive, are we?

"Truly. I did not get any voicemails I didn't listen to. I swear. I really didn't know you contacted me at all."

"I believe you."

He stands from the couch as I put my coat on the rack near the door and kick off my shoes. I might be moving a little slower than normal as I approach.

"Maria, I am not a regular Dom or a Daddy Dom. I won't punish you for letting your phone die."

"But you're still pissed that I did."

"Yeah. But I also know you don't make a habit of it. I can't remember the last time that happened. I was worried, and I wish you'd used one of the guy's phones to call me yourself. I'm just glad you're all right."

"I'm sorry. I hate making you worry. And I know you're being extra vigilant right now, and not knowing that I was okay must have made you really anxious."

"You could say that."

Not knowing I was okay, or rather not being able to hear me say I was okay, left him feeling out of control. He needed to hear my voice. He needed to know directly from me, not from one of my guards or from Gabriele, who was my family guard. Matteo is not a man who panics. Just the opposite. I'm certain he developed at least four different plans to find me if something had gone wrong. And that's fucking stress he doesn't need.

I slide my arms around him, and he gladly pulls me close. We kiss, and I press my pussy against him. He groans as his hands slide down the back of my pants. I pull my left arm back and slide my hand between us to cup his dick. He's getting hard for me, and I still marvel at how we fit together. I'm not tiny by any stretch, but I am still smaller than him. Thank God I have what they'd call good birthing hips in the olden days. The man is more than just endowed. He could be a fucking porn star.

"Daddy, I think I earned a spanking."

"Maria, I am not punishing you for this. You are not a little, and I'm not a Daddy Dom."

"I know. And I don't see it as you punishing me. I made a mistake, I'm owning it, and I'll try not to do it again. But you spanking me gives you back the control I accidentally took from you. I want that. I want to stop worrying that I've upset you, and I want to help you let go of that anxiety. You dominating me, and me submitting to you does that."

"What about your bruises? They haven't gone away, and neither has the road rash. You still have stitches."

"Daddy, I trust you completely to know what to do. I'll safe word if I have to. Transom."

Matteo watches me for a moment, then nods. We move into our bedroom, and I'm already unfastening my pants when he gives the command.

"Strip."

He knew I had toys. We talked about it. He admitted part of him—a part he believed was utterly unreasonable—hated the idea that we would use toys I might have used with someone else. He said he felt so ridiculous confessing it, but we were both horny and feeling extra possessive. I admitted hating that he'd done any of the things we'd share with someone else. I love that he knows what he's doing. I hate how he gained that knowledge. We're like a pair of matching socks.

We solved the problem by picking out pretty much every sex toy or implement we could think of, then used overnight shipping. We tossed everything I had and everything he had—which turned out to be handcuffs, a flogger, and Shibari rope.

As I peel off my clothes, I take a quick sniff. Despite dancing and getting sweaty, I can still smell my deodorant and perfume. Phew. But then I think of something else.

"Daddy, I've been out all night. Let me take a quick shower."

I cock an eyebrow and look down. He laughs and nods. I'm in and out in five minutes, feeling much more refreshed. We pick up where we left off, but he already has things laid out on the bed. A shiver of anticipation shimmies down my spine. He unwinds the Kelly-green silk Shibari rope, and I can't wait to see how he binds me with it. I wait patiently as he creates a

Lark's Head Single Column around my wrists, ensuring he can still fit two vertical fingers between my wrists.

"Wiggle them, *piccolina*."

I move my fingers to prove that everything is still going well. He makes sure the rope doesn't catch any pressure points or trap any nerves before he draws my arms up and over my head until my hands are between the tops of my shoulder blades. My bent arms supposedly look like bunny ears hence why this is called a bunny tie. He brings the tail of the rope around my lower chest and pulls it through the loop he made at my mid-back.

I feel him draw the tail through more loops that he makes below my breasts, but I can't tell exactly what he's doing. He brings the rope over my right shoulder and slides it beneath the rope just below my breasts. He passes the loose end over the part that's already connected in the front. He's constantly mindful of my bruises and road rash. That kind of pain isn't what he wants to inflict. I know he wouldn't forgive himself for causing me harm.

I'm not looking down, but I can guess what he's doing now. He's tying more knots than a sailor as the rope loops through itself and comes up over my left shoulder. It crisscrosses my back before he continues to bind my breasts until he has a diamond harness. My hands are out of the way, and my tits are on display. He turns me to peer into the mirror, and I love how the rope looks, and I love how I'm now completely at his whim. I can't move my arms, and my tits are sticking out, inviting him to suck them.

And he does. He leans forward and suckles the left, then the right one, making them ache. The rope's tight enough to squeeze without hurting. He keeps alternating sides, nipping at and tugging my nipples with his teeth. Because my arms are over my head, I can't let it tilt back. Instead, I watch everything he does. When he's had enough of my tits, he draws me to the bed and sits. He eases me over his lap, and his hand lands across both cheeks. My instinct is to arch my back, but the harness doesn't allow me to.

"You've been planning this all night, haven't you, Daddy?"

"Yes."

His tone is gruff, but I know it's largely from anticipation and a struggle for control. I can feel his cock pressing against my hip. I hear a bottle snap open, then I feel lube drip between my ass cheeks. Yes, please. I know what's coming. It's only a moment later that a slick plug eases into my ass.

"Wiggle your fingers again, *piccolina*."

I obey immediately. My breasts hang past his left thigh, so he reaches beneath my shoulders and tweaks each of them as he spanks me with just his hand. But I saw the paddle on the bed. He pinches and tugs my right nipple as he brings the paddle down with a ringing thwack.

"Ten. Count each."

"Yes, Daddy. One."

Thwack.

"Two."

Thwack.

"Three."

He twirls the butt plug, and I clench.

Thwack.

"Four."

He tugs and presses the plug three times before he resumes my spanking. All the while, he's still pinching and pulling my nipples. The pain is intense, and I kick my feet in between spanks. After the sixth one, he pauses again.

"Wiggle."

I move my fingers and my wrists.

"How're you doing? Can you handle four more?"

"Yes."

It comes out as a sob. I know he's felt my tears drip onto his wrist.

"Maria."

There's a real warning in his voice this time. He's going to stop if I don't get my tears under control.

"Daddy, I'm all right. It fucking hurts like fucking hell. But I want this. I like it."

"How close are you to safe wording?"

"Not at all."

I'm not. Mind over matter. But I don't think he cares for that answer because the last four land much softer than the first six. As I lie across his lap with an inferno in my ass, he's quick to unbind me. He eases me up to take all the rope off, then he helps me move my arms around, getting all the feeling back into them. When he's certain I'm all right, he sits on the bed again, drawing me onto his lap. He's incredibly gentle as he wipes my tears and cradles me against him.

"Shh, *piccolina*. Only you wanted it as a punishment. I was never angry. But thank you for letting me do that. I know you enjoyed it, and I feel much more at peace."

"I know, Daddy. That's what I wanted. You to be in control and for me to just think about the here and now. Not all the what-might-have-happeneds or the what-could-have-gone-wrongs. I know I didn't need your absolution. I needed to absolve myself. After Miami, I never want to make you worry like that again. When I woke up, all I wanted was to be in your arms. But everyone was there. I needed this. What we have right now—I didn't think I would ever have it."

"It's always been you, Maria. It was just a matter of time."

"I wasn't sure if you felt that way. I didn't want to ruin our friendship, so I just sucked it up."

I grin as I wriggle, making him groan from the pressure against his dick.

"I think *piccolina mia* needs a little more attention."

He puts me on the bed and yanks my legs apart before he settles between them. Even when he's rough, he's still gentle compared to how he can be. He's ever aware of my injuries. I grab his pillow and put it under my head with my own. I want to watch as he goes down on me. He's just about to swipe his tongue along my pussy when his phone rings. It's just twice. We look at it on the bedside table where he'd placed it before lying me over his lap. It rings again, only twice.

I sigh, and my shoulders droop as Matteo gets up. It's work. It's just a question of who's calling and why. The more-than-one-call with only two rings each is a signal.

"Uncle Sal—"

I can hear him through the phone, and I immediately scramble off the bed.

"Get here now. It's Sylvia. She's gone."

There's not a chance in hell my aunt would go anywhere without letting Uncle Salvatore know, and she sure as fuck wouldn't go with no one being able to reach her in case something happened to Pia and Natalia. Something is seriously fucking wrong.

I dash across the bedroom to the closet and pull out a sweater top and loose yoga pants that fit over my stitches. Now that my mind isn't on Matteo and the sex we were about to have, I remember how badly my knee hurts. I'm tugging clothes on as I hobble to the bathroom to grab some painkillers. I swallow those down with a little water and am dressed as Matteo slips on his shoes. I slide on a pair, and we grab our coats.

"What's happening?"

"Uncle Sal got home, and the girls were fast asleep. He

went to his room, but Aunt Sylvia wasn't there. He checked the entire house, but he didn't find her. The guards outside didn't let anyone in, and no one left."

"Did he check the basement?"

"Probably."

"Call him back."

We listen as the phone rings twice before Matteo hangs up and calls again. He does it twice more, and I fear my uncle won't answer. He does just as Matteo's about to end the call. I talk over his greeting.

"Uncle Sal, did you check the bootlegger's door?"

"What?"

"The bootlegger's door. It's in the back right corner of the basement. There's a door in the wood paneling that leads into a cement room. That has a half door leading outside to a set of stairs that end just outside your wall. There's a door there that's inside the oak tree. It's what they used during Prohibition when your house was built. We used to use it when we played hide-and-seek. It was my favorite spot in summer."

We have the call on speakerphone as we ride in the back of the SUV Giuseppe is driving tonight. There's no privacy glass in the SUVs, but it's no secret among our most trusted men that something happened to Aunt Sylvia. They'll all be looking for her. I can hear Uncle Salvatore's feet pounding down the wood stairs to the basement.

"*Merda. Porco Giuda! Che due coglioni!*"

Only the first curse has a true literal meaning: shit. The second translates to Judas pig, but it means fuck. The third literally means what a pair of pricks, but Uncle Salvatore means what the fuck.

He must have found the doors.

"Sylvia's engagement ring is on the floor by the wood door, which is open. I'm going through."

"Uncle Sal!"

Matteo calls out to him.

"I've got a gun." There's a pause. "I've got her wedding ring, too. She wanted us to know she went this way. Hold on. I'm going to use my phone flashlight."

There's some shuffling as I hear the outside door creek open, then there's a pause before it opens some more. Uncle Salvatore's silent. I don't know if he's still inside or is going up the steps. Then I hear him tap his phone. He must have turned on the flashlight.

"I'm going up the steps."

There's a pause as we hear him moving.

"Maria, text your brothers and tell them to meet me out there. They must know about the tree."

"We all do. We always assumed all the grownups did, too."

I look at Matteo as Giuseppe speeds toward Queens. It's the middle of the night, so the streets are quiet for New York. My phone's still dead since I haven't plugged it in. Matteo shoots off the text. I can see his phone when Lorenzo replies.

"Uncle Sal, Enzo says they're almost to the tree."

There's silence except for Uncle Salvatore's footsteps.

"Stop!"

I recognize Gabriele's voice.

"*Sono io. Vedi qualcosa?*" It's me. See anything?

We all learned Italian before we learned English. My generation learned English just before kindergarten, so we could understand our teachers and classmates. My parents' generation basically learned English in kindergarten. They knew enough—numbers, letters, phrases—but they weren't fluent. They all revert to Italian when they're upset. Only Aunt Sylvia was born and raised in Sicily, and not only is she the most progressive, she's got the best English grammar of them all. The rest of them, every once in a while, will stumble and say things as they would in Italian. The words are a little out of order.

Lorenzo answers for all of them.

"*Niente.*" Nothing.

I hear Marco next.

"*No. Aspetta. C'è del sangue qui.*" No. Hold on. There's blood over here.

"*Cosa?*" What?

Uncle Salvatore sounds like he's running. Fucking-a. Can we not get there faster? I hate this. I lean to whisper in Matteo's ear.

"Text our parents. Make sure they know."

I see him pull up a thread that has Uncle Domenico, Uncle Cesare, and Papa on it.

MATTEO

> Get to pantera's now. S missing. Guys there.
> M and I on the way.

Pantera. Panther. It was Uncle Salvatore's nickname when he was younger. Very few people would call Don Mancinelli that to his face these days simply because he's not a man you'd use a nickname for. He's too commanding for that. But with his dark hair and suave style, my dad and Uncle Domenico used to call him that when they were teenagers. It's his code name in texts or emails. In situations like this, we never use full or real names. Who knows who might tap our phones or hack our texts and emails?

PAPA

> We're here. Mama's upstairs in case the girls
> wake. The rest of us are in the office.

Matteo's dad responds, and I breathe a little easier. I'm glad Auntie Carlotta is there too. If they find Aunt Sylvia before I get there, at least there's another doctor already at the house. Plus, she's a general surgeon. I can sew up a wound as well as the next doc, but she's better suited for the more severe wounds that the guys get. I can take out bullets, but I prefer not to.

I'm trying to hear what's going on, but the call is really muffled now.

"Uncle Sal?"

"I'm still here, Maria. There's not much blood, but we're following it. Looks like whoever it was, was dragged. The body was a lot heavier than Sylvia."

"No one heard any gunshots or screams?"

The tree and bootlegger's entrance aren't that far from the house. It's right outside the wall where guards patrol. Someone had to hear something.

"No."

I hear a whizzing sound.

"Is that one of Car's drones?"

"Yeah. It's mine."

Carmine's voice is distant but clear. It goes quiet except for the sound of the machine flying over their heads. I'm wiggling my toes in my shoes and trying not to jiggle my legs, but I'm impatient to get to my family. Matteo's expression tells me he feels the same way. He puts his phone on his thigh, and we wrap our arms around each other.

What the fuck is going on?

Chapter Thirteen

Matteo

I can't believe this is happening again.

First, Maria. Now Aunt Sylvia. I want to blame Carmine and Luca for this and lump Gabriele in as an accomplice. If they hadn't gone after Anastasia Kutsenko, then no one would think our women are fair game. But I know what they did snowballed far past what they planned. And before they did anything, the Irish targeted other bratva wives. That's why I immediately wonder if this is Dillan's doing.

As we approach Uncle Salvatore and Aunt Sylvia's house, the headlights show us a group gathered at the far end of the property. I tell Giuseppe to drop us off down there, so Maria and I get out where Uncle Salvatore and the others stand, their phone flashlights on as they search the ground. No one's talking right now, so Maria and I join the line as we comb the area systematically, our pace matching everyone else's as the light from our flashlights sweeps side to side.

When we reach the street, we turn and double back, but approach the tree from a different angle. We do that until we've covered all the ground leading from the tree to the street. I spotted the trail a dragged body made, and the smattering of blood on the grass. Uncle Salvatore was right. Aunt Sylvia wasn't the one dragged. Whoever it was compacted the grass way too much for it to have been her weight.

We finish none the wiser. We make our way to the house via the tunnel, moving our flashlights along the walls, hoping to find another clue. There are some smudged fingerprints that Lorenzo will dust as quickly as he can. He and Carmine will run them and see if they get any hits. Between Lorenzo's hacking expertise and Carmine's intelligence gathering skills, we'll know if anyone who was down there has a record. We just have to be patient as we make our way from the basement to upstairs, where Uncle Massimo, Uncle Cesare, and Papa wait for us with Auntie Nicoletta, Auntie Paola, and Mama.

We catch what Uncle Massimo is saying as we enter the living room.

"If Sylvia dropped her rings to let us know she went that way, it was because someone came into the house and took her."

Uncle Salvatore whimpers. I doubt the man has ever made that sound before in his life. We all pretend not to hear it, but when he sits in his favorite chair, his head hangs forward as he grasps it and rests his elbows on his knees. The man is distraught. It's unnerving since I've never seen him in a situation where he hasn't appeared in control—even when we all knew he wasn't. He jerks to his feet.

"Massi, I can't right now. I need to see my girls. It has to be you."

Uncle Massimo draws his older brother into a tight hug,

and Auntie Paola joins them. Uncle Massimo whispers something to Uncle Salvatore before letting him go while still holding onto Auntie Paola. Our don heads upstairs, looking completely wrecked.

Uncle Massimo issues orders, and even though Luca is the underboss and second in command, I can tell my friend is happy to let his father take the lead.

"Luca, get Enrique and Dillan on the phone. I want them to hear each other. Marco, get Maksim on a call. We know he didn't order this, but he might know who did. Enzo, get those prints."

Carmine shoots me a look before he speaks up.

"We need to look into Papa's side of the family. We found out that a guy Maria knows who was into her is my third cousin through the Ciccones. He's the one who clipped Maria on her bike yesterday."

Carmine watches his dad and offers Uncle Cesare a sympathetic smile. As though the older man's connection with this family hasn't been hard enough for nearly thirty years, now there's a new wave of suspicion. Uncle Cesare's face drains of all color, and Auntie Paolo rushes over to him. They might be separated and will never reconcile, but they've become close friends since they started their own lives. She guides him to the sofa and sits beside him. She entwines her fingers with his and pulls his hand onto her lap as she leans toward him.

"Papa is dead. Your dad is dead. No one is blaming you or your family for this. We'll find out who it is—your family or someone else's—then we'll deal with it. My brother never assumed you were the villain in anything that happened to us. He doesn't think it now. They're barely your family, anyway. They're so distant now they could be strangers."

Uncle Cesare inhales and nods, but I can tell years of being accused of trapping Auntie Paola and hostility between his father and father-in-law have left him raw whenever his family and the Mancinellis tangle.

Maria tugs my hand, and I lean toward her.

"Should I call Jordan? Maybe see if he'll give any clue about if he's involved. I didn't see him at work today, and I haven't confronted him about the accident."

I consider what she's asking. Marco, Luca, Lorenzo, and Carmine all have work they're doing. Lorenzo disappeared into the basement. That leaves Gabriele, Papa, and our uncles—neither of who are actually related to Gabriele or me by blood, but we've just always called them that. Marco can wait to call Maksim since we don't suspect the bratva.

"We can go in Uncle Sal's office and bring Marco and Gabe with us. Who knows what he might say if he feels backed into a corner? I doubt you want your dad hearing anything about your past sex life."

"I definitely don't want that."

"Gabe, Marco."

I jerk my head toward the converted den. My dad and the others watch as the four of us head down the hallway. It's Maria who speaks first.

"Look, you probably already figured out that Jordan wasn't just some guy I was talking to at work. We never dated, and I never wanted to. He was a fuck buddy."

I catch myself from wincing. I don't want to hear that, and neither do the guys. None of us thought Maria was a virgin—obviously, I didn't. But I don't want to think about her past. Her brother and cousin's best friend don't want to have it pointed out that she isn't the angel we usually consider her.

Gabriele clenches his jaw and crosses his arms but speaks before Marco.

"Are we going to visit him now?"

"He comes from money, Gabe. I told Matteo this already.

He can't just disappear. You can scare the shit out of him, but make sure it can't come back on any of you. He hit me where there were cameras. Make sure you don't make the same mistake."

Marco, Gabriele, and I stare at her. I know she's worried, but she's stating the obvious. Something we've known since we were each twelve and started carrying a knife.

"Maybe I should talk to him first. Maybe Carmine has his charger, and I can get my phone back on."

Gabriele shoots her a reproving glance, and Marco's eyebrows shoot up. She's the only one doing the talking right now.

"I know. I fucked up. I let my battery die. I just didn't notice and wasn't thinking about it. Gabe was never out of arm's reach, Marco."

"And I texted Matteo on the way to their place."

Maria looks up at me. I give her a look that says what did you think happened. She just nods. I pull my phone out of my pocket.

"Do you know his number?"

"Not by heart."

Marco hurries out of the office, and I assume he's asking Carmine for his charger. He's back in a few minutes with the cord. Maria plugs in her phone, and while we wait, we all sit. I wrap my arm around Maria's shoulder as I talk, and she relaxes against me.

"We let Maria talk to him. We use what he says against him when we see him. Or we know we have to get something out of him."

Gabriele looks at Maria. He's strategizing like an enforcer now. Not as her friend of nineteen years.

"You said he comes from money. Does he have any? Or do his parents control it?"

"He's doing well on his own, but I think his parents helped him get started. They didn't get him into the med school he wanted. But I think they're connected enough to have gotten him his position at the hospital. I'm certain they can hire any lawyer they want."

We all fall quiet. Aunt Sylvia is our family attorney for all things legal. It reminds us we're having this conversation because someone took our aunt. Maria's phone flashes back to life, and she immediately unlocks it. I watch her pull up her contacts. I squeeze her shoulder when I see she changed Jordan's name to Fuck Face. She puts it on speaker, and we listen to it ring.

"What time does my little whore want me there?"

I fist my free hand as I control my temper. Barely.

"Jordan, we aren't going anywhere. Don't speak to me like that. I—"

"You don't decide. It's yes, sir, or nothing at all. I'm tired of your fucking bullshit. You fucked him a few times. Now it's time to come back to who you always come back to. Be at the club in thirty minutes."

Maria's eyes fill with tears as she looks at Marco and Gabriele. Shame pulses off her. Her shoulders slump. That wasn't something she ever wanted confirmed to anyone in the family but me.

"You do not tell me what to do. Especially not after you hit me with your fucking car. You're lucky I didn't call the cops. There are street cameras. I'm certain it was recorded. What the fuck were you thinking?"

"You always come back, you little cunt. It was bad timing. I didn't see you. Now be at the club—"

"No. I'm not going anywhere near you. Don't test me, Jordan. You figured out who my family is. It won't be good for your health. You followed me into the garage. You followed me on my ride. You won't get a third strike. You'll just be out."

"Are you threatening me?"

"Promising you. I have a boyfriend, three older brothers, a cousin, and a friend. That doesn't even count my dad or uncles. You know who one of them is. Do you really want to test what happens when you go after his niece?"

"Mancinellis. Your fucking family acts like you own New York. You don't own shit but some construction companies and junkyards. Fucking low class jobs. Lipstick on a bunch of pigs. Flaunt your money like the bougie *nouveau riche* you are. Your whole family is a bunch of whores sucking off city officials. No one would take your uncle or any of your lowlife family seriously if you didn't bribe them. My family has connections yours wishes you had. Connections we made generations back that you wanted but still don't have."

Maria looks up at me. Was that a confession that he believes his family should still run New York?

"Connections? Do you expect your parents to buy your way out of trouble with my family like they bought your job? Like they bought your college degree?"

"We know the right people."

This escalated fast. It makes me wonder how he's spoken to her in the past. What made him so aggressive so quickly? If this is how he's always spoken to Maria, or if he's said even a tenth of what he is now, I'll kill him. Then I'll have a little chat with Maria about why the fuck she allowed it. This isn't Dom/sub shit. This is fucked-up shit.

"What're you going to do next? You tried to scare me. That didn't work. You tried to injure me, and I'm still here. You going to try to kill me?"

I squeeze Maria's shoulder hard enough for her to look up at me again.

Little girl, don't give him ideas.

I hope she can read my mind.

"You're not worth killing. You're his niece, but you don't matter that much."

"Got someone else in mind?"

Maria makes it sound like a sarcastic joke, but I get what's she's doing.

"Maybe. Or maybe I'll get you fucking fired. Maybe I'll make sure you lose your license. Maybe you can end all of this and be a good little sub and do as you're told."

"I was never your sub outside the club. You don't get to tell me what to do. Jordan, you're digging your own grave. I already told you who will come after you. If you're just threatening me, stop while you're ahead. If you have something else in the works, tell me now. I might convince them not to kill you."

"No one's coming near me. You talk a big game. You're nothing more than a cock tease. Your cunt wasn't that great. I'll find someone else to fuck. But you shouldn't have picked someone else, Maria. You shouldn't have taken him to our place. That wasn't cool."

What the fuck? How did he know that? He followed her to our place. He followed her on her ride. Did he follow her to the club too? Does he have someone watching her? Us? I want—no, need—answers. But I can't grill him now.

Maria's voice is pure ice when she speaks again.

"You're punishing me for that?"

"Since you won't let me birch you."

"You try to run me over instead."

"Clipped."

Maria's still looking up at me. She can't look at the other guys anymore. I can't blame her. I don't want to make eye contact with Marco or Gabriele, either.

"Maria, your family may think they control New York, but

my family has a long memory. I knew who you were the moment I met you. Your family might think you're better than mine, but I bent you to my will plenty of times. I bent you over and fucked you plenty of times."

My girlfriend is looking to me to help her as tears stream down her face. The only thing I can think of is killing the motherfucker. But I can't do that through the phone. Maria needs me now. I tuck her head against my chest as she continues to speak. I'm proud of how even her voice is despite her tears.

"Jordan, just how far are you willing to go to prove you're better than me?"

"Your family took from mine. Now I've taken from yours."

I look at Marco and Gabriele. That's a fucking confession. But to what?

"If you hurt her—Jordan, you can't imagine the pain you're going to experience."

"Hurt who?"

There's confusion in his voice, and I don't think it's fake. Maria must hear it too because she wants clarification.

"What did you take from me?"

"I hope your family is as close to the fire department as they are NYPD. It's hard to sell buildings that are piles of ash."

All of our brows furrow.

"You set fire to properties my family owns?"

"I didn't. Your family isn't the only ones who can afford bribes. I paid a lot of men a lot of money to remind you that you shouldn't have been such a fucking bitch and to remind your family that what they once took can be taken back."

We hear the call end, and we sit in silence for a moment. Maria speaks to anyone or no one as she surmises what we must all be thinking.

"He's fucking batshit crazy. Like completely insane. He's

never spoken to me like that at all. I mean, he's called me some of those things before, but only when we were—"

Maria's face is flaming, and I feel so horrible for her. She still doesn't want to look at Marco or Gabriele, and I'm not eager to meet their gazes either. But there was a lot of shit that just came out, so I dive in.

"Sounds like he doesn't know about Aunt Sylvia, but if he's gone after our construction projects, then maybe he does. We can't rule it out. We need to find out what he's fucked up, though. We can't ignore business, or it'll just draw more attention, and make more people ask questions."

"This is all my fault. What if he did this, and he's punishing Aunt Sylvia because of me?

Maria pushes off the sofa and hurries toward the door, but I snag her arm and drag her back. I pin her against my chest as her arms come around me.

"Shh, *piccolina*. Don't go out there yet. We keep this to ourselves for a moment while we sort it out. You're only going to upset everyone else, and then you're going to have to explain things that only four people ever need to know were said."

I look back over my shoulder, and Marco and Gabriele are already nodding before I can shoot them a warning look. I relax a smidge. Maria feels it and tightens her hold on me. Her voice is muffled as she speaks because she doesn't move her head, staying nestled against my chest.

"Marco, Gabe, I'm so sorry you heard all that. Matteo knew, but I didn't want anyone else in the family to know about that part of my life. It's so humiliating. I'm so ashamed."

Marco clears his throat as he walks over to us.

"Maria, we all belong to them. Who knew there were that many BDSM clubs in New York that we're members at different ones? At least, I assume we're members of different ones since we don't run into each other."

Maria pulls back, her eyes enormous. She looks at Marco then Gabriele. Neither man looks comfortable, but they aren't ashamed. She looks up at me. I knew about the guys. It was learning she was a member that came as a surprise. Marco grimaces before he continues. What he says next was *not* something I knew.

"Remember when I came home from college and surprised everyone during my fall break sophomore year? Mama and Papa definitely weren't expecting me. I didn't hear or see them or anything. I was about to go into their room to surprise Mama, but I saw what she was putting away. I have never run downstairs and slammed a door as fast as I did that day. She and Papa—"

I have never seen Marco's face that shade of red before. I've seen him sweaty from working out and sports. I've seen him red from anger. I've even seen him red from embarrassment. But this is five alarm, firetruck red. His parents are into kinky shit. I close my eyes before I confess.

"I had something similar. Except I heard my parents talking about a couple of—items."

Gabriele scoffs.

"At least you didn't walk in on yours. I didn't see shit, but I heard something. Carmine was with me. We turned around and ran out of the house like our asses were on fire. I spent the night at his place. We were in eighth grade."

Maria, Marco, and I stare at our friend. Maria gathers her thoughts the fastest.

"Fucking hell. Gross."

Gabriele's lip curls.

"I know."

"Ew. I don't want to know anything else. At least I don't feel quite so shitty now."

I stroke her hair back and whisper to her.

"I'm pretty certain there are two couples our age who are into it, too."

Maria looks like she has a ton of questions now, but she shakes her head. She inhales, and I feel her chest expand. Then it's a slow exhale.

"So, that brings us back to what are you going to do about Jordan?"

Chapter Fourteen

Maria

I have never been so mortified in my life. Not when I walked out of the church bathroom with my skirt tucked in my panty-hose when I was twenty-two. Not when my period came with a vengeance right after swim practice in college, and I stood gushing in the locker room. Not when I had doctors poking and prodding every single inch of me for weeks when I was fifteen and in the hospital from my horseback riding accident. Nothing has been more horrifyingly humiliating than listening to Jordan speak to me with Marco and Gabriele listening. I felt horrendous for Matteo since it was my past not only thrown and smeared in his face, but fully rubbed in.

But never in a million years did I think he would speak to me like that, even if he didn't know we were on speakerphone with other people listening. He's called me a slut, a whore, a cunt, and a bitch before while we were doing scenes. I tuned it out. It wasn't a turn off, but neither were those words a turn on. I'm fucking glad Matteo has said he will never ever use them with me. I think it would truly hurt me to have him think I'm any of those things, even if it's during roleplaying. But now I'm not so sure. Maybe he does. He's not holding me any differently than usual, but what if he's disgusted with me?

I watch Marco as he approaches us and the door, Gabriele on his heels.

"We're going to make calls and see what the fuck's going on with the sites. See if Jordan did interfere."

Marco opens his arms to me, and I let go of Matteo. I step into my brother's embrace, and it feels like it always has. Comforting. I used to annoy the snot out of my brothers, and they still annoy the piss out of me at times. But never have I had a moment's doubt that they love me as much as I love them. Never have I doubted they will always take care of me and protect me. Not just because our family expects it. But because they're just those kinds of guys—they will protect what they cherish, and I'm fortunate to be one of those things. The same is true the other way around. There's nothing I wouldn't do for them. When Gabriele hugs me, it's the same as with Marco. Same as with Carmine. As far as I'm concerned, Gabriele and Carmine are my brothers too.

The guys leave, and I'm standing alone with Matteo. I gasp when he picks me up and carries me to one of the three sofas. He sits and cradles me against him. He tilts my chin up, and his kiss begins gently. It's tender and reassuring in its softness. Then his hand rests heavily on my throat as he plunders my mouth. It's aggressive and reassuring in its possessiveness. I cling to him, unable to get enough. I shift to straddle his lap. He's careful of my bruises as he grips my hips and rubs me against his cock. Everything this man does makes me sopping wet for him.

"*Piccolina*, nothing changes. I don't want you to worry about it anymore. I saw your face, and I know that expression. I don't think less of you. I was your friend then, not your boyfriend. I would defend you just as fiercely as your friend as I would as your boyfriend. Nothing will make me stop loving you. Nothing ever has."

"I love you too. Thank you, *amore mio.*" My love.

"Are you all right to go out there now, or do you need another minute?"

"We need to go out there. They'll be wondering what's keeping us."

"I didn't ask what we need. I asked what you need."

"Just you. Please stay with me if you can. If you have to go, then you have to go. But while you're here, I just really need you next to me."

"Of course."

He gives me such a light peck on the lips that I almost don't feel it. I climb off his lap, and we go out to the living room to face everyone else. It's only been a couple hours, but the worry is already clearly taking its toll on people. It gives me insights into how things must have been when I was missing.

Uncle Salvatore is back down here, and he doesn't look any better. His eyes are red rimmed. Marco's quietly talking to my other brothers and Carmine. I suspect he's filling them in. No one's looking in my direction, but I see how they keep tensing. Serafina and Olivia are here now, so I'm tempted to go to them. But I don't want to let go of Matteo, and he probably needs to go to the guys. If he does that, then I probably shouldn't go because they'll talk about stuff I shouldn't hear. I'm so torn. Matteo decides for us and steers us toward Sera and Olivia.

We hug, so I have to let go of Matteo's hand, but he's there as soon as I step back. I can tell Sera's taking things in stride since she's *Mala del Brenta*, Venetian Mafia, on her dad's side and *Cosa Nostra* on her mom's. Her mom is Aunt Sylvia's older sister. She's keeping it together for the sake of appearances because this isn't the first or last time a Mafia family has feared for a loved one. Olivia's still really new to this world. She got a crash course when I was abducted in Miami. But things have been relatively quiet the last few months. This reminds her of what she married into.

Sera's watching Carmine, but I get her attention when I speak.

"Have you talked to your mom?"

"Yeah. On the way over here. Carmine was on the call too, and so was Papa. They said they were coming here, but I told them to hold on. They don't need to fly from Venice if we resolve this in a few hours. But after *Zia* Sophia..."

Sera's mom, Allegra, and Aunt Sylvia had a younger sister, Sophia. She was murdered about seven years ago. She was pregnant and running from rivals after getting separated from her guards. She knew she had no one to turn to despite passing other Mafia families. They were all rivals, so she was raped and killed. I understand why Allegra wants to be here.

Olivia keeps her voice low as her gaze continues to scan the family gathered here.

"What do we do? Just wait?"

I glance up at Matteo before I answer.

"The guys will probably leave soon. I don't know whether Papa and our uncles will go too or stay here. At least two of them will stay with us since Pia and Natalia are here along with our aunts, Mama, and us."

The moment someone marries into our family, they're one of us. No so-and-so-in-law. When Sera and Olivia married into the Mancinellis, they gained aunts, uncles, cousins, and brothers. They call their husbands' parents Mama and Papa, too. I suppose the only spouse who won't do that is Matteo. My parents will still be Auntie Nicoletta and Uncle Massimo. Actually, that includes me too. His parents will always be

Uncle Domenico and Auntie Carlotta. We're not engaged yet, but we always talk as though we'll be married in the future.

As though my words were a signal, Carmine and Luca join us. They wrap their wives in their arms, and the women practically disappear. Olivia's only five-feet-two, so she's tiny with a husband a foot taller than her. Sera's Rubenesque, as Carmine loves to call her—says she's so beautiful only a master painter could do her justice—but Carmine's broad shoulders make her almost impossible to see. It's our signal, so Matteo and I hug too.

"Be careful, Daddy. I know no promises, but do your fucking damnedest to come home to me."

"I always will. I love you, *tesorina mia*." My treasure. "Stay here. Papa and Uncle Salvatore are staying. Uncle Massimo will wait for us there."

There. That place they go to when they're taking care of people who need to disappear. No one says it out loud in front of the women and kids. But I've overheard that it's a garage, and Matteo's admitted that to me. We can tell who's coming and going from which of the older couples are kissing and hugging.

"What about Uncle Cesare? Is he going with you if the sites were damaged?"

Uncle Cesare is a senior supervisor at an insurance company. I don't know specifics about his dealings, either. But I know that claims always work in our favor.

"He's coming to inspect, hopefully before the police get too involved. Then he'll either come back here or wait with Uncle Massi."

I glance over to where Sera and Carmine are now standing with Auntie Paola and Uncle Cesare. The older couple was like vinegar and baking soda for years, but no matter how they felt about each other, they were always parents first and foremost for Carmine. No one—except for Serafina now—is more important to them than their son. They were always unified when it came to him. I admire what they sacrificed to make sure Carmine always had two parents with him who adored him—even when he wasn't easy to love.

I get another goodbye from Matteo after the other men make their rounds, hugging their parents last. Carmine and Luca get one more kiss from their wives. Then the men are gone. Mama, my aunts, Sera, Olivia, and I are left staring at one another. While my kidnapping was the first in several generations, this isn't the first time the men have left us behind. Auntie Paola gets out a dominos set; she, Olivia, and Mama set them up. Sera, Auntie Carlotta, and I set up a game of Scrabble. None of us completely focus on the games, but it's enough. After two hours, we decide on a movie, and we've just sat down with popcorn when my phone pings.

It's Jordan.

There's a photo, and I almost drop the phone when I see it. I cover my mouth to stifle my gasp, but it's not enough. Auntie Carlotta is at my side immediately. I don't move the phone in time. We both stare at a photo of Matteo badly beaten and bleeding. I zoom in, but I can't tell where he is or whether anyone else from our family is there.

"Mimmo!"

Auntie Carlotta screams for Uncle Domenico. She's the only one who calls him by that nickname. Uncle Salvatore and Uncle Domenico come running from Uncle Sal's office. I hold up my phone, but neither looks surprised. Uncle Domenico wraps his arms around his wife.

"We just got it too. How'd you get it?"

I speak up.

"That guy I know who's been giving me trouble because I turned him down. He hasn't taken it well. While Matteo, Marco, Gabe, and I were in the office, I talked to him. He said some outlandish stuff and got nasty toward me. He's the one who said some of your construction sites would need the fire department. He alluded to the old rivalry with the Ciccones. I don't understand how he got to Matteo, though."

Uncle Salvatore shakes his head, looking at Auntie Carlotta then me.

"He didn't. This is an old photo. This was from a fight with *Tres J's* about four years ago. Matteo put Javier and Jorge in the hospital. This is what Joaquin did to defend his brothers. Back then, Joaquin sent it to Marco, who sent it to me. I sent it to Enrique right before I sank three of his cargo ships coming up from Venezuela. We took some cargo before they went down just to make sure Enrique understood Matteo means as much to me as any of the other boys."

Boys. They're all men over six feet tall and over two-hundred-ten pounds. Luca, Marco, and Matteo are in their thirties. Lorenzo is thirty. But that's how our parents and relatives still see them. With no sons of his own, Uncle Salvatore has six honorary ones.

ME

How'd you get this old photo?

I want to know for real, but I also want Jordan to know that he isn't freaking me out—at least not anymore. Now I'm just pissed. We wait for an answer, but I start to think it isn't coming. I stare at my phone as Uncle Salvatore pulls out his.

"What's Jordan's last name?"

"Ryan."

Uncle Salvatore and Uncle Domenico stare at me before Uncle Salvatore says something.

"Irish?"

"I guess. He knows who I am, but we never got into his family. His ancestry didn't come up."

I force myself not to look away, but it gets super uncomfortable when Mama joins us. She's Auntie Carlotta's best friend, so I know she came to check on us both. Mama rests her hand on my shoulder.

"You were just having fun together."

Fucking hell. Just what does she know? This is so fucking humiliating. I would have preferred my parents to never ever think of me having sex and that any children Matteo and I have are the product of immaculate conception—just like me and my brothers.

All I can do is nod. Uncle Salvatore unlocks his phone and taps a contact. I can guess who he's calling. They all have each other on speed dial. Another fucked-up part of our lives.

"Enrique, who'd Joaquin give or sell the photo of Matteo to?"

The call isn't on speaker, but now that someone turned off the movie, it's possible to hear since Uncle Salvatore doesn't press the phone to his ear.

"Always a pleasure, Sal. Why can't your family call during business hours?"

"Answer me. Someone got a hold of it and is trying to scare Maria and me."

"Maria? Why her?"

"They're together. You already know that, Enrique. Don't play games. *Tres J's* supposedly helped the Kutsenkos and us. Then Alejandro fucks with a woman in my family. You're having a hard time keeping your word that women and children stay out of our business. Who?"

"I don't know. Let me call you back."

"Put me on with Joaquin."

Enrique snorts.

"I'll call you back in a few."

The call ends, and we're all left looking at each other. I

don't want to say anything to upset Sera or Uncle Sal, who are standing next to each other. I think everyone else feels the same way since we wait in silence for at least five minutes until Uncle Salvatore's phone rings. My uncle shows us his phone before he answers. It's Joaquin. He speaks before Uncle Salvatore can.

"I didn't give or sell it to anyone. My accounts were hacked today. I've been dealing with it all fucking day. That's not the only photo that doesn't need to see the light of day."

My nose curls. Except for a very few, like the one of Matteo, no man from any syndicate takes and saves photos like that. It's incriminating. He means women.

"Any idea who?"

"Yeah. And you won't like it."

Uncle Salvatore's barely holding onto his temper.

"Who, Joaquin?"

"Sergei."

I sweep my gaze over everyone gathered together. There's no way the bratva is connected to Aunt Sylvia.

"Why?"

"I don't know. How'd you know, anyway?"

"Someone sent it to Maria, and we don't know how he got it. Domenico and I got it from an unknown number."

"Then call Sergei and ask him."

No shit, Sherlock. Now it's my turn to rein in my temper, but Uncle Salvatore keeps doing the talking.

"What about Sylvia?"

There's a pause. It's Enrique who speaks next.

"What happened to Sylvia? You wouldn't ask if there weren't something wrong."

Uncle Salvatore looks at Auntie Carlotta and my mom. They both nod. They trust Enrique to know.

"Someone took her."

There's someone speaking in the background. It sounds like Pablo.

"*Por eso me alegro de que no haya mujeres en esta familia.*" This is why I'm glad we have no women in this family.

Enrique's voice is clear when he speaks.

"How long ago?"

"Almost two hours ago, at least. I can't be sure. I got home, and she was gone."

"Your girls?"

"Asleep upstairs."

"*Gracias a Dios.*" Thank God. "Sergei might have sent the photo to mess with you, but you know they didn't touch Sylvia."

"Dillan?"

We're all wondering if it's the Irish, but Uncle Salvatore says it out loud.

"Maybe. Have you tried calling Matteo? See if he knows why someone sent you that photo?"

Uncle Salvatore and Uncle Domenico look at me, then at Auntie Carlotta. It's Matteo's dad who responds.

"He didn't answer."

They must have gotten the text before me because Auntie Carlotta saw it only seconds after me, and she called for Uncle Domenico immediately. I narrow my eyes at them. They can go back and forth all they want. Matteo can be pissed with me later. I move to the other side of the living room.

I listen as the phone rings, and it doesn't surprise me when the man answers after the third one. Curiosity and shock. I knew it would make him answer.

"Sergei, why did you send that photo of Matteo to Uncle Salvatore and Uncle Domenico? Or why did you give it or sell it to Jordan? He sent it to me."

"Maria, slow down."

The heavy Russian accent floats through the phone and fills my ear. I used to think it was so sexy. Then I got to know the Kutsenkos and Andreyevs. They're psychopaths, and the voice lures you to your death like sirens. I know I'm safe from them, but if I were a man, I wouldn't believe a word that comes out of their mouths. I don't believe half of them.

"We know you hacked Joaquin today. You found an old photo of Matteo from when he and the *Tres J's* got into it a few years ago. Why'd you give it away or sell it to Jordan?"

"Maria, honestly. Who is Jordan? I allegedly hacked Joaquin because he took something from us. But whatever I allegedly found wasn't sold or given to anyone."

"Allegedly." I snort. "We aren't being bugged, and you know it. Stop with the allegedly bullshit."

There are too many signal jamming devices around each syndicate member's home for any wiretapping to gather something useful. It's when one of us is away from home that we're worried. At this time of night, I'm certain Sergei's at home. The clubs his cousins own are closed, just like Lorenzo's. So, he's not still bouncing at any of them.

"Maria, who is Jordan?"

"A guy I know who isn't thrilled that I'm not interested in him."

Sergei's voice drops to a whisper.

"The one from your club?"

I freeze. I might be sick.

"How the fuck do you know about that?"

"You're not the only person who wears masks and is a member there. Someone we both know recognized you a long time ago."

"And they told you. Who?"

"They asked a favor. Obviously, you didn't want anyone from your family to know since you only go with your guards, except for last time. You went with Matteo. Once this person knew who you were, they asked me to keep an eye out for you."

"You follow me?"

"No. I know people there I trust. They keep an eye out and report to me. No details, Maria. Just that you're safe. If you're in a situation where your two guards aren't enough, there are people there who will get you out and to your family or to one of our houses if need be."

Aunt Sylvia has her sanctuary policy for all syndicate women. She told a bratva wife that, and they've adopted the same one. If a woman needs shelter, then she will find it among our homes and the bratva's. It won't shield the men, but the women are untouchable until their family can get to them. She never wants what happened to her sister Sophia to happen to another woman.

"How long have you known?"

Sergei pauses. He knows why I asked.

"Two-and-a-half years."

"Laura."

That's his cousin's wife. She's married to Maksim, their *pakhan*. He's equivalent to Uncle Salvatore. Sergei remains silent. He won't confirm or deny, but the lack of response tells me everything.

"Tell her thank you."

"I will tell that person."

"Hmm. So, you know about Jordan. How did he get that photo? He texted it to me. I texted back asking him that, but he hasn't responded."

"I don't know. I have to dig. No one else should have access to what I was doing."

"The hacker got hacked."

He grunts.

"Appears so."

"Do you know who has my aunt?"

"Which one?"

There's real concern in his voice when he asks. I realize Marco never had the chance to call Maks because he came into the study with Matteo, Gabriele, and me. I don't know all Sergei's family history, but I know he and his family fled Russia after his uncle died. His aunt Galina is beyond gorgeous. Like steal your breath, pinch yourself to be sure it's real, knock you on your ass gorgeous. When her husband died, she was in danger of being trafficked like I nearly was. She and her four sons fled here with her sister's family and her late husband's brother's family. The eight sons of those three families now lead the bratva. They have absolutely no tolerance for sex trafficking, or even a hint. Not after what their parents sacrificed to keep Galina and her sister, Svetlana—Sergei's mom—along with Galina's sister-in-law, Alina, safe.

"Aunt Sylvia."

I have to hold the phone away from his ear.

"Maksim! Maks!"

A moment later, I hear another man's voice.

"Why're you screaming? The twins are sleeping."

They must be at Maks and Laura's house. They have toddler twins.

"I'm on the phone with Maria. Someone's taken Sylvia. Maria, I'm putting it on speaker."

"Hi, Maks."

"Maria, are you all right? Were you there?"

"No. Wait a moment. Uncle Sal's coming." I cover the mic with my hand. "Uncle Sal, it's Sergei and Maks. Sergei must have been hacked, too. He didn't send the photo to anyone. Someone found it through him."

Uncle Salvatore nods, and I hand him my phone.

"Maks, Sergei."

Maks responds.

"What happened, Salvatore?"

"I came home from a meeting, and Sylvia wasn't here. Someone got in and out through the basement. She left her rings behind to let me know that's how she left. There was blood in the yard and a trail from someone being dragged. Whoever it was, was heavier than Sylvia. There were prints on the wall, but none Carmine or Enzo could match."

I wondered about that. They must have run them while I was in the study with Matteo, Marco, and Gabriele.

"Dillan?"

Everyone always goes straight to guessing O'Rourkes, and with good reason. They stirred up shit with more than half of Maks and Sergei's family, breaking the no women and children code each time. I'm calling Finn when I get my phone back.

No one has a chance to speak because the front door bursts open. One of Uncle Salvatore's guards, Dante, rushes forward carrying Aunt Sylvia. She's missing her shoes. What must have been a gag is around her neck, and severed zip ties are around her wrists.

"Sylvie!"

Uncle Salvatore drops my phone and bolts to his wife. He scoops her out of Dante's arms and dashes to the sofa. Auntie Carlotta and I push through the others.

"Salva, I'm all right. Just let me catch my breath."

I scan my eyes over her, and I know Auntie Carlotta's doing the same. We glance at each other. Neither of us sees anything, but that doesn't mean there isn't something wrong. She rests against my uncle as he cradles her much like Matteo did with me earlier. He keeps kissing her forehead and stroking her hair. They were arranged, but they were a match made in heaven.

Everyone wants to know, but no one wants to push. Olivia brings me my phone, and I realize the call with Sergei and

Maks is still live. I step away and keep my voice barely above a whisper.

"Aunt Sylvia just got home. She doesn't look good, but she's not obviously injured. Uncle Sal or Luca will call if anything comes up."

Maks is a man of few words.

"Good."

Sergei says goodbye and ends the call. No one else has pulled out their phones, so no one's calling or texting the guys. I press Matteo's contact number. I don't recognize the voice that answers. It's definitely not my boyfriend.

"Who's this?"

I want answers. I don't like the woman's tone when she does.

"Who're you?"

"The girlfriend of the owner of the phone you're using. Where's Matteo?"

She giggles. Fucking giggles. What the fuck?

"He's busy right now. Can he call you later?"

"Busy doing what?"

"Reba."

My ears are ringing. The fucking cunt stripper from the club he owns.

"Put him on the phone. Now."

I wait, and when Matteo answers, he sounds breathless.

"Maria?"

I don't want to think he's breathless because he just stopped fucking the whore to come talk to me. He wouldn't be doing that while he thought Aunt Sylvia was missing. There's no way. But the rational part of my brain isn't moving fast enough to shut down my irrational brain.

"What're you doing, Matteo? Why are you at a club when Aunt Sylvia was missing?"

"Was? Is she home?"

"Yeah. Answer me, Matteo."

"Hang on."

The phone's muffled, but I think I hear him speaking Italian. Maybe he's talking to my brothers or Carmine or Gabriele.

"Matteo, answer me."

"I'm headed there now."

I look around, and everyone's paying attention to Aunt Sylvia. I run down the hall to Uncle Salvatore's office and lock myself in.

"Matteo, why are you at one of your clubs?"

"Maria, I'm headed to Uncle Sal's now. We'll talk about this when I get there."

"Talk about what? If you weren't doing anything wrong, then just say so. There shouldn't be anything to talk about."

"I said we'll talk when I get there."

"Matt—"

The call ends. He's never hung up on me. Ever. Even when we've argued before, which we've done plenty of times. Usually, when he's being overprotective. Now it feels like he doesn't care at all. I sink into one of the wingback chairs and stare at the window, but with the curtains drawn, I can't see the yard. I'm being ridiculous and selfish not being out there with my family. But my chest aches.

I must have been sitting in there alone for at least thirty minutes because suddenly I hear Matteo banging on the door, calling to me. He was in Manhattan, so he had to get to Queens. Maybe I've been here longer.

"Matteo, stop pounding."

I open the door, and he steps into the office. Immediately, I get a whiff of cloying perfume. My nose curls, and I take one, then two steps back. I feel nauseated. I wipe my clammy hands on my yoga pants. Why the fuck does Matteo smell like another woman? He cannot possibly think I won't notice. That makes my stomach knot to where I think I am going to be sick. I can't ignore it. I dash down the hall and into the downstairs half bathroom and heave.

"Maria?"

Matteo's shoes pound across the marble floor before he skids into the door, then pushes it open. So much for privacy. The door slams shut behind him, making me wince right before I heave again. Nothing's coming up, which only makes my throat burn.

"Maria, what's wrong?"

He approaches slowly and rubs my back. I swat his hand away. I like to vomit in peace. He takes the hint and pulls open a drawer beneath the sink. He dampens a washcloth and passes it to me. He's folded it into thirds, so I push my hair out of the way and drape it over my neck. It does nothing for me, but I force calming breaths before I stand. I pull the washcloth off and dab at my mouth, turn it over, and run it across my forehead and cheeks.

Then I burst into tears.

Matteo pulls me into his arms, and I nestle against him despite the perfume. His cologne is just strong enough that it still comforts me. The scent is so familiar that it's a balm to my suddenly battered soul. He strokes my hair and just holds me. That's what I need. I can't form words right now. I don't want to hear him making excuses. I just need his silent strength for the moment.

I whimper when he lets go with one arm to reach back and opens the bathroom door. Then I yelp when he lifts me into his arms. I bury my head in the crook of his neck when he walks past Lorenzo, Marco, and Luca, who just came inside. No one says anything as he carries me upstairs to the room he uses when he stays here. We all have rooms here.

I marvel at how strong he is. I've never dated a man who could carry me up stairs before. Others could pick me up and hold me if they had a wall to brace us while we fucked. But none has done what Matteo does. I remember once he said he can carry Gabriele. That makes me wonder what situation has arisen where he's had to. Just how badly hurt was Gabriele?

We remain quiet as he kicks off his shoes and shuffles onto the bed. I pull loose and climb onto the bed with my feet over the edge to kick off my shoes, too. Once he's leaning against the headboard, he half pulls, and I half crawl back onto his lap. I close my eyes as he smatters kisses on my forehead. After five minutes, he whispers to me, and I'm glad because I don't think I can manage anything louder.

"What is going on, *piccolina?* Something isn't right, and we're up here instead of downstairs with the others."

"Why did a woman answer your phone? And why did she say you were doing Reba? And why do you smell like a perfume that isn't mine?"

"We tracked Jordan to the club. The fucker didn't know I own it. He was getting a lap dance from Reba when we found him. Actually, he was getting a lot more than a lap dance from the skank. I pulled her off him and put my suit coat on her. It might be a full nude club, but I wasn't going to stare at another woman while I fucking fired her. That's why I smell like her. I sent her to my office while I dealt with Jordan. I was breathless when I got to the phone because he swung at me, and I broke his arm and shoulder. I must have put my phone on a table when I went to pull Reba off his dick. I don't even remember."

"That woman made it sound like you were the one fucking Reba. When you were practically panting, I thought—"

"You thought I was fucking another woman while I'm supposed to be finding our missing aunt. That I was fucking an employee at the business I own."

"The reasonable part of me knew you weren't. I really did. But—we already have so many secrets that you can't tell me. You've never given me a reason to believe you'd cheat. But I don't know how far you'd go to coerce info from a woman. I know you wouldn't beat her."

"You think I'd fuck another woman and be okay with that just to get information."

"No... Yes... What the fuck is wrong with me that I would even think that, let alone question you? It's completely irrational. But I can't help it."

"Maria, are you not convinced that I love you as much as I say I do?"

"I am. But I know enough to know there aren't many limits to what men in our world do to get what they need."

"And you think I'm morally bereft enough to cheat on you? That I have no limits at all."

"Can I plead temporary insanity? The sane part of me knows you didn't and would never. But apparently, there is a monumentally insecure person lurking inside me. And she's terrified that you might not be as into me and committed to me as I am to you. That you might leave, and I'll—there'll be nothing left of me because I'll shrivel into nothing."

"What do you need from me to not feel that way?"

"It's not your responsibility to fix my fucked-up mind. I'm sorry and so ashamed."

"I know, and I'm so sorry this happened. You know there's so much I can never tell you. You know I won't answer some of your questions. You know I'll tell you half-truths and lie by omission. You escaped that for a while by being with guys outside our lifestyle. Is it really what you want to go back to?"

"I was too quick to judge you despite how I questioned myself. But I'm in this room with you because in my heart, I know you are not a liar. At least, not to me. You lie as an occupation, and I get that. I accept everything you said because I already know that. But I think you've told me the truth. I choose to believe you have. And that makes me horrible that I doubted you for even a millisecond."

"Shh. You had your sexual desires and history broadcast in front of two family members you never wanted to have know about those things. Someone you once trusted insulted and degraded you. You've been here in a stressful environment with other stressed-out people. You heard a woman say I was with someone else. I smell like perfume that isn't yours. And I probably sounded out of breath like I'd just fucked someone since you didn't know I'd just beaten the shit out of a guy. And you were clipped by a car driven by a rejected lover yesterday. I can give you a little grace for being out of sorts tonight."

I pull out my phone and show him the text.

"Fucking hell. One moment you think I'm the one getting the shit kicked out of him. Then the next you think I'm fucking someone. Maria, neither of those things happened. This is a really old photo."

"I know that now. Uncle Sal explained that. Apparently, Sergei hacked Joaquin, but someone else hacked Sergei."

He kisses my head, and I snuggle closer.

"We need to go downstairs, *piccolina*. At least, I do. Do you want to stay up here and sleep?"

"Are we going to stay here tonight? Or will we go home?"

"What do you want?"

"Home. But if we're needed here..."

"Let's go find out."

It takes us ten minutes to get out the front door. Matteo said hello to his parents when he came in. That's how he found out where I was. At least, I don't feel guilty that he ignored them to come deal with me. Uncle Sal's offering rooms to anyone who wants to stay. Marco, Lorenzo, and Gabriele accept. The couples all want to be alone in their homes. Matteo and I are quiet on the drive. I sit on his lap, and he continues to hold me. I'm questioning how I could be so stupid. I feel utterly worthless and shitty. I've struggled with depression and anxiety for as long as I can remember. Now is not the time for me to have one of these bouts of self-hatred and self-recrimination.

We get inside, and Matteo leads me into our bedroom. He slides my coat off and lays it across the bench at the foot of the bed. I wrap my arms around him. Practically for dear life. Like I'm scared I've fucked up enough to have ruined it all.

"Maria, I can practically hear your thoughts. You are being way too hard on yourself. You are not the horrible person you're telling yourself you are."

"How do you know I'm thinking that?"

"Because I've known you since you were five minutes old. I've always listened to you and watched you. I know your challenges with depression and anxiety because you've never kept that a secret. I know the little things you've said about yourself over the years. The things you've done or the way you've retreated. I never wanted to invade your privacy by confronting you about it, but you are so much harder on yourself than anyone else is. I'm not angry or hurt now that I've thought about what your night's been like. But you haven't let it go."

"I can't. I was horrible. What kind of person thinks their boyfriend is cheating when they know their boyfriend is trying to deal with someone who's fucking with them? What kind of person thinks their boyfriend is cheating when they know their boyfriend is trying to find a kidnapped family member? How fucking selfish can anyone get? I think I've proved what level I can stoop to. I don't want to be like this. I don't want to be insecure and jealous. I don't want—"

"Maria, I know. *Piccolina*, I love you. I have for nearly thirty years. You know I know you. I know how you see yourself and how you feel about yourself sometimes. I haven't walked away yet. I'm not going to. I think I hid it pretty damn well, but I was terrified you'd be happy to see Jordan at the movies that day. That you'd realize you didn't want something serious with me because you wanted him too—wanted him more. I beat the shit out of him tonight, not just so he'd stay away from you to keep you safe. I did it to make sure he can never be a rival. Logically, that's fucking ridiculous. I know that. But it doesn't mean I want to imagine I could have any competition for your affection or desire. We're human. We have insecurities. It's all right."

"I didn't believe you the first time you said you minored in psychology. Then I assumed it was so you could understand people when you're *there*. Maybe you picked up enough abnormal psych to understand your girlfriend."

"There's nothing abnormal about you, little one."

I nod. A moment of fear and regret flash through me. I want to marry Matteo, but what if he changes his mind? Reasonably, I know that if he did, then we shouldn't be together. Unreasonably, my brothers might guilt him into it.

He tucks hair behind my ear and cups my cheek.

"I'm not going anywhere, Maria. You're stuck with me."

I whisper to him, and way too many emotions rush back to me. What the hell? This is worse than PMS.

"Don't say that. I'm not stuck with you. I want you. Are we good, Matteo?"

"Yes, but I don't think you're okay yet."

"I'll get there, Daddy."

He watches me for a moment.

"*Piccolina*, let me take care of you."

Chapter Fifteen

Matteo

And I will. Right now, that's what she desperately needs. She needs me to be in control and take care of all of this. Take care of her. That's why she's thinking of me as Daddy and not something else. She feels safe in my arms.

I tilt her head back with my finger under her chin. She gazes into my eyes and exhales. I hope she sees my gaze as loving and earnest. That it's steadfast. That it's reassuring. All the things she probably never imagined from me as her brother's best friend, but what she craves and knows will never change. I love her. I press a soft kiss to her lips.

I stare at her for a moment, then she's suddenly on her back with me pulling down her pants. She raises her hips to help me. I stifle her moan with a kiss as my fingers plunge into her. She fumbles to unfasten my belt and undo the button to my pants. The moment she gets the zipper down, I spring free. She wraps her hand around my cock and sighs. But she has to let go a moment later as I pull her top over her head and practically rip her bra off. She pops a button off my shirt in her haste to get me naked, too.

"Put your hands over your head, Maria. Hold on to the headboard."

She follows my command without hesitation. I kiss along her shoulder and up her neck until my lips press just behind her ear. My warm breath sends a shiver through her.

I settle between her legs the moment she puts her hands over her head. Then I thrust into her with enough force to make the headboard bump into the wall. I know she could feel my cock pressing against her pussy while we spoke. She tries to tilt her hips to rub against me. But I decide on the right moment, and I'm not wrong. The feeling of being buried inside her makes everything right. I gave myself to her the moment we had sex for the first time. I knew then that there would be no going back. I knew then that I'd found what I'd searched for. I want nothing and no one else. I've waited eleven years to have everything I've longed for.

I've been rocking my hips as we kiss, but kissing isn't all we need right now. I'm careful not to fuck her hard enough to make the bed creak or hit the wall again. We don't need to confirm what our guards must be thinking. They stay out in the basement, lobby, and security room, thank God. It's embarrassing to have our men guess, but it would make me ashamed for anyone to know for sure. Maria deserves privacy. We've been discreet while we're around other people. We've made love, and we've fucked, but we haven't broadcasted it to everyone.

"Daddy, may I touch you?"

"Do you want to be fucked? Or do you want to make love, *piccolina*?"

"Make love."

"Then touch me however you want."

"Is that what you want?"

"Yes."

From the slight furrow of her brow, my response must make her wonder why I told her to put her hands over her head, but seeing her like that stirs my passion. As I thrust harder, her hands roam over me as I kiss her. She runs her hands through my hair, cups my jaw, slides them over my back, and grips my ass. Anything she can touch, she wants. It's exciting. It's gratifying. It makes me feel loved.

My muscles bunch and relax as I surge into her over and over, reminding myself to be careful not to be too rough. I push up on my forearms, and I can tell she enjoys the view of my abs and shoulders, but she wants my body against hers. I can deny her nothing as she pulls me down to her, putting us chest to chest again. She says what I'm thinking.

"I love looking at you while we're together, Matteo. Your body is better than anything I could ever imagine. But I don't want anything—even air—between us."

I slide my arms beneath her, and she wraps her arms and legs around me.

"Daddy, may I come?"

"Yes, baby. As many times as you can."

We move together, and I can tell her orgasm is just beyond her reach. Every time my pelvic bone rubs her clit, I sense she gets a little closer until she can no longer hold on. She arches beneath me, her eyes drifting closed. She's barely caught her breath when her core tightens again, and I imagine the waves of pleasure coursing through her. She grips my ass and tries to draw out the sensation. It's intoxicating to know I have that effect on her. That I can make her happy.

"Daddy, I want to make you come."

"I'm close, but not until you're done."

"No. I want us to come together. Please."

"Tell me when you're close again."

I continue to thrust into her, my hips in rhythm with hers. I go balls deep, then grind over and over until her nails bite into my ass.

"Now, Daddy."

Three more hard surges, and we're both coming. This is one of the best I've ever had. Not just with Maria. In life. I close my eyes to catch a breath, then they snap open, and our gazes meet. I know without a doubt that I'm where I belong. We kiss to silence our ecstasy. We lie together panting for a moment, then I slide my left hand between us, resting it on her belly.

"Tell me when, Maria."

"I don't want to share you any more than I have to. Can we have a couple years together first?"

"We can have as long or as short as you want. But one day we are having a family together."

"You don't know how happy it makes me to hear you bring this up."

I roll us until she's straddling me. I hold her hips and rock them. Fucking hell, I'm still hard enough that it feels amazing.

"Do you slip little blue pills?"

I laugh at how serious she sounds.

"I don't need any help getting an erection. All I have to do is think of you in passing, and I'm a fucking tent pole. Seeing you, hearing you, touching you...You have no idea what it's like to spend most of my day fucking rock hard. Then to be inside you. It's a fight not to be done within the first five seconds."

"Really? I do that?"

She's not being coy. She really didn't know.

"Maria, I know you're gorgeous. Yeah, your looks are part of it. But I can think of the way you smell. Your voice. Your laugh. The way your slight accent gets thicker when you're tired or with certain words. I can do just about anything, including just breathe, and you make me hard."

"You're such a romantic, Daddy."

She giggles, and it makes me twitch inside her when she tightens around me. I wonder if I can go again, but we hear one of our phones buzz. We ignore it. It's not the two-ring pattern, so if it is our family, it's not urgent or about work. But it makes both of us look toward the clock. We have to get some sleep.

It was Veronica who texted just before we were out cold. She was just getting up to go to Pilates when we were finally going to bed. She wanted to see when we could go on a double date. Maria showed me the message before we got out of bed, but I said nothing. Probably better that way. We're standing at our sinks, brushing our teeth. I watch her in the mirror, and her gaze is on her medicine bottles that sit between our toothbrush holders. I spit and rinse.

"What's the matter, *tesorina*?"

"I don't like how I felt last night. The catastrophizing. It wasn't reasonable to think you were cheating. And I didn't like how I reacted to myself. Things have been shockingly okay since Miami. I thought I would have a harder time getting over that than I did. But something was off about last night, and I don't know if I should chalk it up to just a stressful night, or if it's a sign of something else."

"Do you feel more anxious? Or is it more sadness? Or something else?"

"Unsettled. I'm not really sure. I mean, I'm anxious because of what happened with Jordan and especially with Aunt Sylvia. We'll learn more when we head over there. I already texted a colleague to switch shifts with me. I don't have to be in until later this afternoon. I didn't feel rage last night, which is something I've struggled with for the past few years. When I've been behind on my refills, I've felt anger bubbling up inside me, and it's been harder to tame. But that wasn't last night. I guess sad is the best way to describe it. Then crushing guilt. It's been a while since I've felt that level guilt for just —existing."

"Do you want to make an appointment with your doctor?"

"I have one in a week. I think I can make it that long. Hopefully, last night was just an off night."

"Does it make you uncomfortable to talk about this with me? Would you rather I didn't bring it up?"

"No. Matteo, my mental health isn't a secret to anyone in our family. I definitely don't want it to be a secret from you. I don't want to burden you with it, but I'm also grateful that I can turn to you, and I know you'll never judge me. I wouldn't and don't blame you for getting frustrated with me, but you have the patience of a saint. No one gets me the way you always have. I know Marco's your best friend, and how in sync you two are would make most people assume you're twins. But you and I—I don't know—just clicked at some point."

"Because we've always been meant for each other. You're mine, Maria. I'm yours. It's just been a matter of time. I've loved you for as long as I can remember. I'm going nowhere. And unless you tell me you want out, you're going nowhere too."

I watch as she bites her lips, exhales, and nods.

"Maria?"

"Just thinking."

"About our future?"

Our gazes meet before she grumbles.

"I'm not sure how I feel about the mind reading."

I laugh and nod.

"It usually pisses you off. Let's get through whatever happened to Aunt Sylvia and dealing with Jordan. Then let's go away for a couple weeks."

"I can't. I've used up all my vacation time for this year."

"Then a long weekend if you can arrange your shifts."

"I can try to do that. Where do you want to go?"

She cants her head and laughs. We answer together.

"Galapagos."

"You read my mind too, *piccolina*."

"You've been talking about those turtles since you were like five. I remember having to listen to you practice reading the same book over and over. You'd put it in my lap and point to each word. I couldn't get up. One time, I had an accident because you wouldn't listen to me when I said I had to go. Auntie Carlotta was *not* thrilled about that on her rug."

"And I admitted what I did. She put that book where I couldn't reach it for three days and told me that the book and I both needed a time out for being so inconsiderate to our—"

We both shift, then laugh. She finishes for me.

"Your little sister. Little did anyone know."

"Bah. Ask our mothers, and they'll say they've known all along. That if we were in Sicily, they would have arranged our marriage at your christening."

We step into the shower, and it's a herculean task not to touch each other. We know if we help scrub each other or wash each other's hair, we'll be in here for at least an hour while I fuck my girlfriend into next week. We need to go. But I want us to get away sooner rather than later. I have a question to ask, and I want to ask it somewhere special.

Aunt Sylvia looks exhausted. She has dark circles beneath her eyes, and she appears pale. But she's smiling when Maria and I arrive. Only Carmine and Sera still need to get here, so at least we aren't the last ones—last couple—to get here. I don't know. That would just be awkward. Like people might assume we can't be on time because we can't stop fucking long enough to be punctual.

Now that everyone is here and Pia and Natalia are at school, we gather in the living room to talk. I'm certain Uncle Salvatore has already heard all this, but the rest of us barely breathe as we listen.

"There were four of them. They came in through the basement and into the kitchen. I thought I heard something and was waiting for one of the girls to come downstairs. I was getting the dough ready for today's bread. I saw someone approaching, so I grabbed the gun from the drawer."

There's a drawer in every family's kitchen that the children know that if they touch it, it will be on pain of death. Some might argue that would just make children more curious. Not with our parents. Pia and Natalia know the same thing we all did growing up: it's not worth discovering the full repertoire of punishments our parents could devise if we disobeyed. The forbidden drawer always has a gun in it. They also have a special childproof latch as the true precaution against anyone getting into it who shouldn't. Our parents made sure they completely hid the latch unless you knew where to feel. There are other drawers like that in every household in case someone is alone, and there's an intruder.

"I had it in my pocket by the time they came in. I didn't shoot because I didn't want to wake the girls. I didn't want them to come downstairs. They were going to take me regardless because they outnumbered me. They said nothing about the girls, so I didn't want to let them know I wasn't alone.

Either they didn't know or didn't care. I kept it that way. I didn't fight at that point. I couldn't get a guard's attention, and I needed to focus and save my energy."

She's sitting next to Uncle Salvatore on the loveseat, and they're holding hands. She pauses to kiss his cheek and rests her hand on his biceps. He still looks wrecked.

"I don't know how they knew about the tunnel. No one's used it in like twenty years. Cocky bastards. They didn't gag me or restrain me, so I let them take me through it. When we got outside, I pulled the gun. I shot two of them before they could get the gun from me. I hit one in the upper chest near his shoulder, and the other in the stomach. It was hard to see and judge their height in the dark. The one I shot in the stomach collapsed, and they had to drag him. What I didn't think about was the silencer on the weapon. I thought it would alert the guards, but I doubt anyone heard it."

"I'm taking all of those off. If anyone is shooting inside the house, it's because they need help. The men should hear it. I'm doing that today."

Uncle Salvatore is talking more to himself than anyone else. Aunt Sylvia pats his arm before she continues.

"Two of them had to drag the guy who went down. The third guy yanked the gun away from me, and the last one gagged me and zip tied my hands in front of me. *Idioti.* They underestimated me, even after I shot two of them. They shoved me into the back of a minivan with the guy with the bullet in his stomach. He was gushing blood and uncon-scious. The one with the shoulder wound kept moaning from the front passenger seat. He was the one in charge. One of the uninjured guys drove while the other was in the third row. You'd think he'd have a gun pointing at me, but I glanced over my shoulder several times. He was on his phone, texting. These guys knew enough to get in the house and get me out, but they weren't pros. They argued about where to take me."

Argued? Going after the don's wife isn't a job a syndicate leader would give to some low-level flunky. The risk and danger necessitate experience. Sounds like these guys lacked that and probably why Aunt Sylvia got away.

"They had a meeting spot planned with whoever hired them, but the guy behind me and the guy in the front seat wanted to take me somewhere else. They wanted more money once they realized how wealthy we are. They thought they could bribe Salva *and* still get paid by their employer. They argued for more than an hour, just driving around Queens. Maybe they thought they could confuse me. While I listened, I noticed the guy next to me was dead. He'd bled out, and they didn't realize it, or they didn't care because no one said anything about getting him help."

Aunt Sylvia relays this story so calmly, not flinching and not mincing words when talking about sitting next to a dying man who was gushing blood. This is the only life she's ever known. Just like Maria. Just like Mama. Just like Auntie Nicoletta. Just like Auntie Paola. Just like Serafina. *Cosa Nostra* since birth. So fucked-up.

"The one with the bullet in his shoulder complained, but the driver said he'd get it out. Since I knew the guy next to me couldn't stop me, I eased the gun from his hip near me. With my hands tied in front of me, I could. When we came to the next stoplight, I tested the door handle. I felt the door open a little. The driver immediately saw the light flash on the dash. He turned to look toward me. I shot him in the head. I shot the guy in the passenger seat. I didn't wait for the one behind me. I got the door open and bolted."

She looks down at her feet. She arrived barefoot, so she must have run at least part of the way without shoes. Her slippers cover them, so I can't see what condition they're in, but they probably hurt. She confirms it.

"I kicked off my shoes since they kept slipping. Despite driving around, we were only a half-hour walk from the house. Once I was certain no one followed me, I stopped running. I couldn't keep going. When I got to the gate, Dante let me in. I'd already pulled my gag down, but he cut the ties and took the gun. He helped me wipe blood off my face, hands, and neck in case the girls were awake. I was so relieved to be home that my knees gave out. He carried me in here."

Uncle Salvatore switches the hands he's using to hold his wife's so he can wrap his free one around her shoulders. She leans against him, and he kisses the top of her head. The movies might have been right about the old Mafia families. I don't know. But they're outdated. Or, at least, we aren't like the old families. Life's too short not to show people how much we love them. If any of us could die today, then we should make sure the loved ones we leave behind never doubt how much they mean to us. It's why we never go on a mission without saying goodbye to at least our parents, if not the entire family. It's why we say I love you before we end most calls.

Uncle Salvatore and Uncle Massimo have always been demonstrative with their daughters, but there isn't a son in this family who doesn't know his parents love him as much as they would or do a daughter. Uncle Salvatore has never shied away from letting Aunt Sylvia, Pia, and Natalia—nor the entire world—know how much he cares. Watching the older couple makes me tighten my arm around Maria as I perch on the arm of her chair.

Now that we know what happened, Aunt Sylvia answers the question we must all have.

"None of them had accents at all. They just sounded like New Yorkers. Maybe Brooklyn, but no hint of speaking a second language. I've been in America for twelve years, but some accents still sound too much alike for me to tell. I wish I could be more helpful."

"You have been, *mia bellissima tesora.*" My beautiful treasure.

Uncle Salvatore looks at Luca then Uncle Massimo. It's obvious that he isn't leaving Aunt Sylvia's side any time soon, so it will fall on his underboss and *consigliere* to ferret out who did this. There's no doubt in my mind that once the culprits are caught and at the garage, Uncle Salvatore will deal with them *very personally.*

Carmine speaks up, and everyone's attention turns to him.

"Fina and I were slow getting here because Sergei called just as we were about to leave. He hasn't pinpointed the exact location of the person who hacked him, but they were on Long Island. They bounced around ISPs, which eventually led to a VPN he hasn't been able to crack. He's working on it. I told him to talk to Enzo, but you know he won't. He and Anton will work on it. He promised to call if he learns anything."

Fucking snobs. They went to an Ivy League—UPENN—so heaven forbid they ask a lowly MIT grad for help. Granted that was for his masters in finance. He went to Rutgers for computer science. But still. I shift my gaze from Carmine to Maria. She's looking up at me, and I know she's scared what came out last night in the office will wind up public knowledge for everyone in the family. I know I don't want my parents to know what I got up to before Maria and I got together, so I can't blame her for wanting her privacy. On top of that, she knows her dad and uncles will lose their shit if they find out she went somewhere like her club with only two guards. She doesn't want to get the guys in trouble, either.

I look at Luca, who handles scheduling the men who guard our family members and our various properties.

"Who do we have watching Jordan?"

"Alfonso, Michael, Aurelio, and Vinny are rotating two on-two off."

"Who's with him now?"

"Alfonso and Vinny."

Those are four of our best *soldati*. I trust them to take this seriously and to know how to act without needing supervision. None of them are rash.

"Where'd he go after I threw him out last night?"

I haven't told Maria any more about my confrontation with him than I did last night.

"He took an Uber home. He went to work this morning. Vinny sent me a photo. He looks like shit. You definitely didn't keep the bruises where no one can see. His shoulder and arm must be bad since he's in a sling."

"Let people ask him what happened. He can have a constant reminder not to screw dancers at our clubs and to stay away from my girlfriend. We know how he's related to the Ciccones, but what about the Irish? His last name's Ryan. Does he have ties to them?"

"We haven't discovered any yet. I dug a little last night when Fina and I got home, but nothing came up. Seems like he's more interested in his Mafia roots than his mobster ones."

Can you blame him? I wouldn't want to be associated with that gaggle fuck.

"Car, can you hack his email?"

Maria's voice doesn't sound anywhere near as confident as it usually does. I don't like it. It claws at the doors that keep my unreasonably protective and possessive side locked away. I've kept that part of me behind chained, locked, and bolted mental doors, fearful ever letting it out would permanently drive Maria away. That it would be so over the top that it would terrify her.

But anyone who makes her question herself makes me want to tear them apart.

Lizzy answered the phone last night, and I'm still pissed at her. I texted my manager and told her to fire the bitch. She shouldn't have touched my phone in the first place. Lying about anything to anyone is a fireable offense, and every employee knows that. Lying to my girlfriend and making it sound like I'm cheating? If I had to deal with her, I'd rip her a new asshole. It's better someone impartial let her go.

"He said he was going to get me fired and make me lose my license. He said he has connections. Can you see if he's trying to do that?"

Carmine hesitates. I don't like that.

"He sent something last night. I got in and deleted it from his account and from the recipient's. He claimed sexual harassment. That you intimidated him into an intimate relationship by threatening to have our family extort money from his and that you threatened him with physical harm if he didn't cooperate. He attached—"

Carmine looks more uncomfortable than he's ever looked in his life. He hates saying any of this as much as the rest of us hate hearing it.

"Audio that's clearly been tampered with, but it sounds like you telling him when and where to meet. The quality isn't good, and there are breaks and uneven volume that signal the recordings have been spliced. But they're clear enough to be incriminating."

"He recorded our conversations? He's been stockpiling evidence against me. He's been doing this to either cover his own ass or to come after me all along."

If he is taking this much interest in hurting Maria, then what's he going to do with that info? That's the really important question to answer for Maria and for our family. For me, personally, the really important question is whether he's going to force Maria and me apart. If he's targeting her and is connected to what happened to Aunt Sylvia, I don't know if he has any limits to what he'll do. If he's doing this to punish Maria for not choosing him, being with me will only make him crazier.

The main priority has to be keeping Maria and the others safe. I can't let her pick me over her family, even if that's exactly what I want. It'll create bad blood, and I don't want her caught in the middle. I don't want to ruin my parents' friendship with hers. I don't want to end my friendship with Marco. I don't want to piss off Uncle Salvatore and lose everything.

I take a breath. My spiraling thoughts need squelching. This won't get me anywhere but pissed.

If Jordan just wants to be a squeaky wheel and isn't connected to Aunt Sylvia's kidnapping, he can. But that doesn't mean it'll end things between Maria and me. That may make him shit a brick. I don't know, and that makes me worry he's going to keep escalating past clipping Maria and sending emails to her boss. I don't like to think Jordan is capable of kidnapping anyone, but he's the frontrunner for culprits.

However, if it's not him, the list of other candidates isn't short. It could be any of the other Mafia branches in America. I don't think the Diazes would actually touch Aunt Sylvia, though Enrique and Pablo wouldn't mind watching our downfall. But they'd just send *Tres J's* to fuck up our shit or turn us over to the IRS. Dillan and his family wouldn't mind dragging us through the gutter before cutting out our hearts. That's exactly what they'd do if they caused any permanent harm to any woman in our family. They'd dance a fucking jig.

I haven't forgotten that the Kutsenkos still aren't pleased with us, despite Carmine helping Misha and his wife. But I've had my mind elsewhere since Jordan started causing trouble.

They definitely have the resources to fuck us over, but I pray they know nothing about Maria's private life. We don't need that to spread.

Is Jordan connected to Aunt Sylvia's attack? Or do we have two enemies—no, two *more* enemies—to fight?

Chapter Sixteen

Maria

I can't stop thinking about Sergei knowing about my club membership. It rankles. If he knows, then they all fucking know. The fucking Kutsenkos. There's eight of them. Two of them are actually Andreyevs—Sergei and Misha—but they're cousins with the four brothers who lead. They're related through their moms. There are two Kutsenkos who are cousins and related to them through their dads. They're all ridiculously handsome. They're also always the largest men in any room. They're like the starting lineup of a pro-American football team. It's shocked me to see all but two of them married now. The women have rocks on their fingers you could see from the moon. It's an Andreyev and a Kutsenko cousin who are single. Their presence is always memorable. Such a shame God wasted so much hotness on so many cold-blooded killers.

They're as close to one another as the members of my family are to one another. That means they have no secrets. We don't have many, but the ones we have, we prefer to keep to ourselves. My history of going to a sex club is a prime example. If Sergei knew, did members of the other syndicates? Is this a weakness they'll exploit one day? Do I tell anyone in my family that I figured out Laura was a member too?

These questions keep playing on a loop while I try to concentrate. What if this gets out and humiliates my family? What if knowing I'm into kinky shit makes me a target for a new round of sex traffickers? What if—

"Maria?"

Matteo whispers to me. I nod, but I'm still in my head.

What if I go missing again? That'll kill my parents. I know they both still have nightmares about it. I don't want that. Carmine and Luca have wives they shouldn't leave to go chasing me. I saw Olivia's hand press on her belly for a moment last night. I don't think anyone else saw it, but that pretty much confirmed my suspicions. Luca doesn't need to be chasing after me when his wife needs him more. I never want him or Carmine to have to choose between me and their wives.

"Maria?"

Matteo's voice is a little more forceful. I look around, and everyone is staring at me. I want to crawl into a hole. I need air. As usual, Matteo reads my mind.

"Let's go outside for a couple minutes."

I offer a jerky nod. I see sympathy and understanding in everyone's eyes. I know it's not pity, but it feels that way with everyone watching me. Matteo and I grab our coats and step onto the back patio.

"What if Jordan is behind what happened to Aunt Sylvia? What if he isn't, and it's someone we have no idea about? I didn't have time to tell you last night, but Sergei knows I'm a member of the club. Or was. Laura was, and apparently, she recognized me after we officially met. She asked Sergei to keep an eye on me in case anything ever went wrong there. What if other syndicates know what I'm into? I have so many what-ifs swirling around in my head that I feel dizzy."

"*Piccolina*, I'm thinking many of those same things. There is some honor among thieves. Sergei and his family know the danger you'd be in if it got out that you belong to a BDSM club. They won't say anything outside their family. I don't know about the others. But we will deal with everything. We always do. That's why our family still leads the *Cosa Nostra* in New York. It's why other branches don't shit without us knowing. We get through everything together. I know you hate that the others are figuring out what you're into, but we're family. We accept everything and everyone."

"Not your brother."

I whisper my response. Emilio is a touchy subject for everyone. He's the one who gave Luca the scar on his face. He was a selfish asshole as a teenager and endangered other people with his recklessness and disregard for the family. At least Carmine didn't nearly kill innocent people during his years of hating half the family. Emilio's the real black sheep of the family. He's been exiled to Jersey. Only Auntie Carlotta, Uncle Domenico, and Matteo have anything to do with him outside of business. He comes to most holidays, but it's uncomfortable. He goes on missions, but only when the guys absolutely need him.

Matteo stiffens, and I wonder if I've just started our first fight as a couple.

"Leo's made choices that hurt people outside the family and drew way too much attention. He hurt Mama and Papa by disregarding their rules and making them fear for his life because of his selfish recklessness. He left Luca to bleed and has never owned what he did. I love my brother, but I don't respect most of the choices he's made. I see his faults just like everyone else. I'll always defend him and protect him, but I don't like him. I miss the brother I had when we were kids. He's had so many chances to reconcile, and he's refused them all. We'd all welcome him back if he'd own what he's done. He doesn't do the stupid shit he used to, but he's too jealous of Luca to ever apologize. He is not the same as you. You know that. You know all of this. Your situation and his do not equate. Yours is embarrassing, but it doesn't harm anyone."

I sigh. I'm catastrophizing again. But in my mind, I'm preparing myself for the worst, so I can handle it when it happens.

"So, what do we do now?"

"The two of us? Or the family?"

"Both."

"We can go home if you want. Uncle Sal, Uncle Massi, and Luca are probably going to be on the phone for a while. Enzo is likely hacking shit. I'm going to ask Carmine to send one of his drones to watch Jordan inside his place once he's home from work. I don't know about Gabe and Marco. Chances are they'll be handling our regular business. There was only one fire last night, and it wasn't a big deal. Enzo tracked Jordan to one of the strip clubs once we knew the fire didn't do any real damage. No one's been called about any others."

"What are you supposed to be doing?"

"Taking care of my girlfriend."

"No. For real. If we weren't together, and this happened to Aunt Sylvia, what would you need to do?"

"I'd be your guard at work. Today would have been my day in the rotation, and you'd be at work right now."

My brothers, cousin, and friends cycle through regular bodyguard rotations to make sure protocols are still being used and are effective for everyone in the family. When the women go to work, at least one of our male family members comes with us once a week. If we're going pretty much anywhere other than work, one of them is with us.

"I still have to go in at two. Can we go home for a couple hours? I think I want a nap."

"Let's see what's going on inside. If we can't go home, I'm sure you can nap here."

I nod, but I hesitate to let go.

"Do you want me to stay with you, *piccolina?*"

"That would be nice... Actually, instead of a nap, I think I'm going to call my doctor. See if I can get a last-minute telehealth."

I don't like how I'm being right now. My doctor is the granddaughter of one of my paternal grandfather's most trusted men. She's closer in age to my parents, but she's been my psychiatrist for years. I can tell her things I could never even whisper to someone outside the *Cosa Nostra.*

We head back inside, and an hour-and-a-half later, I feel worlds better. My doctor squeezed me in, and I got a thirty-minute nap. I feel like a new person. I'm already in scrubs since I figured I might go straight to work from Uncle Salvatore and Aunt Sylvia's. I'm driving Matteo and myself to the hospital. We have an SUV in front of us and one behind. The four men between the two cars will rotate their stations throughout my ten-hour shift today.

Aunt Sylvia's resting at her house. Auntie Carlotta is already at the hospital since she had surgeries scheduled for this afternoon, and she's on call to the Emergency Department if anyone comes in who needs cutting. Mama is a financial analyst, so she's working from home but at my aunt and uncle's since Pia and Natalia will be home in an hour. She'll help with them, so Uncle Salvatore can be with Aunt Sylvia if she needs him. I'm not sure what Uncle Domenico and Papa are doing. Maybe making calls with Luca.

"You said you want us to go away for a long weekend, but

the Galapagos isn't realistic for three or four days. Where else would you like to go?"

I look over at Matteo as I pull into the hospital staff lot.

"We could go down to the house in the Keys."

Matteo owns a beachside house on Islamorada, the most expensive and exclusive island in the Keys. He knows I love it there.

"That sounds perfect. I wish we could go right now, but I know that's not possible."

"Actually, I talked to Uncle Sal and Uncle Massi about that while you were on the call. I think we should get away until we know what Jordan's doing. I'd like you to be out of sight, out of mind for him."

"Let me see what I can do. I still have some favors I can call in from last winter when the flu was crazy, and I had to keep covering for people."

We head inside, and the four bodyguards head to their designated posts. Matteo comes with me. Radiologists are like moles within the hospital. Our offices are dark rooms that make it easier to read the imaging. We don't have those old-fashioned x-ray lights on walls. It's all on the computer now, so some things have advanced with time. But just as many things remain unchanged. I like the solitude to be honest. I enjoy working mostly undisturbed.

We don't have rounds like most doctors, but we have peds rounds where the pediatric team will come in to review all the peds studies from the past day. We also read out our studies with our colleagues to make sure nothing's missing or in case there are differing opinions. That's starting in twenty minutes. As a resident, I still have senior doctors who review my reads and correct or add to them if needed. That's pretty rare, but it happens.

"I need to head in and get ready for everyone to read out their findings."

"I'll be around the corner like always. Love you."

I bounce up on my toes to give Matteo a quick kiss.

"Love you too, Daddy."

I wink, and he gives me a slap on the ass that leaves me giggling. I hurry to my desk and pull up the files I have to review before I head over to the larger black hole where we meet as a radiology team.

My shift passed in a blur, and so did the four days between the morning after Aunt Sylvia's abduction and us now arriving on Islamorada. Everything's been quiet during that time. I spotted Jordan in the cafeteria during that first shift, but I stayed out of sight. He looked like shit. It's not like Matteo mangled his face or anything, but there was clearly bruising on his right cheek, and I could see hints of a bruise just above his shirt collar. My guess is Matteo nearly choked him out. I didn't ask, and I don't want to know. He wasn't in a sling, but he wasn't moving his left arm either. I almost had to deal with him when I saw an imaging request with his name on it come in. I did what I had to, then I passed it on to the attending. She sent the final findings, so I didn't have to even communicate with him.

No one found anything tying him to Aunt Sylvia, and he hasn't tried to contact me. Lorenzo is certain that, not only did someone hack Sergei, but they made it look like the texted photo came from Jordan's number when it didn't really. That's a plus. We're back to thinking he's just a crazy sorta-ex. We don't think he issued completely empty threats, but he isn't on my family's short list for hits.

We know nothing more about Aunt Sylvia's kidnappers

though, and that's driving everyone nuts. I'm glad to escape the tension for a while. I need the breather before my anxiety amps back up. A change in doses is already helping. I don't need a backslide.

"What do you want first, *piccolina?*"

"Sex on the beach."

"The drink?"

Matteo waggles his eyebrows.

"After, once I've built up a thirst."

Hell, I'm already thirsty but of a way different kind. I'll do just about anything to get him naked right now. My brothers came with us, and so did Gabriele. There was no way Matteo and I were going to have sex in the private jet cabin with Marco, Lorenzo, and Gabriele right outside the door. I knew they would have to come, and I'm fine with that. I'm glad for it after Miami. But I realized after we took off that I wouldn't be inducted into the mile-high club on that flight or the one home. Matteo said the same thing. We've both traveled with past partners, but neither of us has done *it* on an airplane. I've had some boyfriends. Matteo's had his subs. I don't want to think about that right now.

We drop our luggage in our bedroom, and we hurry to change into bathing suits. Matteo's eyes narrow as he takes in the barely-there bikini I put on. I twist and pull off the tag, then hold it up.

"Only for you, Daddy."

"Better be."

His arms engulf me, then I'm slung over his shoulder as he slaps my ass. He dashes down the stairs, then walks out of the sliding glass door onto the back veranda. I press my hand against his back enough to lift myself so I can look around. Marco's at one end of the private beach, and Lorenzo is at the other. Gabriele's in the house. My brothers will patrol the property while we're out here. As Matteo runs with me toward the water, my older siblings pretend not to notice us. But I guarantee they could tell you exactly how many steps Matteo took from the house to the water.

Matteo charges into the surf, splashing me in the process. I squeal as the cool water hits the back of my legs. Then he's lifting me off his shoulder, and I'm sailing through the air. I have just enough time to hold my breath before I'm under. I pop back up and brush the hair away from my face.

"Again!"

The guys have been tossing me around since we were kids. Usually, it was in annoyance because I could dive the farthest and fastest for the coins our parents would toss in pools for us. Then they learned that I'm way better at chicken than any of them, so they'd argue over whose shoulders I'd sit on. I could push all of them—even Gabriele—off their partner. I'm strategic and wily when I have to be. It was the only way I could keep up with the six of them—seven before Emilio's banishment. But without fail, a loser always managed to scoop me up and toss me. I loved it.

If any of the other three guys were in the water, they wouldn't come near me in this bathing suit. It barely covers anything. I bought it just for Matteo, though I thought I'd have a cover up. Apparently not. Matteo wraps his hands around my waist, lifts me to kiss me, then launches me backwards. He's careful not to hurt me, but he isn't what most people would consider gentle. Fine by me. He does it twice more before I swim back to him, then pulls me against him as I wrap myself around him.

"Thank you for bringing me here, Daddy. I love it, and you know that. I'm sure there are other places you want to go, but you did this for me. I love you."

"Anything for you, *tesorina*. I want to give you everything you need and hopefully most of what you want. You have my heart, and I'm at your mercy. You have more control than I think you realize."

"Same. You give so much to everyone, especially me. I never want you to feel like it's one-sided or unbalanced. I want to give you what you need as your partner in all ways. I hope I can always give you what you want, too."

"You do, little one. Especially when you call me Daddy. You know I crave it."

"I'm not a little, and you're not a Daddy Dom. But you do take care of me. I have always felt safe with you, and I like being able to let you know that without worrying someone will take it the wrong way. I'll still be able to call you that if we have kids since they'd call you Papa, I suppose."

Something flashes in his eyes, and I wonder what I just said wrong. We've talked about kids in the past, but I don't know if I'll get pregnant easily or have successful ones. I pray I do, but I know better than most what a miracle a healthy pregnancy and healthy baby are.

"Daddy?"

He brushes back hair plastered to my cheek as he leans forward and presses a tender kiss to my lips. It's languid as our tongues explore each other's mouths. I focus my attention entirely on the kiss and Matteo. I love how he feels in my arms. The rightness of our bodies pressed together. But when we pull apart, reality comes back to me.

"Did you kiss me to distract me? Did I say something wrong?"

"You said 'if' earlier. I don't know if you're less certain than you were before, and I don't want to ask since I might not like the answer."

I cup his face and kiss him with everything I have. I loosen my legs enough to reach between us as he supports my weight.

I tug at his boardshorts until they loosen enough for me to push them down his hips until his cock's free. Then I reach to move my bikini bottom aside.

"Come in me, Daddy. There's little chance I could get pregnant, but it's not impossible. If I didn't want kids with you, then I wouldn't let you fill me with your cum over and over. Fuck me."

"If the guys didn't know we're out here, I would fuck you until you can't see straight. You think to give me commands, little girl? Apparently, you took hearing the idea that you can control me to heart after all."

He gives me a smacking kiss before he pulls back.

"I love you, Maria."

"I love you, too. Please, Daddy. With the waves, they won't know what we're doing."

He chuckles, and it's that dark, delicious sound.

"They're guys. They'll know."

"So what?"

I waggle my eyebrows at him. He grins and winks at me before adopting an exaggeratedly stern voice.

"Maria, I'm warning you. Stop making me want to fuck you. Your brothers will never forgive me if they spot us practically naked in the ocean, or if our bathing suits float onto the beach."

"Us? We? That's all on you, Daddy."

I purr the last word.

"I can't spank you while they're around. I don't even know if I can have sex with you in the same house. Your safety is more important than getting off, but this may truly be what finally kills me."

"Do you think they expect us to have separate bedrooms?"

"Probably not. But—I just can't. What if they hear us?"

I laugh so hard I choke. His expression is like he's twelve

again and has to appear before his parents with the vase he broke wrestling with Marco. I can't believe this shyness that's suddenly overcome him. I know my brothers can see us, but he can't see them. Maybe that's what makes him nervous. I'm not fucking abstaining during our entire romantic vacation, but I do respect his sudden bout of virginal nerves and help him pull his boardshorts back up.

"Are your children going to be the product of immaculate conception?"

"As far as your brothers are concerned, yes. That's exactly how *our* children will be made."

He slides his hand over my shoulder and up to my throat. He tightens it as his gaze holds me in place as much as his hand and his body.

"Do you want children, Daddy? I know neither of us would have them without being married, and we'd never divorce. But do you want them? Or do you feel like it's expected?"

I think back to when he rested his hand on my belly a few days ago. I don't know if it was just a spur of the moment, post coital glow or what he really sees happening.

"I don't feel it's expected. I can think of plenty of people who probably pray I never procreate. I've wanted kids in a vague sense because I adore Pia and Natalia, and I wouldn't mind daughters like them. Until a future with you became possible, I did everything I could to never get a woman pregnant. Maria, even with a condom on, I usually pulled out. Now I think about our family all the time."

His hand leaves my throat and goes to my belly.

"When the time is right, we'll get married. Then, when the time is right, we'll have children. I've never wanted them with anyone but you."

"I've always been super careful, too. I've been on birth control since I was eighteen and moved out of my parents' house. I went on it a month before we were together. You know how things are at clubs. The men always wore them, and I had an IUD then too. But I feel the same way as you. I want my future with you, and I want that to include kids. Daddy, I said 'if' because there are so many things beyond our control that could keep it from happening."

"Not having sex in front of your brothers is the right thing to do right now. Not having sex in front of your brothers is the right thing to do right now. Not having sex in front of your brothers —"

"Are you trying to convince me or yourself?"

"Definitely me. Come on. Let's go have lunch before we wind up with you bent over the bed with a welted ass and my dick in it."

I knew it would only take a few hours before Matteo got over his sudden bout of nerves. His house has a master suite downstairs and two big bedrooms upstairs, at opposite ends of the house. We're in an upstairs bedroom since any intruder would have to get through two guys before they could try to get up the stairs. Then there's another guard and Matteo to protect me up here. Marco and Lorenzo have the master suite, and Gabriele's is on the second floor. At night, when one's on duty, the other two sleep. They have three-hour shifts.

We've just come to our room after a beautiful dinner at a local restaurant we both love. Now we're finally truly alone. We're not in anyone's direct or peripheral line of vision. Once we're naked, I step into his arms, and he grabs my ass with both hands. He squeezes hard enough to pull me onto my toes. I rub my pussy against his hard on.

"I'm going to fuck you from behind tonight, Maria. I want

to see all of this as I slam into your pussy. I know you don't like doggy style because you don't get off as easily. But nothing makes me want to fuck you into next week more than watching your ass move as I pound you."

Before Matteo, I was all right with my far-from-skinny ass. But I didn't love putting it on display either. He can't get enough. If I judged him solely on the women I've seen him with at Lorenzo's club, I would never believe he'd desire me the way he does. He walks me backwards until I bump into the bed. I sit, then push myself backwards until my head is on the pillow, and he follows me. His shoulders push my legs apart as he licks my pussy.

"Do you want to fuck me in the ass, Daddy?"

"Oh, that's coming. Don't you doubt that, little one. I'm using all your holes tonight. There will be no doubting I christened this bed, and you're mine for good. You are going to be a sloppy mess by the time we leave. Cum dripping out of your cunt and ass. The taste of you still on my tongue."

He's never brought another woman here on a romantic getaway. I don't know if he realizes how special that little phrase about christening this bed makes me feel. His head dives back down, and he licks me over and over as his hands pinch my nipples. He delves his tongue inside me before sucking on my clit, his teeth brushing against it. He lets go with his right hand and thrusts three fingers into me. I lift my hips higher and undulate them, but his free hand presses down on my belly. His lips close around my clit and press before they tug. Then his teeth graze it again. Fuck me. I'm so close so fast.

I moan the name I love most for him.

"Daddy."

He does it again, and I repeat myself.

"Daddy."

His fingers toy with me, gliding inside my pussy, barely

touching my g spot. Only long enough to torment and make me whimper. I drop my left leg until my knee rests on the bed. A fourth finger enters me, and I pinch my abandoned nipples until I cry out.

"May I come, Daddy?"

He doesn't even look up.

"No."

He works my pussy, stretching me. Is he going to do what I think—hope—he will? I've asked him before, and he's worried it would be too much. His hand is not small. His fingers aren't fat, but neither are they bony. His palms are long and wide. They dwarf my hands, and I don't consider mine particularly small, at least not for a woman.

His thumb rubs my clit before it disappears. His fingers spread inside me, and his wrist twists. Then he does it. He's completely inside me. I've felt nothing like this. I don't even know how to describe it other than I feel full. There's pain, but the kind I like. The kind that makes me beg for more while needing it to stop. His fingers find my g spot and stroke, making me squirm with need. He keeps working me while he kisses the inside of my thighs, the crease where they meet my hips, my clit. All of it over and over.

"Daddy, please."

"No."

He reaches up with his free hand and covers mine over my right nipple. He tweaks it, making me roll it between my thumb and index finger. He's unrelenting as the minutes pass, and it's not until later that I realize I've been moaning loud enough for at least Gabriele, if not all the guys, to hear me. Suddenly, I have a sensation I've never experienced but have heard about. I feel like I need to pee, and it's urgent. I fight against it.

"Daddy, I think I'm going to squirt. I'll make a mess."

He rubs my g spot one more time before his magic fingers

explore until they find my cervix. He withdraws his hand and eases just his index and middle fingers back into me. He knows I'm getting sensitive, and he doesn't want to harm me. He works my cervix, and it's another unusual but pleasurable sensation. The needing to pee was odd, but somehow still enjoyable.

"Daddy, I have to come. I can't stop."

"All right, *piccolina*. Come for Daddy."

I squeeze my eyes shut tightly. This orgasm truly feels like it's coming from the depth of my core. It seizes control of me, and it's even more intense that a regular clit rubbing orgasm.

"Fuck, Daddy. You spoil me."

I tell him that when I can finally open my eyes and catch my breath.

"Always."

He licks his fingers and shoots me that wolfish grin. He helps me pull down the covers.

"You didn't come."

"I know. That wasn't part of my plan."

I don't know about that. I think he decided to focus on me, and it warms my heart. My previous partners weren't selfish, but they didn't give my orgasms the same undivided attention Matteo does. But I'm not satisfied with that.

"Daddy, we're not done. You promised me in the ass."

He chuckles, and I grin. Not the most romantic thing I've ever said.

"I mean, I don't want this to be over yet. I don't want this to just be about me. I appreciate that you're satisfied with getting me off and only making it about me. But I'm not satisfied with it only being about me. I want it to be about both of us."

I push back the covers and swing my left leg over his waist. I lean forward, pushing my tits together, encouraging him to lick or suck or bite or all of those. His hands cover mine as he alternates sides, sucking hard enough to make me moan. When his mouth lets go, he kneads them, and I almost forget my plan. But I pull away, lowering myself so my tits trail along his chest and abs until I'm kneeling between his legs. I lean all the way forward and lick him.

"I'm going to have my way with you tonight, Daddy."

"Who am I to tell my *piccolina* no?"

I snort.

"You tell me no all the fucking time."

"Not in bed, I don't."

"Or against a wall, in the shower, in the backseat of a car, on a sofa."

He sits up suddenly and reaches around me. He spanks me, and I push my ass into his hand and wiggle my hips.

"Cheeky, *piccolina*."

I cock an eyebrow as I wrap my hand around his dick. I practically swallow him, and I love the way he groans. His hand lands on my ass every time I slide up his dick. His free hand goes to my head as he presses. He's not applying any real pressure. I'm still in control of how much I take. But he's reminding me he's in control of the situation. I love it.

"Let go, *cuore*. I'm not coming yet." Sweetheart.

I sit up, then turn around. I feel the bed move as he kneels behind me. Then his hands are on my hips, and he's impaling me.

"Daddy."

I whisper it over and over with every thrust.

"Fucking hell, Maria. Goddamn your ass if fucking fine."

He squeezes and pulls the cheeks apart. Then I feel his spit on my asshole. I've never been into that. I think it's gross in pornos and in real life. But with Matteo, pretty much everything almost makes me come. I feel his thumb pressing into me. Even now, the doctor in me often thinks how unsanitary this is.

But the woman who's getting fucked by the hottest man she's ever seen tells the bitch to shut the fuck up and not ruin the moment.

His thumb slides in, and I fist the sheets. The bed creaks beneath us, and it's a good thing the master bedroom downstairs is beneath the other upstairs bedroom. I have to reach out with my left hand and grab the footboard to brace myself.

"Rub your clit, *piccolina.*"

I try, but I already know it won't do anything for me.

"I can't concentrate on that enough to come."

I squeak as he pulls me back and twists us until I land with my head on the pillow, belly on the mattress. He slides his free hand between the bed and me, then rubs. All of it: the feel of his thumb in my ass, his fingers rubbing my clit, his balls slapping as he pounds me, and the rocking motion of his thrusts—they push me to the edge.

"May I come?"

"Yes. Now... I can't hold on... Fuck, Maria."

I clutch the bedding again, my back bowing as I orgasm. I feel him pull out, and he's pulling my ass cheeks apart. I feel his cum drip into my ass, then he's carefully easing into me.

"I told you I would have it all, and I am. You're mine. Your cunt. Your ass. Your mouth. Your body, heart, and soul. I won't let go unless you tell me to. I will never leave you, Maria. God help anyone who tries to get between us. I'll leave nothing left of them."

I look over my shoulder, and his expression is so intense. It makes my heart race faster than the sex we just had. I believe him. All of what he said.

"That's what I want too. There's nothing I won't do to protect you—us. You give me all of you, and I treasure that. I want you to have the same from me."

He pulls out and rolls onto his side. I cup his cheeks as he pulls me against him. I scoot closer. I could propose to him right now, but I think he already has plans for that. But I can hint that's what I want.

"Matteo, my future is with you. Only you. I want the world to know that. May God have mercy on anyone who interferes because I won't."

God, please don't let there be a reason for either of us to prove we mean that pledge.

Chapter Seventeen

Matteo

Today's been perfect. Maria and I slept in, which I never do. I went downstairs before she woke to make her breakfast only to find Marco already had. He made a shit ton of food. Even though I know he made most of it for him, Lorenzo, and Gabriele, he made Maria's favorites. Eggs poached hard, French toast, yogurt parfaits, bacon, sausage, and ham. Groceries arrived while Maria and I were in the sea yesterday. I'm grateful for the delivery. I fixed plates for Maria and me, then I went back upstairs to have breakfast in bed.

We spent the morning on my boat, fishing. It's the thing Maria enjoys most down here, but she didn't get to the last time she came because Veronica gets seasick. Gabriele and I caught nothing. All the fish decided Maria and Marco's bait was better. It was one after another for them. Maria stood between Gabriele and me. She swears she whispers to the fish. Gabriele had to help her reel one in. Even the harness wouldn't have kept her from going over. After a picture, we tossed it back.

Right after that, what could have been a minnow in comparison nibbled on Gabriele's line, but it dropped off before he could get it above the water. We didn't count that as a catch—well, we being Marco, Maria, and me. Gabriele swears he got one today.

This afternoon, we laid on the deck and soaked up the sun. We're all olive-skinned and tan easily. Maria knows better than any of us that we shouldn't have been out as long as we were, but she's the ringleader when it comes to sunbathing. She loves the feeling of the sun soaking into her skin and would practically bake herself if she could. I have a pool as well as the beach, so taking a dip now and again made staying out for three hours pleasurable. With the guys out there too, Maria had a way more appropriate bikini on today. Much to my disappointment.

We're coming home after dinner at Maria's favorite little fish shack. She always eats with moderation, except for a few places. The person who brought out our food wasn't the same server who took our order. The guy looked at our table and started to put the biggest meal in front of Gabriele. Maria practically reached across the table to snatch it. The guys in our family usually have a three to one ratio with the women. We have three plates to their every one. Maria had a four to one tonight. But I haven't seen her this happy in ages. The last trip to Florida almost got her sold to a sex trafficker. The one before that ended early because she had to go back to work. She hadn't had a vacation before that one in nearly a year-and-a-half because of med school then residency. If she wants to eat all the grouper the restaurant has, then I'll make sure she gets that.

"How about a walk?"

I help her off the golf cart and slide my fingers between hers.

"I definitely need that. I'm so full but so happy. Thank you, guys, for waiting while I finished. I seriously don't know how I can eat as much as I do at that place. Something comes over me."

Her brothers and Gabriele choke and snort. I shoot them a warning glare. Maria looks over her shoulder.

"Oh, God. You guys are disgusting. I'm your sister."

"Yeah, and Matteo's my best friend. You think I enjoy knowing what he's doing to my baby sister?"

Marco points an indignant finger at me, then her. Maria rolls her eyes. We pass the house and head to the beach. Maria stops to slip off her sandals while the rest of us take off our shoes. We leave them on the veranda and walk toward the water.

"Who moved the loungers?"

Maria looks up at me, her brow furrowed. The tide's coming in, and there are two chairs with a cabana pushed together just where the water ends. In fifteen minutes, the water will surround them. I don't answer. I lead us over there, and Maria gasps when she sees the bottle of champagne. Her eyes are wide as she looks at me again. The guys stayed closer to the house, so we're alone now. When we get to the water's edge, we stand looking out at the sea.

"I know how happy you are here, *piccolina*. We've made a lot of memories with our family on the Keys ever since we were kids. I'm hoping that tonight makes your happiest memory yet. I remember when we were younger, I thought looking out to sea was boring. To me, there was nothing out there. Just an abyss. You saw completely the opposite. You saw adventure and possibility, things to explore and discover. Truly a world of possibility. For years, my future felt the same way I used to think about the ocean. The future was an abyss I hoped I would live long enough to endure. Then we finally admitted how we feel. We finally plunged in. But it's not an abyss. It's a new world I've dived into, and you're with me to explore it because there's so much more than I imagined."

I turn to face her, and she moves, so she's looking at me. I drop to one knee.

"I'm hoping instead of saying I told you so, you'll say yes. I love you, *piccolina*. Will you marry me?"

"Yes."

She's practically saying it before I finish. I took her hands in mine while I asked, and now she's tugging me to stand. I resist and reach for my pocket.

"I don't care about that. Kiss me."

"Gladly."

I lift her off her feet, my arms beneath her shapely ass as she cups my cheeks. This kiss is everything. It's happiness. It's love. It's lust. It's hope. It's life. My life is her life. We've been one for longer than we realized. Now we're making it official.

"Matty, I love you so much. I always have in one way or another. I feel whole when we're together. What you said is the most beautiful thing I've ever heard. I was eight, and you were ten when we had the conversation. I'd say I can't believe you still remember that, but that memory is as clear to me as if it were happening right now. I felt so sad for you while you talked, but you agreed with me in the end. You really listened. Really considered what I said. I'd never felt that way with the other guys. I think that's when I fell in love with you. Then Marco came over and got your attention, and I went to play with Carmine and Enzo. I didn't think the conversation mattered that much to you."

"It's meant more and more to me as we've gotten older, and I've come to understand the role I can never leave. If this is the life we both must lead, then I want no one else by my side but you."

Maria grins down at me and jerks her head toward the house.

"How're you going to break that news to Marco?"

"Who do you think moved the chairs for me?"

I put her down and reach into my pocket and pull out the jewelry box. I flip open the lid, and Maria's jaw drops. She covers her mouth with both hands. Her gaze darts from the ring to me three times before she finally sticks her left hand out. I slide the ring onto her finger, and she just stares.

"*Piccolina?*"

"This is just like the ring I pointed out to Roni in a magazine like four years ago while we were sitting by that pool."

She points in the house's direction.

"It was five years ago. The summer between college and med school. I can still feel the unexpected jealousy and anger that spiked through me at the thought that some guy you'd meet in med school would give you a ring like this."

"I can't believe you remember what the ring looked like. You were just walking behind the chairs when I mentioned it. Even Roni wasn't paying that much attention."

It's my turn to cup her cheeks.

"I remember a lot of things you say, Maria. I'll never forget exactly how you sounded when you said yes."

"I love you, Matty."

She's called me that twice. She did it seven months ago when she woke up after being drugged. The last time she did was not long after that trip where we looked out at the ocean. I wanted to be grown up like Emilio and Luca, so I decided I would only answer to Matteo. She was really the only person who called me that. I was a dick to her when I told her and Carmine that only babies had nicknames like that. She and Carmine just nodded. I knew I'd hurt their feelings, especially hers, but I felt way more grown up than I was. I don't think she's realized she's said it here or when she came round.

"I love you, Bambi."

Maria laughs, and she's never been more beautiful than she is now as the moonlight shines on her chestnut hair and makes her eyes twinkle.

"You called me that until I was like six."

Bambi was short for bambina. Baby.

"Do you remember why you stopped calling me that?"

"Yes."

"Tell me why."

She taunts me, and I shake my head and pretend to huff.

"Because you beat me at the fifty-yard dash after school."

"And what baby could do that?"

"You're not a baby anymore, but you're still my little girl."

I lean forward to kiss her as the water swirls around our ankles. I pick her up again and ease us onto the loungers, careful not to hit either of our heads on the cabana. Unless someone is watching us from out at sea, we're shielded from anyone's eyes. As the water laps around us and rises, it's almost like having sex in the ocean. Sort of like a hammock over the water or one of those South Pacific houses on stilts in the ocean.

We fumble as we pull off each other's clothes. I'm not even sure where half of them land. I thrust into her, and we both sigh. Then our movements are frenzied, and we can't get enough.

"Mine."

I grunt the single word like a caveman, but she is. My ring is on her finger. My cock is inside her, and soon my cum will be too.

"Yes, Daddy."

I flex my hips harder and harder, knowing I'm being rough.

"You're going to be sore by the time I'm done with you,

piccolina. Every move you make, every step you take tomorrow, you will remember what it feels like to have your fiancé inside you, claiming you."

"I want that. Harder."

The chair creaks and shakes as I give her what she wants, what we both need. My right hand rests on her thigh as she wraps her leg over mine. My left hand entwines my fingers with hers over her head. Our eyes lock, and we gaze at each other. Nothing in the world exists except for my fiancée, my *piccolina.* No one matters the way she does. I'll burn down the world and everyone in it before I let anything happen to her.

"May I come, Daddy?"

"Yes. I can't hold on much longer."

"Come in me. I want to know *I* made you come. That'll get me off."

I make sure I never finish before her, but I know she's close. I grunt again before I feel my cum shoot from my cock. She arches beneath me as she moans. She squeezes her pussy around me as I continue to thrust.

"I'm the only one you fuck. The only one you make love to. The only one who gets your cum. You're mine."

My kiss steals our breath. As the second youngest of eight kids who grew up like siblings, Maria's always had to share. I love the way she sounds when she's possessive of me. I love that she claims me and would never share me. I keep moving, pushing her into another orgasm. My hand leaves her thigh and wraps around her throat. I squeeze, tightening incrementally until her nails claw my back, and her body goes rigid as her cunt holds me inside her. I let go immediately, kissing behind her ear.

"Has anyone ever told you you're an intense man? Like you have no low simmer or low gear."

I chuckle as I roll us, so I'm on my back with her draped over me.

"You might have once."

"I love it."

I think she's talking about my intensity. Maybe she is, but I follow her gaze and see her staring at her ring. It's a four carat round in a double halo setting with a ring of diamonds and a ring of emeralds encircling the stone to create a bed for the center stone to sit in. Sapphires cascade down the band. At least, that's the way the jeweler described it to me. Even though it's the one from the magazine, I customized the stones around the diamond.

"The emeralds. They're my birthstone. The sapphires are yours. I love that."

"My heart is that diamond, *piccolina*. You hold it just like the emeralds hold the diamond. But I'll always be there to support you just like the sapphire band holds up the diamond."

"You are the most romantic man in the whole wide world."

She smatters kisses across my cheeks.

"Only for you."

We shift and pull the blanket at the foot of the loungers over us; the champagne forgotten, while we hold each other and stare out at the water. Would that we could always stay like this. But we're headed back to the real world tomorrow, and I'm sure that's going to blow.

We've been back for four days, which is a day longer than we had on Islamorada. Our family is ecstatic for us, which is a far cry from how we feared they'd originally take our relationship. There won't be a long engagement. We don't have a date, but I'm not waiting any longer than we have to.

I'm at the garage taking care of a couple low-level associates who thought they could run an underground card ring in Brooklyn without paying for the privilege. If they'd just paid their taxes to us, they'd be alive tomorrow. But they doubled-down and refused, lying to my face, telling me it was just their grandpas playing penuckle. Two of those fuckers don't even have living grandfathers. This is what happens when we open the door too wide to non-Italians and non-Sicilians. Sometimes, shit blows in.

I just got in the shower to scrub off blood and other—stuff— when the satellite phone rings. I lean out and look at Luca. Something's fucking really wrong. I can't leave with DNA evidence on me, so I hurry to scrub myself from the tip of my hair to the soles of my feet. I'm methodical despite my speed. I strain to hear what Luca's saying.

"Maria, slow down. Where are you?"

The moment he says her name, I flip the water off and push open the shower curtain. There isn't a man in this family who hasn't seen everyone else naked. I couldn't give two shits. I snatch the phone from Luca, who has the sense to let go.

"Maria? What happened?"

"Matteo, we were shot at. Mama and Papa were taking me to visit venues for our engagement party."

Not something either of us wants, but we understand it's more about work than pleasure. Since Carmine and Serafina had their wedding abroad, there hasn't been a big celebration since Easter of last year, when we hosted a dinner party for New York's high and mighty. The other syndicates have, so we need to remind everyone we're still the wealthiest.

"We just got to the Beekman. As soon as Francesco opened Mama's door, someone shot at us. They hit Ciccio in the throat. Beppo was still in the driver's seat, so he rolled down his window and fired. I think he hit someone. Papa climbed into the backseat while Mama and I dove into the third row."

My heart's racing. I'm struggling to get clothes onto my wet body. Luca's handing me items as fast as I can get them on.

"I had to shoot, Matteo. I had to kill them. They were going to kill Papa and take Mama. I heard them."

I freeze. Maria's the best shot in the family. There's nothing the woman doesn't excel in except patience. The only time she has any is athletics. She could be a sniper if we allowed her to come on missions, which there isn't a chance in fucking hell that's ever motherfucking happening.

"Are you still at the Beekman?"

"No. There were six of them. Beppo took out one. Papa got one. And I got the other four. I saw them approaching from the other side. I got one of the rifles and climbed back into the second row. I swear I only opened the window enough to get the muzzle out."

That's still wide enough for a bullet to her brain. I take calming breaths as I try not to picture that.

"Where are you, *piccolina?*"

"Your parents'. They got Papa in the arm. Once they were all dead, we got Ciccio in the back and headed here. Your mom's sewing him up right now. Turns out it was only a graze. Why were they after Mama? Why not me? First, Aunt Sylvia. Now, Mama. It should be me."

I can't tell her no the fuck it shouldn't. Her voice drops low, and when she speaks, I narrow my eyes at Luca. He can hear everything, and I can tell he's trying not to freak out as he listens to his sister describe how she and their parents almost died.

"Daddy, I heard them talking. They were from Boston. I'm sure of it. Boston Irish."

Just like there are specific New York accents—don't let

anyone tell you there aren't—there are definitely specific Boston accents too. But that's not the only thing that registers. Either Maria forgot about Luca or assumes he can't hear because she called me Daddy. He leans over to whisper in my free ear.

"Livy calls me that. Sera calls Car that."

I give him a jerky nod.

"Are you safe at my parents'? All the guards are there?"

"Yeah. Can you and Luca come here?"

Luca stripped after I got dressed, and he's in the shower right now. I moved closer, so he could hear over the water.

"As soon as Luca's out of the shower. I'm ready to go. We're coming, little one."

"Hurry. Papa was bleeding so much. He's stable. The bullet passed through, but there was so much blood. I did what I could in the car for Papa and Ciccio, and your mom's stitching Papa up right now."

"We're on our way. Where's everyone else?"

"On their way too. Your dad was here already."

Luca cuts in.

"How's Mama?"

"She's fine. She helped Auntie Carlotta."

"*Piccolina*, I have to hang up. I can't take this phone with us."

"I know. Love you."

"Love you."

Luca and I speak at the same time just before I end the call. He doesn't bother to button his shirt, and he'd barely zipped his pants as we run to the car. I have mine, so I slide in behind the wheel. I look at Luca as I turn on the car.

"Marco and I are having clam chowder for dinner. Call Raffaele."

He's one of our pilots. Marco and I have a trip to make.

Chapter Eighteen

Maria

I don't know why I screamed when the bullet hit Francesco in the throat. It's hardly the worst thing I've seen, especially considering that wasn't the first time I've been caught in a gunfight, and I had rotations in the ER. But it was the first time —that I know of—where Mama was the target. It became really real when I saw all the blood. I've never been so relieved to see anyone as I was to see Matteo.

I'm so lethargic now. Giuseppe pulled into the garage at Auntie Carlotta and Uncle Domenico's. I was in the living room when Luca and Matteo arrived. I called from Matteo's room. He carried me to his car after I sagged against him as we stood next to the bed Papa's resting in. I can't believe I fell asleep during the fifteen-minutes Matteo and the other men met with Papa.

Both sets of parents sent us home, so Matteo and I are on our way to our place. That's still taking some getting used to, even though I've been daydreaming about it for years.

"Maria, I know you're a good shot, but you should have stayed down and let your dad and Beppo deal with the shooters."

I stare at him for a moment as I grit my teeth. I try to calm my temper, but I fail.

"A good shot? The only person better than me is Aunt Sylvia. The shooters were approaching from both sides. Papa and Beppo could only shoot in one direction at a time."

"You tell one of the men that you see more shooters, and they deal with them. You stay down. The SUVs are purposely practically indestructible, but that doesn't do a shit bit of good if you put your head in front of the open window. Those bullets wouldn't have come into the car from that side with bullet proof glass to stop them."

"I know all of that, but I have as much right to protect my family as any of you do to protect me."

"And distracting your dad is probably why—"

"Don't you dare finish that fucking sentence. I didn't distract him. He got shot before I got the rifle. That's why the fuck I did it. We needed to get Ciccio in the car, and we needed to get Papa to your mom. If you fucking blame me for my dad getting shot, I won't forgive you."

"I'm sorry. I shouldn't have said that. I know he got hurt first, but can you imagine how it felt to hear you say that you had to kill someone? Four fucking someones. Do you understand how much I want to hold on to you and never let you go near anyone who can hurt you? Do you know what it's like to think the person you love most is about to die? To go through that twice in only a few months?"

"Of course, I fucking do. Now you know how every woman in our family feels when you guys leave. How I've felt saying goodbye to you for years."

He snaps his mouth shut and glances at me as he drives.

"Matteo, I wanted two things in those minutes that felt like hours. I wanted my parents safe, and I wanted to live long enough to get to you. I knew I was safe at your parents' house, but I didn't *feel* safe until you got there."

His hand covers mine as it rests on my thigh. He squeezes it before lacing our fingers as we pull into his underground garage. Our conversation pauses as we ride in the elevator with two guards assigned to us for tonight. We don't start talking again until we're inside our condo.

"I need to be able to trust that you're going to follow protocols, Maria. They're there for a reason. The men train for this. There is so much more that could have been happening that you didn't know to look for or things you wouldn't know how to do. You didn't trust your family or our men to do their sworn duty. Protect the don's family at all cost."

"I'm not reckless. You know that. At least, not in situations like this. If I wasn't confident I could hit them, I would have stayed hidden. I wasn't trying to be a hero. I had nothing to prove. But don't underestimate what I'll do to protect my family. I have no limits and no boundaries or lines I won't cross. Be pissed at me and think what I did was stupid. But I won't apologize, and I don't regret it."

We stare at each other, and I'm worried it's about to become a standoff. But he leans forward and kisses me. It's like I can taste his fear. He's holding me as though I'm fragile. I knew he was worried and scared for me, but I don't think I understood the depth of that until now. I cup his jaw as we pull apart.

"I did what I thought I had to in that moment. I knew I was supposed to stay hidden, and you're right. I didn't trust the protocols I've known since I was a child. I know I got lucky that it worked out to our advantage and that so much could have gone wrong. I'm still not sorry for what I did because I protected my parents. But I am sorry I scared you, Daddy."

"Maria, I know the exact feeling you had. I've experienced it plenty of times. Part of me is so fucking proud of how brave you were and that you have the skills to protect your family and you. But there is just so much that could have gone wrong. Your dad needed a doctor. If they'd shot you through the brain, who was going to save you? Who was going to save your dad and Ciccio? By opening the window, you gave those shooters a clear path to Uncle Massi's and Beppo's heads. A bullet could have gone straight past you and into the back of either of their skulls. Things worked out this time, but I'm scared it won't the next time."

"Where does that leave us? Am I forgiven or is this unforgiveable?"

His face hardens, and I don't know what to make of that. Matteo's stripping me, then practically ripping his clothes off. I glue my eyes to the belt he drops on the floor until he's guiding me to step into the massive soaking tub once he's gotten in. His tone is stern, and it actually soothes me.

"Maria, my love is unconditional. I'll always forgive you. You made a mistake, but with the best of intentions. I'm not going to hold this against you. I just want you to understand the gravity of your role. I don't agree with what you did because your safety has always been paramount to me—more so than anyone else's, and I know I shouldn't admit that because Uncle Salvatore, as our don, should come ahead of everyone else. But no one comes before you. No one ever has. I would tell you the same things even if we weren't together. But I hope, now that you know how I feel about you, you'll understand why I'm so protective of you. I didn't think I was going to make it through Miami. I can't lose you."

"I love you unconditionally, too. I should have trusted the

system, but I truly just wanted my parents safe and to get to you. We're really okay?"

He sits, and I maneuver myself to straddle his legs. He strokes my back and my ass as I lean against him, and I kiss his chest over his heart. I saw his hard on, and now I feel it pressed against my clit. I rub it twice before he lifts me and impales me. Right now, we need the connection, our bodies one to show us both that nothing will ever separate us. Getting off isn't our priority.

"We are going to argue, *tesorina*. All couples do. Anyone who says they never disagree is lying. Maybe they keep it to themselves, but no couple always thinks the same. That's all right. What I need is your trust, and it frightens me that it shattered so easily. But I understand."

"I know, and that's why I can't believe you forgive me already. That wasn't just a little mistake. I knew I could have gotten myself shot, but I didn't think about how I made Papa and Beppo targets. In the moment, I thought I was doing the right thing. But—"

"Shh, Bambi. I know. Can you imagine how you would have reacted if you saw me, and our roles were reversed? Me taking risks like that?"

"Yeah. I'd say your reaction was pretty fucking tame. And I know it's completely unfair and hypocritical that I'd expect you to be okay with what I did when I'd be shitting a fucking brick if you were me, and I were you."

"I can't tell you all the things I know or all the things I'm trained to do. I get that's part of why it's hard for you to see things completely from my perspective."

"But I know better."

"There's a world of difference between knowing better and how you feel when you're suddenly in the situation. I've watched Uncle Massi and Uncle Sal kiss my aunts goodbye.

How my parents were. How they lingered, not wanting to let go of their wives. I knew they understood it might be the last kiss they shared. But until I was on the way to my parents' house, I didn't have a clue how hard it is to wait to see if the person you love most really is safe."

We sit together silently until the water cools, neither of us wanting to get off so much as to just be close. We step out of the tub and into the shower. One kiss leads to another and another until Matteo drops to his knee. He guides my leg over his shoulder. Then his lips are around my clit.

"Matteo, fuck that feels amazing."

"Once you come, I want to feel your hand on me, jerking me off. I want to feel you sucking my dick until I'm so close to coming that I can barely pull out long enough to get my dick in your cunt before I blow."

My fingers go to his hair, and I try to press his head closer. He slaps the back of my hand and pulls it away. He moves them to my lower back, and I know better than to fight him. He'll edge me if I do. When he feels me cross them, he lets go. He licks my pussy before delving his tongue into me. He rubs the heel of his left hand along my pussy lips while his right hand reaches up to pinch my nipple. He increases the pressure on my nipple until I'm moaning, unsure if I can bear any more. Just when I'm about to safe word, his fingers replace his tongue. He strokes my g spot over and over.

"Come, Maria. Let me taste you."

"Yes, Daddy."

He redoubles his efforts. I know how much he loves hearing me call him that. I love it just as much. The more I say it, the more I want to say it. I'd say it with every sentence. I chant it in my head until I feel that tightening low in my belly, the ache in my pussy, then the pleasure.

"I'm coming, Daddy."

He licks me again and again. When I stop moaning, he stands and spins me around. He pulls my hips back and thrusts into me. He squeezes my ass as hard as he did my nipples. He spreads my cheeks, and I know he's looking at my asshole.

"Maria, you know I forgive you for putting yourself at risk. But are you upset with yourself now that I've told you how I feel?"

Of course, I am. I feel like I've disappointed him. And I don't enjoy knowing I scared him. I nod.

"I didn't intend to make you feel shitty, *piccolina*. I just wanted you to understand the other outcomes that you didn't foresee. I know what you think about yourself when you feel guilty. I don't think you need to be punished for putting yourself at risk. I know you're punishing yourself enough. But are you going to forgive yourself like I forgave you?"

I shake my head. He's right. Guilt is a powerful emotion and one I've struggled with a lot as part of my depression. I still don't regret that I killed those men. And that's what I feel guilty for—the lack of regret. But more than anything, I feel guilty for scaring Matteo. I haven't spoken about my part in all of this with my parents yet, and I can only imagine how I must have made them feel, especially once they have time to reflect on what happened. That really makes me feel shitty.

"Do you want to try the belt, Maria? I saw you eyeing it earlier, and that's when I realized how your guilt was starting."

"Yes. Absolutely."

"Then I'll give you what you want. Once your ass is pretty, pink, and puffy with the welts, I'm going to fuck you here."

He presses his thumb against the hole.

"Yes, Daddy."

"I'm going to come inside your pussy now. Later, I'll come inside your ass. You're going to sleep with my jiz in both holes."

"You said I was also going to jerk you off. I want to see and feel your cum on me. You said I was going to suck you off. I want to taste you like you tasted me."

"Why do you want that?"

"Because I'm yours."

"Why else?"

I grin even though I know he can't see it.

"Because you're mine. No one else gets what I have. Your cum and your orgasms are mine to give."

He leans forward, his lips against my ear.

"That's right, little girl. No matter what happens out there, I belong to you. Every single part of me. Heart, body, mind, and soul. You felt out of control earlier, and it didn't feel like I was on your side. I realize that now. You sought to get that control back by arguing that you did the right thing. But you picked the wrong part of our relationship—your safety—to push me on. I will never ease up on that, and I will never let you think any danger to you is acceptable. But you have so much more control over me than you realize, *piccolina*."

I stop meeting his thrusts, and he pauses, too. I twist to see him.

"I know. But I'm not sure I like the idea that I can control you. Part of what makes you desirable is that there's an element of you that feels like no one can control you. I know, in reality, Uncle Salvatore has a lot of control because he's our don. There's an aura around you though that is just so masculine and dominant. I don't want that to change."

"I just want you to know we're equals in this. I'm all in, Maria. We might not agree with each other's choices some-times, but we will always be okay. We will always work it out."

The next time he surges into me, he uses so much force that it presses me against the wall. My cheek rests against the cool tile as steam fills the air. I'm back to thrusting my hips to take him. His fingers bite into my skin.

"Fucking come, Maria. I can't hold out."

"Don't. Come in me."

He reaches between me and the wall to rub my clit. I moan.

"Louder."

He barks the command, and I obey. The sounds of pleasure echo throughout the bathroom until I scream.

"Matteo!"

He pins my hips in place, and I feel him pulse inside me.

"Maria!"

I sag forward, but he pulls me up, my back to his chest. His arm wraps around my waist as he nuzzles my neck. I reach back and slide my fingers into his hair before we kiss. I sigh. Things feel back to normal between us, but I still don't feel great about myself. I'm used to a lot of stressors in my life. But Jordan, Aunt Sylvia's kidnapping, and my dad getting shot are testing me.

I want the spanking with the belt. Not only so I can absolve myself, but so I can let go and allow Matteo to have control. I know hearing me on the phone say someone shot at me and that I shot back had to leave him feeling helpless. He may not realize it, but he needs to spank me as much as I need him to. He needs to feel like he's in charge and able to protect me, just as much as I need to know that he can handle all of this, instead of feeling like the weight of these stressors is grinding me into the ground.

Once we're dry and in the bedroom, Matteo points to the bed. I cross my wrists against my lower back again and lean over the mattress. My feet are apart and turned in. I watch as he goes to the dresser drawer where we keep all our sex toys. When we have children, we're going to have more than one kind of secret drawer. The same safety latch that goes on the gun drawers we're all forbidden to touch as children—the one that would have gotten us punished until we were old enough to have our own kids—will need to go on our sex drawer.

Matteo prowls back to the bed with a sleep mask, ear plugs, and handcuffs. As he looks at me in my prone position, his dick hardens again. I push my hips back farther as I wait for him. He puts everything on the bedspread beside me before he picks up the belt and coils it around his hand, the buckle against his palm. He leaves a tongue about eight inches long. I swallow my nervousness as he positions himself beside me.

"Put the mask on and the ear plugs in, *piccolina*."

Fuck. I won't know when each lash is coming, and there's something hot as fuck about making me do that myself. I follow his directions. What's he going to do with the handcuffs? I find out a moment later. He easily lifts me off my feet and turns me before letting me land lengthwise on the mattress with my head on the pillow. He pulls out one earplug.

"Hands over your head."

I obey immediately, and he cuffs my wrists together and to the headboard.

"If it's too much, say your safe word. Do not take more than you can manage because you already feel guilty and feel worse because you think you're failing. I will be so monumentally pissed if you do. It'll take me a long time to cool off, and we won't do anything like this again soon.

"Daddy, I know. I never want what we do to make you feel bad or to break your trust. When we're like this, I enjoy being yours to do with what you want. The idea of ruining that hurts. I love you too much to do that to you."

He kisses between my shoulder blades and slips the earplug back in. I relax. But a moment later, the belt nails my ass, and I kick my feet. Holy fuck. That hurts like a mother-fucker. I barely recover from the first spank before the next one lands. He does it three more times, and my ass feels like a fire is trying to burst up through my skin. He yanks my right leg until it hangs over the side. I brace myself. The belt slaps my pussy, and I cry out. Then I feel my arms freed from the cuffs. He whips off my mask and lifts me onto his lap. I pull out the ear plugs and look up at him.

"Daddy?"

"It's done because you wanted it. We can try the belt again for mutual enjoyment. But I will never punish you again with it. I can't."

"Why?"

"I'm not angry with you, and I wasn't a moment ago. But I never want you to see the welts that are forming and think I hit you out of anger."

"You didn't hit me. You never have and never ever would."

"Fine. Struck you."

I scramble off his lap and hold his face in place.

"Look at me."

There's command in my voice that I don't use with him. He tilts his head back, and our eyes meet. My thumb brushes against his cheek.

"You gave me what I needed. I don't know why I'm like this. Why we're like this. But you understand me, and I'm grateful for that. But you did not hit me or strike me. You spanked me because I asked for it. I know you're not angry with me. I know if you ever punish me, you'll be calm and rational when you do it. You know how much stronger you are than I am. You know how you could harm me if you wanted to or if you were reckless. I know without a shadow of a doubt in my mind, you would never punish me while angry. You would never risk being too rough with me. I know you're scared I wouldn't forgive you. I'm scared you'd never forgive yourself. If I didn't trust you, I wouldn't submit."

He pulls me close, and I straddle him. I guide his cock into me. I set the pace as I ride him. I'm rough and fast, grinding my clit against his pubic bone. He holds onto my waist as he lets me do what I want. I ache to come. But when I feel him move me faster, I stop. I stand and reach for the bedside table. I pull out the bottle of lube and quickly lean over the side of the bed, pulling my ass cheeks apart. He stands and pours some of the cool liquid into me, then I hear him lube his cock. The tip presses into me, and I shove my hips back. I inhale a deep breath before he's pushing all the way in. Then he's fucking me. He's neither rough nor gentle. He reaches around me to find my clit, but I catch his wrist.

"You did what I needed without getting off. I want the same for you."

I move his hand to my hip. He grips it like he is the other and pounds into me.

"Fucking hell, Maria. Fuck... You're so tight... Your ass looks so good with the welts *I* gave you."

He runs his hands over them, and I moan with arousal, not pain. I meet each of his thrusts, encouraging him. When he comes, he squeezes my ass with a viselike grip. He pulls out and rolls me over before sinking to his knees. He latches onto my clit and sucks until I writhe.

"Daddy!"

"That's right, piccolina."

We finish breathless, and he once again lifts me onto his lap, cradling me against him.

"Maria, I feel closer to you than I ever have anyone else. More than I imagined I could be with you. I don't know why I am like I am, or why we're like this. But there's no one in this world I would ever share this with."

"Same."

We wind up back in the shower, then we crawl into bed.

We curl up together and are soon asleep. When morning comes, I feel settled again.

When I wake and roll over, I'm alone in bed. That doesn't happen often, so I wonder if Matteo slipped out to go to the gym with the guys or if he's already working in his office. I brush my teeth and head out to see if he's still home. My ass still stings, but each step reminds me how much Matteo loves me. That's probably totally fucked-up in most people's mind, but I couldn't give a flying fucking shit. It works for us.

I hear his voice, so I follow it to the living room and find him on the phone. He's quiet as I approach, so he must have heard me. He turns toward me and offers me a tight smile.

"We'll head out tomorrow morning. I'll take her to my parents now that she's up."

Who's he talking to? I don't like the look he's giving me or his tone.

"Maria's awake. I'll explain everything to her, Uncle Massi."

He hangs up, and I'm ready with my questions.

"What? Why?"

"Because there isn't nearly enough security here while I need to head to Boston and find out who did this. Yeah, I have guards who work the front desk, and nothing comes up here without being x-rayed. I have men in the basement and the lobby, but that's not enough. I like the elevator opening into here because no one can skulk around and catch me unprepared. But now that we're living together, it's too much of a risk. If they make it up here, then you're in way too much danger. My parents live in a gated community on a gated property with twenty-four-hour security patrolling. It's that or

Uncle Salvatore and Aunt Sylvia's. You're not staying here. Your place is obviously completely out of the question."

"Why can't I stay with my parents?"

I accept his explanation for why I can't stay here. It's reasonable. Some of the guys live in penthouses with elevators down the hall, and some live in ones where the elevator opens directly into their condo. Ours is the latter.

"Because your dad has things to take care of. He may not be at the house. I think your mom is coming to my parents', too. That or Luca's."

"All right."

What else can I say? We head out to the car. Each step I take reminds me of last night, and it gives me that reassurance we're okay, and Matteo will support me no matter what as we head to his parents', so I can face them. But I still worry about what my mom and dad are going to say as Matteo parks at his parents' house.

"Maria, there's still something wrong."

He whispers as we cross the driveway and step up to the door.

"I still feel crappy about how I acted. I could have handled it so much better."

"*Piccolina*, regardless of whether my mom shows us to separate bedrooms, I'm here for whatever you need."

His parents are old school too. Emilio lives with his girl-friend, and I'm living with Matteo. But neither he nor I assume they'll let us share a room tonight. We hope we will, but we're prepared not to.

"You need to make peace with this and yourself. We both fucked up. I should have figured out a better way to let you know why what you did was so risky. Neither of us is innocent, but neither of us needs to continue punishing ourselves. We're together, and there's no more questioning that."

"Yes, Daddy. That part makes me so happy."

His arm is around me as we walk in. Our parents leave the kitchen as we enter the foyer. One look at them, and all I can think is what the fuck have I done? Both of my parents rush forward and engulf me in a hug. Papa kisses my forehead as Mama squeezes me. He speaks first.

"We're proud of your bravery yesterday, but we're both upset with the risks you took. You ignored Mama and me when we told you to get back into the third row."

I wince. I didn't mean to leave that part out when I told Matteo what happened. I look over my shoulder at him and see he's pissed.

"What you were saying didn't register with me. I was focused on what was happening outside the car."

"All the more reason you shouldn't have been shooting. If you can't be aware of everything around you, then you're risking your life."

"I'm sorry I scared you both. I just wanted to make sure we could get Ciccio back in the car and get both of you to Auntie Carlotta."

I look at Matteo, and I know he remembers what I said about needing to get to him. He gives me a little nod. Mama lets go and leans back to look at me.

"I was just as capable as you were to shoot, and it wouldn't have been the first time I've done it. But I knew opening that window was a bigger risk. I wish you'd listened to me, but I know what that tunnel vision is like. I know what it's like to only focus on protecting the people you love. We're upset about the risk, but we aren't upset about your need to help."

Something about what Mama says makes me think she's been in that position more than once. But this doesn't feel like the right time to ask. Matteo slides his arm around me when my parents let go, and I step back next to him.

"Mama, I don't know how long Maria'll need to stay here."

"This is still your home, Matteo, and Maria knows this is her second home, too."

"Thank you."

It may still be his, but house guests are like fish. They're only good for two days, then you want to throw them out.

"Maria, make a list of any foods you want for the next week or so. Domenico can pick them up."

"I'm certain I'll be happy with whatever you have."

"You will starve if you say that. Matteo will whip through the fridge like a Tasmanian Devil. It'll be empty before bedtime. I recommend you make that list."

"Mama."

He sounds so aggrieved.

She rolls her eyes.

"Maria, look at the size of the fridge. I don't have that because I need all that space with just Domenico and me living here. I keep it stocked for when he and Marco come over."

I didn't think he'd seen his parents in days, but I know he used to visit frequently.

"He usually stops by at least three times a week. Even if it's for fifteen minutes, he still eats a meal's worth."

"You make me sound like a *porcellino*." Little pig.

She just cocks an eyebrow.

I pinch his ribs, and he shies away. There's nothing to grab.

"I think he burns it off."

He gives me one of those heated stares again, and I know he's thinking of one way to burn those calories. But he's the one who said we might have separate rooms here. I pray that isn't the case. Even if we don't have sex, I want to sleep beside him tonight. Who knows what's going to happen in Boston?

Chapter Nineteen

Matteo

We just touched down in Boston. We didn't have a private airfield we could land at, but Logan Airport has an area for private jets. Only Marco came with me. We don't want to draw too much attention. Greased palms mean we don't have anyone looking too closely at what we have aboard, which is an array of weapons that would make any guerilla army jealous. We'll outfit the Boston *Cosa Nostra* men who come with us. If I could, I'd control everything they do right down to their toothpaste. But I know our weapons are reliable and silent. I don't want surprises.

While the Mancinellis don't run the Boston *Cosa Nostra*, there's no disputing we're way more powerful than the Vizzinis. So, when I made a call and asked Tommaso Vizzini to lend me some men, he was more than happy to oblige. And by that, I mean he knew he didn't have a fucking choice, so it cost him less to do as I asked. He learned that when Carmine "asked"—

yes, air quotes—to help when we were still dealing with the sex traffickers who took Maria.

Marco and I climb into the backseat of the black SUV waiting for us. Our SUVs back home are unbelievable. Thank God. They're veritable tanks. Bullet proof, roll proof, bomb proof basically. The tires will still roll even after being shot. The windows are shatter proof. The auto body shop reinforced the undercarriage with metal plating. The crazy part is that all the syndicates get our vehicles customized at the same place. The same fucking guys do the work on our cars along with the bratva's, Cartel's, and mob's. Fucking irony. I just wish we had some of those here.

I look over at Marco as we leave the airport and head to the hotel. He and I strategize on the way. I share my thoughts about the Vizzini don.

"Tommaso was more agreeable than I expected."

"You said you'd pay him a hundred grand to his personal account. Of course, he was agreeable."

"Eh. I assumed he'd try to keep me dangling for a while."

"Anyone else in your family, even Uncle Salvatore, yeah. But he knows he'll never out bullshit you. He'd rather just get the cash."

Which we brought plenty of. That's another one of those things we don't want airport security looking too closely at. We're also killing two birds with one stone. The deal Carmine came up here to do fell through by no fault of his. We're making sure that doesn't happen a second time by negotiating a new deal. Instead of with the Albanians, it's directly with the mob.

"Well, we have to get those kilos before they go anywhere else. Luis is back from Colombia, and I think he got wind of this deal. There's no way he kept this from his *jefe*, and there's no way Enrique is going to ignore anything his brother tells him.

It's not that I want to beat them to this deal, but I've made headway with Riley. If I buy the drugs from them, then they'll help me ferret out Jordan."

I grimace saying the shitwad's name. But I continue, even with the sour taste in my mouth making it sting.

"I heard Riley's half-Italian, half-Irish friend has ties to Bogota. He's been digging around to make friends in all our rival syndicates. Enrique's going to take that personally and want to get involved since he doesn't want any other Colombians making deals up and down the Eastern Seaboard. He's going to try to score this deal for the product to make sure he keeps his monopoly over anything coming out of South America. I don't want this spilling into New York. We deal with this here and end it."

Motherfucking Jordan. Who could have guessed the connections the half-Italian, half- Irish bastard started making once he met Maria? Slimy piece of shit. He listened to his family's tales of their glory days and thought he could make himself the next Don Corleone by trapping Maria. Fuck that shit. His last name, Ryan, isn't just some generations old connection to Ireland. It's fucking fresh. We discovered that his family used to vacation on Cape Cod and has ties to the mob up here.

"Are you sure part of it is that you don't want the Diazes to sweep in and take over this deal, making us look like idiots?"

"Sure, that's a bit of it. But Jordan sucked us—you, me—everyone—in, too. I wouldn't mind my slice of the revenge while *we* make the profit off the shipment, not the Diazes. Just what the doctor ordered."

"Doctor? Thinking about Maria?"

"Always."

I look out the SUV window as we approach the hotel. We're at one of the nicest places in the city, and I wish I were here on a romantic getaway with Maria. Instead, I'm dealing with small-time Italian and Irish syndicates and possibly having to buy mob-owned coke just to sell it. That makes my stomach turn. I know I'm not actually buying it to keep it. We always buy directly from the source, so it feels like buying product from the Irish makes me nothing more than a *sfigato*—loser— even if I'm doing it to get to Jordan. I don't know. It just doesn't sit right with me.

"How pissed was Rowan when Jordan swooped in and took over the negotiations? He doesn't know it's with us, right?"

I shift my gaze back to Marco before I answer. Riley O'Malley is my contact among the Irish here. We went to Cornell together and lived in the same dorm. His older brother, Rowan, runs the Irish in Boston. I can't stand the prick.

"I don't know. I offered Rowan a ridiculous amount for the coke in exchange for the information about Jordan, but he didn't act fast enough. Now Jordan's in the picture, and I have to jump through hoops for shit that's already meant to be ours. The ships carrying the kilos went to Texas, and now they're being brought up here. That part I don't get. A visit to Rowan better explain all of it."

My phone pings, and I see it's Riley. Perfect timing.

RILEY

The asshole you're after is here. He must be hiding from you. I heard what he did to your girl. Dumb fuck.

ME

Is Rowan helping him?

RILEY

Sorta. He's not hooking him up with shit but he isn't telling you he's here either. He knows what the guy did.

ME

Where's he at?

RILEY

Haven't seen him so not sure. Rowan knows.
I want him gone. I don't want him sucking my
brother into his shit.

ME

Does Rowan know we're here?

RILEY

Yeah

ME

How?

RILEY

We know people at Logan.

ME

Is Rowan going to help hide him?

RILEY

No. If you ask he'll tell. Family favor not to
volunteer the info but neither of us cares
about him or his family enough to fight you.

ME

Keep me posted.

I show Marco my phone, and he reads the thread.

"Is Riley ratting out his brother? Or is Rowan incompetent and needs someone pulling the strings?"

Good questions. In our world, there's not much lower than a rat. Those are fighting words.

"I'm not sure. Rowan's always struck me as a competent leader, but maybe it's always been Riley. Maybe he's just protective of his older brother and their people. Maybe he's setting me up. Rowan's a douche, but he's not stupid. Sounds like he's playing Jordan. Hopefully, he remembers the mob's heyday came and went decades ago. They're no match for us. Pissing me off won't be good for his health."

I look over at Marco, and he nods. We might be avenging his sister, mom, and dad if Jordan had anything to do with the shooting the day before yesterday, and we're definitely avenging the shit Jordan's pulled on Maria, but he's letting me lead. I'm Maria's fiancé now, so it's my right to decide how we handle this.

"I need to call Uncle Sal. I have to update him that we know Rowan's letting Jordan stay in the city. He needs to prepare in case the O'Rourkes find out and think to come to the O'Malleys side."

I unlock my phone and tap my uncle's contact.

"*Ciao.*"

"*Ciao, zio.*"

"Everything going well so far?"

"Yeah. I can't say much more over the phone. Jordan is definitely here."

"Do you think he knows you're there?"

"I haven't asked."

I know what my uncle is going to say next.

"Should you?"

"Probably. But I need more information before I make any moves."

"Tread carefully, Matteo. I'm hearing things about this half-Irish, half-Italian shit. We do not need the O'Rourkes involved. If the Irish up there are fucking over the Vizzinis and us, we take care of that first."

I know all this, but I didn't tell Uncle Salvatore everything about Rowan and my suspicions. Until I know what game Rowan's playing, I'd rather not speculate and blow this up in all our faces. Uncle Salvatore waits for me to say more, but I keep quiet. What he says next is a relief.

"Call me back when you know more. It might be time to have a sit down with Dillan and Enrique. Things have been quiet with them since we reminded them who we are."

We struck back hard against the O'Rourkes for their latest attack on our family, and the Diazes know we'll keep taking from them if they stick their noses too far into our business. The cost of dealing with both is barely a drop in the bucket to our income. They get that. Up here, we know about the Irish underground gambling, their loan sharking within their own community, their extortion rings. Everything. The Boston Irish are even more insular than the New York Irish, so it'll be satisfying to insert ourselves where they can't kick us out. Now we'll do business in their communities.

"Will do."

Marco and I check into our hotel, have dinner, and I have way too brief a call with Maria. She's working tonight, so we didn't have long. I miss her. I know she's safe at my parents' house, and I know my uncles posted extra men to go to work with her. But I want to smell her perfume and feel her hand in mine. I want to talk to her without either of us having to rush away. Soon. I'm dealing with this bullshit and going home to my fiancée. I love how that sounds in my head. I climb into bed, and I'm asleep way faster than I expected.

"Fucking Riley. The shitbag's been lying to me all along. He didn't want to warn me about this shit for the sake of helping his brother. Oh, no. He did it to distract me from the fact that Rowan's turning a blind eye to what Jordan's really doing here in Boston—which is trying to recruit the Vizzinis to help him against us, which will never happen. That's on top of lying about the shipment of coke Rowan's supposed to sell us."

I'm fuming, and Marco might be silently listening, but he feels the same way as we head to Rowan's house. We need to have a little convo. Fucking hell. Fuck. I'd rather be with Maria right now than dealing with this bullshit.

I just got off the phone with Rowan about the drugs. When I tried to confirm the deal with him, that blabber mouth, boasting sack of shit admitted he's letting Jordan stay in Boston, even though he knows I'm here for Jordan as much as I am the coke. Except, it isn't kilos, as in hundreds. It's more like kilos, as in a couple at this point. Not that it surprises me they sold most of it in Texas. I gave him the chance, but he's trying to back out. Now I'm going to take what I want.

I don't know what happened to the cocaine once the ships got to Texas, but they probably disappeared across the border. Rowan knows I'm sure Jordan is here. But for some reason it's personal to Rowan that he doesn't want to get involved with what's happening between Jordan and me. The fucker already is.

The problem is—among way too many—Jordan's hidden somewhere, and I don't know where. He's fucking around with me. I think he's probably suggesting to Rowan that he holds onto the remaining drugs, then tries to get me to pay more for a new shipment. I'm not paying shit. Who fucking knows at this point? Maybe Jordan is involved with the O'Malleys, and maybe he isn't. I'm running all possibilities through my head.

But Rowan is going to tell me what I want to know. He basically stole the drugs to extort more money from me. I'm taking what I'm owed. He doesn't have nearly enough men to stop us, and they're worthless from what the Vizzinis tell us.

Fucking son of a bitch. Just deal with Jordan for Maria's sake.

Yeah, I want to stick it to Riley and Rowan now that they've tried to dick me over, but the bigger reason I'm involved is to stop Jordan. I never would have ignored something happening to Maria, but now my heart won't stop screaming to wipe out anyone connected to anyone who tries to hurt her.

Riley's being shady as fuck, too. He's known about Rowan backing out and helping Jordan, despite how he claimed he didn't like or trust the guy. That day he took my call about finding Jordan is fresh in my memory. He wanted me to take out Jordan, so his family didn't wind up in my family's crosshairs. He even gave me a heads-up that Jordan might plan more shit against Maria and use his Irish connections to help him. He neglected to mention some of the other things he knows. I want to understand why, but first I need to deal with his brother.

We're at Rowan's place five minutes after we leave the hotel. We scout the neighborhood before I get out of the car. Marco's going to hang back for now. No need to appear aggressive. Yet.

"Rowan!"

He's just come outside and looks like he's on the way to work. He looks up from locking the front door. Cute house. Very quaint. Makes it look like he's a family man. I heard he's even married. Lord only knows how he managed that.

"What're you doing here?"

"Came to pay a little visit, Rowan. Seems you and your brother only gave me the first chapter of your little story. Now we're getting to the good part where I learn how the hell you're involved in all this."

Before I know what's happening, he pulls his gun. I'm just as fast. He gets off one shot. Why doesn't he have a fucking silencer? Marco, our men, and I get off several more. He bursts back into his house. My men approach, but the garage door opens. He peels out, and I can see someone bending down in the passenger seat. It's a little girl.

"Don't shoot. You'll hit her."

My men pull back as his car speeds away. I jerk my chin, and men return to one of our SUVs. They take off after them. I make my way to the front door.

"Toss it. I don't care if you find anything. Fuck it all up."

The men still with me rush forward. In a matter of moments, they tear the place apart. My phone buzzes in my pocket as I turn back toward the door. I almost ignore it, but I pull it out to see who's calling. It's Uncle Salvatore.

The entire conversation goes sideways within moments. He wants me to pull back and leave Rowan's home, but he gives me no real reason. I'm forced to obey, even though I believe it's a mistake. I order the men to head back to the SUVs and hang up once I'm outside. The place is in shambles. They found nothing, but it left a message. Fuck you, Rowan. You want to play? Now you're in the major leagues.

"Was that Uncle Salvatore?"

Marco asks me as he watches me hang up.

"Yeah. He wouldn't tell me why we had to leave. He just said something's come up and changes things."

I just don't know why, and that's fucking annoying as hell.

"We got him. He went to some abandoned looking shithole, but it's his office. Do we take him to our place?"

Their equivalent to our garage. I'm talking to a Vizzini Made Man on the phone. He's one of Tommaso's *capos*, and I've known the guy for years, but not that well. So far, I trust him as he explains what he knows about Rowan.

"No. Depending on how things go, we may need him to do shit for us."

If he goes to their place, he can't leave. Same rules apply

there as they do at our garage. Guests check in but they never leave. Ought to call the place Hotel California.

"Okay. We've got guys surrounding the building. We'll keep him there. I'll text the address."

We learned this morning while Marco and I had breakfast that Jordan's at a hotel. We sent a couple guys over. I shot off a text, and when I heard back, the guy said Jordan had left. We got into the hotel room where he's staying, but we found nothing interesting. We were just about to head to Tomasso's office to see what he could find, but I got the call from his *capo*.

Marco's waiting by the back driver's side door.

"So, what now?"

"We visit Rowan again. This isn't over. He may not know everything about why I'm after Jordan, but he knows I'll be visiting him because I know he's part of this. Uncle Sal said to leave his house. He didn't say to leave Rowan alone."

We sit in the car as I try to plan. If we can't get Rowan, then we go after Jordan.

Uncle Salvatore saying he was hearing more about Jordan just amped everything up. Now I'm really pissed because we didn't get to the fucker in his hotel room. When I see Rowan, he better speak fast. I'm not as patient as I was in New York.

When my phone pings, it's the Vizzini man I sent after Rowan. He shoots me the address, and we head over to the sketchy office in a shitty part of south Boston. There's plenty of them, so his office is actually inconspicuous. No wonder he's working out of an abandoned building. It takes us twenty minutes to get there; I have my gun drawn as I approach. Marco shoots two of Rowan's men when they try to get off a couple rounds at us. I saunter in, my gun pointed at his head.

"Tsk, tsk. Sucking half-Irish, half-Italian dick is going to get you killed. Tell me everything, and you might go home to that pretty little girl who was in the car with you."

"Stay away from her."

"Testy."

"Fuck you."

"No, thanks. But I've got a metal pipe that'll fuck you up the ass if you don't start explaining. Not cool shooting at us, Rowan. We came for a friendly visit. Now I'm going to hurt you. You abetted a crime. You could have avoided this the moment you knew Jordan was in town. If you know this much, then you know I'm going to kill him and take the coke. I'm not paying a cent.

"I don't know anything."

"Tell us where he is, and we'll forgive the shit with the shipment."

"I'm telling you. I know nothing."

"Liar. Why are you involved?"

I walk forward and plow my fist into his sternum before I step back. He wheezes and splutters for a moment. I raise my fist again and take another menacing step forward. I flick open my knife with the other hand. I point it at his eye. I can tell Rowan's weighing his options. I can tell when he realizes he'd better tell me at least something, or his death is a guarantee.

"Jordan threatened to tell Dillan I'm the one running the drugs to Texas then up here. I know more about Jordan's plans than he thinks. I had collateral, so I told him I wouldn't say anything to you."

Collateral. Guess he's using it with us instead of against Jordan.

"Speak, Rowan. Now."

"Doing that deal with the Cartel in Bogota fucked me in more ways than one. I thought I could run the drugs up from Colombia to Texas and into Mexico without Dillan. In exchange for Jordan's connections in Bogota, I made sure Jordan had a place to stay here. He heard Riley on the phone, talking to our guy at the docks. Jordan thought he could bribe me into helping him against you if he threatened to tell Dillan about the drugs. Except the Diazes already found out that I'm running drugs for a Cartel they're connected to."

Fuck. They're already involved, after all. They haven't really come up since Marco and I got here. I keep my expression neutral.

"And?"

"And I'm trying to keep the peace here for my people and keep my head on my shoulders. It's the whole keep your friends close and your enemies closer deal. If you want to shoot each other up, take it to New York. I'm not getting in the middle."

"But in the middle is where you're already at. The pasty-ass middle of this fucking Oreo. Where's Jordan now? He wasn't at his hotel."

"I don't know."

"Wrong answer. Again."

I nod to Marco. Rowan was afraid when I held the knife toward his eye. Now, he's terrified as my best friend approaches his desk and flips it with ease. Rowan tries to back his desk chair away, but Marco wraps both hands around his throat and picks him up. Rowan's not light, but Marco pulls him onto his toes and shakes him before Marco's fist moves Rowan's nose halfway across his face. Marco knew what to expect, so he'd already turned Rowan away. Blood squirts out barely missing my friend.

"Try again, Rowan. Jordan went after my woman and got to you about the drugs."

He hesitates, so Marco drives a fist into his left ribs over and over. If he doesn't break them, he'll bruise them badly enough that it'll feel the same.

"I heard a rumor, but I don't know for sure. He's got some chick he's been fucking since they were teenagers here in

Boston. She's Brazilian, and her family supplies the Cartel in Bogota with the shit they need to make cocaine. She's been opening doors for him with the Colombians lately. He's waiting for you to pay me for the drugs, then he's going to tell the feds you're in town. He's going to say you tried to force him to smuggle them down to New York or some shit like that. I know him. He'll come up with something. His grandfather's a dirty judge. They'll lock you up and have you bumped off."

"The address. Now."

He stays quiet, but one of the Vizzinis comes in. He worked over a guy Rowan employs. He got an address, and he said he knows where it is.

I turn away and let Marco continue. I hear his knife flick open, then Rowan's screams fill the air. Good thing there's no one in the neighborhood. I turn back around and cross my arms. My gaze meets Rowan's, and I smile. My best friend, who's still a skilled top enforcer, stabs him in the abdomen, twisting the knife and pulling it down. It may not be deep, but it's painful. He gives him several more shallow cuts.

"You're going to live, Rowan. That way you're a lesson to anyone who thinks they can fuck over the Mancinellis. You owe us and will do whatever the fuck we say. Fuck with us, and we will drag you."

Marco's fist slams into Rowan's temple, and he crumbles. There's a bathroom in the building, so Marco gets cleaned up. He got some blood on him, so one guy brings the clean clothes we put in the trunk just in case. Once Marco's changed into tactical gear, he puts everything else in a bag a guy hands him. They'll take care of burning it all and sanitizing the bathroom plus cleaning up the blood in Rowan's office.

"Let's get him."

Chapter Twenty

Maria

It's not that I can't survive without him. That's not it at all. It's my feelings' strength that makes me realize just how serious I am about Matteo. I admit I've questioned how things will work out, loving a man who has a life like his. But I want the ordinary, not just the spectacular, with him. I know there are going to be other trips. I know I'm going to miss him again. And I want that. I want us to be together, so I can experience it all. I much prefer the happy times and not fearing for his life. But this is part of our life. It's what being a Mafia wife is.

But I won't jump the gun on that. We still have to set the date, and I need him to live long enough for that. I've been into other guys, and when I believed nothing could ever come of being with Matteo, I tried to picture myself with some of them. Yet none of those daydreams were even remotely like this. I liked some guys a lot, but I always had reservations. I just kept telling myself I just needed a little longer to get over him. I didn't. As the years went by, I had to force an image of being someone else's wife and having a family with a guy who wasn't Matteo. The daydreams were always murky, even in the beginning. It's crystal clear with Matteo.

I hoped Lorenzo would ride in the back of the town car with me in case Matteo calls for some reason, but he gets into the front passenger seat. I recognize Alfonso as I walk out of Auntie Carlotta and Uncle Domenico's house. He's one of our most trusted bodyguards. He closes the door behind me, and I'm alone. I rest my head back and close my eyes. I hate how little time I had to talk to Matteo last night. I miss him so much. I was so excited during the call. Now I'm miserable.

I'm meeting Olivia at her ultrasound appointment. She finally admitted that she and Luca are having a baby. He's stuck at the garage and can't get away, so they asked me to come. I know part of it is that she wants company, but I suspect some of it is so I'll see what's happening as the imaging checks out their little peanut. I ride in silence until we get to the medical complex. Alfonso opens my door again, and Lorenzo escorts me to the obstetrician's office. He looks around inside, nods to Gabriele, Olivia's guard today, and steps back outside.

"Maria, you look exhausted."

I didn't when I woke up this morning. I must look like shit now. Matches my mood.

"Yeah."

I don't want to say anything more.

"You miss Matteo, don't you?"

I did.

"I do."

My mind wanders to when Matteo might be home and whether Jordan is still a threat. I chide myself for not concentrating on what my sister-in-law's saying. I focus, and we're soon called back to the ultrasound tech's room. Watching the baby inside Olivia's belly is amazing. And bittersweet. I'm so excited for her and Luca, but I'm a little envious. I'm also sad that maybe I won't be doing this with Matteo if anything happens to him. I've fantasized about having babies with Matteo.

"Can you believe it, Maria? Look how perfect my baby is."

"I know. Oh, this is so incredible. I can't believe that's a real little person in those pictures, and that real little person is inside you."

I grin at her, and I can't help but be happy for her when I see the joy in her eyes. It soothes me and puts things back into perspective. She convinces me to have lunch with her before I head back to Manhattan, where I spend the rest of the afternoon hanging out with my mom at her office. We're both working, but it's nice to keep each other company. She's a financial analyst and going over investment statements. I'm reading imaging reports. Of course, I can't help but wonder if Matteo will be back in time to join me at another charity event. It won't be some momentous occasion, but I was looking forward to dressing up and seeing him in his tux again.

I'm writing my reports to send to a fully board-certified doctor for review, so my mind's occupied throughout the afternoon. Lorenzo is as unobtrusive as the other men in our family. He stays in the hallway with a clear view of the office and doors. I stay in his line of sight, too. Carmine is Mama's guard today, but he's outside the building in a town car, keeping an eye out down there. The time is ticking by, and I don't notice when it gets to five o'clock.

"Are you ready to go?"

I look up when my mom comes to stand by the conference table where I'm working. I haven't been to work with her since I was a little girl.

"Yeah. Let me save and pack up."

I'm gathering my things and looking out through Mama's

office door. There's no one left in the office since people leave at four-thirty. They have mostly European clients, so their days start early and end early to better coincide with their overseas accounts. The door to the office suite bursts open, and Lorenzo is racing toward us. He's signaling for us to come, so I scramble to grab my stuff. He gets to the conference room door, yelling at us.

"Leave it! Come, now!"

Mama and I grab our phones and the small pistols we carry in our purses. Then Mama pushes me between her and Lorenzo. We leave everything else behind as we run toward the elevators. Lorenzo's talking a mile a minute into his earpiece, telling Carmine we're coming down and to have the car doors open at the curb. He's telling the other men guarding different parts of the building that he's already taken down two assailants. My eyes widen as I look behind me to where the stairwell door across from the elevators is open. A man's leg props it ajar. I see the pool of blood he's lying in. Just beyond him is a man on the stairs, blood surrounding him.

The elevator pings and opens. Lorenzo shifts to block Mama and me as six men appear. The three of us each get off a round, each taking down a guy. Lorenzo's forced to fight one as the other two surge forward. Neither is looking at me. They're after Mama. I fire twice more, hitting one guy in the ribs and the abdomen. But I can't aim at the other and guarantee I'll hit him instead of my mom. They pull her into the elevator as I rush forward. The man who isn't bleeding raises his foot and kicks me in the belly, shoving me backward as the doors closed.

"Maria?"

"They got Mama. Go."

Lorenzo helps me to my feet as he yells commands into the earpiece. He wraps me in his arms as we enter the stairwell. He helps me past the two corpses, then lets go. He leads, his gun pointing downward as I follow with my gun pointed up. I may not have the same training as my brothers, cousins, and friends, but every woman knows how to get out of a building. The men in our family make sure of that. I see someone. I know none of our men are on floors above us, so I don't wait. I shoot. I hear the scream, then the thump.

"You okay?"

"Yeah, Enzo. Keep going."

We have six flights to get down, but we see no one else until we ease through the door and into the lobby. Our men swarm the place, and Carmine runs toward us.

"They took her out through the backdoor and into a van they pulled up practically into the building. It's bulletproof."

"Pros?"

I ask as I look between my brother and cousin. They both look at me, and I know the answer without them saying anything.

"Did anyone hear them speak? Were they Bostonians too?"

Lorenzo nods.

"Yeah. The two who tried to get into the office spoke. Thick Boston accents, but neither sounds like Italians or Irish. Hired men."

Carmine's phone rings, and he pulls it from his pocket.

"Luca? Is her tracker pinging?"

He puts it on speaker as we rush out to the SUV. I hear my oldest brother, and he sounds angrier than I've ever heard him.

"Yeah. Headed to the tunnel and 95."

The interstate. Jersey? Connecticut? North to Massachusetts? At least Mama's tracker is working, unlike mine did when the men in Miami took me. I get into the second row between Carmine and Lorenzo, and they practically smother me, but I feel safest between them. I don't want to sit alone in any row. Lorenzo wraps his arm around my shoulder, and

Carmine holds my hand. I give it a squeeze, then unlock my phone.

"Has anyone called Papa?"

Carmine nods as he now scrolls something on his phone.

"Him, my dad, and our uncles. Uncle Dom and Uncle Massi are on their way to Uncle Sal's. Our aunts are headed to Mama's with Papa."

Fucking hell. This must be a big deal if they want the husbands and wives separated. They don't want the whole family in the same place.

"Where are we going?"

"To Luca's."

My brother has a house in Queens that has a gated wall and security patrols. I think about Olivia and our morning together.

"What about Olivia and Sera?"

Carmine glances at me.

"Already on their way there."

I see the fear in his eyes as he mentions his wife. I hit my contacts, but my phone rings before I can hit the one that's calling me.

"*Piccolina!*"

Matteo's practically screaming through the phone.

"I'm here. I'm with Lorenzo and Carmine. You're not on speaker, but they can hear you if you keep screaming."

He lowers his voice to practically a whisper.

"Did they touch you? Are you hurt? I'm on my way."

"I'm all right, Matty."

I know a bruise is going to form on my stomach, and he'll lose every bit of his shit when he sees it. I'm not going to amp him up more by telling him someone kicked me. I've noticed that I've reverted to calling him Matty when I can't call him Daddy or when I'm happiest.

"I'm coming home, Bambi."

He's gone back to calling me that, too. I didn't know I missed it until he started saying it again.

"No, finish whatever you have to. Enzo said they sounded like Bostonians. Whatever you're dealing with isn't done."

"I'm not leaving you—"

"You have to. You and Marco are already up there. I'm safe. I'm with Carmine and Enzo. They're taking me to Luca's. He's already tracking Mama. Our dads and uncles are at Uncle Sal's. Our moms and Aunt Sylvia are heading to Auntie Paola's with Uncle Cesare."

Lorenzo leans, so Matteo will hear him.

"Every available man's headed to Auntie Paola's or Luca's. Carmine's staying at Luca's with Sera, Olivia, and Maria. I'm headed to Uncle Sal's after I drop off Carmine and Maria. Gabriele's already on his way to Auntie Paola's. Maria's right. Stay up there and find out what the fuck is going on."

Something niggles at the back of my mind. A memory that's struggling to come forward. I force myself to focus on Matteo.

"I'll text you every couple hours to let you know we're fine."

"Every hour, Maria. I swear if you miss a single one..."

"I know, Matty. I promise."

"I'll be home as soon as I can."

"I know. Just please be careful. If this is Jordan's doing or someone else's, and it's all connected, *and* they're willing to take Mama, then they're definitely willing to kill you."

"I know, *piccolina*. Remember to text me. I'm going to talk to Marco and figure out what we do next. I love you."

"I love you, too."

"Enzo. Carmine."

My fiancé says nothing else. The warning in his voice means he doesn't have to. If anything happens to me, he's holding them responsible. I hang up and immediately pull up my texts.

ME

> I'm all right Daddy. Promise. Be careful. Please. I love you and need you.

I get a response immediately.

MATTEO

> I need and love you too. No getting involved. Hide or stay down. Promise me.

ME

> I promise Daddy.

I don't get a response, and I don't expect one. I tried to shield my phone screen, but I'm pretty certain Carmine and Lorenzo saw at least part of what I typed. I don't even give a shit right now. Them knowing I call Matteo Daddy is the least of anyone's concerns.

All three of us put our phones away. Lorenzo's arm stays around my shoulder. Carmine takes my hand again, and I rest my head against him. We ride to Luca's in silence. Thank God I have my brother and cousin. I'd be a shaking and sobbing mess if I didn't. So many times, I wished I had a smaller family just so I could have a moment to breathe alone. Now is not one of those times. We need each other, and no one faces the world on their own. Whoever did this is about to find out that vendetta and vindictive aren't just words the Romans came up with. They're the words this Italian family lives by.

Sera, Olivia, Carmine, and I are sitting in Olivia and Luca's living room, pretending to watch a movie. None of us are concentrating on it, but it's better than staring at the walls or each other. My phone buzzes in my pocket, so I pull it out. I don't recognize the number.

"Carmine, I don't know who this is. Do I answer it?"

"Yeah. Put it on speaker."

I nod as I slide the screen to answer.

"Hello."

"Is this Dr. Mancinelli?"

"Who may I ask is calling?"

"Maria?"

I don't respond. I watch Carmine. For a moment, I wondered if they meant Auntie Carlotta. He nods and gestures for me to go on.

"Yes. Who is this?"

"I'm Kate Ryan."

Hell. It's Jordan's sister. I can't keep the bite out of my voice.

"What do you want?"

"I want to know what your mobster family did to my brother."

"What?"

"What did they do to him? No one's been able to reach him in two days."

"My family did nothing to him. But he hit me with his car. Did he mention that?"

"I don't believe you."

"I don't care if you do."

"You're going to regret going after my brother just because he didn't want you."

"Is that what he told you? We weren't dating. We hooked

up when we felt like it. I'm engaged now. I've never been interested in a relationship with Jordan."

"You cheated on your boyfriend with my brother. Then he
dumped you."

I laugh. I can't help it.

"Even if I wasn't with my fiancé, I wouldn't have chosen
Jordan over anyone else."

"You're lying because he rejected you."

"Whatever. Defend your brother. But my family did nothing
to him. I know where all of my family is, and none of them are
with Jordan. If you can't find him, that's your problem."

"Your Mafia family took him. If you don't let him go—"

"If you believe we're Mafia, then you should know why
threatening me wouldn't be a good idea. Do you really want to
piss me off if your brother is allegedly missing, and I allegedly
caused him to allegedly go missing?"

I know no one is listening, but in case she's recording this. I
pull up my texts and shoot one off to Matteo.

ME

> J's sister called me. Talking to her now. She's
> accusing us of doing something to J.

I wait for a response. Nothing comes in, so I focus on the
call again as Kate screams at me.

"Tell your family to let him go or you will pay even more
than you are now!"

My hackles go up.

"What did you do?"

"Nothing your family isn't doing to mine."

"Where is my mother?"

"Wouldn't you like to know?"

"Yes, I would."

"Ask your father why my family doesn't like yours."

"I already know. You're my cousin's third cousin through his father. You don't like that my family rose to the occasion, and yours failed miserably."

"No one gives a shit about that ancient history. This was way more recent. Ask your dad who your mom was really supposed to marry. Who she loved."

I laugh again.

"My parents have been in love since they were kids. She never dated anyone but my father. My grandfather tried to arrange a marriage for her, but my parents eloped."

"And who was she supposed to marry? She didn't love your father back then."

I look at Carmine, but he shrugs. He stands up and moves to a corner. I'm guessing he's calling my dad or his dad. Maybe both. That niggling sensation of a memory comes back to me. A story I probably heard as a kid.

"I don't know. You tell me since you know so much."

"My uncle."

My brow furrows as Carmine and I watch each other. She rambles, so I mute the call. Carmine comes over and has my father on speaker. I hear him speak.

"Mama was supposed to marry Antonio Morelli. He was related to the Ciccones, and my father thought it would be an olive branch. But Mama never wanted to marry him, and I wasn't going to let that happen. Mama and I knew we wanted to marry since we were teens. My father relented and arranged something between Mama's father and mine. We'd already eloped, though."

I'm still half listening to Kate. She's still ranting, and I needed to know this little piece of family history that probably would have been no big deal from now until eternity. But I wound up fucking the wrong guy. I turn my attention back to her and unmute.

"You're pissed because my mom chose my father just like I chose Matteo. No one ever wants your family. Doing this won't help your family's chance to rise. You will never match mine, so you should let my mother go."

"Once you give me back my brother."

We're going to go around in circles.

"You're not making a good choice. I seriously recommend you reconsider."

"Or what? They'll come after me?"

"The men in my family don't hurt women and children."

I leave the unsaid dangling in the air. Let her interpret that how she wants, but I won't say my threat aloud. She probably is recording this.

"Goodbye, Kate."

I hang up. I look at Carmine, who has his laptop open now. I noticed he got it once he brought his phone over to us.

"She's in Parsippany."

That's north Jersey and not that far outside the city.

"Mama or Kate?"

"Kate. I tracked the call."

My dad speaks up.

"Mama's tracker is going off there. Luca and Lorenzo are already on their way. They'll have her soon, and then we'll deal with this woman."

I'll fucking deal with this woman. The men won't hurt her, but I will.

Chapter Twenty-One

Matteo

After we visited Rowan, we search for Riley. The man is predictable and has been since college. It's four in the afternoon, and the guy is working out. More specifically, he's running along the Charles and easy to spot. The SUV slows as he reaches a stretch of the sidewalk along the river where there are few people. When we're a few feet ahead of him, Marco, two Vizzini men, and I hop out. We're all in our tactical gear, but we hide most of it with our hoodies. We have ball caps and sunglasses on with our hoods up as we join him on the sidewalk, jogging toward him. We box him in, and before he can do anything, we corral him into the SUV.

As much as I wish we could take him to the Vizzinis' place to interrogate and finish him, we can't. Just like Rowan, Riley may still be useful after this conversation. Instead, we head to Tommaso's dry-cleaning business in the North End. We pull up out back, and Riley has the sense to know fighting us won't do him any good. He didn't make a sound in the car on the way here, so we didn't have to say anything either. None of us took off our sunglasses or hats, but I'm certain he knows exactly who has him. I know he had to recognize me, even if we haven't seen each other in years and only spoken on the phone.

Marco shoves him out of the car and leads him inside. I follow, after looking around to make sure no one's getting nosey. There are no street cameras in this area, and the only one I spy is the one on Tommaso's business. The place is empty since this is a front for the Vizzinis' less than legal money laundering. They pay the Boston cops who have this beat well to pretend the only thing happening here is a bunch of shirts getting starched.

"Riley, you were never good at playing cards. You can't bluff for shit. Or maybe I just read you too well. I gave you the benefit of the doubt this time. I tried to keep this civil, letting you tell me what you knew. If you hadn't lied, you and Rowan would have gotten several grand for the product you were supposed to sell us. But then there was less for us, and now there's nothing for you."

"Nothing?"

I laugh at Riley's perplexed expression.

"Why the fuck would I pay you and your brother fucking shit when the shipment's a fraction of what you promised? And now you're so far up Jordan Ryan's ass that you're licking the back of his teeth. I'm not giving you shit after helping him. I'll take whatever the fuck I want, and there's not a damn fucking thing you can do to stop me."

My fist slams into his jaw. He staggers backward, and Marco's hands clasp his shoulders before pushing down. Riley lands on a chair and nearly falls off as it tips. Marco rights him and has his hands tied behind his back in a flash. I'm trying to keep my anger in check because if I don't, I'll kill him before I get anything useful from him.

I couldn't respond to Maria's text when it came in because I was in the middle of beating the shit out of Rowan with Marco. I had to call her back, and it was one of the worst conversations I've ever had. The only one worse was telling the others that someone had kidnapped Maria. Talking to Maria, learning they have Auntie Nicoletta almost pushed Marco and me around the bend. I want to know who the fuck this Kate Ryan is and how connected Riley and Rowan are.

"Who's Kate Ryan?"

Riley freezes for less than a heartbeat. There's the tell I'm looking for. He knows exactly who she is.

"Jordan's sister."

"And what's she to you?"

Riley's eyes narrow.

"Why do you want to know?"

"Because the bitch took my aunt."

Riley fights against the chair but quickly realizes he's going nowhere. Marco leans over and whispers in his ear.

"You have thirty seconds to tell me why the cunt took my mother."

"Give me a phone or let me get mine. Let me call her. She doesn't know what she's done. She doesn't get that none of this is fucking Hollywood."

I lean toward his other ear.

"You still haven't answered me. Who is she to you?"

Riley's inhale whistles. I crack my knuckles.

"My girlfriend."

I snort.

"By choice?"

"It was until now. I warned her not to get involved."

"Tell me everything she knows and thinks about our life. *Now*."

I stress the last word. I know Marco as well as I know

myself. He's on the precipice of losing all sense of reason. I know I have to do the talking because it'll come out a jumble if he has to talk about the bitch who took his mother. I'd be no different, and I'm barely any better.

"Her mom's side of the family claims the Mancinellis basically shot that Ciccone don in the back way back when. That they ratted him out to the feds, stole everything, then had him bumped off."

That's not entirely far off. Except, no one in my family ratted out anyone to the feds. That implies we were friends, or at least allies, and crossed them. Maria and Marco's paternal great-grandfather was a rival to Carmine's paternal great-grandfather from the very beginning. They both tried to build their businesses at the same time, but the Mancinellis did it better.

When the Ciccone don back then thought he could circumvent paying taxes completely, the Mancinellis called the cops on an illegal gambling ring. That signaled the Ciccones' downfall. Didn't they fucking learn shit from Al Capone and Mickey Cohen? From there, the Mancinellis' businesses gained ground, took over, and prospered. Maria and Marco's paternal great-grandfather—and actually, Carmine's maternal great-grandfather—did kill Carmine's paternal great-grandfather after the Ciccone don tried to knife his rival.

"And what? Jordan and Kate believe they can come for the Mancinellis and single-handedly take us down? Did they think your family could take us down?"

Riley shakes his head and closes his eyes as he tilts his head back.

"Jordan started it all when he realized he could hook up with Maria. He wanted to worm his way into your family, but I guess she never took it further than sex. He got impatient, then you entered the picture. That really pissed him off and spurred him to act. He thought he could make friends with the Colombians in

South America and New York. He was certain that if he started doing deals with them that not only would he have more money to get what he wanted, but he'd make allies who'd do the dirty work for him. He couldn't get anyone in New York to pay attention to him, so he's relying on his Colombian connections up here."

"And Kate?"

"She got greedy. Her family already has money, but I guess she's seen how your family lives and wants that. She wants us to have penthouses in Boston and New York, houses around the world. But she won't work for it. She thinks if Jordan takes you down, then as his sister, she's entitled to some of the spoils."

Marco practically snarls when he speaks.

"And you let her think this?"

"Let her? Kate does what Kate wants. I warned her this was a horrible idea. Hers and Jordan's. I told her that if she sucked my family into this bullshit, we'd be over. I told her she's more likely to wind up dead than living in a penthouse. She argued the syndicates don't touch women and children. I told her the shit that's gone down recently. She didn't care. I warned her that the men might not come after her, but the women might. And that's why I think she took your mom. She doesn't believe anyone can stop her."

He looks at Marco as he finishes. He appears a defeated man. He's probably wishing he never stuck his dick in Kate. Marco crosses his arms as he steps in front of Riley.

"A preemptive strike against us?"

"I guess."

I step next to Marco, my arms crossed too. These fucking families. The O'Malleys and the Ryans. Fucking hell.

"So, Kate got impatient that Jordan wasn't moving fast enough. He thought to undermine us from the bottom up, and she thought to go straight to the top."

"Pretty much. Look. She's not evil. She's ambitious. Her head's been filled most of her life with how she should be a Mafia princess. She didn't know my ties until only recently. She wondered if her Irish side of the family was linked to the O'Rourkes. Instead, she discovered her family is linked to mine. That's when she started plotting, thinking I'd do her dirty work. Like I said, I told her to lay off, or I'd break up with her. Clearly, she either thinks I won't, or she doesn't give a shit. Let me call her. I can convince her to back down."

I look at Marco, and we silently communicate just like we have since we were kids. The barely there twitch of his left eye tells me he's considering Riley's suggestion. The way the right side of my mouth pulls up slightly tells him I don't think we have much to lose at this point. Marco pulls his phone from his pocket.

"What's her number?"

"I don't have it memorized. She won't answer your number, anyway. Let me call from mine."

Marco tips the chair almost completely sideways while I yank Riley's phone from his back pocket. Marco lets the chair drop, and it wobbles as Riley tries to keep his balance. I swipe the screen and press Riley's finger to it to unlock it. Before I dial, I go into Riley's texts and start reading any that might connect the pieces. I show Marco the ones with Kate. At least Riley hasn't lied.

The last like thirty messages between them were her ranting and him begging her to stop. We skim a few more from Rowan, but there's nothing about Kate in them. Just vague ones about Jordan, the Diazes, and the Colombians in South America. The ones between Kate and him are way too clear. Riley tried vagueness in the beginning, but his dumbass girlfriend spelled out everything. I tap her contact, and we wait while it rings. Just when I believe it'll go to voicemail, a woman answers.

"Riley, I got her."

He looks up at Marco and me. I see him gulp. Good. If he fucking pisses himself, even better.

"Kate, you have to let her go. You are in way over your head. You don't understand that they won't stop until Mrs. Mancinelli is back with her family. They will take everything from you. Your family. Your money. Your life."

"Let them fucking try. They took Jordan."

There's a pause as Riley's brow furrows.

"No, they didn't."

"Then where is he? He hasn't answered any of my calls or texts."

"He's been at a hotel with that Brazilian woman. My guess is he's had his phone off to try to keep the Mancinellis from tracking him. He's going out with her, so he's not trying that hard to stay hidden. I've told him a hundred times to drop this. I'm telling you the same thing. Let this go before you both wind up dead. You will not win against the Mancinellis."

"No. They'll give me what I want to get the bitch back."

Riley flinches before he looks up at Marco, then me.

"Kate, let her go, or we're done. I'm not looking to die, and I'm already halfway there."

"What do you mean, halfway there?"

"I'm with Marco and Matteo, and we're not having beer and wings. Let her go, or we're through. My family is not going down for this, which is exactly what'll happen if I stay with you. I'm not getting my brothers, uncles, dad, cousins, mom, and everyone else within six degrees killed for you."

"They won't do shit if they want Nicoletta alive."

"Kate, you answered my call. You have your phone on. I can guarantee you they know where you and Mrs. Mancinelli are. It's only a matter of time. Let her go and come up here. I'll do what I can for you."

He looks between Marco and me, banking on the fact that we won't do anything to her as a woman. God help her if Maria gets to her. Auntie Paola, Aunt Sylvia, and my mom won't be any more forgiving. Serafina's from this world, so she won't be any less vindictive, and from what I've seen, Olivia won't have any trouble supporting a vendetta against Kate.

"Kate, this is Matteo Mancinelli. You have my future mother-in-law. You should listen to your boyfriend. You're banking on the men in my family not touching you. You're banking on the women in my family being like you. Untrained. You are seriously mistaken. There's nothing my fiancée won't do to protect her mother. Let Nicoletta go, and you might live if you come up here to Riley. Persist, and not only will you lose Nicoletta when the men in my family come for her, you'll lose your life when my fiancée, mother, and aunts get to you. Have you ever watched the nature channel? Lionesses hunt in packs at night. They will strike when you can't see them coming. They will circle you until there is no way out. They will rip you to shreds, so there's nothing left of you for anyone to recognize."

"I can defend myself."

Riley groans while Marco and I laugh.

"You have no idea what you've gotten yourself into, little girl."

That phrase doesn't mean even remotely the same thing as when I say it to Maria.

"I'll take my chances."

"You're a fucking idiot. Riley, any last words before she dies?"

"Kate, seriously. End this. Come up here while you still can. They aren't exaggerating. The Mancinelli women aren't to be toyed with. These are women who spent their entire lives with the Mafia. These are women who have survived multiple attempts on their lives. These are women strong enough to have raised the sons who will come for you. These are women who aren't afraid to argue with husbands who kill for a living. You are underestimating them and overestimating yourself. Please, Kate."

"I only like it when you beg during sex, Riley. You sound like a little bitch."

Riley leans forward as he looks at the phone.

"I'd say screw you, but that's never happening again. Marco, Matteo, send your family to Chestnut Street in Parsippany. The last house on the right before it intersects with Hazelnut. It's a two-story colonial with a red door. There's a porch swing."

"Riley!"

Kate screeches through the phone.

"You had your chance, Kate. You chose yourself over me. Now I'm doing the same. I'm not dying for you. Good luck."

He sits back and scowls at the phone. I offer the phone to Marco, but he shakes his head. I speak next.

"Sounds like you're out of friends. Your brother's ignoring you, and your boyfriend just gave us directions to you. Between my family already tracking you and Riley confirming your address, you're done. The women in my family will handle you. Since the men in my family won't touch you, we'll punish Jordan. I'd call him one last time. Leave a message and let him know he has thirty minutes until he dies."

I look at Marco, and he nods. I hang up before she can say anything else. I look down at Riley. Marco reaches out and wraps his hand around the *stronzo's*—asshole's—neck. He squeezes until Riley's face takes on a tinge of red that borders purple. He lets go.

"Take us to Jordan. Fuck around with us, and we'll get

Rowan. Then we'll torture the two of you. We'll kill him first and make sure you watch."

"They're probably at *Céu e Terra*. Her dad owns it. It's a front for some illegal import/export business."

Heaven and Earth. I know the restaurant. I didn't know about the illegal shit, but it doesn't surprise me. It's in a good neighborhood, and the food is excellent. It's the clientele that makes me question it. I've never heard anyone but the kitchen staff speak Portuguese, which tells me Brazilians don't eat there. Not a good sign when people from the same culture won't eat at a place.

Marco unties Riley and leads him back out to the SUV. While Marco handles Riley, I send Luca a lengthy text explaining as much as I know for now. If anything goes sideways, and Marco and I can't finish this, then someone needs to know what's happening. He offers to come up here with his brother, along with Carmine and Gabriele, but I'm confident we can handle this. Texting him is just part of a contingency plan. I really am not worried.

It takes a half-an-hour, but we're soon pulling up to the restaurant and heading toward the doors. Before we stake out the place, the rest of Vizzini men with us change, too. Now we're in all black with bulletproof vests. Russians aren't the only ones who can wear balaclavas. With the weapons we supplied, the Boston *Cosa Nostra soldati* follow Marco's and my orders as we branch off to cover the various exits and the parking lot. The Vizzini soldiers are almost as well trained as ours. I'll have to let Don Vizzini know they impressed me.

We have to wait an hour until most of the customers leave the restaurant. In for a penny, in for a dollar. Or whatever that old phrase is. I just want to be done with this and get home to Maria. What I need to do is figure out what the hell I can tell her. I can tell this shit won't end with a few phone calls and quick explanations.

We bring a lot of different equipment with us when we go on missions like this. We get Riley situated with a wire, so we can see and hear what's going on. It's nearing nine at night, so the restaurant is dimly lit. Before we can see anyone clearly at the table he approaches, we hear just enough to know the men are Latin American, and we hear Rowan too. Maybe he's trying to protect his family. Should have done a better job.

We have earpieces in to communicate. We take only a moment to end the inept men the restaurant owner assigned to the alley and doors. Marco lets me know the back is clear. He's entering through the kitchen. I'm headed in through the front door. I spot Jordan, Rowan, and Riley immediately. They're seated in a back booth with men I recognize from surveilling the Diazes in New York. I strip off my balaclava. I approach slowly, my hands where the Colombians can see them. None of them reach for weapons. That's a good start.

The woman next to Jordan turns toward me. Up close, I see her face.

Oh, fuck me. Fuck me. Fuck me. This is *soooo* much worse than even my worst nightmare could conjure.

"You're Giselle, aren't you?"

"Yes?"

She speaks English, but with a strong accent. Her brow furrows. Her gaze darts around as she takes in the *Cosa Nostra* men. She doesn't appear surprised at all. I know little about her, but my guess is she's familiar with the Cartel. It's not a stretch to understand the Mafia if Giselle knows about our Latin American equivalent. This shitstorm is building, and it's about to dump all over us.

"I'm Carmine's distant relative and friend."

There's something I wouldn't have said a year ago. We

could barely tolerate being in the same room. Now I actually really enjoy his company. This woman went out with Carmine a few times, but Alejandro Diaz was dating her then too. The pieces are falling into place. I bet he's her connection in Bogota.

"Carmine. I know that name. Why?"

"Playing dumb is not a good look for you, Giselle. You know exactly who Carmine Mancinelli is."

Her eyes narrow at me, and her attitude shifts. From what I remember, Carmine discovered Alejandro was into her. Like really into her. So, he walked away. Alejandro thought Carmine was being an asshole and suggesting Alejandro take his sloppy seconds. From what I also remember, Giselle wasn't pleased Carmine left her instead of the other way around. She wasn't accustomed to being dumped.

I wait for her to respond, but she says nothing. I supply the answer to her question.

"Enemies of the Diazes."

I'll let Carmine know she's involved since this means Alejandro is, too.

"Are you and Alejandro still friends, Giselle? How well do you really know him? You're playing a dangerous game involving them. They're not like the Cartels you might know from Brazil or the low-level drug dealers you've probably been scoring weed from since middle school. You might be safe with the Diazes, but your family and Jordan aren't. Enrique Diaz is the *jefe*, and you're still toying with his nephew. You can absolutely trust them. You can trust your family is in trouble if you've crossed them. None of the men in any of these families will touch you, but the women in mine will destroy you. They make all of us men look merciful."

I stare at Jordan, who still appears shocked to see me. Then I shift my gaze to the other men at the table. Rowan looks like shit. Riley's glancing at the exits, likely planning his escape.

"Jordan, you getting in the middle of my deal between Rowan and these men wasn't good for your health. You might afford one shipment, but you won't be able to remain a regular customer."

I look at the Colombians. They appear suspicious. Their English must not be great. I switch to Spanish for their sake.

"Rowan sold the bulk of the shipment in Texas, leaving me with a few kilos. Then Jordan got in the middle and negotiated with you instead of Rowan. You're having dinner with him. Seems like you'd rather do business with him than my family. Fine. But know that we will never do business again. The Diazes won't be pleased to learn you're doing deals directly on U.S. soil."

I pull out my phone and hit a contact. Everyone watches me as I wait for an answer. I put the call on speaker as a voice comes out of my phone. I continue in Spanish, uncaring whether Jordan, Rowan, or Riley speak the language.

"Enrique, I just walked in on a very interesting dinner meeting. It seems like the O'Malleys up here in Boston are striking deals with the Muñozes. Did you know that? Is Alejandro around? There's someone here who might want to speak to him."

Enrique says nothing to me, and it sounds like the phone changes hands.

"Matteo?"

It's Alejandro. I shove the phone in front of Giselle and still speak Spanish.

"Say hello."

"Hola, Alejandro."

"Giselle? Where are you? Are you all right? What's the fucker done to you?"

I pull the phone back.

"I haven't done shit to her. She's using your contacts in

Bogota—the Muñozes—to help the guy she's been fucking since high school score coke from your rivals with the help of the O'Malleys up here in Boston. They're all having dinner together right now at her father's restaurant."

"Giselle, is that true?"

From his tone, Alejandro isn't hurt. He isn't even surprised. But he is pissed. I've known him since we were kids. I can tell.

"I'm helping a friend."

"Let me guess. Jordan Ryan."

"How'd—"

"His sister kidnapped Matteo's aunt. My uncle's been on the phone with Don Salvatore Mancinelli for the past hour. Now I find out you're helping Jordan do business with our rivals, men who still technically work for us. Giselle, what have you done?"

"What I had to. You dumped me. Remember? I don't owe you anything."

Alejandro scoffs when he responds.

"What you had to. You're a gold digger. You thought Carmine would worship your golden cunt and that you'd trap him into marrying you. You played the same game with me in case Carmine didn't work out. You want the money our families have. Now you think Jordan is the next best choice. You think he's going to topple the Mancinelli family. Fucking idiots. Both of you. He won't do shit to the Mancinellis except keep pissing them off. His family has been useless for generations. And the O'Malleys?" Alejandro switches to English. "Rowan, you and Riley are dead men walking when Dillan finds out you're trying to run drugs without him. Fucking hell. Plan your wakes now."

Alejandro's laugh has no humor in it. I pull the phone back so he can hear me clearly.

"Oh, it gets better, Alejandro. Guess who Riley was dating just two hours ago. Jordan's sister."

"Rowan, Riley, you're both so fucked. Plan those wakes because you've already dug your graves."

I watch the Colombians, and it's clear they want out of the restaurant yesterday. It's useful being trilingual. Once more, I speak Spanish.

"Enrique, can you hear me?"

"Yes."

"What do you want us to do with the Muñozes?"

"Deal with them the way we would. I accept I owe you a favor."

"The drugs we were supposed to buy from the O'Malleys before Jordan got involved. We get those free without you getting pissed. Agree to that, and we'll call it even."

"Deal."

That was simple. I turn toward the Vizzini men posted just inside the restaurant. I wave them over. They grab the three Muñoz men, and I know they'll be at the Vizzinis' garage and dead within the hour. We need nothing from them, and I doubt Tommaso does either. They'll be quick kills.

"Alejandro, what do you want me to do about Giselle?"

"Send her ass to Rio or São Paulo. Economy. Fuck if I care. Dump her in South Boston if you want. She stopped being my problem years ago. Better yet, let Maria decide. Giselle helped Jordan, and his sister took her mother. I think that's fair."

"I warned her about the women in my family. She didn't take me seriously."

I look at Giselle and cock an eyebrow. She's looking way more nervous than she did a few minutes ago.

"More fool is she. The women in your family scare the shit out of everyone. They appear way too nice for it to be real."

I laugh. Appearances can be deceiving. Anastasia Kutsenko—a woman so thin a good wind could probably knock her over—is the only woman who looks less likely to kill someone than the women in my family, but I'm certain she's not just killed but tortured.

"And Jordan? He encouraged the Muñozes to stake a claim here. He got in the way of my deal, and he hit Maria with his car."

"Qué?!"

I hear at least five voices, so that means *Tres J's*—Javier, Jorge, Joaquin—are with Alejandro and Enrique.

"He clipped her with his car while she was on a ride."

Enrique's voice is like stone when he speaks.

"Do whatever the fuck you want with him, but take your fucking time doing it."

When we all played youth soccer, and it was his family's turn to bring the orange slices, he used to make sure Maria got first choice out of all the teams. With our age ranges, all our families had members on various teams. Totally and utterly fucked-up childhood. We played with and against one another, and now we barely keep from killing one another. He has a soft spot for Maria, so it doesn't surprise me he wants Jordan's death to be excruciating.

"I'll keep that in mind. I'll let you know when it's done."

Rowan and Riley must have understood most, if not all, of what we said since neither of them looks confused. Only Jordan does. I look at the brothers and stick with English.

"I haven't decided what to do with you yet, but that doesn't mean you're off the hook. You can start redeeming yourselves, though. Trash this place, then go to Giselle's place. Trash it too. Drain her bank accounts in the morning and give me the cash. I will know how much there should be. Then drop her ass in downtown or Roxbury without a phone, ID, or cash. Let her figure out what the fuck to do. If she makes it home, dump her ass on a flight to Feira de Santana."

It's the most dangerous city in Brazil. If she survives the shittiest neighborhoods in Boston without being the victim of violent crime, then she can take her chances in her homeland. I don't give a flying fuck what happens to her. She messed with my family twice. There's no chance for a third strike. She's already out. We don't touch women and children, but that doesn't mean we ignore them when they wrong our family. Someone else can do the dirty work. We just set it in motion.

Marco walks up to me and darts his gaze between Jordan and Giselle. I made sure my earpiece mic was on, so he should have heard everything. He steps in front of Jordan and yanks him out of the booth by the front of his shirt. Once Jordan's on his feet, Marco shakes him, then drives his fist into the guy's junk.

"I hate you because of what you did to my sister. You made sure her private life became public knowledge. You tried to intimidate her. You tried to hurt her. You made my little sister unhappy for even a second. You will suffer for that. Your fucking piece of shit sister took my mom. I can't do shit to her that I want, so I'll do it all to you. When I'm done with you, my sister's fiancé will have his turn. I won't kill you, but he will. I can't wait to watch."

I wave a couple more Vizzini men over, and they take Jordan from Marco. They'll make sure he's ready for us at the garage. When Rowan and Riley stand, I clamp a hand on each of their shoulders.

"You don't want to know what will happen if you fail. I can promise you that."

Chapter Twenty-Two

Matteo

We head to the Vizzinis' garage to have a little talk with Jordan. The guys who dragged him out of the restaurant now drag him inside. They strip him as I look around. I see exactly what I want. There's a support beam with knee brace joints that makes the beams connected to it form a Y. It's not very high because it holds up what must be Tommaso's viewing platform or something. It's about seven feet off the floor, so there isn't a whole lot of head room for men as tall as Marco and me, who stand a few inches over six feet.

"Tie him up to those."

I point to the beams while I saunter over to a table with various implements. I know Jordan's watching and wondering what I'm going to do. I make sure I look casual, as though I don't have a care in the world. Like this is something I've done so many times that it isn't a big deal to me anymore. The torture part does nothing for me. I've done it too many times for it to bother me these days. But knowing I'm going to make the man who hurt and scared Maria pay? That makes me almost giddy.

I look over my shoulder as he tries to fight the three men who drag him over. Two of them have chairs they step onto to lift him high enough. They use rope to tie him, and it's not long before it looks like he's being crucified. Just how I want it since that's exactly what I'm going to do. I grab a metal mallet and four three-and-a-half inch nails. The typical ones for carpentry and framing buildings. I signal for the men to leave the chairs where they are.

"Jordan, you made some serious fuck-ups. Do you understand why I can't and won't ignore them?"

"Drugs and a whore. You need to protect your pride because you're a Mancinelli, and all you have are drugs and whores."

My fist slams into his dick and nuts. He howls with pain. Did I mention I slipped on brass knuckles when I got the mallet and nails?

"You wanted into this life so badly. Now you're here. Now you'll know what it means to be *Cosa Nostra*. You're about to learn how we live. Let's see how you handle a little fun at your expense."

I step onto the chair beside his right arm. This is the one I broke, and the shoulder I dislocated. I know he's already in agony. I place the tip of a nail against the inside of his wrist, having to wiggle it in around his cast. Then I pound it with the mallet, making sure I have to strike it three times before the nail impales him. He's screaming loud enough to wake the dead.

"You know, we always talk about the nails in Jesus's palms. But, in actual fact, the nails usually went through the wrists of those being crucified. Way more painful. I took a few religious studies classes between my architecture ones. Fascinating stuff they didn't teach during Sunday school."

I get down and walk around to the other side.

"I'm going to put a nail through this wrist. You decide whether I do it with one mallet strike or five. Did you arrange for those photos?"

Between leaving the restaurant and getting here, we stopped by Giselle's place. We found photos I can't let myself picture right now, or I will go on a rampage. I step onto the chair. He glares at me mutinously. Oh, well. I put the nail to his wrist and tap it with the mallet just hard enough to break and imbed in his skin. He cries out again. I pound the nail a little harder this time, but it's still not enough to drive it through his arm. Luckily, I'm standing to his side because he pisses himself. All the men laugh. Marco scoffs.

"That was sooner than I expected."

"He's a pussy. I didn't think he'd last this long. Answer my question, and I'll put the nail all the way in with one more strike."

He continues to glare at me. All right then. I tap the nail slowly into his wrist, but when I'm certain it's come out the other side but hasn't imbedded in the wood, I stop.

"Fine! I had a PI take them. I paid him cash to keep him quiet."

I look at a Vizzini *capo*, and he nods. He'll take care of the guy. He'll make calls down to New York. I won't risk the man ever mentioning Maria.

"What else do you have planned?"

"Nothing."

"I don't believe you. I'm certain those photos delivered to you at Giselle's weren't the only copies. What were you going to do with them? Where's the other set?"

He hesitates, so I slam the nail into the wood. I climb off the chair and move to his feet. I position them and drive a nail through the top of his left foot.

"I was going to post them on porn sites."

"Was going to or already did?"

"Was going to. I planned to send the second set to her with web addresses."

"What else?"

"Nothing else to Maria."

"Then the rest of us. Did you plan to put hits on the men?"

"Yes!"

He wails as I drive the fourth nail into him.

"Tell me how you got involved with the O'Malleys and the deal I had going with them."

It still shocks me to know he's the one who fucked things up. He was a nobody to me a couple months ago, and now he's fucked up a sale that could have netted us almost a million dollars after we sold the shit ourselves. I'm still not sure if he knew we were the intended buyers, or it was just a shit coincidence that Rowan and Riley kept to themselves. It could have given me info about Jordan without searching, without beating the shit out of Rowan. I'm simmering over that one, so I wait for Jordan to speak up.

"The Columbians in Boston aren't like you. They keep their community pretty tight. They stick to doing business with each other in a lot of cases. But you can't do anything in Boston without someone who claims they're Irish."

Marco and I look at each other. He has said nothing we don't know. The Colombian community in Boston is small, like seven or eight thousand people, and they're all practically in one neighborhood.

"Rowan knew he needed to run some product to you. When Kate overheard Riley talking to someone, that's how I knew I could stir shit up here. I already planned to be here to see Giselle. I figured it was only a matter of time before you connected me to the Irish up here, so I reached out to Rowan before you did. I made him lie to you at first about doing a deal with the Colombians until I could make it true. I didn't have a buyer at first, but Rowan said I could sell it to Dillan O'Rourke. We figured the New York Irish would always want a way to fuck you over. I told Rowan that the deal I could score with Dillan would make whatever shit this stirred up with you seem like no big deal. He refused, so I told Kate to make Riley agree. I didn't know Rowan refused because Riley told him what Kate was thinking about. I didn't know because he was trying to help you. The dumb fuck should have mentioned my sister was involved and trying to get back at you. It wouldn't have stopped me, but I would have planned better with those two."

So, he did know all along. He was more than one step ahead of us. Jordan looks at Marco before he looks at me. It doesn't surprise me when Marco wonders if there's something more.

"Dillan's only involvement was refusing your shipment?"

I nod to Jordan, my gaze boring into him. He better answer Marco's question.

"Not exactly. Riley told him Kate was getting involved and decided to take Marco's mom."

That was something we'd hoped to keep to ourselves, since we hadn't figured out how to use it to our advantage with Jordan. We can't threaten Kate, and I don't want to bring Maria into any conversation with Jordan that doesn't involve him confessing shit. It reminds me of the conversation I had with Riley at the dry cleaners.

Marco and I look at each other, remembering the last time Dillan had anything to do with our business up here in Boston. Carmine was helping a Russian woman who was kidnapped by the same men who took Maria. She was the one who turned out to be the sister of the woman Misha Kutsenko married. Dillan inserted himself into the Albanian's *giak*, or blood feud. Since we don't need Jordan to know shit about the last time we dealt with Dillan before this shit really got going, I speak Italian.

"I truly thought we were done with Dillan and his fucking us over up here. Besnik and his New York counterpart were rivals for years, trying to increase their business with us. Wasn't it bad enough when Dillan found out about this and convinced Besnik to sell to him instead of us? Once he had that shipment, he lied to the New York Albanian leader and told him Besnik low-balled Dillan and got a better deal with Uncle Sal."

Marco nods as we both remember the sit-down we had with the Diazes and Kutsenkos over this. It was all connected to Maria's kidnapping nine months ago. Marco looks toward the door as he recalls the rest of what happened in Italian.

"He poured gasoline on the fire between them, hoping the Albanians would take out Besnik. That would have given Dillan the chance to expand into more of Boston. That would've been bad for us. Is that what he's doing now? That's why Carmine let Besnik live. We only sent a message. We could have killed him, but we wanted to make sure Dillan remembered to stay away from us and to make sure anyone else who thought to cross us knew how we would handle it. Looks like it should have been a more strongly worded message."

Neither of us bothers to mention the part where one of our informants spoke to Carmine right before he and Gabriele left for Boston. The real reason the Boston Albanian leader, Besnik, was in New York months ago was to set up the deal with Dillan. The informant gave Carmine more details about Besnik's deal with a half-Russian, half-Albanian man and about this foreigner's deal with Dillan. We learned Dillan was supposed to off Besnik if the New York Albanian leader didn't do it to end the feud. How the half-Russian, half-Albanian took the money from Dillan to pay for Larisa, Katerina Kutsenko' sister, in Texas and to take her to Boston. Motherfucking

Besnik went straight from Carmine to his meeting with Dillan. Would have been useful if our informant had put everything together a little faster.

When Carmine was up here handling that deal that went sideways, he assumed once Besnik's life was in his hands, Besnik would flip. But Besnik feared the Kutsenkos more than Carmine, apparently. If he'd told Carmine he was helping Misha, Carmine might not have let Gabriele rough Besnik up quite so severely.

I switch back to English as I ask Jordan another question.

"How does Kate play into all of this?"

"We were told about how the feud between the Mancinellis and Ciccones started because your however many great-grandfathers back stole ten grand from my great-grandfather's younger brother and killed my great-grandfather. The head of your family knew, but let his son or nephew hide in Jersey until he could go back to New York. I don't remember all the exact branches of your family tree."

Our family told us a wee more during our childhoods than just our great-grandfather stole and killed a guy. The Ciccone don back then was a boastful idiot. He's the great-great-grandfather Jordan and Kate share with Carmine. Don Ciccone's younger brother assaulted our great-great-aunt when she was barely fifteen. That's how the violence started. Marco's parents and mine shared everything their parents told them about the Mancinelli-Ciccone feud, so we could understand why Marco's grandfather treated Uncle Cesare and Carmine like shit.

"Okay?"

I want him to get to the point sooner rather than later. I want to go home to Maria.

"So, Kate thought the money I stood to make from the drugs would be enough to hire hitmen for all of you. She must have gotten impatient when she couldn't reach me up here and took matters into her own hands."

Jordan's growing breathless with each sentence. Blood's dripping from his wounds, and his face is pale. It surprises me how much we've gotten out of him so far. I'll push him until he passes out. He's nowhere near dead yet. I still have time to make him regret his choices even more.

"How much did Riley know about your sister's plans?"

"I don't think that much. He told me he tried to talk her out of it, but she wouldn't listen. He kept nagging me to talk to her, but I was busy."

Busy. Sure. Fucking Giselle and fucking my family over.

"I want to know exactly what you had over Rowan to get him to back out of his agreement with me. I don't believe it was just your connections to the Muñozes through Giselle."

Jordan pants, and his head lolls to one side. I wave my right hand in a come here motion to a Vizzini guy I see from the corner of my eye. He brings a bucket over. I toss it at Jordan, and he revives enough to pant out more of his explanation.

"Rowan's daughter isn't really his. His ex-wife fucked one of his guys and got knocked up. He didn't find out until a couple years ago when she got sick. Tests came back that he couldn't be a donor for anything and that he wasn't her bio dad. He loves his daughter even though he barely stands his ex-wife. I threatened to blast it across social media."

"Why didn't he kill you for that?"

"Because Giselle would have gotten the Muñozes to kill him and his daughter. They wouldn't have a problem doing that."

That sounds plausible. Enrique's been keeping them under his thumb for years, and they hate it. They think he's too soft because he has limits even he won't cross for retribution against families. He's made sure the Muñozes know he won't touch their women and children, but he'll make up for it with what he'll do to the men. That's why it shocked me to realize the Muñozes were doing a deal with Rowan, and why I wanted it done before Enrique could get involved. I didn't want the Diazes to believe I endorsed the Muñozes.

I need to detangle all this and wrap my mind around it all, so I think out loud.

"I had a deal with Rowan for the drugs the Muñozes were going to sell him. I only agreed to the deal to get more info about you. You stepped in and jacked-up the deal by trying to buy the whole shipment from the Colombians, which you were going to sell to Dillan. You did that specifically to screw my family over."

"Yeah. Not only would it have screwed you over, it would have made me enough money to bribe the right people into ruining Maria's reputation and destroy her chances of working in any hospital again."

He can barely form the words when he speaks again.

"Yes, I remember that threat."

I remember all the shit Jordan's done. I just haven't relived some of them in my mind; otherwise, he'd be dead, and we wouldn't know any of what he's told us today.

"You got Giselle to use her contacts to connect you with the Colombians. You already had plans for the money, and you knew that because of Riley's relationship with Kate, there wasn't much he or Rowan could do to stop you."

His eyes water, and he just stares at me. I draw my knife from my pocket and flick it open. I slide it along his chest. Nicking him enough for the pain to bring him around, but not deep enough to cause more serious bleeding.

"Kate's got a temper. Riley learned ages ago that it's easier to let her have what she wants. I guess she scares him more than you did. But she fucked all this up by going after Nicoletta. If she'd just waited a little longer."

Marco grabs a pair of pliers and puts them around Jordan's dick. He squeezes. Jordan's eyes glaze, and he looks like he's about to pass out. Marco releases him and grabs a bottle from the same table the pliers were on. He tosses the liquid on Jordan, and he shrieks. Immediately, the chemical burns rise on his arms and abdomen. Marco tosses a second round of acid on him before explaining.

"Since you started this shit that clearly made your sister think this was a good idea, I'm going to punish you for her choices."

We both know he knows nothing more. Riley told us as much on the way to the restaurant. We just wanted to see what Jordan would tell us. I step away to call Maria while Marco finishes Jordan. I watch the piece of shit breathe his last, and all I feel is relief that he's out of Maria's life.

I get off the phone with Maria, and I wish I had better news to share. But I had to tell her about the photos first. I just sent Uncle Salvatore and Uncle Massimo a group text to tell them the gist of it. It doesn't surprise me when my phone rings a couple minutes later.

After we finished disposing of Jordan, we headed back to the hotel. I was in the two-bedroom suite I'm sharing with Marco when I talked to Maria. But now we're in the lobby, so I switch to Italian after our greetings.

"*Zio Sal, siamo pronti per tornare a casa.*" Uncle Sal, we're ready to head home.

"*Cosa sta succedendo? Mi serve la storia completa, Matteo. So che sei andato a trattare con Jordan, e ora c'è la donna del passato di Carmine. Come sono coinvolti gli O'Malley?*" What's going on? I need the full story, Matteo. I know you went to deal with Jordan, and now there's the woman from Carmine's past. How are the O'Malleys involved?

"Non ci crederete. Quella donna è quella con cui Carmine e Alejandro uscivano. Quella per cui era così incazzato finché Carmine non l'ha affrontato. Ha avuto una relazione saltuaria con Jordan fin dal liceo e conosce dei colombiani che dovrebbero lavorare per Enrique. Non so molto di più. Puoi farlo sapere a Carmine? Ci imbarcheremo presto sull'aereo." You won't believe this. The woman's the one Carmine and Alejandro dated. The one he was so pissed about until Carmine dealt with him. She's been involved with Jordan off and on since high school, and she knows some Colombians who are supposed to work for Enrique. I don't know much more than that. Can you let Carmine know? We'll be boarding the plane soon.

"No. Devi tornare indietro in auto. Tuo padre ha dovuto fare un viaggio d'emergenza a Chicago. Ho già richiamato l'aereo." No. You have to drive back. Your dad had to make an emergency trip to Chicago. I already called the plane back.

I sigh. That's going to triple the time to get home. I want to get to Maria and find out what she plans to do to Kate. I want to help her when the reality of her actions sets in.

"Bene. Dovremo prendere una macchina." Fine. We'll have to get a car.

Marco only heard my side of the conversation, so I quickly fill him in. We change our plans, heading to the airport for a car instead of a flight. Luckily, paying cash means the car rental place is quick to give us an upgraded one-way rental with few questions. Marco settles in the driver's seat once we have the car picked out. We've already said our thanks and goodbyes to Tommaso.

Neither Marco nor I are feeling chatty right now. I don't know what to make of Dillan's involvement. Maria filled me in on a few things, and it's a stark difference from the last time we had to deal with them. They're permanently on the Kutsenkos' shit list. I don't think things will ever calm down between them. Carmine helping Larisa sorta soothed the Russians after the shit Luca and Carmine pulled that got Anastasia—Nikolai's wife—injured then abducted by a rival bratva from Moscow.

I wonder how Enrique's going to handle the Muñozes in Colombia. The Diazes are on slightly better terms with the bratva these days. We, on the other hand, are not on good terms with the Diazes. Maybe shit will calm down now that Giselle wronged both our families, so neither Carmine nor Alejandro came out ahead. She hasn't been in the picture for years, but syndicate families hold grudges better than most people.

Marco and I switch off driving when we get halfway. I text Maria that I'm on the way home, and she lets me know everyone is back at my parents'. When I called her earlier, she avoided telling me what happened to Kate. It's just as well that she didn't say it or text it. But I'm worried about her. I remember the first time I harmed someone by torturing them. It's way different from just putting a bullet in them.

I nudge Marco as we pull into my parents' driveway. We're both exhausted, but seeing Maria open the door takes the weight of the world off my shoulders. At least for now, until she tells me everything I missed.

Chapter Twenty-Three

Maria

Matteo just texted me Kate's address. He got it from some Irish twat up there. It matches where Luca's getting a signal from our mom's tracker bracelet and Kate's phone. I'm ready to tear this bitch apart.

"You are not going anywhere near this place, Maria."

I square off with Luca, who's giving me orders, and Lorenzo, who's nodding along with what our oldest brother says. I look at our dad, whose expression is grim. He doesn't want me involved, but he has the sense to know it'd be better if I go with my brothers. If they refuse me, I'll just deal with Kate on my own.

We've all convened at Uncle Domenico and Auntie Carlotta's. Carmine and Gabriele remain across the room, having already tried to convince me not to get involved. Fat fucking chance. Serafina, Olivia, Aunt Sylvia, Auntie Paola, and Auntie Carlotta stand behind me. Our family is physically divided in two, men versus women. Luca continues his attempt to dissuade me.

"You can only go as a doctor."

"What're you going to do with her? I know none of you will punish her like she deserves. It's not like we can go to the cops or have Aunt Sylvia file a protective order against her."

Lorenzo holds up his hand when he interjects, and it tempts me to slap it away.

"And she can't die. Her brother's going to. It's one thing for their parents to cover up why the Mafia took out their son. It's another to explain the death of both of their children."

"It's not like I can take her *there*. But I can rough her up and scare the shit out of her for good. Auntie Carlotta goes as the doctor in case Mama needs her. Aunt Sylvia files whatever lawsuit she can think of to ruin their family. Auntie Paola makes sure each of her clients understands their reelection depends on turning a blind eye to this, too."

Auntie Paola is a public relations and campaign manager for several politicians in New York. She's helped get the mayor elected and reelected. She got the governor into the mansion in Albany, and more than one person has enjoyed the power that comes with being a U.S. Senator or U.S. Congressperson. She's the one who makes any and all bad press go away, and Aunt Sylvia is the one who sues the ass off anyone, so they remember not to try making that mistake again. Our family is a business, and everyone works to support it somehow.

Papa steps forward when Luca and Lorenzo appear ready to strangle me. We all look at him.

"Take her. She'll do something on her own, and we don't need the risks that go along with that."

Rather backhanded, but I'll take it. I know he's scared to lose his wife and his daughter if this goes wrong. He's done everything he can to shield Mama and me, but sometimes best efforts aren't enough. I feel my phone vibrate, so I pull it out of my jeans back pocket. I let everyone know who it is.

"Matteo."

I step away and go to the opposite end of the spacious living room before I answer.

"Hi."

"Hi, *piccolina*. How're you holding up?"

"All right. Luca and the guys are going to take me to Kate's."

I wait for the explosion, but it doesn't come. That's way worse. That means Matteo doesn't trust himself to say anything. I whisper when I speak again.

"Daddy?"

There's a pause, but he responds.

"I expected nothing less. But be careful. Do the guys know who's there with Auntie Nicoletta and Kate?"

"Not yet. They're going in first. They'll sweep the place and make sure it's clean. Your mom is going in case we need a doctor, and I can't do it."

I wince. That's not what he wants to hear. I can and have stitched up plenty of members of our family. I've set bones and taken out bullets. But Auntie Carlotta is the surgeon, so she's better suited to those things. I've joked that we should get an x-ray machine and ultrasound unit for her house. I'm surprised they haven't shown up.

"Get her to a place that doesn't have carpet. Put trash bags everywhere. Twice the diameter you think you need. Touch nothing but your tools and her. Don't—"

"Matteo, I know. I've heard the lessons before, even if I wasn't supposed to. I already know exactly what I'm going to do. I've had plenty of time to think about it."

I hear Matteo sigh.

"Just make sure two of the guys are with you in case something goes wrong."

"You know there's not a chance in hell Luca, Lorenzo, Carmine, or Gabriele won't be there. They'll all insist, and that's fine. The cleanup is the only part that makes me a little nervous."

The more I think about what I want to do to her, the sooner I want to head out. I want this over, and I want my mom.

"I have *him* and will deal with the piece of shit as fast as I can. Then I'm leaving this fucking city."

"Do what you have to. I'm not going anywhere."

"Be careful, *piccolina*. There's only one of you, and I can't live without you anymore."

"Hurry up and come home. I miss you, Daddy."

"I love you."

We speak at the same time before we hang up. I wonder what he's going to do to Jordan now that he has him. I run upstairs to change. I have just the right stuff still at my parents. It's a bit of an odd combo, but I have black athletic leggings, a black turtleneck, black socks, and black ballet flats. I wrap my hair in a tight bun. Just before I leave, I remember something in my work bag. I have a black cloth surgical cap. The kind that sorta looks like a bonnet out of something like *Little House on the Prairie*. I rarely take part in surgeries, but I have done intraoperative imaging. I've also been on hand to observe some ablations. I keep it with me just in case. I didn't think I'd use it for a mission, but it pays to be prepared. I put it on as I dash back downstairs.

Uncle Salvatore, Uncle Domenico, Uncle Cesare, and Papa all hug us before we leave. Auntie Carlotta and Uncle Domenico exchange a kiss that makes us all turn away. My parents are probably the most discreet couple in public, but they're no better when they think they're alone. Auntie Carlotta, the guys, and I head out to the waiting SUV.

Luca slides into the driver's seat with Carmine in the front passenger side. He has a drone he'll release a few blocks away. Gabriele and Lorenzo are in the second row in case they need to get out in a hurry. If anyone were to get close enough to open the rear doors, they'll wind up with my brother's and friend's guns in their faces. Auntie Carlotta and I are in the third row. We have handguns while the guys all have rifles. Luca's stands between the back of the center console and Gabriele's right knee. The others have them across their laps.

We ride in silence all the way to north New Jersey. Funnily enough, when we reach Kate, we'll be about twenty minutes from Enrique's home in Short Hills. His family prefers Jersey once they settle down. Of course, Enrique lives in the wealthiest town in New Jersey. I can't help but roll my eyes. There's not a one of us in any of the syndicates who doesn't live in the most expensive or wealthiest places we can. That's one of our many rivalries. Enrique and Uncle Salvatore were on the phone for like an hour earlier. Enrique offered to help since he's so close. Thanks, but no thanks. This is our family, and we'll handle it.

"What the fuck are they doing there?"

My head jerks up as I realize how lost in thought I was when Carmine speaks. It's dark, so I squint. I can't see anything. I lean to see past or over Lorenzo's and Gabriele's shoulders, but they're just too big. I ask what everyone else wonders.

"Who?"

"Moth—the O'Rourkes."

Carmine catches himself before he swears again in front of

Auntie Carlotta. He looks sheepishly over his shoulder and winces. I glance at her, and she cocks an eyebrow. She's the one to absolutely not swear in front of. She used to threaten to wash our mouths out with soap while making us recite the rosary. When we were kids, we totally believed her.

Lorenzo shifts to look at the tablet Carmine's holding. It has images the drone's sending back to him. Now I can see. I recognize the SUV. Since all the syndicate families get our cars customized at the same place, and the vehicles are often at the same place at the same time, the body shop puts slightly different lug nuts on the cars to differentiate the families. Carmine's got the drone hovering close enough for us to see that.

We circle the block and stop four houses down, where there are no streetlights. There are other cars for ours to blend in with. It's not the only large SUV here. Someone's having a party, so no one will think twice about it. We ease out of the vehicle, and the doors barely click closed. Auntie Carlotta and I are in the center with Luca and Carmine leading, and Lorenzo and Gabriele covering us from behind. With so little lighting, we move with stealth and ease. We enter the backyard and come around to the patio sliding glass door.

When we get there, the curtains are drawn, so we don't know what we'll face. Luca gets the door open, and Carmine yanks the curtains back. Auntie Carlotta and I have our guns raised, and Lorenzo and Gabriele are positioned behind us, ready to aim. Luca and Carmine swoop in first, and we swarm the living room. Kate screams, the O'Rourkes draw their weapons, and Mama sits quietly. She doesn't appear rattled in the least, but she does have a black eye, and her cheek is bruised.

I aim my gun at Finn O'Rourke. He's the only one I know

won't do shit to me. He still owes me a massive favor. I got him out of the party where his date OD'ed on the drugs his family sold the hosts.

"Finn, who touched my mom?"

The O'Rourkes relax slightly, seeing we're asking questions before shooting. They move their hands where we can all see them. Finn turns toward me.

"Kate."

I push past Luca and Carmine, my gun now trained on Kate's head.

"Mama, are you all right?"

"Yes, *stellina.*"

Little star. I feel so relieved to hear that one word. It's like I can breathe again.

"Everyone out except for Kate and me."

"Hold on."

I keep my gun pointed at Kate as my gaze shifts to Dillan, the mob's leader. I narrow my eyes at him as I respond.

"Nope. Out. She's not related to you, so you have no claim to defend her."

"Maria, you can't—"

"Do you want to test me and find out?"

Mama stands and walks across the room to me. I lower my gun, then slide it into the holster Carmine gave me as we were leaving. The weapon sits against my lower back. We hug, and I inhale the faint scent of her perfume. I close my eyes for a moment, and it's like being a little kid again. Like my mom can solve all the world's problems. She whispers to me.

"You can't take back whatever you plan to do. Are you certain you can live with that?"

"And sleep like a baby. Mama, did she hit you?"

"Yes."

I lean back and study the bruised eye. Her cheek looks like someone slapped her. I dart my gaze to Kate. She's got fingerprints around her neck. I don't doubt my mom's stronger and better able to defend herself. Something kept her from killing Kate.

"Who helped her, Mama?"

She sighs. But it's Dillan who answers.

"We heard you shot most of the ones who came down from Boston. She also hired some of our guys. They can't do anything else."

They're dead or will be soon.

"Mama, I can live with it. Auntie Carlotta, can you make sure Mama only has a couple bruises?"

My mom gives me a long look before Lorenzo accompanies Mama and Auntie Carlotta into the kitchen. I keep my voice low.

"Carmine, find a bathroom with the narrowest tub."

He hesitates, and I know he's looking over my head at Luca and Gabriele while I watch Kate. I approach her but stay out of her reach. She's sitting on a sofa, so I lean forward.

"You made a huge mistake thinking you can do *anything* to my family. You made a monumental mistake to go near *my mom*. You want to be a Mafia princess? You're about to find out what this life really is. None of these men will touch you, but I will. I will make you pay for even looking in our direction. There's a reason my family rose to power and has stayed there for three, going on four, generations. You're about to discover it. Carmine."

He sounds resigned.

"I'll help you."

I know that doesn't mean just finding a bathtub. Luca steps closer to me, putting himself between the O'Rourkes and me.

"You heard my sister. Out."

Dillan sighs, and he's the sincerest I've ever heard him.

"There's shit you should know first."

We all look at Kate. Dillan waves over Cormac and Seamus, his cousins of some sort. Kinda like how Uncle Domenico is my dad's second cousin, except the O'Rourkes are all related by blood.

"Watch her. Maria, will you and Luca and Gabriele come with the rest of us?"

I look at Luca and Gabriele, who both nod. I follow Dillan, along with Finn and his twin brothers Sean and Shane, into the dining room. Shockingly, he pulls out the chair at the head of the table and steps aside, clearly offering it to me. I watch him sit to my left. Gabriele doesn't like that and glares at Dillan, who shakes his head but moves one seat down. Luca sits to my right. Carmine stands by the door, having followed us rather than find the bathroom. Shane stands on the other side of it while Finn and Sean also sit.

"We didn't know what was going on until two hours ago when one of our men got cold feet and wanted out of this shit storm. Too late for him, but we found out what was going on."

I meet Gabriele's gaze several times when he looks at me before sweeping his eyes over everyone else. Dillan sounds calm—which is still shocking the hell out of me. I'm waiting for the brash or grating tone he usually has. It makes me wonder just how connected he is to the Ryans if he's taking this in stride. That, or he's a more phenomenal actor than he rarely has been before.

Finn speaks up again.

"Maria?"

"Yeah."

"Hear us out. All of it. But only if Kate remains unharmed

while you do. So, you better tell me now if Lorenzo's going to do anything while we're in here."

"Who else knows what's going on?"

"Jordan, and Rowan and Riley O'Malley up in Boston."

The O'Malleys? What the fuck is Kate doing with them? I assumed Jordan had something to do with them since Matteo is up there.

I glance at Sean and Shane, and it's my turn to doubt whether Carmine, Gabriele, Luca, and I should hear what Finn has to say next. I shift to see through the door, and I spy Kate watching us. I know the O'Rourkes are fluent Spanish speakers, just like my generation of Mancinellis are because we had to take it in school. I don't know about Kate. I don't want her to understand what we discuss since it may influence how I handle things.

If the situation were reversed, I know the O'Rourkes would protect their plans, too. I can concede to some things. It won't kill me to change some of my plans. Some. Not all. And not any more than what I feel I must to get their cooperation. No need to get carried away.

Kate watches me throughout this conversation. Her furrowed brow tells me she can't hear well, but I'm still switching to Spanish.

"Try to see things my way, Dillan. We still have a little while longer until her parents wonder what's happening to their children. Matteo and Marco will be back pretty soon, so we need to tie up the loose ends here."

Dillan looks way more agreeable than I expected. I'd doubted whether we'd made the right choice to have this sit-down. I suppose I'm just glad they aren't arguing with us. My family and I want this resolved soon, so I guess we're stuck hearing them out.

Something annoys Dillan when he glances down at his

phone and sees who's calling. When he answers, he puts it on speakerphone and taps his finger to his lips.

"Rowan, this isn't a good time."

"Matteo's in Boston, and he's after Jordan Ryan. He's connected to Maria."

"That confirms what I've heard. Does he know you got yourself into this shit?"

"You need to call him. He flipped out when he found out we're involved."

"I don't doubt that. I will once I'm done with my current meeting."

There's a long pause before this guy talks again.

"Are you with the Mancinellis? I figured you would be soon. Robby and Mikey couldn't find you at any of the pubs."

I remain silent, just rolling my eyes. We can all disappear when we want. We all know that.

"Yeah."

"Dillan, don't waste time. Call Matteo before he can call you."

"I will. But I'm in the middle of talking to some of the Mancinellis. Since you've been involved since things started with Jordan and Kate, you should be on this call too. We won't know what's really going on until we hear your part and put it together. You're on speakerphone by the way."

There's another pause, and I can practically hear the guy shaking through the phone.

"Fine. Let me get Riley on here, too. My brother and I aren't in the mood to get shot today. A few minutes, okay?"

"Nope. Call him now. You're not getting time to come up with lies."

I see Dillan mute the call before he looks at me.

"Rowan runs the Irish in Boston. His brother, Riley, has been dating Kate for a couple years. My guess is Matteo and

Marco have already paid them a visit. They're still breathing because they must still be useful. If they aren't, then I'll let Matteo know."

I nod, then we wait. I wonder if I should get Matteo on the phone, too. Carmine, Gabriele, Luca, and I are just looking at one another when my phone buzzes. It's Uncle Salvatore this time. I glance at the O'Rourkes and decide Italian is the better choice. He tells me nothing I want to hear. Uncle Domenico has to take the plane for an emergency meeting in Chicago. The only choice for Matteo and Marco is to drive back to New York. We hang up, and I explain what's going on to my family in Italian. I sit back while we wait for this Riley fucker. He better tell us whatever he can.

It's the O'Rourkes turn to talk amongst themselves, and they use Gaelic. I can't blame them. I never hear my name, and I'm certain that's intentional. But there's no way they aren't talking about Kate and me since Dillan's looking straight at the witch.

Everyone but Dillan is looking around and already getting annoyed when my phone pings, and I look down to see a text from Uncle Salvatore.

UNCLE SALVATORE

> Matteo and Marco are already on their way
> home. They took care of everything up there.
> Call him before he calls you.

I barely have time to read the message before my phone buzzes again. It's Matteo. I get straight to the point.

"We're at Kate's. The O'Rourkes are here."

"What?"

It's a good thing this call isn't on speakerphone because they'd all hear how much he dislikes knowing I'm anywhere near the Irish. It only takes one word to convey all that.

"Dillan, Finn, the twins, and their cousins are here. Dillan has Rowan on hold, and we're waiting for this guy's brother to get on the phone, too."

"Where are Carmine, Gabriele, and your brothers?"

"Lorenzo's with Mama and your mom in the kitchen. Luca, Gabriele, and Carmine are with me in the dining room."

"Have Gabriele take you out to the car. I need to talk to you, but we need the jammer."

I turn my attention to the biggest of all the guys in our family. Just looking at Gabriele is enough to deter most folks from approaching.

"*Vuole che mi accompagni alla macchina perché vuole che usi i disturbatori di segnale.*" He wants you to take me to the car because he wants me to use the signal jammers.

He stands, and so do the rest of the men. I don't remember the last time I sat at a table with any of the O'Rourkes, so I was unprepared for them to have the same ingrained manners as the men in my family. I've seen the bratva men and know they do the same. When a woman stands or arrives at the table, the men stand too. Old-fashioned, but I like the tradition. I think it's sweet. I smile at the Irish before Gabriele leads me to the front door. I hear Luca explaining that I need to take the call in private. I'm certain they understand why we're headed out to the car. Gabriele and I hurry down the street, but we keep a pace that won't draw attention.

I climb in, and Gabriele flicks a switch up front.

"Matteo?"

"Yeah. I'm still here. I'm going to tell you what I can. If I leave anything out, it's because I can't tell you."

"I know. I won't ask. I'm putting you on speaker with Gabriele here."

"Jordan's dead. We found him and took care of it. He was

with some guys who supposedly still work for Enrique in Bogota. We know Giselle's involved."

"What?"

Gabriele stares at me before looking at my phone. His gaze falls on me next. He's Carmine's closest friend, so he may as well be my cousin too. He recognizes the woman's name as well.

"We found them having dinner together. I found out that he's been involved with her since they were teens. It didn't take long to know that she was Jordan's connection to the Colombians. Her family supplies the Cartel with materials to make their coke. Jordan and Giselle met the Colombians and Rowan at her father's restaurant. Riley went in with a wire, so we knew who was at the table before I went inside. I heard Jordan making an offer to someone. When I joined them, I recognized the guys. Vizzini men came in and took the Colombians away, but I let Jordan stay while I was on the phone with Enrique and Alejandro. He heard Alejandro's suggestions for how to handle Giselle. Once that conversation ended, Jordan, Marco, and I had a private conversation somewhere else."

Somewhere else. I'm certain the Vizzinis have a place like we do. I wonder for a moment if it's a garage, too. But I have a more pressing question, considering I was just sitting with New York's mob leaders.

"How'd the Irish get involved?"

"Jordan approached Rowan and told him he could get the O'Malleys a better deal than with us. We were only doing the deal to learn more about him. That's when he brought Giselle in to connect him to the Colombians. Once we got all we were going to learn at the restaurant, we took him there."

There. The code word in our family. It doesn't matter where "there" is, "there" is always the same. The place where my family handles business. The place I wish I could take Kate.

"We headed to Giselle's after we finished. When we got to her apartment, Marco went to her desk and pulled open all the drawers. I watched him retrieve a manila envelope. He dumped photos on his desk and spread them out. Luckily, only Marco and I were in there because when I stepped closer, my jaw hit the ground. I could barely look at your brother."

"What did you find? Matteo, get to the point."

"According to the concierge, when we went back downstairs, they arrived an hour before we got there. I want you prepared before I come home. I may need to tell Aunt Sylvia about these photos in case she needs to file a protective order or something."

It doesn't surprise me that Aunt Sylvia might know at least some of what's going on. She doesn't get involved in *Cosa Nostra* business, but Uncle Salvatore trusts her opinion. We all do. We learned early on that she's glamorous *and* wickedly intelligent. She's known no life but the *Cosa Nostra*. She understands people on an intuitive level, so she's been invaluable to Uncle Salvatore when he's sought her advice.

Matteo pauses, as though he's gearing himself up to tell me whatever's coming next. It makes my stomach clench.

"I picked up one photo after another. They're shots of you in our condo, in our bedroom. You're partially undressed in all of them. They're even two of you in our room at my parents'.

"How the fuck are they getting these? I don't think I've had the blinds open once at your parents'. And the windows at the penthouse are double-sided, even at night."

I struggle to control my temper, lest it gets the better of me, and I can't think clearly. No one needs me going on a shooting rampage without knowing who to target. Matteo doesn't have an answer to my question, but he lets me know he feels the same way I do.

"Thank God none of them show parts of you a bikini

doesn't cover. I'd go totally ape-shit then. It would have been fucking uncomfortable for your brother to see that. But knowing someone saw you naked to take them would send me around the bend. I keep trying to tell myself the photog might be a woman, not that that's any guarantee the person wouldn't get off looking at my beautiful fiancée."

The compliment is kind, but it does nothing to allay my fear or tamp down my anger. Matteo has more to say, and I wish he would just stop.

"Once Marco had a glance at them, I studied them. I couldn't get any info from them, so I put them back in the envelope. I couldn't stand to see them just strewn on Giselle's desk. I considered destroying them, but I can't until I know who took them."

I dart my gaze to Gabriele, who's averted his eyes, then to my phone.

"Even if you don't know how they're getting them, do you have any idea who sent them?"

"No. The concierge didn't know who dropped them off. I called the courier company, and they said it was a teenager."

I cock an eyebrow and lean my head forward. Gabriele apparently understands what I'm wondering because he speaks for the second time.

"Asian."

I inhale deeply, then sigh. That gives us no hint to who. I highly doubt the Chinese triad or Japanese *yakuza* are involved in this. As far as I know, we're on good terms with syndicates from both countries. They like our weapons and how we run drugs for them. They won't jeopardize that. I shake my head.

"They did that on purpose."

I didn't need to state the obvious, but I'm so annoyed I spit it out. Gabrielle's expression tells most people nothing, but the guys and I know when he's pissed. Not my level pissed, but he's angry. Whoever delivered these photos to Giselle purposely picked someone we couldn't link to the major syndicates: the Italians, the Irish, the Colombians, or the Russians. It doesn't even connect us to some of the lower-level ones like the Albanians. Grrr. This is so fucking frustrating. I have way more questions than anyone has answers. What the fuck next?

Chapter Twenty-Four

Maria

Gabriele and I head back into the house, and we talk to the guys. I can admit I'm way too embarrassed to tell my mom and Auntie Carlotta that there are photos of me half naked floating around. It's uncomfortable enough telling two of my brothers and my cousin, but it'll have to come out at some point because Aunt Sylvia has to know in case she needs to file some motion or suit.

Once we're all seated at the dining room table again, with Mama and Auntie Carlotta now in a bedroom where Mama's resting, we go back to talking to the O'Rourkes. I have a single burning question.

"Why are you helping us?"

Finn's gaze locks with mine, and I know the answer before he speaks.

"We can't stand the men in your family, but you kept me out of prison and likely kept me alive. We won't overlook that favor, and it isn't one that we believe we've paid back. Just like all of us, God's will sucked you into this life by making you have the parents you do. But you've always been kind to us. We know you don't like us any more than we like your family, but you've never wronged any of us. Just the opposite. You helped me, and you deflected plenty of questions from other kids when we were in school."

"Any answer you gave would have involved us, too."

We all know that, and I know I'm being snide when he's being sincere. But I want to know what happens next.

"What now? You ignore what the O'Malleys did? You let me do what needs doing here? You ignore that a fellow Irishman died at my fiancé's hand?"

"Yes."

I cock an eyebrow at Dillan's response. I wait for him to speak, and the guys in my family seem fine to let me lead these negotiations. There's a first time for everything.

"The O'Malleys run Boston, not us. We have influence over them, but they're not vassals or some shit like that. We have close ties, but they are not us, and we are not them. They got involved in this. We ignore what they did, so your family can do what needs doing. Three out of the four syndicates in this city have been shit about respecting the unwritten rule that women and children are off limits. My family's been the worst. Donovan and Declan dug us into holes I couldn't get us to climb out of. I had to do what I had to do to protect our interests. Doesn't mean I morally agree with all of it."

"Morally agree? I'm fucking morally gray at best, along with any other woman in a syndicate family. You—you and your family and every other man in this world—are morally black. Good thing for Matteo that morally black is my favorite color. You know he's going to have shit to say about all this."

"None of us doubts that. He should. You're his fiancée, and Mrs. Mancinelli is his future mother-in-law. That's why we aren't trying to intervene on the O'Malleys' behalf or derail Matteo and Marco's plans."

"And Kate? You can really walk out of here and let me do what I want?"

Shane and Sean have been silent throughout this conversation. Sean speaks up. He's probably the most soft-spoken in his family, but he's the most likely to dig his heels in.

"We'll help you clean up the *fecking* bitch."

I didn't expect that. I narrow my eyes to let them all know I'm suspicious.

"Look, she and her brother tried to get in the way of what would have been a good business deal for us that would have had your family paying us indirectly. *Relying* on us indirectly. We're out the money and the leverage. They're bringing in new players to this game, and the table only seats four. Plus, like Finn said, you haven't wronged any of us. Just the opposite. We haven't done right by women recently because none were women connected to our family. We've known each other since we could barely walk, Maria. It's just different."

Sean sits back and crosses his arms, glaring at Luca then Carmine then Gabriele, daring any of them to disagree with him. I lean forward and stare at Dillan.

"You like being the puppeteer. You like yanking everyone's chain and making everyone dance to your tune. I'm not interested in putting on a show for you. Maybe you have turned over a new leaf, but I don't believe you or trust you. Since you lead, that means I don't trust anyone beneath you. You need to do a shit ton more than show up here to prove to me—to prove to anyone in my family—that you aren't the shitbags you've made yourselves into."

I know I'm throwing their *kindness*—yes, I use that term sarcastically—back in their faces. But I don't trust them, and it is going to take a lot more than a few pretty words right now to make me believe for a second that they're trustworthy after seeing what their family did to bratva and *Cosa Nostra* women.

"You want me to see this as a show of good faith? You need to do more than sit across from me. Since the Ryans decided to play up their Irish side for more than St. Patrick's Day, you can make sure Jordan and Kate's parents understand the mistake they made by going to the O'Malleys against us. You make sure they keep quiet. And if they don't, you don't do shit when *we* silence them. This is on you since you had men come near my mom, and you got into bed with Jordan."

I scoot my seat back. We've already been here longer than I expected. Old habits die hard, so I push in my chair. I turn toward the living room where Kate's still waiting. She looks like shit. Her nose is red and running, and she's sobbing. Her hair looks like she's been pulling at it. I walk over to her and snatch a handful of hair before she can anticipate my moves. I drive my fist into her eye. Then I look at the O'Rourkes.

"Get comfortable. This won't be fast. Carmine, find the narrow tub and fill it."

I shake Kate before shoving her away. I lean forward and whisper to her.

"Jordan told me you were a swimmer. We're going to see how long you can hold your breath."

I stand and cross my arms until Carmine returns and says the tub's full. I jerk my chin, and Gabriele and Luca drag her upstairs and down the hall with me following. Once we're in the bathroom, I look at the guys.

"Leave."

"Mar—"

Luca starts to speak, but I herd the guys out and slam the door. I'm quick to lock it. I spin back around to Kate, knowing she'll fight back if she gets the chance. I pull the gun from the holster at my lower back, flick off the safety, and point it at her twat.

"Strip."

She stares at me for a moment, and I take a step closer, my gun still pointing at her vag. She pulls off her clothes after kicking off her shoes. I grab a bath towel and twirl it until it's rolled lengthwise. Then I snap it at her. She stumbles back, and I spin her to face the bath. I holster the gun again, then shove her onto her knees. I wrap the towel around her throat as tightly as I can before forcing her head under water. She thrashes, but I'm stronger. Before she can pass out, I pull her head up.

"This part of your punishment is for conspiring with your brother to do anything to my family."

I shove her head back into the water, pulling her out and dunking her seven more times. I know she's panicking, sucking in water, and feeling it burn as it enters her lungs. She's expending the air she has in her lungs by trying to resist and scream. Oh, well. She's spluttering and trembling when we get to the eighth time. I hold her down until she stops thrashing. I give it ten seconds, then pull her out. I don't want her dead. Yet. I look around the bathroom and open a couple drawers until I find what I want.

"Get in. All the way. Shoulders submerged. This is for coming near my mom and daring to touch her."

She watches me with pure terror as I pull out a curling iron. I hand it to her, and she knows what's coming.

"Put it in the water."

I want to tell her between her legs, but I force myself to have some limits. I made sure the switch was on before giving it to her. Now, I check my hands and my feet. No water near or on me. I plug it in. She screams. I pull out the plug. I watch her, my eyes narrowed, looking for the signs of an electrical burn. I see the mark on her arm. I plug it in again. She convulses. I pull out the plug. I wait at least five minutes, making her watch me and the plug, wondering what will come next.

"Let the water out, then climb out."

I wait for her to follow my commands. She's quick to comply. She's unstable on her feet, and I take advantage of her leaning forward to wrap the towel around her neck again. I twist and tighten, yanking her to bend in half. I watch her face turn red then purple. Before she can pass out, I pull the towel from her throat. She collapses. I don't mind waiting. I got lucky that I didn't kill her. I was willing to take the risk, and I came out the winner. Barely.

I know the guys are still outside the door, wondering what the fuck I'm doing in here. I'm not yelling, or even talking to her. I'm certain they're getting anxious. I've found patience I didn't know I had. The minutes tick by until she comes round again. I grab her hair and yank her to her feet, enjoying the power that comes from manhandling her. The rest of what I'm doing doesn't elicit a reaction from me. Not nervousness. Not eagerness. Not satisfaction. It just feels right. Is this how the guys feel?

I examine her wounds from the electrocution, and from having the towel wrapped around her throat. Her eyes are bulging, but otherwise, she really doesn't have many outward signs that she's being tortured.

"Get dressed."

I wouldn't care if a house full of men saw her naked, and it humiliated her. I don't want Mama or Auntie Carlotta to see me humiliate her. I saw an electric razor when I pulled out the curling iron, and it tempted me to buzz her head. But that will draw way too much attention with way too many people asking questions since I have to let her live. When she has her clothes on, I open the door.

"The towel on the floor, the door and drawer knobs, the bathmat, the tub, and the curling iron."

That's all I say. They know I'm listing the things either of us touched. The things that will need destroying or scrubbing. They stare at me, each taking a moment to dart their eyes over my head to the curling iron laying wet on the floor. I nudge Kate forward. Fortunately, the bathroom is closer to the stairs than the bedroom where Mama's resting. With my gun out yet again, I instruct her to head to the kitchen. Carmine, Luca, Gabriele, and now Lorenzo follow us. I glance over at the O'Rourkes who are speaking in low tones in the living room.

When we get in there, I go straight to the cabinet beneath the sink and use my shirt to cover my hand as I open it. I grab six garbage bags. I spread two over the kitchen table and the rest on the floor.

"Lean over the table."

I want her to watch and wonder. I sweep my gaze around the room, taking in all I can. I'm not entirely sure what's coming next. It'll depend on what I find. I grab a dish towel and use it to pull open drawers, but there's not much that's useful. Then I get to the bowl with potatoes, onions, and ginger root. Winner, winner. Chicken dinner. I snag the ginger and grab a knife. I grab paper towel and lay it out on the counter before peeling the ginger. When I have it whittled to the size and shape I want, I saunter over to the table. Kate's watching me. She has no idea what's about to happen. Good.

"Pull down your pants, then lean over the table again."

Good thing I'm a doctor and have no aversion to any part of the human body. I grab an ass cheek and shove the root in. I push it as far as I can. She howls. I don't give two shits what damage I may cause to her rectum and colon. Fuck the cunt. I step back and wait. I grin as she whimpers and shifts. I grab a wooden spatula and nail her ass.

"Don't move."

She listens and remains still, but she's back to sobbing. I step where she can see me and fist her hair, pulling up until she yelps from the neck pain.

"This is so you think twice before coming near my family. You want the Mafia life? Welcome to it. Fuck with us and find out. Your brother's dead. We're doing your parents a favor by not killing you, too. Breathe in our direction again, and not only will I really torture you, I will make sure you live a long and solitary life. I won't kill you. Then your suffering is done. Why let the devil have all the fun? You won't go to hell for a long, long time. I will keep you in misery. Never underestimate my family, and especially me, ever again. You will never win. I will fuck with your mind until there is nothing left."

I curb my desire to do way more. If I do, I may very well kill her. But I have one last treat for her. I go back to the knife I used earlier. I move a chair onto the spread-out garbage bags, remembering Matteo's instructions to double the diameter of what I think I need.

"Pull up your pants and sit on the chair."

I grab her forearm and push up her sleeve. Once more, good thing I'm a doctor. I use the knife to cut what looks like tracks on her arm, then I slit her wrist in a way I know will leave a scar but won't cause her to bleed out. I repeat the process on the other arm. Now she practically has the stigmata and something to remember me by.

I step back and examine her. Her burns are bad and really should be treated at a hospital. Too bad, so sad. The cuts on her wrists don't need stitches, but they should have pressure applied to them. Too bad, so sad. Her asshole is probably raw and should have the ginger taken out. Too bad, so sad. She'll survive, but she'll have visible and invisible scars to remember what happens when she crosses a Mafia daughter.

"Vengeance is mine, and I will repay," saith the Lord. *Doesn't mean I can't have a vendetta and be vindictive. We're selective Catholics at best.*

I can justify my own thoughts and deeds. Morally black is my favorite color, after all.

I sigh as I watch Matteo walk toward me. The O'Rourkes did as they said and what I decided. Carmine and Gabriele stayed behind to oversee the cleanup, which the O'Rourkes handled personally. Apparently, Merry Maids would hire them all. Luca and Lorenzo rode back with Auntie Carlotta, Mama, and me. Neither my aunt nor my mom asked what happened to Kate. She was getting into the back of Cormac's car when we walked outside. More accurately, Cormac was laying her across the backseat.

I swept through all the medicine cabinets and found a nice little cocktail of Butalbital, a barbiturate used for migraines and tension headaches—I guarantee she already had a roaring headache, and that ain't gonna make it better—and cyclobenzaprine. That's a muscle relaxant, and what I found is an unusually high dose from a patient in a nonclinical setting. I actually cut it in half. Together, these are two out of three ingredients for lethal injection. The muscle relaxant is a much milder version of the neuromuscular blockers used for capital punishment, and I'm not giving her potassium chloride. I'm not even injecting her. But she's going to feel like shit for a long time.

She's so sedated she won't know her own name for at least a day. She won't give Cormac any shit when he drops her in Mott Haven, which is one of the roughest neighborhoods in the Bronx, which is the roughest borough in New York. If she winds up in a hospital, the tox screen will look like she fucked up self-medicating.

But now that's over, and Matteo is hugging me. I've been waiting two hours for him to get back.

"Daddy."

I inhale his cologne, and everything is back to being right in the world. When we kiss, my toes curl in my shoes. I've already showered and changed. I'm certain someone in my family burned the clothes I wore.

"*Piccolina mia.*"

He nuzzles my neck and kisses behind my ear before our lips meet again. We keep the kiss tame since the entire family is here. We head inside, and it isn't long until we're all sitting in the living room explaining the various sides of the fucktastrophe we survived. I keep looking at my mom, worrying she'll be disappointed in me for dealing with Kate.

She doesn't know the details, and all the guys—Mancinellis and O'Rourkes—agreed what happened in that house will never leave the house. I actually trust Dillan and his relatives to never breathe a word about what I did. Endangering me...Now that Matteo and I are engaged, they know facing Matteo means no one but he will come out the winner. It would be the same if they went after Olivia, and Luca sought revenge. Or if they went after Serafina, and Carmine doled out retribution.

Once the conversation winds down, I lean against Matteo and whisper to him as he pulls me closer.

"Can we go home?"

He hesitates and looks toward the stairs before he nods.

"The only thing I don't know yet is who the photographer was and whether he's still around. I need Dillan to confirm the O'Malleys' hit on the guy went through."

I nod and smile grimly before I respond.

"It did. He got the text just before we left Kate's. The guy went wherever they deal with things, and Dillan's man said it was done."

"Then, yes. Let's go home."

We say goodbye to everyone before getting in the back of a town car together. Alone, I take the time to explain in explicit detail everything I did to Kate, even—or rather, especially—the parts that my brothers, cousin, and friend didn't see. The parts I didn't want to say in front of Mama, my aunts, Olivia, and Sera.

Uncle Salvatore will likely expect me to give him a full report, which means Papa will be there as his *consigliere*. I don't mind Papa knowing, but I don't want him to tell Mama. However, neither do I want to ask my dad to keep anything from my mom. There's plenty he can't tell her, and she totally gets that. But they've always been pretty open about anything that happens to my brothers and me.

Matteo has me cradled in his arms, and he reads my mind.

"We'll deal with telling Uncle Sal everything you couldn't say tonight, along with how and when your dad finds out. Uncle Massi will understand, and your mom knows shit happened."

"Do you think she's disgusted with me?"

"*Piccolina*, if Kate went after you, she would be dead. Your mom wouldn't stop until she was. Believe me, she isn't disgusted or disappointed in you. She understands."

I nod. We're quiet for a long time as we leave Queens and head into Manhattan. It's not until we're in our condo that we really start talking again. Matteo helps me undress as he speaks.

"Do you want to stay in this place? Or would you rather have a house in the burbs?"

"Manhattan is still convenient for my work, but it's not like I can't commute. Do you want to be in Queens closer to our parents, like Luca and Carmine are with their wives?"

He's quick to strip before we climb into bed naked, talking as we go.

"Gabriele, Marco, and Lorenzo still live in Manhattan, so I know they can get to you if I can't. But I would feel better if we lived in a gated community with a gated property. Once we marry, the danger to you increases from just being a Mafia daughter to being a Mafia wife, too. It scares me that someone like Jordan could get it in their head to target you. I don't want to lock you away or put you on virtual house arrest. I won't say don't go cycling or running. But I would just be so much more comfortable if we were in a quieter neighborhood."

"I'd feel a lot better if you were coming home to a gated community and property. I don't like you coming and going from the underground parking lot in the middle of the night, or knowing someone could lurk in the lobby or the roof. You know what happened at Maks's building when he and Laura were dating. That could happen here."

"When do you want to move?"

"When we find the right house."

"And what does the right house look like, little one?"

"Big enough for us to have a playroom that isn't anywhere near the home gym I know you'll put in the basement. The other guys cannot know about it. One that can have a room far away from future kids, so they never hear us in the middle of sex."

"Mmm. Good thing you're marrying an architect. I have ideas. Lots and lots of ideas."

I playfully thwack his chest as I lean against him as we stretch out beneath the covers.

"You cannot have any of our family businesses build it! Carmine cannot oversee this project, and his design firm absolutely cannot decorate!"

"Shh. Anyone can build a house and not know what a room

is for. I can do anything we might want built into an interior wall after the fact. And if anyone would understand some of the décor we might want, it would be Carmine. You know he and Sera are into…"

"Yeah, but he doesn't need to know we are, too."

"That ship's already sailed."

"What?"

I jerk back and sit up.

"My brothers and cousin know?"

"Maria, the guys knew I belonged to a club and that I've had subs. Since the shit with Jordan, they know you did, too. It's not a leap for them to figure out that if we were into that stuff alone, then we'd be extra into it together."

"Yeah, but ew."

"I know. It's not like we'd ever discuss it. Luca and Carmine would both explode if anyone discussed what they do intimately with their wives. Everyone knows I'd do the same."

"When do you want to get married?"

"Nine a.m."

"So, a morning wedding, but what day?"

"Tomorrow."

I sit cross-legged as I stare at him.

"Do you mean the courthouse? How could we get a church service that soon?"

"Either. And yes, we could. Our family has donated enough to the Diocese of New York to rival the riches in the Vatican catacombs. If we want to get married tomorrow at nine in the morning, a priest will be available."

I consider what he's saying. The nine in the morning part is perfect for me. It's logistics that make me wonder how on earth.

"Whether we say our vows in front of a Justice of the Peace or a priest, you know we're going to have a ridiculous reception unless we do it abroad like Carmine and Sera."

"Whatever you want. Uncle Sal and the rest of our family can flex their wealth at the next wedding. If that isn't what you want, then it isn't happening. Plain and simple."

"It's never—"

"Yes, it is. You will be my wife, and no one will ever force you to do something you don't want. I will not allow anyone to force you into anything."

I grin and shake my head. Then I collapse into laughter. I lie back down beside him, still giggling as I cup his face.

"I love you, Daddy. You say the most wonderfully ridiculous things. In any other world but ours, you'd probably be right. We both know we have duties we can't avoid. But thank you for being so assertive about protecting me and what I want."

"I'm serious, Maria. I'll work something else out, and we might have to compromise. But so will they. No one forces you. I swore from the very beginning that I would take care of you. I don't mean that any less now than I did then."

The conviction in his voice matches what I see in his eyes. He might not win that argument when it comes, but I know he'll do his damnedest, and he won't back down, even if we have no choice. I inch even closer, and our legs tangle together as he cups my bare ass.

"I'd like a church wedding tomorrow morning, Daddy."

I won't hold my breath, but he twists and grabs his phone where he placed it on the bedside table before we got into bed. I can see the texts he's firing off. Responses come almost immediately and one after the other.

CARMINE

About fucking time

LUCA

About fucking time

My second oldest brother may congratulate his best friend, but he's still my big brother. No one thinks any of us are still virgins, but I'm certain they'll feel better knowing we're married when we have sex. The texts keep going, and I eventually have to get my phone too. We shoot messages back and forth for over an hour. I'm exhausted by the time we finally fall asleep. We hold each other until we wake a few hours later, both needing to feel our bodies connected. Matteo makes love to me, and it might be the best we've ever had.

I arrive at the church at eight o'clock. Money means we have privileges. A bridal shop opened ass early for me this morning, and I was able to get a gown that looks like it was custom made for me. Olivia, Sera, and the other women in my family are here, and we have a team of stylists doing our hair and makeup.

I've barely seen my best friend, Veronica, since Matteo and I started dating. I gave her the briefest rundown last night when I called her to tell her about today. She's *Cosa Nostra* too. She understands secrets and can keep them. She also doesn't ask to know anything that isn't offered. I'm glad she's here now as my maid of honor. No one in my family likes her, especially not Carmine. And Serafina isn't thrilled about seeing her. But everyone makes nice for my sake.

Then it's nine o'clock on the dot, and I hear the organ as I stand in the foyer with Papa. We walk around the corner and make our way down the aisle. All I see is Matteo. He's never been more handsome than in the tux he's wearing now. I vaguely sense the guys in my family standing beside him. Veronica, Sera, and Olivia stand near where Papa and I stop. He gives me a hug and quick kiss on the cheek through my veil. Then the important part starts.

We face each other and recite the vows as the priest prompts us. Tears well in my eyes when I see our rings. From the pride in his eyes, Matteo knows he got it right. I can't believe he already picked out our wedding bands when he got my engagement ring. They're absolutely perfect. But the tears threaten to fall as he slides the band onto my finger. He squeezes my hands and offers me a reassuring smile. I let go of his hands to slip the plain band halfway down his ring finger. I pause and look up. Our gazes meet as I slide it over his knuckle until it stops.

When we're pronounced man and wife, there's no rushing us through our first wedded kiss. It's not obscene, but neither is it quick. When we finally pull apart, I rest my head against his chest as he kisses the top of my head. I know he feels me relax against him, and it eases the tension that's kept me nearly rigid. Everything is better when my husband is holding me. Fuck, I love the sound of that. We look toward the voices, calling our names and waving to us. We walk hand-in-hand to our family, then out of the nave.

I lace my fingers with his, and my nails dig into the back of his hand with excitement. When we're nearly to the building's exit, we gather, so our family can congratulate us. We draw attention from parishioners arriving for the ten-thirty service. People guess who we are. We move away from the entrance, and now we're standing off to the side, close to the garden.

Auntie Carlotta kisses my cheeks, then Matteo pulls her in for a hug that lifts her onto her tiptoes.

"*Paperotto*, are you ready to celebrate?"

I look over at Matteo, and my grin is ear to ear. His mom calling him little duck still amuses me. She couldn't get him out of the bath or the pool when we were all babies. But I'm also simply excited that we're married. Either way, I nod.

Uncle Salvatore takes Auntie Carlotta's place and gives me a tighter hug than I've gotten since I was a kid. I listen to him speak softly to Matteo.

"I'm proud of you, Matteo. I wish you all the best. You deserve it, *nipote*." Nephew.

Our names for each other show how complicated our family tree is since Uncle Salvatore isn't really Matteo's uncle. He's mine, but now "nephew" works for real since Matteo and I are married.

"*Grazie, zio*."

"No one should have to cook for all of us. Let's go to Donatelli's."

It's a restaurant not too far from the church here in Manhattan. It's a family favorite. The owner grew up with Papa, Uncle Salvatore, and Auntie Paola. The guy is everything you'd expect from an Italian American New Yorker. The hair. The jewelry. The accent. All of it. He's also one of the nicest men in the world. Everyone who walks through the door is family. He's the only *Cosa Nostra* business owner I know of who's never had to pay protection money. He's like a cousin to Papa, my uncle, and my aunt, and everyone knows it's Uncle Salvatore's favorite restaurant. No one's going near Mikey Donatelli, so he doesn't need any protection.

Only Marco and Lorenzo ride in the SUV with Matteo and me. Giuseppe is our driver, and Marco sits in the third row while Lorenzo is in the front passenger seat. It's not much privacy, but while Matteo perceives even the hint of a lingering threat, he doesn't trust having less than two other men with us while he's out with me. Our family's other guards are in the cars ahead and behind us, while the rest of our family is in an SUV and limo.

We arrive at the restaurant, and a host immediately shows us to a private room Mikey built to accommodate my family. I love looking around at the quaint place, always enjoying the rustic feel. My eyes dart from the decorations on the wall to Uncle Salvatore. Matteo whispers to me.

"We're lucky it's our uncle's favorite restaurant, and he's known Mikey since they were kids. It's one of the few places where we can all relax."

We can relax because there isn't a man on staff who isn't carrying a gun once we arrive. These men are on my family's payroll to make sure they protect us when we're here.

Matteo and I take our seats at the center of the table, and the wine is soon flowing. It's one toast after another. From my brothers, cousin, and friend, one joke after another is at Matteo's expense, but none have any subtle innuendos that might have come if he'd married someone else. Instead, they're fun quips from when we were kids. From before the men became who and what they are now. It feels good to be happy around my family now that Carmine's reconciled with everyone, and two more women have joined our family. It's only taken twenty years. As Matteo holds my hand and kisses me when everyone taps their wine glasses, I have that sense of peace again.

He leans to whisper in my ear, and his warm breath sends a shiver along my spine. From what he says, we're both thinking about our wedding night.

"You had a long day yesterday. Too much wine will make

you sleepy. I'm going to keep you up as long as you keep me up."

My cheeks surely flush bright pink, and he knows I understood the hint. He moves his hand to rest on my thigh, his fingers between my legs. I wish he could push my dress up and move his hand closer to my pussy, but we're not alone. He won't embarrass me, and he won't let anyone think he doesn't respect his wife.

That sense of peace from a moment ago shatters when nine cell phones ping at the same time. My husband, brothers, cousin, father, and uncles, along with Gabriele, all pull them from their pockets. It's a text from Finn O'Rourke. I'm certain we all feel the same dread.

Matteo locks his screen after a quick peek and looks around. All the men look at me. My aunts, Mama, Sera, and Olivia barely look interested, but I furrow my brow; the question clear in my eyes. I'm worried this will call them away.

"Work, *cuore*." Sweetheart.

I know our entire family's here, so he's discreet. I nod and reach for my wine glass just as all the men's phone's ping again. This is not the time for this shit. Matteo gazes down at me, and I can tell he's scared this is going to ruin my day. But they have no choice; they have to look.

I know what "work" means. I don't want to, and I'm grateful I don't have to know details. From the men's grim expressions, whatever came through these texts requires attention. But at least it won't be during brunch. Once the phones stop pinging, we have a wonderful meal. However, there's still a problem, and they may have to deal with it soon.

While the waiters bring out dessert, I nudge Matteo. He sighs and pulls out his phone, so I can get a better view of the texts. The first was a photo of some men I don't know. They looked Latin American, and from the glance I got, they were dead.

There's another photo attached to this most recent one. It's Kate, and she doesn't look in as bad shape as how I left her, but she definitely looks fucked-up. As I stare at the photo, I realize she's dead. Matteo scrolls, and I read the message beneath the photo.

FINN

C dropped her off in MH but she was already dead when she arrived. Social media posts make it look like she did it herself because her brother died in a boating accident.

I also realize I don't care. Neither photo stirs any emotion in me. I don't feel guilty for getting revenge. I don't feel grateful or annoyed that the Irish seemed to have handled what became of Kate. I'm certain Uncle Salvatore and the others will care since this might jeopardize our connections in Boston for all I know. The Irish got the shit done for us that I decided they owed us. That syndicate family is an enemy and an ally. We prefer them to do the asking, rather than the other way around, but they were useful.

"*Piccolina*, are you ready to go?"

"Yes. What now, Daddy?"

It's my turn to whisper. He turns his head and snags my lips in a kiss that has everyone else walking away.

"I think it's time to consummate our marriage."

I grin as we walk out to the town car, which Matteo decides is fine for us to ride in. He surprises me with a suite at the finest hotel in the city. As we sit in the soaking tub, facing each other as we make love, I keep my voice low.

"I'm certain we weren't ready for any of this eleven years ago. It probably would have blown up in our faces. But the beauty of having a family as close as ours is that no one knows me better than you, husband.

"And despite what your brother—my best friend—may say, no one knows your husband better than you do, wife. If beauty is in the eye of the beholder, then I wouldn't have our family any other way."

The way we read each other's minds proves to me we're soulmates. We are who we are, and we're better for being together. We say as much with our bodies when we move together as we do with our declaration.

"I love you."

Epilogue

Matteo

"Are you sore, *piccolina?*"

"Deliciously. A wonderful reminder of a perfect night with you."

The sun streams into our bedroom as we wake. Maria rolls over in my arms and cups my jaw as she kisses me. I knead her tits, and it's my turn to sigh. We pull apart, and her dazzling eyes lock with mine. Her smile is radiant. I can't believe we've already been married eight months. It's gone by in a flash. Maybe because we took a two-and-a-half-month honeymoon. Maria finished her residency, so we traveled. She applied for a position at another hospital in the city when we got back, and she's been there for a few months.

"You're so beautiful, Maria."

"Thank you. You're pretty damn handsome."

She trails her nails down my chest and wraps her hand around my cock.

"What do you want Daddy to do, little girl?"

"Fuck me."

"Fuck me what?"

"Fuck me, Daddy. Please."

I roll onto my back, and she straddles me. She's already as wet as I am hard. It's always like that. The wonders of same day shipping mean we came home from work to find a package waiting at the door. Apparently, Maria did some online shopping while she waited for some imaging to come in. I reach for the bullet vibrator we opened around the second or third time we had sex in the middle of the night.

She slides along my cock, and I turn on the vibrator. I trail is over her nipples, making them pucker. Her belly clenches as I glide it down to her clit. She moans and speaks with an exhale.

"Yes, *caro*." Darling.

"Do you like it?"

"So much."

"Can you take more?"

"Always."

I turn it up a notch. We move together, and I grab one tit then the other as they bounce in front of my face. There's something both arousing and relaxing about sucking her tits. Freud probably would have said I was breastfed too long or not long enough. I just know that I can't resist the magnificent temptation, and Maria loves it.

"That feels so good. All of it. Just more, Daddy."

"Hold it against your clit."

"Daddy" spurs every dominant gene I have, so my response is a command, not a suggestion. My fingers dig into her hips as I set a hardcore pace.

"May I come, Daddy?"

"No."

She moans in frustration. She's so slick that we hear my

cock slide into her as our bodies move together. It's a good thing we have no neighbors up here. We own the entire floor—she was on the deed to every property I owned before we even got married. I change our rhythm and rock her instead of lifting and pulling her down. I know she likes this so much more. With the vibrator turned up, she's going to explode soon.

"Please. I really need to come."

"Yes, *cuore*." Sweetheart.

I'm unprepared for her to pull the vibrator away and reach behind her. She presses it to my taint, and I can't stop.

"Fuck, Maria. Fucking take my cum. All of it... Fuck. Just like that, little girl. Ride my cock... Who's cock is it?

"My daddy's."

"Well, yes. But guess again."

"My cock?"

"All yours, *piccolina*. Fucking hell. Keep squeezing and riding me."

She Kegels around me, and I'm certain I've shot every ounce of semen I have into her. My dick keeps pulsing. If she's as fertile as I have cum, we're going to have to be careful or Uncle Massimo and Auntie Nicoletta won't be the only ones with four kids in six years.

She collapses against me.

"Was that good, Daddy?"

"Amazing."

I brush hair from her face as we kiss. Then she rests her head on my shoulder. I was never a cuddler before Maria. I fucked and finished. I might have stayed in bed to catch my breath, but there was no affection or sentimentality. At least not on my part, and I don't remember any woman looking for that from me.

"I don't remember telling you to move the vibrator."

"Didn't you like that?"

"I did. I shot my load the second it touched me. But I don't remember telling you to do that."

"It was so good your mind went blank."

I chuckle and spank her before I squeeze the soft flesh. I love the sound of her giggles. It's rare, so it's a treat. I know it means she's happy, and that's what I want most for her. The only thing I want nearly as much is to plan for our future. I haven't forgotten about the threats made to Maria and how either of us could have someone from our past haunt us. The men involved in her Miami kidnapping are taken care of, so Maria's been avenged. We didn't bother fucking with the Colombians other than the ones involved in the deal that flopped—I couldn't care enough to worry about that shit when the Diazes handled it. The men working for Dillan who took Auntie Nicoletta are no longer for this world. Jordan's gone, and so is Kate. But I still worry. We still don't know who took Aunt Sylvia. I don't know what to do to protect the one person I love more than anything or anyone.

"Matteo?"

The bubble is dissolving. I'm heading back into reality, which is not where I want to be. I focus on the feel of still being inside Maria. Her expression shows her worry as she speaks.

"What is it?"

"You know I have businesses I run. I'm not as hands on as you are as a doctor, but I still work. Despite what the world believes. But I have managers I trust because I travel for other work a lot."

"A lot? Still? What are you getting at?"

That's something I haven't discussed since Uncle Salvatore's let me have a honeymoon beyond our trip.

"I did. I don't know about now. Things are changing, and Uncle Salvatore isn't giving me a ton of jobs anymore. And I don't think he will now that I'm married. He'll assign things to the unmarried guys. He won't pull me away from you if he can help it. But you know I had to go to Boston, and I eventually made it to Reno to check on the casino there. Some things are inevitable."

"But you're not usually gone more than you're here."

"No. You know I haven't been gone that often for a while. I was just wondering if you might want to come with me for some trips, too."

"That would be nice. We'll see, I guess. But that's probably going to take a ton of creative scheduling."

I will never ask her to quit working. She loves being a doctor, and she's worked so hard to accomplish everything she has. I wish I could bubble wrap her and keep her beside me all the time. But it's neither practical nor healthy for our relationship. But I would love for her to be with me when I travel if it works with her schedule.

"We won't solve all the world's problems today, but you can check out the places you want to visit near where I usually have to travel. Make a list of which towns or sites, and then I'll make sure we have houses there."

"Houses?"

"Of course. Speaking of which..."

"Oh, my God. Are the plans done?"

She jumps off the bed and runs out of our room naked. She heads straight to my office and stares at the blueprint canister on my desk. I open it and roll out the digital mockups along with the blueprints. She spreads them out and stares at each before turning toward me.

"This is our house, *piccolina*."

She wraps herself around me as I lift her off her feet. She squeezes as tightly as she can.

"It's perfect. You're perfect."

"I try for you, *piccolina*. I'm ready to have a real home with you."

"That's all I've wanted since I was sixteen."

"And you say patience isn't one of your virtues. They say good things come to those who wait. I got the very best, *amore mio*."

Our kiss steals my breath, just like her laughter and beauty do, too. We rest our foreheads against each other when we come up for air. As we do so often, we speak at the same time.

"*Ti amo, amore mio.*" I love you, my love.

Discover how Mafia enforcer, Gabriele Scotto, falls for the least appropriate woman when Sinead O'Malley is hired to defend him. The Irish-American experienced attorney and the newly licensed mafioso lawyer can't agree on anything, except for an attraction that threatens to ruin them both. When enemies make Sinead their target, Gabriele will risk his freedom to protect the only woman he's ever wanted in *Mafia Angel*.

Don't miss the next installment

Preorder and have it ready when you wake on Aug 22nd.

We come from opposite worlds.

I shouldn't trust her.

I definitely shouldn't want her.

But I'll make her mine.

I'll put my life in her hands.

In return, I'll give her everything she wants.

I push her to the edge over and over.

Then bring her pleasure beyond her wildest dreams.

I dare anyone to stand in our way.

I'll burn the world down before I let anything happen to her.

There's nothing I won't do for her.

Mafia Angel is a dark romance with a HEA and no cliffhanger. It contains **EXTRA-STEAMY** scenes that will make your toes curl and your granny blush. *The Mancinelli Brotherhood* is a six-book series that'll keep you warm at night.

Preorder your copy now.

Thank you for reading Mafia Beauty

Sabine Barclay, a nom de plume also writing Historical Romance as Celeste Barclay, lives near the Southern California coast with her husband and sons. Growing up in the Midwest, Celeste enjoyed spending as much time in and on the water as she could. Now she lives near the beach. She's an avid swimmer, a hopeful future surfer, and a former rower. She loves writing romances that will make your toes curl and your granny blush.

Subscribe to Sabine's bimonthly newsletter to receive exclusive insider perks.

www.sabinebarclay.com

Join the fun and get exclusive insider giveaways, sneak peeks,
and new release announcements in
<u>Sabine Barclay's Facebook Dubious Dames Group</u>

Do you also enjoy steamy Historical Romance? Discover
Sabine's books written as Celeste Barclay.

The Mancinelli Brotherhood

Mafia Heir **BOOK ONE SNEAK PEEK**

Luca

This asshole is pissing me off. We've been going around in circles for five minutes, and the longer we stand out here, the greater the likelihood someone will spot us. I have a sixth sense about these things. It's why I'm still alive at the ripe old age of thirty-one.

"Espinoza, enough already. Either sell to us or don't, but we set the price. Your tequila is good, but it isn't nectar from the gods."

I'm watching Carlos Espinoza, some lackey for the Mexican Culiacán Cartel, try to maneuver me into paying more than the agreed upon price. I know it's so he can skim off the top.

"It's as close as you're going to get. You've upped the order, so the price per case goes up."

My uncle, Salvatore Mancinelli, is the New York don. He negotiated this deal, and I warned him it was a bad idea. But what do I know as his underboss and heir? I'm not backing down.

"Haven't you ever heard of a bulk discount? The more I order the better the price should be. No one else around here is buying from you. You know we're your only choice in three out of five boroughs. You aren't going to the Bronx because you won't get more than pennies there. You aren't going to Queens because you don't want to run into the Colombians. You aren't going to Manhattan because then you face the bratva along with us. And what are you going to do in Staten Island? Sell to us anyway? We control Staten Island and Brooklyn when it comes to liquor stores, so take the money and go."

"Luca, there are plenty of liquor stores in Brooklyn that aren't owned by Italians. I'll go there."

We aren't friends. He's patronizing me by using my first name. Fuck him and the horse he rode in on. I have other solutions for this shit.

"And I'll just take what I want from them for free. That's not a half bad idea. The deal's over. Take your shit with the worm in it and go."

"Motherfucking racist. Not all tequila has a worm in it."

"You're selling Mezcal. It's known for the fucking worm. I wouldn't start calling me names, you *penche hijo de puta*." Fucking son of a bitch.

He has twenty-five crates of stolen tequila that he's trying to offload because he knows he can't sell it at his own liquor store.

"What did you call me?"

Carlos takes what he thinks is a menacing step forward, and his two bodyguards do the same. Not smart. Neither of my two bodyguards nor I react, but the three men in each of my cars open their doors. They won't do more than that. It's just a reminder that the Culiacán can try, but the *Cosa Nostra* still run New York City.

"This is the third and final time I say this. Sell or leave."

Every head turns toward the liquor store's back door as it opens. A gorgeous blonde steps out, and I wish I had the time to appreciate her beauty, but she's about to die. Carlos and his men draw their guns and pivot toward her. My men pull their weapons too, but we keep them pointed at the Mexicans. The woman stands like a deer in the headlights for a second before ducking behind the industrial garbage dumpster like a frightened rabbit. Three shots hit the metal almost at the same moment. That's all it takes for my men and me. The two bodyguards standing with me aim for a guard each, and I set my sights on Carlos. We squeeze our triggers, and the men fall.

Screeching tires tell me Carlos's driver takes off. I hear more gunshots as at least one soldier in my cars tries to shoot the escaping vehicle. Glass shatters, but the sedan keeps going. I hear more tires squeal as one of my SUVs takes off and chases the guy. I holster my gun and wave my men to do the same.

I inch forward toward the trash can, but I see the shadow shift. The woman bolts from the other side. She's still the frightened rabbit, but I'm the fox pursuing her. She's fast, I'll give her that. But she has to be at least a foot shorter than me. My legs are a lot longer and cover a lot more ground with each stride.

She weaves among the cars, most likely believing it's harder to hit a moving object. She isn't wrong, but I have no intention of shooting her. I push myself harder and pounce as she darts out and tries to cross the last stretch of parking lot to reach a better lit area near a bus stop. I lunge.

"Stop running, *piccolina*. I won't hurt you."

I wrap my arms around her and pull her back against my chest, but I'm quick to spin her around and put space between us as I grasp her arms. Of course, she fights me.

"If I wanted you dead, I would have shot at you, too."

"It doesn't mean you won't kill me after."

She's breathless as she continues to struggle. I almost let go to take a step back, insulted at what she implied. But I can't blame her. If I were a woman, I'd be terrified of the same thing.

"I'm not going to rape you. I'm going to talk to you."

"Talk? You are not a man who talks if you just killed a guy."

"To keep him and his men from killing you. I told you, if I wanted you dead, I would have shot at you too. And I wouldn't have missed."

She stops struggling against me, but her eyes continue to dart from one place to another, trying to find somewhere to flee. I know I can keep her in place with only one hand, so I release her left arm. I still have a firm hold on her right one, but I haven't held it nearly as tightly as I could.

"I'm Luca. I know you figured out you interrupted something you shouldn't have. Did that man know who you are?"

"Yes."

"What about his driver? Would he know you?"

"Yes."

"Do you have a name?"

"Yes."

"*Piccolina*, we won't get very far if yes is all you can say. Are you willing to answer me with more than one word?"

"No."

I knew that was coming, and I grin. I can't help it. I wasn't wrong about her being gorgeous, but I doubt she wants to know that's what I think. At least, not if I want her to know I won't assault her.

"Fine. I have more than twenty questions I can ask that you can answer with one word. Do you work at the store?"

"Sometimes."

Ah, an improvement.

"Did Carlos know you were still working?"

"No."

"Do you have a car, or do you take the subway or bus?"

She raises her chin and remains silent. Smart but counterproductive.

"The subway or the bus will get you killed. You're too easy to find and follow. Do you have a car?"

"Yes."

"Can you stay with someone instead of going home?"

She refuses to answer.

"If that man knew you and you sometimes work in the store, then he knew where you live. If he found that out, so will someone in his cartel."

"I know. Let me go. The longer I stand here, the more likely someone is to come back for me."

"No one will touch you while I'm here."

"Arrogant. If he shot at me, he would have shot at you."

"And he would have died, anyway. What's your name?"

"Jane."

"Look, I know you won't get in one of my cars and let me drive you somewhere. In most cases, I would say that's a smart move. But you did nothing wrong tonight except for leave work at the wrong time. I know that, and you know that. But the Culiacán won't see it that way, *piccolina*."

She freezes for no more than five seconds before she trembles so much that I can see it. I don't know what drives me next, but it's the same instinct that's made me call her little girl three times. I pull her to my chest and tuck her head against it. I stroke her hair down to her shoulders, rubbing my hand up and down her back. This is the most inopportune moment to notice she isn't wearing a bra. I will my body not to react.

"What does that mean?"

Her voice is barely more than a whisper, but I know what she's asking.

"It means little girl."

"I should be insulted, but the way you say it..."

"It has nothing to do with your height. I know you're not a child."

God, do I know she's not. She feels amazing. Her tits are soft as they press against me, and I can see she has the most delectable ass. I'd love nothing more than to cup it and squeeze until she goes up on her toes and begs for me to wrap her legs around my waist and fuck her. For fuck's sake. Stop, you disgusting asshole. That is not what you need to be thinking about.

"Why didn't you shoot me? Whatever you were talking about, if it was with a Cartel member, then it wasn't completely legal. Carlos didn't want me alive to talk about seeing you together. Why are you letting me live?"

"I told you. You did nothing wrong but try to leave work. He should have checked the building before starting the meeting. That was on him. The only thing I take issue with is you leaving by yourself and walking into a dimly lit parking lot. I suspect you do that often, and that's too dangerous. Jane Doe, I don't hurt women."

Mafia Sinner

Mafia Beauty

Mafia Angel (8.22.23)

Mafia Redeemer (10.17.23)

Mafia Star (12.12.23)

The Ivankov Brotherhood

Bratva Darling

BOOK ONE SNEAK PEEK

LAURA

As I sit across from the four Kutsenko brothers, I press my lips together to keep from drooling. No four men should be so strikingly handsome. Not all from the same family, anyway. I fight a valiant battle against letting my gaze drift toward the eldest, Maksim, whose ice-blue eyes bore into me. After years of negotiating billion-dollar investment contracts while facing countless ruthless businessmen, I've learned to keep my expression studiously blank. But it's a true struggle today. Instead, I focus my attention on the squirrelly lawyer sitting across the conference table. While he's disingenuous with each comment, he's a good negotiator. But I'm better. How cliché am I?

While I feel Maksim watching me, I focus on Dmitry Yakovitch as he continues to argue the merits of the venture capitalist company I represent, RK Capital Group, merging with Kutsenko Partners. What he means is the merits of Kutsenko Partners acquiring RK Capital Group, then stripping it and making it another money-laundering shell corporation. While most people in New York have little awareness of the Russian mafia, I do. The Kutsenko brothers' names appear on no titles or deeds anywhere in New York City, but it wasn't difficult to determine which shell companies likely belong to them. Their assumption that I'm unfamiliar with them is proving beneficial to me as they continue to whisper amongst themselves in Russian. I think they may even believe they're convincing me that they don't speak much English.

The senior partners of RK Capital Group know who I'm negotiating with, though they may not know I'm aware of these Russians' more nefarious operations. They've given me the go-ahead to agree to a merger with an eventual acquisition, but only for the right price. A price to the tune of twenty billion dollars. Considering an investment firm like Goldman Sachs is worth nearly one-hundred-and-twenty billion dollars, my clients' asking price appears reasonable.

"Mr. Yakovitch, I shall stop you now." I raise my left hand, pen caught between my index and middle fingers. When I have his attention, I lean back in my chair and casually twirl the pen over my index finger and thumb. "Fifty billion is my clients' asking price. You know that. Your clients know that. RK doesn't oppose the merger. What they oppose is the insulting offer you've made. It's nearly noon, and I'm hungry, Mr. Yakovitch. I have a delicious ham sandwich waiting for me. I even have three chocolate chip cookies waiting for me. If we aren't going to make any progress, I shall let you go, so I can move onto my eagerly anticipated lunch."

I cant my head just enough for me to appear as though my gaze rests solely on the opposing attorney's face, but I can see each Kutsenko brothers' reaction. My face battles yet again against showing my emotions as I fight not to smirk. Their muted but surprised expressions confirm what I already know.

"Please tell your clients to make a reasonable counteroffer, or I will conclude this meeting and enjoy my ham sandwich and cookies."

Dmitry glares at me before turning to Maksim and his three brothers. In rapid Russian, he doesn't interpret my suggestion. Oh no. There's no need for that. I can't catch every word because his voice is too low. But I catch something along the lines of "The bitch refuses to budge. What now? A fucking ham sandwich. More like a stick up her ass."

Maksim swivels his chair to look at his brothers. In Russian, he says, "Fifty billion is ridiculous. She's not so stupid or naïve not to know that. My guess is they'll settle for twenty billion. We offer fifteen."

"That's barely better than what we already offered," Aleksei, the second-oldest brother, argues. "She'll be eating the fucking sandwich and dipping her cookies in milk before we walk out the door. We need the buildings."

"We offer twenty, Maks," Bogdan, the youngest, insists.

As I watch the brothers discuss, their voices barely lowered, I pull my lunch sack from the black leather satchel by my feet and set it beside my laptop. It's a ridiculously pink floral bag with an embroidered monogram, the L and D overlapping. It's an empty prop, but they don't know that. I watch as five sets of eyes narrow. I offer a smile that would appear innocent in any setting other than this meeting. It's patronizing, and I know it.

Bratva Sweetheart

Bratva Treasure

Bratva Beauty

Bratva Angel

Bratva Jewel

www.ingramcontent.com/pod-product-compliance
Lightning Source LLC
Chambersburg PA
CBHW030221120726
47903CB00005B/1320